Bantam Books by Cameron Judd
Ask your bookseller for the books you have missed

THE

BORDER

MEN

A Novel of the Tennessee Frontier: 1778–1783

CAMERON JUDD

BANTAM BOOKS
NEW YORK • TORONTO • LONDON • SYDNEY • AUCKLAND

THE BORDER MEN

A Bantam Domain Book / June 1992

DOMAIN and the portrayal of a boxed "d" are trademarks of Bantam Books, a division of Bantam Doubleday Dell Publishing Group, Inc.

Map designed by GDS
Jeffrey L. Ward.

ISBN 0-553-29533-0

Published simultaneously in the United States and Canada

Bantam Books are published by Bantam Books, a division of Bantam Doubleday Dell Publishing Group, Inc. Its trademark, consisting of the words "Bantam Books" and the portrayal of a rooster, is Registered in U.S. Patent and Trademark Office and in other countries. Marca Registrada. Bantam Books, 1540 Broadway, New York, New York 10036.

PRINTED IN THE UNITED STATES OF AMERICA

OPM   0   9   8   7   6   5   4   3

*This novel is dedicated
to the memory of
Vesper C. Judd (1913–1977),
my father and friend,
and a marvelous teller
of stories.*

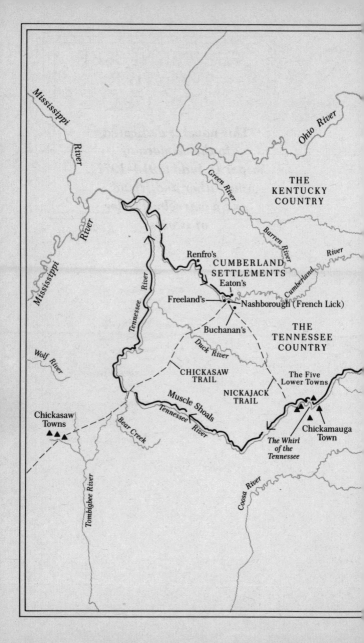

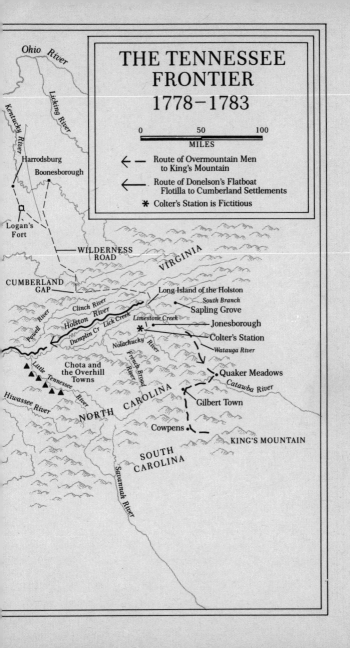

PROLOGUE

She awakened swiftly, as was her way. There was rarely a twilight interim between sleep and alertness; she passed from slumber to wakefulness not like a diver rising through water, but like a hawk bolting from forest to sky.

Her name was Ayasta, and she lay in a log hut in the mile-long town called Chickamauga. Rising now on this early autumn night in 1778, she cast aside her blanket and walked silently across the packed dirt floor to the place where her son of three years, Wasi, stirred and cried.

He sat up as she reached him, his arms stretched out, and she embraced him. His thin body, afflicted again with the intermittent fever that had plagued him for the past two days, was hot against her breast. She could feel it even through her long linsey-woolsey shirt, which had been taken in a some raid against a white farmstead to the northeast and given to her by Atsina, her elderly neighbor.

Atsina gave Ayasta many such gifts. The old woman's desire to goad the young widow into marrying her son was so obvious it sometimes made Ayasta laugh behind

1

Atsina's back; not in mirth, but in mocking irony. Could Atsina really believe her plain, lazy son could replace the brave and handsome John Hawk, Ayasta's slain husband? In the year since John Hawk's death, Ayasta had been given five opportunities to take husbands superior to Atsina's son and had denied them all. None could match John Hawk, and it was Ayasta's conviction that to live alone with her slain mate's memory was better than companionship with some inferior substitute. She and Wasi were fine alone.

Wasi snuggled against his mother and stopped whimpering. Ayasta gently patted his back and sang softly the lullaby that, according to the old storytellers, the mothers of the lost clan of the Ani-Tsaguhi sang in the days before they turned themselves from human beings into bears:

> Ha-mama, ha-mama, ha-mama, ha-mama,
> Uda-haleyi hi-lunnu, hi-lunnu,
> Uda-haleyi hi-lunnu, hi-lunnu . . .

Within a few minutes Wasi was asleep again, soothed by the soft and repetitious music. Ayasta laid him down gently and pulled his blanket halfway over him so that he could cover himself later if his fever heat turned to chill. After that she sat on her haunches for several minutes, looking at her son in the darkness, which was only slightly dispelled by the flicker of the fire. Her thoughts were solemn, deep, even unwelcome, but also unavoidable.

The slender young woman rose and walked to the door. Opening it, she looked out over the sleeping town of Chickamauga, named after the creek along which it had been built. For a town so relatively new, Chickamauga was large and still growing. The ranks of its populace were swollen almost daily by new defectors from the Overhill Cherokees, Ayasta's native people. Other newcomers included malcontent Creeks, Cherokees of the Middle and Lower Towns, and even many whites who sought safety from the violence of the great war being fought between the Americans and the English.

Chickamauga was the town of Dragging Canoe, unappeasable foe of the white settlers, and mentor and guide of John Hawk in his last months of life. Ayasta had lived in Chickamauga almost a year now, yet it still wasn't home. Despite its size and relatively healthy state of supply by the British commissary, Chickamauga and the other allied towns around it had about them an indefinable feel of impermanence, or so it seemed to Ayasta. They were children's play-villages of reeds and sticks, doomed to be blown away in the next strong wind.

Why did she feel this way? She asked herself the question as she looked out over the dark town. There seemed no reason for her pessimism. Dragging Canoe, after all, was strong in his determination to keep his people's lands and even to regain those already lost through the acquiescence of the Overhill Cherokees from whom he had seceded. Every day, his fighting force grew. And the alliance with the British against the Americans remained firm. Chickamauga Town and the Chickamaugas, as Dragging Canoe's faction had come to be known, should hold fast and remain long.

But it won't be that way, she thought. I know it won't. How she knew it, Ayasta could not say, but she knew it. Danger was coming to the Chickamaugas, to their cabins, fields, and town houses . . . and also to herself and, worst of all, to Wasi. This was the great fear that gnawed at her, making sleep slow to come and quick to depart. The confidence so many of her peers placed in the British was a plant with no root. If the tide of war turned, the British might abandon the Chickamaugas as they had already substantially abandoned the Overhill towns, which now suffered dire need. Ayasta knew that one factor driving many young Overhill warriors to the Chickamaugas was that most persuasive motivator—empty bellies.

Ayasta closed the door and sat down in the darkness, regretting the frenzied activity of her mind. Now she would surely not sleep for the rest of the night. She would remain awake until dawn, chilled by the shadow of foreboding that only she could detect.

She had once cautiously revealed her premonition of doom to Atsina, only to hear it mocked. And her brother,

Ulagu, who by custom would one day train Wasi in the ways of a warrior, had similarly chided her when she had hinted of her worries to him. After that she kept her fears private, and in so doing learned something: Fears, like cave mushrooms, grow bigger when chambered in the dark.

Wasi stirred again but did not awaken. Ayasta went to him and felt his brow. Cooler now. That was good. Perhaps tomorrow he would be well, though even if he was, he would probably fall ill again before another month passed. He was a sickly boy. The old women, when they thought Ayasta did not hear, whispered that Wasi was weak and plagued by the witches of this mystic river country and probably would not live to manhood. And Ulagu, Ayasta well knew, was secretly concerned and perhaps embarrassed by Wasi's sickliness. It was Ulagu's hope that Wasi would grow to be what John Hawk had been: stronger, wiser, braver, better than his peers. Yet Wasi's sickly early childhood was not a promising start toward such an end.

Good, Ayasta thought with a surge of defiant satisfaction. Good. If Wasi is too sickly to be a mighty warrior, I am glad. His father was a mighty warrior, and he did what mighty warriors do: he died. I won't allow Wasi to die too. I'll not lose him like I lost John Hawk.

Closing her arms around herself, Ayasta strode about the cabin, thinking how Ulagu would deplore her thoughts tonight. John Hawk would have felt the same if he were alive, and there again was the point: John Hawk wasn't alive. His warlike life had led him to an early death. And now Ayasta's brother was determined to see Wasi, who was all Ayasta had left of her husband, follow the bloody tracks of his father.

No. Ayasta gritted her teeth fiercely. No. Wasi would not follow a path of death, but a path of life—if such a path existed. One thing seemed certain: It could not be reached from the towns of the Chickamaugas. If Ayasta was to find it, she would have to look at another place and seek the help of others. And she knew where the other place was and who the helpers would be.

She smiled softly, at peace now. The great war within her had calmed. When the right time came, she and Wasi would find that path of life she so wished for. There would surely be a price to pay in finding it, but no sacrifice was too great for Wasi's welfare, even the sacrifice of the only way of life she had ever known.

Ayasta put more wood on the fire, then returned to her blankets and lay down on her left side, her knees drawn up, her hand under her head. She did not seek sleep, having been too often frustrated when she did, but this time sleep sought her. When Ayasta closed her eyes, she did not open them again until morning.

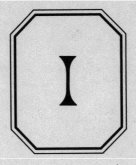

I

THE
BORDER
WAR

The old frontiersman paused and leaned, panting, against a beech, his blood-mottled right hand clutching his wounded left side. Brown autumn-dry leaves, which would cling to the tree until spring, tickled his face in the night wind. More blood oozed between his fingers and dripped to the sodden thatch beneath his moccasins. Alphus Colter closed his eyes a few moments, praying for strength. He opened them again, saw ahead the dark wall of the stockade that bore his name, and was relieved.

Not much farther now. If he could only keep from fainting for a few minutes more, he could make it to his brother's cabin and live. If he passed out, he doubted he could rise again. He would bleed to death on the wet earth, and the Tory raider Elisha Brecht would have claimed one more victim.

"Keep moving," Alphus said aloud to himself. "Keep moving, by Joseph."

He took a breath, winced at the pain of his stab wound, and advanced, using his long rifle as a crutch. Emerging from the edge of the forest, he moved slowly to the empty stockade. He leaned against it as he rounded the front and passed the big double gate. Now he could see the new cabin of Thomas Colter, standing where the more substantial log house of his own late son Gabriel had been until the Cherokees burned it two years ago. Thomas's shutters were closed, but a sliver of faint light shone between them. The light meant hope. Heartened, Alphus advanced a little faster.

At this moment Alphus was immensely grateful that his bachelor brother had come from North Carolina to resettle at Colter's Station. He had been in the settlement a mere five months, but already his presence had brightened the gloom that had often enshrouded Alphus since Gabriel's violent death. Now, if God was willing and Alphus's legs were strong, Thomas would save his older brother's life.

The distance to the cabin seemed triple what it really was. With every step, Alphus felt his feet growing heavier and his head growing lighter. Flashes of light began swirling across his vision, and he had to lean hard on the rifle to keep from falling. The butt piece of the long weapon mashed deeply into the damp earth, causing Alphus to leave behind a peculiar trail of sign: shortly spaced moccasin tracks interspersed with the oval depressions of the rifle butt along with great spots of fresh blood every foot or so.

At the end, Alphus began to believe he would not make it. Thomas's cabin was only yards away and stubbornly refused to draw any closer. His vision swam and his legs grew weaker.

Only one thought kept him from falling, and that was that he was unwilling to die at the hands of Elisha Brecht. There were many men Alphus Colter would find no dishonor in being killed by. Brecht was not one of them. It wasn't solely because Brecht was the most hated and merciless Tory plaguing the American patriot frontiersmen. It was far more personal than that for Alphus Colter. The Colters and Brechts had been at odds long before either family crossed the mountains to this frontier, and Alphus had vowed years ago that no Brecht would ever lay him low.

"Thomas!" he shouted feebly as he forced one more step out of his weary body. "Thomas!"

No sign indicated he had been heard. Tears began streaming down Alphus Colter's face, not drawn by fear or grief, but by exertion. "Thomas!" he shouted again. "Help me, Thomas!"

He advanced another ten steps before white light rose from the back of his eyes and obliterated his vision. He fell but had the paradoxical sensation of rising at the same time. The ground slammed against him like the palm of a great slapping hand.

"Thomas . . ." This time he could not shout, only murmur. The light in his vision began to fade, and in moments was black.

"It was Brecht—you're sure?"

"That's what Alphus was raving," said Thomas Colter. His face was still flushed from the exertion of his ride to Joshua and Darcy Colter's new home on Great Limestone Creek about a mile from where it spilled into the Nolichucky. "Please, Joshua—we must hurry!"

Sina Colter, the lean, weathered wife of Alphus, stepped forward and gripped Thomas's arm. As irony would have it, she had been visiting Joshua's cabin this evening, helping tend to Joshua's little son William while Darcy lay ill with a fever. "I'm coming too," Sina said.

"No, Sina," Joshua said firmly. "Stay here, and come in the morning. Too many people will slow us . . . and Brecht may yet be about."

"I'll not stay behind when Alphus needs me!"

"You will!" Joshua shouted. Sina wilted back, looking tired, frightened, and as old as Alphus, though she was many years younger than her husband. Joshua regretted his loss of temper. "I'm sorry. It's what I think best."

She did not argue further. She withdrew to the fireside and sat down on a three-legged stool, wrapping her thin arms around her middle and gazing into the fire. Zachariah, Sina's nine-year-old son by her previous marriage to the late Levi Hampton, went to her and put his arm across her shoulder, manfully trying to be calm and brave but looking scared. The child had been born in the waning days of Sina's childbearing years, and was her greatest comfort as the shadows of her declining years loomed.

The pale-faced Darcy, clad in a long homespun nightgown, went to her husband and kissed his bearded cheek. Her face was hot against him. "Be careful, dear heart," she said. "Beware of Brecht."

"I will, Darcy."

The front door opened and Cooper Haverly entered. He was damp. The rain had resumed, a foggy drizzle. Despite their differing surnames, Cooper and Joshua were brothers by birth. Cooper had been born eighteen years before to their mutual mother, Hester Byrum, who had died bringing him into the world within the walls of a doomed English fort named Loudoun, and had been named Samuel by Joshua himself. He had been raised through unusual circumstances by a would-be frontier empire builder, Peter Haverly. It was Peter Haverly who had begun calling his adoptive son Cooper, a nickname that had stuck harder than the boy's Christian name of Samuel.

Cooper's path had diverged from Joshua's for many years, only to rejoin it here in this transmountain frontier. Difficulties and differences they had known in their day. Now time had healed old hurts, and they were again the brothers nature had intended them to be.

"The horses are ready, Joshua," Cooper said. "What do you want me to do now?"

"I fear you'll have no sleep tonight, Cooper. Callum McSwain came by today, heading down to get whiskey at Dudley Grubbins and Jim Birdwell's place. He likely put up there for the night. Go fetch him and the others if they're not drunk, then roust out all the other rangers you can who can get to Thomas's cabin by sunrise. Maybe we can pick up Brecht's spoor in the morning and have him done for once and for all."

Cooper turned to leave; Joshua grasped his shoulder. "Be careful—I don't want you mistaken for a Tory raider and shot."

"I'll take care." And then he was gone. Moments later the sound of his horse's hoofbeats receded.

"Let's be off, Thomas," said Joshua.

They rode in silence, swiftly following a trail that the horses knew well. Joshua was in turmoil as he prayed for the welfare of his wounded foster father. As bitter anger at the despised Elisha Brecht flared in him, he deliberately tried to quell it, for Joshua Colter knew that uncontrolled rage made a man careless—and where Brecht was involved, carelessness couldn't be afforded.

He had sensed that something was wrong the moment Thomas Colter pounded on his door. The white-haired merchant had rushed into the cabin when the door opened, almost spilling Joshua over in the process. "It's Alphus," he had said. "Cut and near drained of blood—I heard his voice and found him in the yard. Come quick! Come quick and help him!"

Joshua urged more speed from his horse. A damp maple branch reaching down over the trail slapped his face in the darkness and swept off his broad-brimmed hat. He ignored it, leaving the hat behind and bending lower in his homemade saddle.

Alphus mustn't die, he can't die, not like this. He's the only real father I've known. God above, don't let him die on me now.

Joshua's thoughts raced back across the years. He remembered his first sight of Alphus Colter back in a long hunters' little station camp cabin in 1760, when this country was unsettled wilderness. Joshua had been only a decade old at the time and had taken refuge in Alphus's station camp cabin after a remarkable solitary journey across the wilderness, fresh from captivity among the Overhill Cherokees. That seemed so long ago, yet the memory of Alphus as he had been in those days remained starkly clear.

Now Alphus was much older, just two years shy of seventy. It was a remarkable span of years in a trying land where a man was considered old at fifty-five. Alphus had already outlived most men born at his time. In all the years Joshua had known him, Alphus had seemed younger than his years. Yet of late there was no denying he was not the man he had been. Age had gripped him and now was beginning that viselike squeeze that never loosens. Joshua feared that his father might be too old to survive the knifing Elisha Brecht had inflicted.

When at last the panting horses reached Colter's Station on Sinking Creek, Joshua dismounted before coming to a full stop. He raced to the door of Thomas's cabin and pushed it open, only to find himself staring down the muzzle of Alphus's rifle.

"By Joseph, son, I might have shot you!" Alphus declared. He grinned a grin that was as weak as his voice. The long rifle trembled down and fell to the dirt floor, and Alphus lay back, closing his eyes. He was on Thomas's straw-tick bed, his head propped on a stack of rolled-up blankets. Joshua went to his side.

"How do you feel, Alphus?"

"How do you think? I'm weak as rainwater."

Joshua smiled, encouraged to detect a flicker of lingering feistiness in the wounded old man. It told him that his foster father would live. The thought brought such overwhelming relief that, to Joshua's surprise, he began to cry. He leaned forward and put his arms around Alphus's shoulders, burying his face against his neck.

"By Joseph, boy, you're worse than a blubbery old woman," Alphus murmured.

"I was afraid I'd lost you," Joshua said, growing ashamed, as he always did at those rare times he cried. Tears were for women and children.

"I'll not die until I get the chance to try my own blade on Brecht and see how he likes it," Alphus said, his voice even weaker.

"How did it happen?"

"I was hunting . . . they came upon me before I knew they were there . . . shot at me. I shot back and put a ball in the leg of one of Brecht's redskins . . . I ran and Brecht followed me . . . we scuffled right proper, I'll tell you. He stuck me, but I kicked his pins from under him and rolled over a little bluff. I was able to run from there before they could get down to me. I hid myself until they got wearied of looking, and went on."

"Well, we'll find them, God's truth. Cooper's fetching the men. You rest now—no need to talk."

Alphus's eyes had already closed, and a burst of panic rocked Joshua for a moment until he saw the old man was merely asleep. He examined Alphus's bandage, placed on him earlier by Thomas Colter, then turned. "How much blood did he lose?"

"He had hardly a drop left in him to shed. You see it all down him there," Thomas replied.

"Aye . . . well, thank God he's living. If he rests he'll make it through. I can tell it."

"Praise be. At the beginning I feared we'd lose him."

Joshua went to the fire and added wood, heightening the blaze and knocking off the chill that had begun to creep through the chinked walls of the log house. He left the house and fetched his rifle, which he had dropped to the ground while dismounting. Such carelessness was not typical of him. Desperation to see Alphus had caused it.

Crouching on his haunches in the light of the fire, he began examining the weapon. It was a new rifle, just one of several new things in the life of Joshua Colter. Some months earlier his former home on Gone to God Creek had been destroyed by Brecht's Tory raiders, a mix of renegade whites and Chickamaugas who had begun plaguing the settlements early in 1778. In that fight Joshua's favorite old rifle had been damaged beyond repair. This new one was made in its place by his old friend Callum McSwain, a Scottish blacksmith, gun maker, and farrier.

McSwain had suffered much personal loss of late. In March his homestead had been burned by Brecht's raiders. Shortly after, his wife had fallen ill and died so quickly that her disease was never ascertained. Such things were common on the frontier, far away from medical care and physician's books of medicine. Callum McSwain had since moved north of Colter's Station, building a new cabin and forge, where he worked hard when he wasn't drinking too much whiskey in an attempt to wash away his grief.

It was a great plague to Joshua to see McSwain turn to drink like he had. The habit didn't flatter the man, any more than his recent tendency to loiter about Thomas Colter's store, staring at every woman who passed. Grief and loneliness were changing Callum McSwain, and Joshua wondered how much of the old friend he had known would be left when the changing was done.

Joshua examined the fine Deckard lock of the rifle; it glittered prettily in the firelight. Many a buck this rifle had already brought down, along with one Tory and two Chickamaugas. Though the Overmountain country was more populated now than before, it was as much as ever a land of the gun. The war against Britain still raged full-force, and though the frontiersmen were separated from its seaboard activity by the great mountain ranges, the tendrils of warfare still stretched across to touch them.

But border warfare was different. It was not, for the most part, a battle against redcoated regulars, but a fight between white men and red, and between American patriots and the abundant loyalists who also lived on the frontier. Many of the latter had come to escape the persecutions facing them east of the mountains, to find, ironically, that their growing numbers only served to bring right back to them the same trouble and harassment that they had fled.

Joshua, at twenty-eight years, was firmly on the side of the American rebellion. The Colter clan, which in the minds of most included Cooper Haverly, was known as one of the staunchest Whig families in the region.

Not that Toryism hadn't touched their lives. Cooper's adoptive father Peter Haverly, founder of what was now Colter's Station, had been so firm a loyalist that he had proven willing to betray his own people back in '76, when the British-backed Overhill Cherokees had unsuccessfully tried to drive out the Overmountain rebels. And there were many others of Joshua's acquaintance whose political leanings were ambiguous at best, such as Solomon Brecht, brother of Elisha.

Cooper had only come around fully to the patriot side within the past year, the influence of Peter Haverly taking time to fade. And Gabriel Colter, Joshua's late foster brother and Alphus's only natural son, had also been a secret loyalist right up to the last days of his life.

Joshua took a small rag from the pouch of his hunting shirt and gently shined the beautiful walnut stock of his rifle. He loved this weapon like no other he had ever possessed; cleaning and polishing it like this was an almost-nightly ritual.

Long after midnight Joshua lit up a pipeful of tobacco and smoked in silence. Thomas had gone to sleep on a bearskin in the far corner, near the bed occupied by Alphus, and the two aging brothers were engaged in a snoring match that made Joshua grin around the clay stem of his pipe. When the tobacco burned out, he knocked out the bowl on the hearth, leaned back against the wall, and fell into the controlled light sleep he had mastered as a long hunter. In that state his mind could yet hear and evaluate sounds that didn't even fully register in his consciousness; he could differentiate the nonthreatening skitter of a mouse across the cabin floor from more significant sounds, such as approaching hoofbeats or the sounds of voices.

He heard both of the latter soon enough. As he opened his eyes, experience-honed instincts told him it was about an hour before dawn. He rose and walked to the door, listening to the sound of the coming riders. In the nearing clamor he picked out Cooper's voice, then Callum McSwain's. Joshua opened the door. Cooper and McSwain rode up, followed by Dudley Grubbins, Jim Birdwell, Willie Ayers, and two other rangers.

Cooper swung down from his saddle and lightly darted up onto the puncheon porch beside Joshua. "How is Alphus?"

"Sleeping. He's going to live."

"Praise be for that." Thomas Colter, rubbing his eyes, appeared in the doorway. "Hello, Thomas," Cooper said.

"Good evening to you, Cooper."

"Evening's long gone—it's morning," Joshua said. "The sun will be up soon. With any good fortune we'll be able to track Brecht."

Callum McSwain came out of the darkness and joined the brothers in the faint triangle of light spilling out of the door. His mode of motion was expansive, sweeping; his expression had a life of its own, his thick auburn brows in almost continual motion. Those brows had always seemed to Joshua the most Scottish thing about his friend and fellow ranger. "Joshua, my good companion, I'm happy to tell you that it won't be on good fortune alone we'll have to rely while searching for Brecht."

"What are you talking about, Callum?"

"About Brecht, my dear Captain Colter! We know his whereabouts."

"We do? How?"

Cooper butted in before McSwain could answer, and the Scotsman looked unhappy indeed to be denied the coveted role of newsbearer. "Brecht's hiding place has been found at last," Cooper said. "Willie Ayers saw Brecht and his scoundrels on the move while he was hunting yesterday, and followed them far enough to see where they went. It must have been right after Alphus had his round with them. They've got a cabin in a hollow, long and low and well-hidden. Willie says he could find it again with his eyes closed."

Thomas Colter, himself too old and unskilled to be among the rangers, nevertheless was perfectly suited to feed them. Being a merchant, he kept his house well-stocked, so as sunlight rose he fed the assembled band, which had grown to fifteen by then. They were all skilled horsemen, and each had readily answered Cooper's summons. This was an active group. Its chief duty was defensive: to deter raiders, white and red, from striking the settlements. But when necessary, the band acted offensively as well. That would be the case today.

The morning was cloudy and moist; the sunshine was gray after filtering first through sluggish clouds and then through wet, interlocking tree branches. The rangers, filled to satisfaction with Thomas Colter's bread and salted meat, mounted to begin their ride to nearly certain battle. If the prospect brought fear, not a face showed it.

As they grouped up, Sina and Zachariah arrived by

horseback, coming to tend Alphus. Sina didn't look at Joshua, but young Zachariah flashed him a wry glance that said a lot.

Cooper, carrying his rifle, rode to Joshua's side on his Chickasaw horse. "Did you see that?"

"Yes. Sina's mad at me. She'll probably fume for a month or more."

"Perhaps you should have let her come on last night."

"Perhaps. But at the time I didn't know but that Brecht's scoundrels would still be about, and at times like that I like knowing the women are safe in their cabins after the sun sets." He paused. "And the truth is, I was afraid we'd find Alphus dead. I didn't want her to have to face that."

"Aye. Well, I think we're fixed to go now."

Joshua eyed Cooper somberly. "Coop, I believe you'd best remain behind."

Cooper's eyes widened, then narrowed. "Stay behind? I don't see why I should!"

"Of course you do. It's Hannah Brecht I'm thinking of."

Joshua saw his brother's jaw tighten and clench. The subject of Hannah always brought out the fire in Cooper; the young man seemed so sensitive about it that Joshua usually avoided talking of the girl. This time he had not felt he had a choice.

Joshua had known only one other Hannah in his life, that one being a plump and overfriendly tavern wench back in Salisbury, North Carolina. Hannah Brecht couldn't have been more different in background, age, and appearance. The teenaged daughter of Solomon Brecht, Elisha's brother, she was auburn-haired, strikingly attractive, and adored by every young male within miles. Yet few ever made more than the feeblest attempts to woo her, for two great barriers stood between her and the population of marriageable young men. The first and most fearsome was her father. Tall, stern, overbearing, Solomon Brecht was generally mistrusted both because of his brotherhood to Elisha Brecht and his suspicious lack of activity on behalf of the rebellion. There were widespread rumors, unproven, that he himself was a Tory spy who held clandestine meetings with his brother in the forests. The second barrier was the fact that anyone who knew Hannah Brecht at all knew that her heart belonged to Cooper Haverly alone. To all others she was unattainable.

But Cooper sometimes felt Hannah was unattainable even to him. The problem was the long-standing bitterness that held between the Colter and Brecht families.

Before crossing the mountains, both families had last lived in the Yadkin country of North Carolina. There, a squabble over land had divided the families and driven them to court, where the Colters prevailed. The dispute didn't die, however. Instead it grew far more intense than its origins justified. Ever since, the Colters had little use for the Brechts, and the Brechts outright hated the Colters. Joshua had never figured out why Solomon Brecht had ever been willing to settle near a place named Colter's Station, of all things. He theorized that it was either because Solomon was indeed a Tory spy and wanted to be at a place where his subterfuge could sting the Colters in particular, or, more likely, simply because the settlement had still been called Haverly's Fort at the time Solomon began seeking land there. It amused Joshua to imagine how livid it must have made Solomon when he discovered the area he was about to move to had been renamed after the family he hated most.

Cooper Haverly might have escaped the brunt of the Brecht-Colter hostilities had his kinship to Joshua not been so widely known. But it was known, and he was generally perceived as a Colter, even though truly he wasn't. For that matter, even Joshua was a Colter by adoption only. His original surname, and Cooper's, had been Byrum.

None of that made any difference to Solomon Brecht. Both Joshua and Cooper were part and parcel with Alphus Colter in his book. And no Colter, he had vowed, would ever have his daughter.

All this was in Joshua's mind when he suggested that Cooper drop out of the expedition. Why should Cooper unnecessarily heighten his own troubles with the Brechts?

There were rangers enough for the task without Cooper coming along.

"Don't you fret over Hannah or old Solomon," Cooper responded with noticeable ice. "I can hold my own with Solomon Brecht on my worst day."

"A man oughtn't fight the very family he's hoping to marry into," Joshua replied. "You ought to stay behind today."

"I don't want to stay behind. Elisha Brecht cut Alphus, and I want my chance to take a slash at him."

Joshua looked into Cooper's handsome, determined face. In it he saw flashes of his and Cooper's long-dead mother, their turbulent father, and even himself. Cooper would not be denied, and Joshua knew it. He exhaled resignedly.

"Very well. Come along, if you must. But mind you be careful."

"Don't talk to me like I'm a lap-child, Joshua. I don't like that."

"By heaven, Cooper, you're as stubborn as any little bugger I've ever trotted on my knee! Now mount up. We have Tories to chase."

Down the alternately peaceful and broken Sinking Creek they rode, passing cabins and farmsteads, and the mill built the previous summer by Alphus Colter. Willie Ayers led them. At the upper bank of the Nolichucky they bore right and followed the contours of the river for a few miles, then forded at a rocky shallow and entered the rugged country beyond. Here mountains loomed, barren and brown monoliths covered with innumerable leafless trees interspersed with evergreens and gray faces of stone. Will Ayers was a good woodsman, as were all the rangers, and led the riders with a minimum of talk, sometimes using hand signals as the Cherokees did.

They began climbing a narrow trail, and Joshua saw the first clear sign of other horsemen. His skin pulled tight on his shoulders—a phenomenon he often experienced when danger likely lay ahead. Joshua was far too experienced in frontier military affairs to assume they would reach Brecht's stronghold without detection. Ambush was a strong possibility, especially if Brecht used sentries.

A rock-filled creek tumbled down the mountainside; mossy, dripping boulders rose on the far side of it. Laurel and ivy crowded the creekside between the massive trees. The noise of the creek masked to a large measure the sounds of the now-weary horses.

For a long time they proceeded, until at last Ayers stopped. Joshua came up beside him. "Up the ridge, through that gap, and into the hollow," Ayers said in a low voice.

"How far in?"

"Not a mile."

"I'm surprised we've seen nothing of them yet," Joshua said. "I don't like the feeling of it."

"If you were a Cherokee I suppose you'd be telling us to turn back because the signs aren't favorable," McSwain teased, having ridden up beside Joshua and Ayers. He reached back and swung up a small crockery bottle that was tied with a long whang to his saddle and lodged beside a small but well-stuffed keg of gunpowder. He uncorked the bottle and lifted it to his lips. Joshua smelled some of Dudley Grubbins's strong whiskey.

"Don't laugh off Indian notions too quick, Callum. I was amongst them enough to wonder if there isn't something to their way of thinking," Joshua replied. "And put away that whiskey. I don't want you drunk in the midst of the fight."

McSwain brought the bottle back out, opened it, turned it over, let the last drop fall from the rim, then put the bottle back in place. "There went the last of the fiery demon, so you can spare me more preaching." He was smiling, but his tone was not entirely playful. His worsening tendency toward drink was a tender subject between him and Joshua. "A good swallow of whiskey does no more than steady my nerves." He held out his hand and clenched the fist. "See that? Strong and steady as the cornerstone of an old-country kirk! Don't you worry about me, my friend!"

Joshua ignored McSwain. He looked up at the gap. "A

long and low cabin, you say, Willie? How lays the land around it?"

They talked quietly of such matters for a long time, until at last Joshua knew they were as ready as they would be. There was no evidence they had been detected, no hints they were being watched.

"Check your powder and rifles," he said. "We're going in."

They began their climb, horses falling into single file on the narrow, rocky trail that led up to the notchlike pass through the ridge above.

2

The rangers abandoned their horses shortly after crossing through the narrow gap, hobbling them behind a thicket and leaving a man to guard them. Then, with rifles ready, shot pouches swinging from shoulders, and moccasins creeping silently on the wet earth, they advanced through the stalks and brambles of the leafless forest, led by Willie Ayers with Joshua at his side.

They were good and experienced woodsmen to the last man, and Joshua never quite figured out how they failed to detect the presence of the two hunters until it was too late for surprise. Emerging into a clearing, Joshua and Ayers found themselves face-to-face with two riflemen traveling on foot with strings of freshly killed squirrels hanging across their shoulders. Joshua knew they were of Brecht's number, for he recognized both from previous encounters. For a moment all four men were too surprised to react; then others of Joshua's band emerged behind him and Ayers, and one of Brecht's hunters lowered his rifle in a panic and fired. Joshua heard a grunt and felt a man slightly behind and to the side of him fall back. He knew even before he looked that it was Cooper.

Heartsick and fearful for Cooper's welfare, Joshua lifted his rifle and fired. The hunter who had fired the first shot took the ball in the chest and fell back, writhing. In a moment he was dead. The other hunter, eyes white and wide in a broad face so dirty it was black from brow to beard, cried out in alarm, cast down his rifle, and fell to his knees with arms uplifted.

"Please, no, please, no!" he said. "I'll not fight!"

Others rushed in to claim the prisoner. Joshua wheeled and knelt beside Cooper; Callum McSwain was already at Cooper's other side, lifting him to a seated position. Blood streamed down the young man's left arm.

"Cooper, are you—"

"I'm fine, Joshua, I'm fine." Cooper's voice bore witness to his pain. "It nicked my shoulder, that's all."

"That's more than a nick," McSwain said. He had ripped open the sleeve of Cooper's hunting shirt with his knife to expose the wound. "The ball plowed quite a furrow."

"There'll be no surprising them now," Cooper said to Joshua. "They surely heard the shots."

"Aye, but maybe they'll think it was just their hunters," Joshua replied. "We'll go on—except for you, Coop."

"What? I'm as ready for this fight as any man here!"

"Ready to go back home, you mean," Joshua replied. "You're in no shape to fight with a fresh wound. You'd endanger yourself and others besides."

"Not bloody likely you'll drive me off so easy! I can fight with the best of you."

"Let's see you lift that arm, then," McSwain said.

Cooper tried; his hand rose a little, pain flashed across his face, and he stopped. He looked angry and disappointed, but knew the futility of arguing further.

Joshua was already pulling a linen rag from beneath his hunting shirt; he carried a few on all such excursions for binding wounds or for making new ball patches in a pinch. In a few moments the cloth was tight around Cooper's bleeding arm, staunching the blood flow. The pain went away with the bleeding, as Cooper's arm grew numb from its trauma.

"Off with you now," Joshua said, helping Cooper to his feet.

Cooper was sullen. "You've got no call to send me home like some pap-sucking baby. It's shameful to me." He turned and began tramping angrily back to where the horses were hidden—now carrying his rifle in his right hand, Joshua noted.

As Joshua reloaded, he realized that Cooper's wounding had been fortuitous in a way, for it had forced the youth out of a battle Joshua had not wanted him involved with in the first place. Israel Coffman probably would have called it a kindness of providence.

The prisoner was standing now, looking very frightened and pleading not to be hanged. Joshua walked up and faced him. "You'll indeed hang, my friend, unless you choose to help us."

"Anything you ask—I'll do anything!"

Joshua smiled coldly. "That's a fine and charitable spirit," he said. "I'll tell you what you're going to do. You're going to be bait on our line, and the fish we'll catch is Elisha Brecht."

"What do you have in mind, Captain?" one of the rangers asked.

Succinctly Joshua outlined a plan he had handily knitted together. As the captured man listened, he went pale beneath his coat of grime, but the rangers smiled. Captain Joshua Colter was a quick and keen strategist; that was why his men respected and followed him. Their devotion was a grand compliment to their captain, for frontiersmen did not give allegiance for long to any leader who did not earn it, no matter what his rank or title.

Joshua's fingers fidgeted on the stock of his rifle while the captured hunter advanced, no doubt mindful of the fourteen cocked ranger rifles behind him. Smeared with blood from one of the squirrels, he stumbled up the slope toward Elisha Brecht's well-concealed refuge, crying out that he was hurt. As hoped, several men emerged and raced down toward him. When they were well away from the long poplar-log cabin, from which a thin line of chimney smoke wafted, the rangers rose from their hiding places with rifles at ready; Joshua shouted down a call for immediate surrender.

He knew better than to expect to get what he asked for. The human decoy he had sent out obviously was equally pessimistic. He dropped on his belly, putting his hands behind his head and mashing his face into the earth as if trying to mole himself into the ground. Two of Brecht's surprised men fired off their rifles, neither striking any human target. Ranger rifle fire answered at once, and three of those below—one Chickamauga and two whites— fell dead. A fourth man tried to flee, and Callum McSwain impressively proved his claim of a steady hand by bringing him down with a fatal shot through the middle of the back. The two Tories still in the open dropped to their bellies and spread their arms outward in evidence of surrender.

A great cry arose from within Brecht's refuge, and rifle barrels probed out through windows and loopholes, spitting smoke and rifle balls toward the besieging rangers. Joshua was surprised by the amount of fire. He counted a full dozen rifles thrusting out of the cabin.

Most of the rangers dropped back into their hiding places; a previously designated few, who had been instructed not to fire in the first volleys, began creeping around under cover to approach the long cabin from the sides and if possible, the rear. Joshua reloaded, aimed through a crotch in the deadfall that hid him, and fired carefully at a Chickamauga who showed himself for a moment too long at one of the three front windows. Through the smoke of the shot Joshua saw the Indian fall back; he was sure he had hit him. Quickly he reloaded.

The initial phase of the battle dragged on longer than Joshua had hoped. The complication was the unexpected size of Brecht's band, and the fact that the Tory refuge was a virtual fortress with walls of thick, closely set poplar logs. Even though one of the rangers had driven off all the Tories' horses early in the battle, lessening the odds of Brecht's men making an escape, it appeared that a standoff might hold for a long time. Then came an event that made Joshua ponder whether Callum McSwain was the bravest or most foolish man he had ever known. Or perhaps simply the most reckless, for indeed McSwain had become reckless since the death of his wife.

The Scotsman had disappeared in the midst of the fight. Joshua, knowing McSwain would never flee a battle, assumed he had simply taken a new position elsewhere. Joshua himself retained his initial position, which was as safe as could be desired while also in easy range of the cabin.

Since the onset of the battle, the smoke from the cabin chimney had increased. Someone inside either had hurriedly overstoked the blaze about the time the first shots were fired, or perhaps had built up the fire to heat irons to be used for quick cauterization of gunshot wounds. It was obvious the chimney was poorly made and drafty; even from this distance Joshua could tell the cabin was quite smoky.

As Joshua now was sighting in on another figure—was it Brecht himself?—who showed himself furtively at one of the windows, he was astounded to see McSwain appear on the roof. He had climbed on from behind.

Under McSwain's left arm was the little powder keg that had been lashed to the back of his saddle earlier. Over his right shoulder was the bedding blanket he always carried on horseback. Obviously McSwain had rushed back to the horses to fetch the items—and his motive quickly became clear.

McSwain squatted on the roof, used his belt axe to crack open the well-stuffed powder keg, then poured its contents down the smoking chimney. Hurriedly he threw the blanket over the smoke-gushing stick-and-mud chimney top. He gracefully leaped off the back of the roof, rifle in hand, and made for the closest cover. Sulfurous power smoke gushed out of the windows and loopholes. Joshua laughed aloud at his friend's brave and clever ploy.

The cabin door burst open moments later. Tories and Chickamaugas emerged, burned, coughing, but still fighting. The rangers laid down a volley, then leaped from cover to meet their foes man to man. The battle was no longer one of long-distance rifle siege, but individual hand-to-hand combat.

Joshua rose and loped down to join the fight. He brought down one already wounded Tory with a swing of his rifle; then he saw a man scrambling away to the left, making for the hills. It was the stocky Elisha Brecht himself, hatless, his bald pate and fringe of long dirt-brown hair making him instantly recognizable.

Joshua began immediate pursuit; around the far side of the cabin he met Callum McSwain similarly in chase. Speaking not a word to each other, the two rangers chased Brecht into the forest and up a slope. For a stocky man, Brecht was fleet. Joshua figured with a sense of satisfaction that Brecht was driven by pure fear, for now he did not have his usual band of marauders around him to protect him. He was alone.

They raced ever upward, through the thickets and across stony ridges and shelves. The mountainside undergrowth, though mostly leafless, was thick and slowed them. Joshua was dismayed when Brecht found a convenient gap in the brown foliage and went out of sight.

Together McSwain and Joshua climbed, until at last they were atop a high ridge. There they stopped. Brecht was nowhere to be seen, and on the ground they saw no sign. It was stony here, and Brecht had taken to the rocks to avoid leaving a path.

Gasping for air, McSwain said, "Let's separate, Joshua—one of us is sure to find him."

"Aye," Joshua said. "Aye."

Joshua headed west, McSwain east, and both hoped Brecht had not gone north. That was the only other possible direction for him. To the south was the very battle site he was trying to flee. Joshua loped along, keeping watch for both ambush and sign. At length he found a trace of the latter: disturbed leaves where the rocks gave way to thatch-covered forest ground, and a moccasin track in dirt.

Joshua followed the sign down into a little hollow, then up another steep slope. As a far-ranging hunter, he was fit and used to hard travel, but so rugged was the terrain that by the time he reached the top he had to pause for air. He leaned against a massive boulder, letting his straining lungs fill again and again. Suddenly he caught his breath and froze in silence. Cocking his head, he listened to a peculiar sound, and a grin spread across his face.

On the other side of the boulder someone else also was panting for breath. He heard fumbling movement, then the sound of liquid striking leaves. From the evidence first of ears and then nose, Joshua realized that Brecht was taking advantage of a moment of perceived solitude to empty his bladder.

Joshua began edging around the boulder, grinning. What a riotous fireside story this would make—capturing the most hated Tory on this frontier while he was distracted by one of nature's necessities! Poising himself, Joshua darted around the rest of the way.

And then, just as he faced Brecht, he slipped. He maligned himself for a fool even as he fell. How could he have been so careless? He had made the ludicrous blunder of setting his foot right on the wet urine spot Brecht had left on the leafy earth. To make it all the worse, as Joshua fell, his rifle smacked against the boulder and was knocked from his hand.

As clumsy as Joshua's attack was, Brecht was surprised by it and leaped back. He recovered quickly. Because Brecht still held his rifle, Joshua rolled to avoid the gunshot that surely would come. When it didn't come, Joshua knew then that Brecht's rifle was empty. He leaped to his feet and scrambled for his own weapon, but as his arm groped out for it, a sharp pain racked his right shoulder and his arm went numb. He fell on his face, rolled again, and saw the grinning Brecht above him, knife in hand. He had stabbed Joshua in the shoulder.

"Captain Colter!" Brecht said in triumphant pleasure as he recognized his foe. "The very captain himself!" He came forward and down, knife in motion.

They grappled for several moments, grunting and gasping. Joshua cried out when the blade cut him again, worse this time, and in the leg. Brecht was strong and determined, and did not give Joshua opportunity to reach his own knife. Somehow the Tory managed to force Joshua's head back, hard; the frontiersman's skull cracked hard against a stone, stunning him.

"Give greetings to my friends in the fires of perdition, Colter!" the Tory exhulted as he lifted his knife for the fatal stroke.

A rifle shot cracked. Brecht tensed and jerked back. Joshua tried to focus his eyes but couldn't. For a few moments he blacked out. When he came to, Cooper was beside him.

"Are you alive, brother?"

"As best I can tell, yes." Joshua sat up, bloodied and dizzy. "Where is Brecht?"

"Gone. Scampered off into the forest. But I got him, Joshua! I put a ball into him, and me wounded and shooting one-armed! You should have seen his face when he saw me! He ran like a scared buck."

Joshua rubbed his head. The back of his skull was tender and sore, and his stabbed leg bled and throbbed. "Where the devil did you come from, Cooper? You are supposed to be long gone from here."

"I couldn't stay gone, Joshua, not after I heard the shooting begin. I turned back. By the time I got here you and Callum were chasing Brecht up the ridge, so I followed. And it was to your good fortune that I did, eh?"

"I ought to have you whipped for disobeying my orders."

Cooper's eyes twinkled. "I wouldn't do that, Joshua. If you do, I'll feel obliged to spread word that the famous Captain Joshua Colter almost got himself killed by a puddle of piss."

Joshua looked chagrined. "You saw that, did you?"

"No, but from that big smeared track yonder, and the smell of you, it wasn't hard to figure what happened. And now you've owned up to it!"

"You needn't tell anyone, Cooper. If you do, I swear I'll flail you, I truly will!"

Cooper grinned, and Joshua did too. It really was a marvelous joke even if it was on him. "A fine soldier I am, eh?" he said. He paused. "Listen! The shooting has stopped. Help me bind up this leg, and we'll go see what's come of our fight. How bad did you wound Brecht?"

"Not bad enough to keep him from running, clear enough. He was struck in the side, I believe."

"Let's hope it putrefies and puts him right into his grave," Joshua said.

They met McSwain halfway back to the battle site and told him what had transpired, omitting the embarrassing details. "By the way, Callum, that was quite a clever job you did, dumping that powder in the chimney."

"Well, it was certainly no waste. That powder was made with Sicilian sulfur, very impure. It could have found no better use."

The trio moved as fast as Joshua's stabbed leg would allow down to the emptied Tory refuge. The clouds began to break, and the sun spilled through.

Joshua's relief at being alive was tempered by disappointment. This expedition had been only a partial success. Elisha Brecht was still alive and free. Maybe the wound Cooper had inflicted would prove fatal, but Joshua couldn't assume that it would. Brecht seemed too sorry a snake to die that conveniently, anyway.

Though news of Brecht's escape disappointed the other rangers, most felt the venture had been worthwhile regardless. Not a ranger had been lost, and only two others besides Cooper had suffered wounds, all of them minor. Brecht's raiders, on the other hand, had suffered several woundings and an astounding eight deaths—including one by hanging at the close of the battle, before Joshua returned. Joshua regretted that his overeager men hadn't closely interrogated the prisoner. As for the rest of the Tories, they had been scattered.

Analyzing the outcome, Joshua's dissatisfaction yielded to relative contentment. Brecht's force had been broken up, Brecht himself had been wounded, and his hidden stronghold found. Today's battle would hardly put an end to Tory ravages, but it would certainly slow them down for a time, at least where Brecht was concerned. The rangers were in high spirits, and cheered Joshua's command that Brecht's former refuge be put to the torch.

McSwain tended Joshua's wounds as the flames leaped skyward. Joshua stared into the fire, feeling its searing heat even from many yards away. When McSwain was finished with him, Joshua sat on a stump and rested, fingering the ancient Roman coin that he wore on a thong around his neck. The coin, a boyhood gift from his blood father, the late Carolina trader Jack Byrum, had become an identifying mark, even a symbol, of Joshua Colter to both his friends and enemies.

To Joshua himself the symbolism ran deeper. The coin reminded him of his childhood as a trader's son among the Overhill Cherokees, and of his relationship to the late Cherokee-Chickamauga renegade, John Hawk. John Hawk once had been a great friend, and later a great enemy. The friendship was what Joshua remembered and treasured.

On the darker side, the coin also symbolized a secret that Joshua had not shared even with Darcy. No one but he knew of John Hawk's last battle, fought with knives and muscle on the place where the Overhill Cherokee town of Tikwalitsi had stood. There, Joshua had met John Hawk as a child; there, years later, he took his life as a man. This was Joshua's greatest secret, guarded as closely as the Roman coin itself.

Cooper strode over to Joshua, grinning, waving toward the burning cabin. "There's one rat hole I'm glad to see eaten by the flames."

"Aye. We should have less trouble from Elisha Brecht now—I hope." Joshua looked somberly at Cooper. "But I'm afraid that all this will only mean more trouble for you from Solomon Brecht."

"What does it matter? Old Solomon already despises me."

"I could tell the others not to speak of your part in this . . ."

"No. No need. I don't mind Solomon knowing. I can put up with the old cur. Besides, I'm right proud of having been the one who actually shot Elisha Brecht."

"I doubt he knows who you are."

"Oh, he knows. I yelled my name for him good and loud while he was running off and you were passed out."

"I wish you hadn't. I'm afraid Solomon Brecht will take his rifle to you."

"Let him try," Cooper said coldly. "Just let him try."

Most of the rangers, including Cooper, returned to their homes that night; Joshua told Cooper to give word that all were safe and would return the next day. McSwain tried to lure Joshua home with Cooper, but Joshua declined, wanting to remain in case any of Brecht's dispersed force returned. McSwain remained too, and five of the other rangers. All passed a long and restless night. By morning Joshua was convinced there was no reason to stay any longer.

Upon returning home, Joshua was happy to learn that Sina's anger at him had cooled substantially. She now seemed almost jovial, or as close to that as the dour woman ever came. Alphus was doing well; he had already been moved from Thomas's cabin to his own, which stood down the creek and in sight of the mill, near Cooper's little cabin hut. Though Cooper had no true kinship to Alphus, he had become almost a second son to him over the past year, helping him run the mill and keeping an eye on him, Sina, and Zachariah.

Darcy remained feverish but was up and active again, driven by worry over Joshua's welfare. So accustomed was he to battle that Joshua often failed to consider the worries such activity brought this wife. When she greeted him with a tremulous kiss and fought back tears when she saw his wounds, he felt especially tender toward her. "Don't cry, Darcy, don't cry," he said, patting her shoulder as he hugged her close. "I'm always careful when I'm off fighting."

"Careful or not, it scares me," she said. "I lie awake every night you're away, and wonder if I'll ever see you again. This time I felt so sure you'd not come back."

Joshua was sorry for Darcy's worries, but what could he do to spare her from them? He wasn't a man to sit idle in a time of danger. Any man who did was held in the lowest esteem on the frontier. A man had to back up his talk with actions, or else he was held in suspicion, as was Solomon Brecht, whose inactivity in the revolutionary effort was as much a black mark against him as was his brotherhood to Elisha Brecht. "I'll always come back to you, Darcy," Joshua said clumsily, feeling quite uncomfortable. "I love you a heap too much to go and get myself killed."

He had hoped the words would please her. They didn't. Darcy let go of him and went out into the yard, where she began gathering an armload of wood from the woodpile. Joshua went to the doorway. "Come back in here and let me fetch that for you, Darcy. You're still fevered."

"Go sit down," she said gruffly. "You're stabbed, and that's worse than fevered. Anyway, I reckon I'd best stay accustomed to fending for myself. Lord knows I'll have to do it aplenty once I'm widowed."

Joshua sighed. She was in one of those impossible moods again. He hobbled over and sat down beside the fireplace, and began playing with little Will, who cooed in his cradle, waving chubby hands toward his father.

"You're friendly, at least," Joshua muttered, reaching down to his son.

The boy chirped babyishly, wrapping his hand around Joshua's forefinger. After a few moments of play he blinked and closed his eyes, going off to sleep with his grip still intact. He was strong for such a little one, Joshua noted proudly. He would grow up to be big and strong. A good woodsman, a good fighter . . . and then, he realized, Darcy would have two men to worry about.

"Will, what we need is a little girl around this place," Joshua said. "Somebody to take your mother's mind off her menfolk."

Joshua slipped his finger out of the baby's fist, loaded his pipe, and smoked thoughtfully. Maybe another baby really was what Darcy needed. He'd discuss the idea with her . . . but not until she calmed down a bit.

Women were hard creatures to figure sometimes. No matter what a man did or didn't do, they found something in it to get worked up about. He recalled a piece of Alphus's advice from early in his marriage: Sometimes, by Joseph, the thing to do is just get out of the house and leave the females alone for a while.

Joshua wished he could do that right now. But his wounded leg needed rest, and Darcy probably would dislike him leaving so soon after his return, anyway. So he just stayed where he was, smoking his pipe, feeling restless and dissatisfied and put-upon by the worrisome nature of women.

Cooper, meanwhile, was smoking his own pipe outside his own little cabin. Like his brother, Cooper was pondering womankind, but his thoughts were much more positive than Joshua's, and for good reason. Hannah Brecht had just left him. Her kiss still burned on his lips, and his thoughts were still repeating the wonderful declaration of love for him that she had finally made. It had been the first time in their relationship that she had actually told him she loved him. Cooper had feared until today that he would never hear her say the words at all.

Hannah had plenty of reason to be slow to pledge affection to a man. Life in her home was often tense and combative; the picture of husband and wife she had grown up with was a contradictory one: spouses as lovers and spouses as enemies. Hannah had described to Cooper the many times she had seen her mother gently caress her father in the morning and rage in fury at him before nightfall, for unpredictable swings of emotion characterized her mother, Repentance, who some whispered was mad. Whatever the state of her sanity, Repentance's violent changes brought a constant atmosphere of insecurity to the Brecht household. Hannah loved both her parents, but Cooper had detected that her devotion to her father was strong—ironic, in that Repentance didn't seem to hate Cooper like Solomon did.

Cooper had been in the foulest of humors before Hannah came to him today. He had been struggling to clean his rifle and had grown frustrated because his wounded arm made it enormously difficult. He was almost ready to cast the rifle to the dirt when Hannah emerged from the forest, having followed the trail off the wagon road that led past the southern edge of her father's farm down to Colter's Mill.

Immediately Cooper's bad mood had turned to happiness. He ran to Hannah and greeted her with such an enthusiastic hug that his momentarily forgotten wound made him yelp in pain.

"Cooper, how bad did they hurt you?" Hannah asked, stepping back to eye him at arm's length, as if to make sure he was missing no ears, eyes, or fingers.

"I'm fine, fine." He paused. "My rifle gave your uncle Elisha a lot worse than what the Tories gave me."

"Yes . . . I heard."

"So the word is spreading?"

"Father knows, if that's what you mean."

"And I suppose he hates me all the more for it."

Her silence was an uncomfortable affirmative.

"And how do you feel about it?" he asked.

She looked directly into his eyes. "I hate it, like I hate everything to do with war and battles—but you know I could never hate you, Cooper Haverly. I could never hate the man I love and want to marry."

That was how she said it, and before she left she said it twice more. As always, she had left him far too soon, but such quick departures were essential, for her father had forbidden her to see Cooper. Only when Solomon Brecht was occupied on his farm or off in the forest on a hunt was Hannah able to see Cooper at all, and even then she had to evade her mother.

Cooper finished his pipe and knocked the ash from it, wishing Hannah were still here. No one could rouse in him the kind of warm, half-hurting, half-wonderful ache that Hannah Brecht did. Someday and soon, he vowed to himself, I'll not be apart from her anymore. We'll be together forever, whatever her deuced father thinks of it.

With nothing to do at the moment, and his mind too distracted by thoughts of Hannah to allow him to work, Cooper saddled his Chickasaw and rode the full twelve miles or so to Joshua's house, pleasantly surprising his restless brother when he came riding around the wall of the partially finished stockade Joshua was building around his place. He and Joshua talked, and try as he might, Cooper could not restrain himself from talking about Hannah and what had just transpired between them.

Joshua looked serious but not surprised. He had known something big was on Cooper's mind simply from the fact he had ridden so far for no obvious good reason. "Marriage, then. Is that what you're thinking of?"

"Aye . . . why are you asking in that kind of voice?"

"Because I worry for you if you marry her. Solomon Brecht will be an eternal burden on your shoulders."

"I don't see that he need be. When I marry Hannah, I'll take her away. Then we won't see old Solomon anymore, and there'll be no more trouble."

"You think she will be willing to choose between you and her parents?"

"Why wouldn't she? Her father's hated by everyone, and her mother is addled in the mind. Why would she choose them above me?"

"Peter Haverly was hated as well in the end, but you stood by him, Cooper, because he had raised you and you were loyal. Hannah is a loyal person as well."

"Daughters leave home and marry all the time, Joshua," Cooper said defensively. He hadn't expected the conversation to go this way. "Beth did it, didn't she?" The reference was to Beth Haverly, Cooper's adoptive sister, no kin to Joshua. In February she had married a young frontiersman named Abe Pellmar and had moved with him back across the mountains into the North Carolina Piedmont country.

"Yes, but Beth is not estranged from her kin by her choice of a husband. Hannah would be." Joshua paused. "I'm saying naught but that you and Hannah had best think hard before you make plans she might not be willing to keep in the end. If you force a choice on her, you may not like what she chooses."

Cooper stood. "It seems I've come many miles just to hear the wind blow through your skull, Joshua. You've got it set in your mind that Hannah and I can never marry, and I won't stay about to hear such as that. Good day, Joshua."

Darcy had been outside, and came back in as Cooper rode away. "He wouldn't stay to eat?" she asked.

"No. I'm afraid I've made him mad."

Darcy lifted her brows in a way that said without words that there was nothing surprising about Joshua Colter making those around him angry, then she went to the corner and sat down at her spinning wheel.

Joshua lit his pipe and smoked, wishing he were out in the forest with dogs, horse, and rifle, where a man could be himself and not have to please anyone else at all.

He wanted in the worst way to leave, Callum McSwain admitted to Joshua Colter over a pipeful of tobacco. Outside it was snowing lightly, blanketing the early December landscape in a shallow coating of white. Callum and Joshua were standing side by side, leaning on the handhewn mantelpiece above the stone fireplace in Alphus Colter's mill on Sinking Creek. Joshua's wounds from the autumn battle were substantially healed, though he still felt twinges of pain when he moved in certain ways.

Callum was in a mood of confession, talking of his feelings and emotions with unusual openness. Since the death of his wife, he said, life hereabouts hadn't been the same. It had taken him a long time to realize he not only wanted to leave this region, but needed to. The memory of his lost Jean made it too difficult to stay, and had driven him too deeply into his whiskey cups of late. As long as he remained here, she would haunt him.

Joshua was sad to hear Callum talking so. "You'll be much missed when you're gone, not only for your work, but for the man you are," he said.

"Aye? Well, that's a fine thing to for you to say, my friend, and I thank you. But I must go."

"Where to?"

"I don't yet know. Kentucky, I had first thought. Now I'm thinking more of going with Robertson to the French Lick, if he'll allow me along, just to see how I like the Cumberland country."

Joshua's brows went up. He blew a ring of smoke toward the ceiling. "The Cumberland country! Now, there would be a fine place!"

The Robertson whom Callum had named was James Robertson, one of the most noted leaders of the Overmountain settlements. Robertson, one of the region's earliest settlers, had lived first in Watauga but had since moved to a stockaded home on Big Creek in Carter's Valley, down the Holston and closer by the river route to the Indian towns. He had made the move after North Carolina named him Indian agent for its lands west of the mountains. As Indian agent, Robertson now spent much time away in Chota, the sacred Overhill town.

Joshua, like Callum, had known and respected James Robertson for several years. With Robertson, he and Alphus had once participated in an important diplomatic mission to Chota; with Robertson, he and other notable frontiersmen, such as the handsome and flamboyant John Sevier, had led in defense of the settlements during the early Cherokee onslaughts against them.

Now Robertson, following through on plans that had brewed even before North Carolina jurist Richard Henderson's controversial 1775 "purchase" of Cumberland River land from the Cherokee headman, was planning a presettlement journey westward to explore the wide, rich bottomlands of the Cumberland River. That fertile country had already attracted other explorers and hunters, and even some settlers. Already about French Lick was a French-descended hunter and trapper, Jacques Timothe Boucher de Montbrun—whose tongue-twisting name had been simplified in usage to Timothe Demunbreun. A huge hunter named Thomas Spencer had hunted the region extensively, living for a time in a huge, hollow sycamore tree. There was also rumored to be a colony of Tories, exiled from North Carolina, and other assorted individuals and families. Overall, however, settlement was sparse and the potential of the Cumberland frontier unrealized. Robertson and others hoped to change that. If his exploratory journey showed the Cumberland country to be as promising as expected, he would return there with a settlement party at first opportunity.

Callum looked intently at Joshua. "A fine place indeed . . . maybe the perfect sort of place for a man like yourself, eh?"

Joshua felt a sudden pang of longing. He had wandered all his life, and the lust for exploration hadn't left him. To find a new home, to start anew, to see lands as yet mostly unsettled . . . the prospect was immensely attractive. Still, he shook his head.

"I can't," he said. "There's too much holding me here now, especially with Elisha Brecht still a threat."

"Brecht is dead, Joshua. I'm sure of it. If he wasn't, we would have seen more of him by now."

Joshua shrugged. He did not know why he remained intuitively certain that Brecht was still alive. Perhaps it was because he couldn't afford to think otherwise and risk the disaster that comes from overoptimism. And in one way Brecht's status hardly mattered; even if he was dead, there remained plenty of other Tories to worry about—entire nests of them along the Nolichucky.

Thanks to the Tories, the past year had been an active one for Joshua, his band of Whig rangers, and other bands like them. Captain William Bean and a group of patriot riflemen had driven a troublesome loyalist named Isam Yearly off the Nolichucky earlier in the year, and later had driven a second Tory band that had at least one killing to its credit, back across the mountains. Joshua was himself a stern punisher of Tories, but others were even harsher. Many were the Tories who had died in the noose, and many more were there who had felt the sting of fire-tempered hickory whips on their backs. Tories were subject to confiscations of land and property, tarring and feathering, and being driven to the farthest borders of the frontier. Sometimes Joshua secretly regretted individual instances of overharsh Tory punishment, but at heart he had no real love for the breed, for he had seen too many loyalists willing to fatally betray their neighbors, or like Elisha Brecht, to become "outliers" and take advantage of warfare as an excuse for criminal gain. And for every story of degradations suffered by Tories, there were equally as many of degradations inflicted by them.

"We'll hear from Brecht yet—mark my words," Joshua said. "And besides, Callum, I've got other concerns holding me here." He lowered his voice. "You know how Alphus is anymore. If I headed for French Lick, he'd want to go as well, and he's too old for it."

Joshua couldn't have picked a worse time to make that comment, for around the door came Alphus, face reddening and eyes snapping. He was moving in the gingerly, careful manner that had characterized him since his wounding by Brecht. His healing was proceeding more slowly than Joshua's, though he was improved enough now that all Sina's pleading couldn't persuade him to stay home, leave the milling and hunting to others, and avoid exertion.

"Old, you say? By Joseph, is that what you think of me now, Joshua? I reckon you think I'm deaf as well. Well, I'm not. I've heard every word you said."

Joshua grew angry; Alphus often made him angry these days, for reasons he sometimes couldn't put his finger on. "Alphus, anything I've said is no insult," Joshua snapped back. "I'd never speak ill of you. But a lot of years have walked over you now, and they leave tracks on any man, no matter how strong he is."

"So I'm an old man now, and ought to content myself with a chair by the fire? By Joseph, I can still keep pace with you on your best day, Joshua Colter!"

Joshua waved his hand in exasperation. He didn't want to argue with his foster father, even though Alphus's last statement was blatantly untrue. Alphus was far slower, and much less the woodsman, than he had been as recently as a year ago. Everyone knew it, including Alphus. The old hunter simply refused to admit it.

"Forget I said anything, then," Joshua replied, forcing back his irritation.

Alphus sat down heavily on a stool in the corner and leaned forward on the walking stick he had used since his wounding. He looked up though his bushy brows at Callum. "I might just go with you to the French Lick, Callum," he said. "By Joseph, I'd like to see some new country." He glanced quickly at Joshua. "In new country a man is judged by what he does and what he is, not by how many years he's got behind him."

"I'd best be going," Joshua muttered, emptying his clay pipe into the fire and tucking it away. Callum looked pleadingly at him, regretting having unwittingly sparked a family squabble and dreading being left alone to deal with Alphus while he was mad.

Joshua left the mill and walked through the lightly falling snow up the dirt road along Sinking Creek. He felt badly about having angered Alphus. Anger wasn't healthy in a man so old. Alphus worried Joshua lately, and worried Sina even more. The terrible death of Gabriel Colter had marked a significant change in Alphus. Sometimes he would be lost for an entire day in silent broods over his son. So deep were some of these spells that he wouldn't respond even when directly spoken to. And when finally he did snap back into the world of reality, he often would be crotchety and restless and go off for hunts of two or three days' duration, Sina worrying all the while that he wouldn't return. Several times Joshua had been compelled to go out and find Alphus, who when found would complain about being treated like an old man in his dotage— even though that's exactly what he had become. Joshua found the entire matter very frustrating. Dealing with Alphus these days was like playing a game that couldn't be won.

Joshua looked around him. This land, so marked with cabins and farmsteads, blockhouses and stockades, had not long ago been an empty wilderness. He, Alphus, and their old partner Levi Hampton had hunted here when no one lived within countless miles. Even the Overhill Cherokees hadn't lived here, though they hunted and traveled back and forth along ancient war and trading paths. Their residential towns lay to the southwest, along the Tennessee River.

Now this no longer seemed a true wilderness to Joshua. The land was divided by invisible surveyor's lines that marked off property, and Indian treaty boundaries that white men were not supposed to cross. Only a few miles west of where Joshua now walked was one such boundary, agreed to in council with the Cherokees on the Long Island of the Holston in 1777. The line marked what was supposed to be the western boundary of white settlement. Yet even now some whites had settled west of the line and violated the treaty. Of course, the Cherokees themselves had violated the treaty as well, failing to return horses that had been stolen, as the terms required. This very failure Joshua had heard given as justification for settlement beyond the line. Joshua had lived among both Indians and whites long enough to know that dealings between them were no more pure and clear-cut than any other affairs of men. There was bad will, dishonesty, and failure enough on both sides to keep matters eternally unsettled. A man could grow cynical thinking about it.

White settlement had deeply changed the land. Many formerly forested hills and levels had become stump-filled open fields, and fast-running streams now turned great mill wheels. And there was government now, passing laws and setting the prices of corn, whiskey, hay, and pasturage, and in general making life much too complicated for a simplicity-loving man like Joshua Colter. What had been an empty frontier in which the only law was that of God and nature had evolved into a political entity called Washington County, and was represented in the North Carolina assembly. Another body, a county court, dealt with local legal matters. It expended much of its energies condemning and seizing Tory property, and in sending off convicted criminals to fight the British.

Valentine Sevier was sheriff of Washington County, succeeding himself in the same job he had held under the authority of the earlier Watauga Association government. Joshua had been undersheriff back in those days; now he held no such official post, but was as involved as ever in keeping the peace; that was one part of his life that hadn't much changed. Though Joshua had gone through a time of disrepute before his marriage, his good reputation had since been restored and the Overmountain people again thought of him as a leader.

Leader. Joshua accepted the designation only with reluctance. He had never had much interest in civil affairs and responsibility; he wanted merely to be free and unencumbered, making his living as best he could off the wilderness itself. For many years he had earned almost all his livelihood from the deerskin trade. Now his living came mostly from farming, dealing in land and property, occasional work at Alphus's mill, and surveying, a skill he was still learning. The irony was that none of these things appealed inherently to him, yet he was forced to cling to them . . . this while Callum McSwain was about to embark on what promised to be a spirited, rewarding adventure. Joshua realized right then that he was jealous of his friend.

There were compensations that came with this more settled life, of course, Darcy and little Will chief among them. Joshua snorted in self-contempt. Compensations! His loved ones were far more than mere compensations. They were his lifeblood, the reason he lived and worked and put up with burdens he otherwise might shrug off. He felt ashamed to envy Callum's freedom when he considered that Callum had gained it only through the death of his wife. Surely, if Callum had the choice, he would throw away that liberty in a moment and take on the chains of matrimony and responsibility again, if only his beloved one could miraculously return.

Joshua took a deep breath and stopped, leaning on the rifle he carried everywhere he went. He decided that he didn't envy Callum when it came down to it. He simply missed the freedom he had gradually lost. What had happened to the old times? When had they vanished, and why hadn't he noticed them fading away? It made him feel old to think of such things . . . old, and he still hadn't reached his thirtieth year.

Thoughts of age again brought thoughts of Alphus. He

realized that his own sad feelings at the moment were nothing more than watered-down versions of what Alphus surely felt. No wonder Alphus seemed unhappy! The world he had known was washing away in the current of change, like an eroding creek bank. Joshua was still young enough to anticipate new adventures and experiences. Alphus was not, and Joshua could hardly fault him for being bitter as his life moved from twilight toward night. It was as he had heard Israel Coffman once say in a sermon: In this fallen world, even happy stories turn to sad ones as they near their end, if for no other reason than that they are ending.

Joshua hefted his rifle, sighed, and crossed the foot log across the icy cold creek. On the other side was forest, stretching for miles. A few hours of hunting was what he needed to turn his mind off bleak thoughts. Maybe he could bring down a buck—if he could find one. The bigger game was harder to find anymore. Likely he'd have to satisfy himself with a string of squirrels—another case of settling for what the world was instead of what he wished it could be.

Shifting his shot pouch on his shoulder, he stepped off the log and vanished into the snowy woods.

Darcy Colter looked out over the peaceful, snowy landscape beyond Great Limestone Creek and noted that on days like this, one could hardly imagine there was a war going on. The only visual reminder that these were not peaceful times was the wall of the stockade Joshua was building around the yard, and over near the creek the pile of logs that would someday make up a blockhouse.

Often life on this side of the mountains gave little evidence of the massive rebellion that had caught the eye of the world. Days would roll past, one after the other, with nothing marking them except the eternal repetition of domestic labor.

That was the way Darcy liked it. She could abide the mundane, for her life was a good one. She had a fine husband and a beautiful young son, and every uneventful day that passed was one more day that she could give thanks for in her evening prayers.

It hadn't always been that way for her. Before her marriage to Joshua, she had been the wife of Joshua's foster brother Gabriel, a jealous and abusive man. It was too bad, Darcy had often reflected, that the good side of Gabriel had not shown itself until the last days of his life, far too late for it to make a difference in their marriage. She might have actually loved Gabriel if only he had given her the smallest chance.

Joshua possessed a quality his foster brother never had, and that was the capacity to receive love—something that Darcy had learned was as essential to a marriage as the ability to give it. Joshua, though quiet and undemonstrative, gave and accepted love with effortless grace. He was an easy man to live with, most of the time. He had given Darcy what she wanted most: a peaceful life.

A peaceful life. There again was the deception, the facade that sometimes made her forget the grimmer reality behind it. There really was no peaceful life here for anyone, no matter how calm individual days or weeks might be, and there would not be a truly peaceful life for anyone until the war with Britain was settled.

Darcy was deeply interested in the progress of the war, though she seldom talked about it. Joshua didn't like her to worry about matters mostly beyond her control, nor did he consider it a woman's place to take on such manly concerns as war. Darcy thought that a silly notion; did not Joshua realize that women and children were just as affected by war as men, and even more victimized by it? It was women and children who were left husbandless and fatherless every time a militiaman or soldier fell and died, and women and children who sometimes fell and died themselves—a tragedy worsened by its injustice.

War, in fact, seemed to Darcy a demon with a particular hatred of women, and which reserved certain tortures specifically for them. Darcy personally knew three women who had watched husbands ride off on one military expedition or another, only to have them vanish into a limbo from which neither they nor any word of their fate ever returned. Darcy could not imagine a more hellish thing than that: to lose a man and never know to the day of one's own death what had happened to him.

News of the war elsewhere in the country was slow to come across the mountains; often the frontier people had to rely on information that was old before it arrived. What information Darcy could find she mentally tucked away and pondered as deeply as the outdated broadsides and tattered newspapers posted occasionally on the wall of Colter's Mill.

She cared deeply about the outcome of the war for very personal reasons, fearing that if the British prevailed, such outspoken and militant Whigs as her husband would be treated as traitors, jailed, shot, or hanged, and their wives and children turned over to the vengeance of the Indians. Darcy had a deep terror of Indians, having lost her mother, brother, and first husband to them, and having gone through a brief but terrifying Cherokee captivity of her own, in which she escaped the fire and stake only by the intervention of Nancy Ward, a Cherokee woman of rank who favored peace with the whites. Now, beyond her deep gratitude to Nancy Ward, she had nothing good to say about "savages." Even though Joshua often tried to persuade her that she was wrong to "pickle every Indian in the same barrel," he had failed to change her mind.

Darcy wrung her hands together out of habit, her strong left hand clasping her undersized and slightly misshapen right one. The hand had been badly maimed in a wagon accident in her girlhood, and had never grown correctly thereafter. She had always been ashamed of her "withered" hand. Even though Joshua never seemed even to notice the deformity, she wondered sometimes if he secretly found it repelling. Gabriel certainly had; he had never allowed her to touch him with her right hand.

Darcy heard a distant rifle shot and jumped involuntarily. It sounded like Joshua's rifle, firing a light squirrel charge. Probably he was out there hunting. Darcy was glad no one had seen her startled by so relatively distant a sound. But one could never know if a rifle's crack meant a hunter's success and supper on the table, or the end of a human life at the hand of some wartime border raider.

Lord, she prayed silently, please bring this war to an end. So many die, so many suffer on all sides. Have mercy on us, Lord, and bring us peace.

Darcy had prayed for peace all year. So far it had not come except in short, deceptive lulls, and even those were ruined by rumors of new violence to come.

The most recent whispers were the most frightening. Rumor had it that the Chickamaugas were to launch a major attack on the settlements in the spring. Some even said the Overhill Cherokees, enticed by promise of renewed British aid and angered by the continuing advance of white settlement, might join their estranged offspring in the effort. Joshua discounted that, noting that many people still confused the Chickamaugas and the Overhill Cherokees, attributing to the latter intentions and actions actually belonging to the former. Darcy wasn't as discriminating as her husband. To her an Indian was an Indian, and all were equally fearsome and unpredictable.

A couple of nights before, Darcy had prompted Joshua to talk some about his views of the border war. He gave much credence to fears of springtime warfare, and hinted that it was his preference, and that of most patriotic men of merit in these parts, to carry war to the Chickamaugas first. All throughout the year, the Chickamaugas had been helping the British chastise Georgia and South Carolina, which kept their towns substantially reduced in number of fighting men. Bit by bit the location of the main Chickamauga nests had been discovered, and a strike against them while their ranks were diluted seemed a good option.

Darcy was chilled at the prospect of Joshua departing in the spring to fight, for he would surely take part in the campaign. She would make no attempt to argue him out of it, of course, for Joshua never shirked any fight he felt was his duty. Only rarely did he miss out on any major battle expedition. One such occasion had been this very year, when he remained behind while several other men from the region went off to the Illinois country to help

George Rogers Clark take Kaskaskia from the British. Joshua would have gone but for a fractured rib suffered in a fall from a neighbor's cabin he was helping roof. As it turned out, the attackers of Kaskaskia got by just fine without Joshua Colter; Clark and his band took the stronghold without firing a shot.

Darcy heard the crack of a rifle again, this time closer and making her react even more than the first time. She walked around the side of the cabin to investigate the origin of the shot, so close had it sounded. She was surprised and pleased to see Cooper Haverly striding across toward her through the open gate of the unfinished stockade, a big grin on his face and five squirrels tied on a string.

"You're fixed fine for supper meat now, Darcy Colter!" he called.

"Why, thank you, Cooper. But Sina might need them worse than we do. I'm expecting Joshua in soon, and likely he'll bring meat with him."

"So he will. There he comes yonder."

Darcy turned. Sure enough, Joshua was coming down the footpath through the delicate snowfall, bearing a string of squirrels identical to Cooper's. He had a broad smile on his face; the sight of him made Darcy's heart race, like it always did.

"Well, Coop, it appears that between us we've struck grief into a heap of squirrel families today," Joshua said.

"So it appears. I think mine are fatter, though."

"That's 'cause you can only hit the lazy ones that are too fat to run. Me, I can spot the fastest squirrel in the woods at dead midnight with no more light than the flash of a lightning bolt, drop him on the jump from one tree to the next, skin him with my fingernail, and roast him for breakfast over the coals of my pipe."

"Why, you're going to have to let me see you do that one of these evenings, Joshua," Cooper said. "Tell you what, you show me that, and I'll show you my new hunting hound. He trees liars."

Darcy smiled at the brotherly banter. "Cooper, can you stay for supper?" she asked.

"I can, and I'll be obliged forever to you, Darcy," he said. "If you're cooking, I'm skinning."

"Thank you, Cooper. I'm going in—I hear Will starting to fuss."

Joshua set to work with his knife on the squirrels, removing the skins with the attentionless ease that comes from familiarity with a task. Cooper joined him. Picking up a squirrel, he cut through the tail up to the skin of the back, flipped the animal over, and cut slits down each ham. Putting his foot onto the tail, he pulled until the skin was stripped from the forelegs, then peeled the skin off the hind legs. After the feet were cut off, he finished skinning the head, the entire job done in less than a minute. Cooper had not a trace of stiffness remaining from his shoulder wound. He began to whistle as he labored.

"You're in high spirits today, Cooper," Joshua commented.

"And well I might be."

Joshua waited for Cooper to go on, which he didn't, then smiled slightly as he realized Cooper wanted to be prompted. "So what's got you grinning?"

"I saw Hannah this morning."

Joshua stopped smiling. "Where?"

"It don't matter. We have a place we meet where old Solomon can't find us."

Joshua suddenly was uncomfortable with the conversation. Since the expedition against Elisha Brecht, Solomon Brecht had been more forceful than ever in his hatred of Cooper, or so everyone said. It had reached the point that Joshua had hoped Cooper and Hannah would have a falling out so as to put Cooper out of burning range of Solomon Brecht's hot temper.

"How's Hannah?"

"Fine, though not nearly so fine as she'll be come springtime."

"What do you mean?"

"I mean I'm going to marry her, that's what. First blush of spring, I'm making Hannah my wife and we're going to go off to the French Lick or Kentucky or any other place we want—any place that old Solomon and Repentance won't be."

Joshua took a deep breath. All his old worries and objections to Cooper's romance with Hannah remained; Cooper had never satisfactorily answered any of them. But clearly Cooper's mind was made up. Joshua painted a smile on his face and nodded. "Best wishes to you, then, brother." He put out his hand.

Cooper grinned and stuck his hand into Joshua's.

"Can Darcy know?" Joshua asked.

"Yes . . . but no one else. Not yet."

They worked for another minute without words. Cooper whistled happily through his teeth. Joshua laid aside another skin and said, "You might need to know something, Coop—I heard just yesterday that Solomon Brecht's lands might be taken from him."

Cooper stopped whistling and looked up sharply. "The county court?"

"There's some ready to swear that Solomon's a Tory and spies for Elisha."

Cooper frowned and shook his head. "I've got no love for Solomon Brecht, but I don't believe he's a spy. Not for a minute. I'm not even persuaded he's a Tory—Hannah surely isn't."

"You may not think he is, but plenty of others do."

"Including you, Joshua?"

"I don't pass judgment on what I don't know about."

Cooper fumed silently a few minutes, skinning another couple of squirrels, then said. "Let's forget about Solomon Brecht for now—it ain't him I'm going to marry anyway."

"I reckon it's not," Joshua replied, laying aside the last skin. "Let's get these into Darcy's kettle. I'm hungry enough to eat them raw, bones and all."

Supper was a fine one, followed by pipes and conversation about Cooper's upcoming married life. Joshua had to force his joviality a little, worried as he was about Cooper's plans, and Darcy seemed distracted. At length Cooper departed for his own cabin, and Joshua and Darcy retired.

Joshua lay in bed a long time that night, looking up into

the darkness and thinking about Cooper until at last he decided such fretting wasn't properly his job. He was Cooper's brother, after all, not his father. And after that he lay awake another hour, worrying over him all the same, while Darcy slept.

But she really wasn't sleeping. She was lying on her side, back to Joshua, wide awake, thinking the same thoughts that had distracted her at supper: thoughts about springtime, Chickamaugas, and military expeditions. Most of all she wondered how hard it was to be a widow, and if she would be one of the unfortunate women who had to find out.

Cooper crawled through the damp leaves like a snake, wriggling on his belly beneath the brush. His horse was hobbled on the other side of a little knoll far behind him; his rifle was gripped tightly in his right hand, and he was trying his best to make minimal noise as he advanced. It had been cold throughout the morning on this early January day in 1779, until the late morning sun warmed the earth above the freezing point and left the land damp and chilly.

Cooper had heard the voices like distant whispers on the wind, and one of them was familiar. At first he thought it was Alphus, out hunting and talking to some partner— or perhaps to himself, as he sometimes did lately. The closer he drew, however, the less like Alphus's the voice sounded, and the more like Solomon Brecht's. At that point Cooper had grown very careful, and began approaching as slyly as he could.

There was no question now that the voice indeed was Solomon's, and that he was talking to at least two other men. Every instinct warned Cooper that this situation was dangerous to him, and he considered turning back. For Solomon Brecht to find him alone in the forest might tempt the man to rid himself of the young whelp who threatened to take away his beloved daughter. Out here that could easily be done, and no one would be the wiser as to what had happened to Cooper Haverly.

But Cooper was a young man in whom curiosity was as strong as caution, sometimes stronger. He had not departed. Just a few more feet of careful crawling and he should be able to see Brecht and whoever he was talking to.

The smell of horses was so strong now that Cooper began to suspect the party ahead was larger than he had first thought. He heard hooves moving on the forest floor, and a man's cough. The wind rustled the forest branches enough to help mask any noise Cooper made, but also enough to keep him from understanding what was being said. Wet, cold, and strained from his unnatural mode of travel, he edged forward the final yard and lay as flat as he could, looking down into a wide ravine.

Solomon Brecht was there, almost directly facing Cooper. Behind him was a frightening-looking group of mounted men, three Indians and four whites, the latter dirty to the man and clad in woodsmen's garb. Cooper recognized none of them.

The man Solomon Brecht was talking to had his back to Cooper. He was much shorter than the lean, lanky Solomon and seemed to be stocky, though that was hard to be sure of in that he wore a long bearskin cloak. His hat was made of raccoon fur, with the long tail still attached for show and hanging down onto his right shoulder.

Cooper lay very still and let his breathing slow. He wished he hadn't come this close, for one of the red men was looking with a suspicious expression toward the thicket that hid him. Cooper began to shiver, and not from the cold.

Solomon Brecht was talking in a low voice and standing close to the unidentified man, a very serious expression on his face. Meanwhile, the suspicious Indian heeled his mount forward, toward the thicket.

Cooper's hand tightened on his rifle, ready to draw up and fire if need be. He felt sure he could shoot the Indian off his horse, though if he did, he would be no better off, just unarmed to face all the others. Fear swept over him in a great wave; he had to fight down the insane temptation to rise and run.

The Indian did not seem to have actually seen Cooper. The young frontiersman didn't even blink, not daring to move at all. But move he did, and almost yelled in alarm, when something broke out of the brush beside him and angled across in front of the advancing Indian's horse.

A rabbit. Nothing but a rabbit. Cooper hoped his startled movement hadn't betrayed him.

Then he saw that the Indian had stopped, watching the rabbit dart into a dried-up briar thicket on the other side of the ravine. The Indian smiled slightly, turned his mount, and rejoined the others. Cooper breathed in relief and sank even deeper into the cold leaves, thinking that he would never be able to bring himself to shoot or snare another rabbit again. He owed the species his life.

Solomon Brecht's conversation with the stranger ended moments later. Solomon turned and walked back to his own waiting horse, passing so close to Cooper that he might have seen him had he been more woodsman than farmer.

Cooper's eyes shifted back to the others. The stranger had advanced back to the waiting band and mounted. For the first time Cooper saw his face. Elisha Brecht.

Cooper waited until the riders were long gone before he rose and returned to his own horse. He was glad he was alone so that no one could see how scared he was. He mounted and began riding north, back toward his home. When he had put a mile behind him, he felt better and his trembling lessened. He began to think over the implications of the meeting he had witnessed.

It proved beyond question that Elisha Brecht was alive, as Joshua had suspected, and close by. Cooper wondered if Brecht had been about this region all along, and if so, why he had not been actively raiding. Perhaps he had been elsewhere, as Joshua had speculated, and had only recently returned.

The most shattering aspect of the meeting, however,

was that it proved the rumors about Solomon Brecht were correct. He did in fact keep contact with his infamous brother, which gave great credence to the suspicion that Solomon was a Tory spy.

I ought to tell Joshua, Cooper thought.

Surprisingly, a great resistance to the idea surged in him. Cooper stopped the Chickasaw and dismounted, crouching down on his haunches beside the horse to think.

Surely it was his duty to tell what he had seen. But to do so might carry a great personal cost. Hannah truly believed that her father, while not a fervent Whig, was no Tory, and certainly not a spy. How might she react if the very man she wished to marry brought condemning information about her father? Cooper had noticed lately that Hannah seemed a little colder, a little more distant, than she had before. It had worried him considerably, and the prospect of putting further pressure on what might be a weakening relationship seemed intolerable.

Cooper knew why Hannah seemed somber: Her father had barely escaped seizure of his lands and property by the county court. Solomon Brecht had been officially accused of being a Tory spy, and only through a sworn vow of innocence and a declaration of his support for the American cause had he overcome the charge.

None of the Colters had been involved in the proceedings against Solomon Brecht; but Solomon himself, Hannah had confided, believed Joshua was the ultimate source of the charge, and resented it. He must have talked up his bitterness quite a lot at home, for it had clearly affected Hannah, who seemed unpersuaded by Cooper's defense of his brother.

Cooper stood, his mind made up. I'll just keep what I saw to myself for now. All I saw was two brothers talking. I don't know what was said. And if Brecht hasn't raided here in all this time, there's no reason to believe he's about to start again.

He mounted and rode home, feeling better for his decision, or at least telling himself he did.

* * *

My brother is a fine-looking man, Ayasta thought to herself as she watched Ulagu pick up Wasi and hold him high. The child laughed as the powder-tattooed warrior began to toss him up and down in a way that looked careless but that worried Ayasta not at all. Ulagu was strong, rugged, and rough, but also thoroughly devoted to Wasi, and that made the difference. In his big hands Wasi was safe in even the roughest play.

Ulagu, wounded in the leg and temporarily left unable to fight, had returned to the Chickamauga towns two weeks before, but had come to Chickamauga itself only today. Accompanying him had been Elisha Brecht, who had long ago recovered from the wound that had been given him by a young ranger who Brecht swore was the younger brother of Joshua Colter. Brecht had been raiding for many months with the remnants of his band in Georgia and South Carolina, but had gone on temporarily to the Nolichucky and Watauga country to see his brother, who was rumored to be in some kind of trouble. Ulagu, not having gone farther than the Chickamauga towns with Brecht, did not know the outcome of that matter, and didn't care in any case. Brecht's family problems were his own.

Ulagu, mostly recovered now, was eager to leave soon to resume the warfare that was his life and happiness. Already he had outlined to Ayasta the progress of the war as he had followed it for the past many months. John McDonald, the British commissary to the Chickamaugas, and Alexander Cameron, British Indian agent, had guided the Indian war efforts throughout the year. At their request, Dragging Canoe had sent as many warriors as he could to aid the British in battling Georgia and South Carolina rebels.

Ayasta fed Ulagu a big meal that evening. While he ate he talked optimistically of the war. In the pleasant dialect of the Overhill Cherokees from whom he had seceded, Ulagu said, "Before this season comes again, we will have destroyed the unakas. This will be a year of blood. I wish John Hawk were alive to join us in shedding it, and that

Wasi were a man and not a child, so that he could fight by
our sides."

There was no way Ulagu could know the way that
statement made Ayasta feel. She did not let it show.

"The unakas believe they cannot be driven back, but
they are wrong," Ulagu continued. "John Hawk's spirit
will be glad when what he fought for in his life is finally
achieved. He will be satisfied then—the land will be as it
should be when the unakas are gone. Wasi will grow up
in a better place and have a better life than his father ever
knew."

"Yes, he will," Ayasta said. The words carried an irony
Ulagu couldn't detect.

Ayasta hoped her brother would find subjects other
than war and bloodshed and Wasi and the spirit of John
Hawk to speak of, but she was disappointed. Ulagu
seemed happy, excited by his vision of a world free of
white encroachers. The evening dragged on until the
warrior's talk became a droning in Ayasta's ears that she
could no longer abide. When Ulagu yet again began
talking of Wasi's future as a warrior, Ayasta stood. "Wasi
will not be what his father was," she declared bluntly.

Ulagu looked at her in puzzlement. "What did you
say?"

Ayasta was aware of one fractional moment when she
might alter her statement and avert what was sure to be
anger on her brother's part. She let the moment pass.
Ayasta's temper was too stirred for her to hold silent.

"Your ears aren't filled with mud, Ulagu," she said.
"You understand what I said."

"But—"

"There's nothing for you to say. If Wasi lives the life of
his father, he will also die the death of his father. I will
not allow it."

Ulagu had been crouched comfortably on a bearskin
pallet. Now he came to his feet as smoothly and easily as
a levitating ghost, despite the soreness lingering in his
wounded leg. Although his face was not as thin now as it
had been two weeks ago, when he was still lean from the
deprivations and exertions of warfare, his features looked

strangely gaunt and chiseled as he stared darkly at his sister. Ayasta saw her brother in a new way at that moment, and realized that this must be his face as it had been seen by many of his enemies in the final moments before he took their lives.

"You talk foolishly, sister. As Mother's brother I am Wasi's discipliner."

"It wasn't your body that nested him and then pushed him out into the world," Ayasta replied. "It wasn't your breast that fed him."

"Old woman's talk!"

"No! Mother's talk . . . and even more than that, a widow's talk. I'll not lose my son as I lost my husband!"

Ulagu looked at Ayasta with contempt. "Wasi's future will not be your decision. I know what John Hawk's will for him was, and I know that it is my duty to make him into a great warrior. You won't keep me from it."

Ayasta stepped forward, opening her mouth to speak even more defiant words. She stopped short and closed her lips tightly together, then turned away. Wasi, who had been asleep in the corner, woke up, disturbed by the loud adult voices. Ayasta went to him and picked him up.

Ulagu watched his sister and nephew silently for a few moments, then stomped to the door. Though the night was cold, Ulagu was a typical warrior, seemingly oblivious to physical stresses, and had brought nothing but a thin blanket to protect him. This he tossed across his shoulders as he exited.

Ayasta closed her eyes and began to regret her loose tongue. Had she said too much? Only at the last moment had she caught back the words that would have revealed her secret plan to Ulagu. She went back and analyzed her statements, searching her words until she was content that she had not revealed anything to endanger her plan.

Wasi went back to sleep in moments, but Ayasta continued to hold him. His body seemed small and frail; his frequent illnesses had kept him from growing as he should. Also, Ayasta was convinced, the lack of a male presence in Wasi's life somehow contributed to his frailty. Wasi needed so much more than his present circumstances were able to give him.

The fire that had been burning brightly dwindled until the flame was about to play itself out. Ayasta laid Wasi down and covered him with his blanket, then stoked the blaze. As the flames brightened, her spirit darkened.

Did she really have the courage to do what she planned? It had now been more than three months since she had made her resolve—yet here she remained, her plan still nothing but a thought in her mind.

Maybe now is the time, she thought. Maybe tomorrow, or the next day, or next week . . .

Or perhaps the spring. Yes—the spring, when the weather is warm and Wasi won't grow sick in the cold. I'll gather food and weapons, take a horse, and then we'll go, just he and I. We'll ride fast and far and be out of reach long before Ulagu knows we are gone. We'll ride until we reach the places where the unakas live, and search until we find the unaka my husband called Colter, who wears the amulet around his neck. If I cannot find Colter, I will seek out the God-man called Coffman. John Hawk said both were good men, far better than most of their race. I'll find one of them, perhaps both, and they will help me give Wasi the life I want him to have.

Her spirit brightened as she reaffirmed her plan. She decided to speak again to Ulagu in the morning, and profess to be sorry for the "foolishness" she had displayed tonight. She would tell him that of course Wasi would grow to be a great warrior, as John Hawk would have wanted, and would attribute her earlier words to the contrary to the approach of her menstrual issue, which always distressed her mind.

And Ulagu would believe her. If there was one skill Ayasta possessed, it was the ability to convince her brother of whatever she wanted him to believe. She had honed that ability since their childhood, and it would serve her well as she healed the damage done by her angry words tonight.

She went back to Wasi's side and smiled at the sleeping

boy. "When the spring comes," she chanted softly, improvising a song. "When the spring comes, my son, we will go, we will go, we will go together."

Many long miles from Ayasta and unknown to her, there were others waiting for the spring to come, and they also had plans.

Virginia Governor Patrick Henry had long been aware of the continued danger posed by the Chickamauga towns to the white settlers, and today had moved to deal with it. At about the same time Ulagu had set foot in Ayasta's house, the governor was putting his seal and stamp upon a letter addressed to Richard Caswell, his political counterpart in North Carolina. In the letter, he informed Caswell that he had already instructed Colonel Evan Shelby of the Holston country in Virginia to raise a three hundred man force to assault the Chickamauga towns. Could the honorable governor of North Carolina add two hundred volunteers from Washington County to the Virginia force? The assembled forces would combine and travel by river to the Chickamauga towns and lay them to waste.

The letter was delivered to Caswell; days rolled past as its request was considered, first by the governor, then by the North Carolina general assembly. On January 21 the decision was made: Washington County would accept Henry's request and furnish two hundred volunteering militiamen, to be commanded by Major Charles Robertson, one of the county's representatives in the current assembly. His rank was increased to lieutenant colonel, and the lower-house assemblyman from Washington County, Major Jesse Walton, was named commissary for the venture.

The two appointees accepted their posts readily and prepared to leave the assembly at once, Walton being given nine thousand pounds to finance supplies. Colonel Shelby, they were told, was to prepare a fleet of small craft that would carry the militiamen downriver.

As the Washington Countians were about to leave, one final directive was given them. This was to be no malicious enterprise. No friendly Cherokees were to be harmed, if at all possible; the only targets were the Chickamaugas. And of those, women and children were to be spared and respected. Was this clear?

Both Robertson and Walton nodded. Yes, they said, it was clear.

"The finest thing about this country in early spring is the sweetness of the wind," Joshua Colter exulted to Alphus as they rode side by side along the dirt trace. It was indeed a particularly blustery day, clear and beautiful. Sometimes, Joshua said, he wondered if a man could take some feathers and make himself a big pair of wings and fly off a mountaintop with them on a day like this.

Alphus shook his head, his eyes twinkling. "Don't try it, Joshua. I did, back in 'seventy-three. It worked fine until the ground sprung up sudden and smote me a hard one on the mouth."

Joshua chuckled politely at Alphus's joke. The old man was in a good mood today, playing his droll sense of humor like Callum McSwain played his fiddle: somewhat irritatingly. He had been cracking jokes all day, most of them bland as bread crust.

Joshua put up with it gladly, happy to see Alphus more like his old self. Alphus's moods were always better when he had traveling to do, even such mundane traveling as accompanying Joshua, Cooper, and a score of other militiamen up to the Long Island of the Holston. There had been no reason for Alphus to come other than his simply wanting to, but Joshua had agreed to it, knowing Alphus would come whether needed or not. What worried Joshua was whether Alphus's good humor would linger after he was forced to watch the militiamen head off for Big Creek and leave him behind.

That worry was momentarily forgotten when at last the riders came in view of the Long Island. For Joshua the tree-covered spit of land in the Holston seemed as special as it did to the Cherokees themselves. For years this Holston landmark had been both a stage upon which the history of the region had been played and a backdrop against which battles had been fought and diplomatic maneuvers played out. This was an ancient treaty ground for the Cherokees; in 1777 Joshua had last come here to see the working out of yet one more treaty between the whites and Cherokees. Here he had seen his old Cherokee mentor, Attakullakulla or Little Carpenter, for the last time; here he had listened as Cherokee spokesman Old Tassel had made one of the most moving pleas on behalf of his people that Joshua had ever heard.

The island, though best known as a treaty ground, also was an important military site. On its northern bank in the violent summer of 1776, Dragging Canoe and his warriors—including John Hawk—had made camp before their ill-fated battle at Island Flats with riflemen from Eaton's Station, a fort some six miles away. At this island, less than a month after that battle, an army had gathered for the punishment of the Cherokees, and Captain William Russell had built the existing nearby fortification, Fort Patrick Henry.

The fort stood about the same place as an earlier stockade, Fort Robinson, enclosed about a hundred square yards, and had but three sides, for the riverbank itself provided sufficient protection on the fourth. It was bastioned on each corner and within its walls was a storehouse and a home for the fort commander. The river and several small springs provided an abundance of water.

The Long Island also was home to Joseph Martin, the Indian agent for Virginia, and his mixed-blood Cherokee wife Betsy Ward. Joshua hoped to meet Betsy, for he owed the debt of Darcy's life to Betsy's mother, the Cherokee Beloved Woman Nancy Ward of Chota, originally Nanye'hi. She was niece of Little Carpenter and, ironically, cousin of Dragging Canoe, whose viewpoints on dealing with the whites could hardly be farther from hers. The Ward surname came from Nancy's white husband, Brian Ward, a trader from South Carolina.

It struck Joshua that he seldom saw the Long Island when it wasn't buzzing with activity. In 1777 the island and its vicinity had been crowded with hundreds of whites and Cherokees gathered for the treaty-making. Now the activity was mostly boat building. Joshua and his fellow militiamen dismounted and examined the long canoes and larger craft on the riverbank. A quick examination of the workmanship gratified Joshua. These were boats that could survive the swift and lengthy journey that would be required of them.

Alphus's mood began to decline. He stopped his joking and fell silent. "I wish I could go with you," he said quietly.

Joshua was about to tell Alphus he ought to consider himself lucky to be avoiding the inconvenience, difficulty, and danger of the coming expedition, but the words died on his lips as he looked at Alphus's sad face. "I wish you could come too," he said. The old man turned away and walked off to examine an unfinished dugout being burnt and hewn from a long poplar log.

Joshua watched Alphus a few moments, then noticed Cooper was looking around with an intent expression, as if trying to find someone. Joshua shifted his rifle to his left hand and walked up to his brother.

"Who you looking for, Coop?"

Cooper replied, "Nobody . . . well, Solomon Brecht."

"Solomon? Why'd you think he'd be here?"

"Because he's a good canoe builder, or so they say."

"They also say he's a Tory, and if that's true, he's hardly likely to be here today."

"I know what they say. I just hoped that maybe . . ." Cooper let his sentence die.

Joshua walked away to rejoin Alphus, leaving Cooper alone. Ever since the day he had seen Solomon and Elisha Brecht together in the forest, Cooper had kept his resolve to remain silent about it. At first he had maintained silence through sheer will, deliberately putting the welfare of his relationship with Hannah above the concerns of his neighbors. After a while that got to be too heavy a burden on his conscience, and he had started rationalizing, trying to convince himself that Solomon's meeting with Elisha was innocent, and that he was not the Tory that everyone suspected he was.

Cooper had so thoroughly rationalized to himself that

he had honestly hoped to see Solomon here today, putting
his boatmaking skills to use for a frontier army determined
to smite the Chickamaugas a fierce blow. Now he was
embarrassed at the nonsensical expectation and wished
he hadn't told Joshua about it.

Alphus remained with the militiamen at Long Island
only one night, then mounted and rode toward home,
saying he might hunt along the way. Joshua worried for
him even as he rode out of sight, and prayed for his safety
on the homeward journey.

The bustle of activity around the island as new parties
of militiamen arrived soon took Joshua's mind off anything
but the task at hand. He put his hand to helping finish
the boats—he and all others had, as directed in the militia
call-up, brought an adze and axe. Occasionally he introduced himself to men he hadn't met, and in most cases
found his identity already known because of the Roman
coin about his neck, and his reputation.

As always, such recognitions left him vaguely bewildered. Joshua had never been able to fully comprehend
how well-known he was, and that his reputation as a
woodsman and fighter rivaled that of many men he himself admired, such as his old friend and senior Daniel
Boone.

One of the strangers he met, a young man named Hugh
Frost, told Joshua they had a mutual friend, Callum
McSwain, and asked why the Scotsman was not here.

"Callum's gone off to the Cumberland country with
James Robertson and some others," Joshua replied. "Him
and Zach White, William Overall, Will Neely, James
Hanley, and one or two more I can't name right off. Lord
only knows when they'll be back. If they hadn't gone, I
can tell you certain that Callum would have been right
here with us."

"He may not return at all, if he likes the land," Frost
replied. "When Callum sets his head, he's stubborn as a
redskin."

Frost, five years younger than Joshua, proved to be a
pleasant, if slightly naive, young man. He seemed eager
to be seen with the famed Joshua and all but asked for his

friendship. This actually tended to put off Joshua, but the
frontiersman abided Frost out of kindness.

The neophyte was a fount of information about the
coming expedition and gushed it out even though Joshua
already knew most of it. Captain Isaac Shelby, Frost said,
was in charge of the boat construction and was already at
the Big Creek fort farther down the Holston, where most
of the smaller craft were being made. On the first of April,
still some days away, the actual muster would take place
at Big Creek, final details would be worked out, and the
flotilla would set off to follow the waterways to the Chickamauga towns. Great effort had been made to keep the
expedition secret, in hopes that the towns would be
surprised and substantially defenseless.

"I've never fit redskins before," Frost said. "I want to
bring me back Dragging Canoe's scalp to show to my
woman."

"You get close enough to the Dragon to scalp him, and
your brain will be axe-split before you know what's happened. And I doubt he's there. Most likely he's off somewhere with the British. Wherever he is, he's a fierce man,
Frost, and not to be took lightly."

"Maybe he can't be took lightly—but I do believe he
can be took!" Frost said, laughing at his words.

Joshua had no comment. He recognized Frost as falling
into one of two categories of men who craved war. Joshua
had differentiated the categories through his own wartime
observations.

The first category—Frost's—was comprised of young,
overeager, untested men, men who knew nothing of how
harsh war really was and therefore dreaded it insufficiently. Those in this category seldom remained there
long, unless their war experience proved exceedingly
brief and superficial.

The second category of war-cravers was in one way the
opposite of the first. Comprising it were men who had
known war too well for too long and had developed a
peculiar need for it, like some men developed a need for
liquor.

Joshua merely pitied men of the first category, but

those in the second group he feared, partly because he recognized his own potential for becoming one of them. He had seen too many men, both white and red, come to love warfare, to believe himself immune from the addiction. He had watched the souls of such grow callous and cold as a dead thing. One more battle, one more killing, and his own soul might similarly harden. He might find too late that he had developed a taste for what was still, thankfully, repulsive to him, even if sometimes necessary.

In time the work at the Long Island was complete and the men headed downriver toward the fort at Big Creek. Joshua left without fulfilling his intention of meeting Joseph Martin and Betsy Ward. Inquiry had revealed the couple was off at Chota. Well, no matter, Joshua told himself. I'll come back sometime after this is through, and meet them then.

It was good to have a postexpedition plan in mind, he decided. Alphus had once told him that it was advisable for any man going off to battle to have at least one piece of unfinished business awaiting his return. Such a thing tended, in some miraculous way, to keep a man alive. Or at least that's what Alphus Colter had told Joshua, and Alphus was seldom wrong about anything.

5

Forty-five-year-old Solomon Brecht, unlike his infamous brother Elisha, was a towering man, taller by the length of two thumbs than Alphus Colter—a despised man to Solomon—had been before age put a curve into his spine. Usually surrounded by men much shorter than himself, Solomon had developed the habit of slumping his shoulders to minimize his height. He had to stoop to enter most cabin doors. His own cabin was different; he had built the door and ceiling high, declaring that for once in his life he was going to have a home he could live in without worrying for his noggin every time he stood.

Solomon was at that door now on this mid-April night, peering out a loophole he had augered through the riven planks and shielded on the inside with a wooden slide piece. The hole and slide were recent additions, put in place for the sake of vigilance after the court hearing in which Solomon had scarcely escaped official stigmatization as a Tory and loss of his property. The verdict had displeased many people; several times since it was rendered, Solomon had received threats both veiled and open. Now he spent most of his evenings either seated

70

tensely near the door or window, listening for commotion
among the hounds outside, and leaping to the loophole,
rifle in hand, whenever any occurred.

His wife, Repentance, silently watched him peeping
out the hole. Her expression was one of mild contempt.
Solomon Brecht did not see the expression at the moment, yet knew full well she wore it. She seldom looked
at him these days in any other fashion.

"What is it this time—rebels with torches . . . or
another 'possum?" she asked cuttingly.

Solomon did not answer her; he continued peering out
the hole.

Repentance laid down the hunting shirt she had been
embroidering with patterns in red thread. "I asked you,
is it rebels with torches, or—"

"In the name of heaven, woman, hush your yap so a
man can keep his mind on what he's doing!" Solomon
stormed without looking at her.

She gave no reaction to the rebuff except to lift her left
brow in a queenly display of offense. Sighing loudly
enough to make sure Solomon heard it, she picked up her
stitching and began working again. From the loft of the
cabin came a murmured childish voice—that of ten-year-
old Andrew, who shared a loft bed with his older brother,
Perrin. On the opposite side of the loft slept Hannah, the
Brecht's only daughter and without doubt the favorite
child of her father. That favor Solomon displayed in many
ways, including his giving Hannah fully half the loft to
herself, allowing her the same amount of space her two
brothers were forced to share. Solomon had divided the
loft with a big piece of sailcloth he had purchased several
years before. The division of the loft had given Hannah
privacy that few frontier youths enjoyed. Her curtained-
off chamber was a luxury she prized and protected. She
sent up wails of protest if either of her brothers dared set
foot in her space without permission, or allowed some
item of their own possession to slip beneath the sailcloth
into her domain.

Solomon finally closed the loophole cover. Leaning his
rifle against the wall, he sat down on a hickory chair

bottomed with white oak strips. Picking up his thick Bible, he began to read by the light of a tallow candle on the table beside him. It was a nightly ritual for him. Minutes passed. As he read he occasionally looked up sharply when he heard new noises outside, and a few times started to rise again to investigate. Only the sharp glances of Repentance kept him in his chair.

Even when she appeared to be fully concentrating on her sewing, Repentance actually was slyly watching her husband, evaluating him, sizing him up, and finding him wanting. Solomon could feel it. Repentance had always been critical of him, impatient with him, reflexively in disagreement with whatever position he took on any issue, including his loyalist political stance. He knew the sting of her tongue quite well, and no longer sought to persuade her toward his views. Sometimes he wondered why he loved her so much. And love her he did, more than anything or anyone else, except perhaps Hannah. He rationalized Repentance's harshness by attributing it to her trying girlhood.

Repentance Brecht had been born outside wedlock, daughter of a Virginia harlot who upon her bastard daughter's birth declared her errant ways at an end. She named her baby Repentance, a common name for illegitimate girls, and contrived to reflect the penance of the sinning mother. The name, of course, punished the child as much as the mother, perhaps more, for it was a veritable brand of illegitimacy.

In the happier days of early marriage, Repentance had told her husband a little of her childhood. Solomon was saddened that his wife's mother had inflicted so much suffering on the daughter. Society had given Repentance no respite, either. Her stigmatic name told the world what she was, and she was ill-treated for it.

"Those who have suffered the most merit the greatest patience and mercy," Solomon's scholarly, clerical father had instructed him in boyhood. Solomon had tried to follow that dictum in dealing with his wife, though it had become more difficult as she grew hard and sniping with age. Now he more often lost his temper and snapped at her, as he had tonight. In stronger periods he endured her backbiting and harping without response, believing that having been given little but poor treatment in her own life, Repentance had little else but the same to give others. But sometimes, when she was at her most bitter and biting, he secretly wondered if his wife was fully sane.

Whatever her condition, Solomon was determined to remain loyal to her. Loyalty was in his blood and nature. He clung to what he loved and believed in with a tenacity that was unshakable. His religion, his family, his duties, his few friendships—these he was faithful to in all circumstances. And he was equally faithful to the king of England, the country from which his roaming branch of the originally Germanic Brecht family had come to the colonies.

Though the Washington County court had failed to prove it, Solomon Brecht was in fact as much a Tory as his militant brother. He saw no wrong in his falsely sworn declarations of American support. This was wartime, and in wartime lesser duties had to yield to greater ones. By living among the rebels and pretending to be one of them, Solomon was occasionally able to obtain information useful to the British cause, and this he had passed on secretly to Elisha. That was at an end now. When Elisha had surprised him by reappearing in the region in January, Solomon had told of his legal trouble and said it was too dangerous for them to meet again. Elisha had departed, heading to the Chickamauga country.

Solomon knew his brother was a violent man, cruel and lacking almost all moral restraint, but he had aided him even while disliking him. Elisha Brecht, despite his evil, represented both kin and kingdom to Solomon, and to both he held fast without qualification.

This position was often hard to maintain, for it required lying to his own children, who knew nothing of his true politics. Only Repentance knew the truth, and though she had declared herself in agreement with the American rebellion, she promised Solomon she would not betray him, "for the sake of wifely duty," as she airily put it.

Solomon's main problem was very simple: He had to

live a lie, and he was not a particularly good liar. His claims of support for the rebellion didn't seem to convince many of his Whig neighbors, and Solomon spent much time in sincere fear of the tar bucket and feather bag, even of the noose.

A flurry of barking outside the cabin brought Solomon to his feet. He snatched his rifle and went back to his loophole. Seeing nothing, he cautiously unbarred and cracked open the door, only to see an opossum waddle off into the woods. He closed the door again, embarrassed before his wife.

"I thought maybe it was that deuced Cooper Colter come 'round after Hannah," he muttered feebly, making up an excuse. It wasn't a bad one; he knew Cooper had been seeing his daughter on the sneak—a fact he deplored, and one that threatened his close relationship with his daughter.

"His name is Haverly, not Colter," Repentance replied. "And he's far away from here tonight."

"He's blood brother to Joshua Colter and therefore a Colter to me, whatever name he uses. And what do you know of where he is tonight?"

Repentance presented her husband a smug look. "Perhaps I know more about what goes on hereabouts than the secret Tory who fancies himself the spy," she said in a low tone.

"Woman, say what you mean!"

"Are you blind, husband? Have you been so busy listening for Whigs outside the cabin that you've failed to see the empty houses and missing menfolk, the women working alone? Have you heard no whispers of the riflemen in boats going downriver to scour out the nests of the red savages that your brother loves so dear?"

Solomon came toward her, hand uplifted. He had already begun to bring it down at her face, fingers cupped for a hard slap, before he realized what he was doing and stopped himself. He stood trembling in fury over her. Her face had grown fearful for only a moment, then resumed its look of haughty defiance.

"You will not speak to me so in this house," he whispered with forced restraint, not wanting the children to hear. "I'll not abide it. Now you tell me, Repentance, exactly what you are speaking of."

"Oh, I'll happily tell you, for now it's too late for you to do aught about it. There is an army—six hundred strong, I hear—that mustered on the Holston at the first of this month and is descending upon the Chickamauga towns. The deed is surely done by now—and you've known nothing of it!" She laughed heartily.

Solomon looked down at his scornful wife and felt a greater rage rising in him. This time her defiance was too much to endure. Repentance was a mocking, intolerable creature. His hand cupped and went back again, and again swung down. This time he did not hold back the blow.

The sound of the slap was loud in the cabin, louder than the yelp of surprise and pain it brought out of Repentance. Up in the loft Andrew stirred and murmured in his sleep, disturbed, and Hannah shifted on her bed, making the corn shucks rustle.

Below, in the silence that followed, Repentance began to cry, rubbing her reddened face. It was the first time in their years together that Solomon had struck her.

The tall man knelt, his feelings turned from fury to deep sorrow. He touched his wife's teared face.

"Oh, dear wife, I'm sorry," he said. "God forgive me, I'm so very sorry I hit you. I love you, Repentance, I love you."

She turned her face and would not look at him. After a few moments he rose, picked up his rifle, and walked to the far end of the cabin, undressed, and climbed into bed, feeling tired, helpless, and discouraged. He lay there for a long time, listening for alarms from the hounds and hearing the soft crying of his wife, before he fell asleep.

It will come today, Joshua Colter thought in the predawn darkness as his hand-carved oar dipped silently into the water of the Tennessee River. Whatever is to come of this, it will come today.

Joshua was perched at the head of a long dugout. He

had ridden in this posture for hours every day since April 10, when the floating army had disembarked down the Holston from the Big Creek fort. Piloted by a capable man named John Hudson, the six hundred man flotilla had made good time, for the river was high from spring rains and flowed rapidly.

Down the broad freshet the dugouts swept, steered by their frontiersmen passengers, all of whom were almost as adept at this sort of water travel as they were at land travel. If anyone in the number lacked river expertise, he had gained it abundantly by the time the flotilla at last entered the hostile territory. Joshua had gotten so accustomed to his rower's perch and to handling his oar that when he lay down at night, he felt as if he were still in motion.

In the east the sky began to pale, and gradually cool light spread across the river, turning it from black to silver. The music of the morning forest began, a peaceful sound that made the warlike intentions of the waterborne men seem incongruous. Joshua glanced to his right; in a dugout almost even with his own rode Cooper. The young man nodded and grinned at Joshua. Like Hugh Frost farther back in the flotilla, Cooper was young enough to be slightly overeager. But he was maturing quickly. As a member of Joshua's rangers who had known what it was to be wounded, he was a step ahead of the few novices among the force.

Joshua and Cooper were among the expeditioners who expected to drub the Chickamauga towns and then return home. Others would be going farther. Along with the flotilla were troops under Captain John Montgomery, who had aided George Rogers Clark in the celebrated capture of Kaskaskia. Clark had sent the officer back to gather more troops from Virginia, and as that effort proceeded, a realization had come that Montgomery and his troops could effectively help with the Chickamauga campaign on their way by river to the Illinois country, and the two ventures had been conjoined.

Scarcely had the dawn spread its light before Joshua lifted his finger and pointed ahead. The mouth of Chickamauga Creek was in view. Silently the boatmen advanced through the water, turning their craft into the creek.

Cooper was the first to spot the lone Indian who sat on the bank near a sunken fish trap. His head lolled to one side; the sound of his snores carried across the water to the boatmen. By the time Cooper signaled, Joshua too, had seen the man.

Joshua and his fellow oarsmen steered their dugouts close to the bank downstream from the sleeping man, then Joshua and three others slipped out into the water and up onto the bank, rifles in hand.

The Indian didn't cry out when he awakened to find himself staring at four silent unakas with rifles pointed at his head, but his expression showed that he anticipated quick death. Joshua spoke to him in Cherokee.

"Keep silent and help us and we'll let you live. Raise a sound and you will be the first of many to die today."

The Chickamauga looked from solemn face to solemn face, and nodded.

"Stand up," Joshua ordered, and the man complied. "Look across the water. You see how many we are, and how foolish it would be to defy us?"

"Yes," the Indian replied.

"You will guide us to Chickamauga Town," Joshua instructed. "You will give no warning of our approach, and you will take us by the swiftest route that is also hidden. Do you understand?"

By now other boats had been rowed to shore and dozens of frontiersmen were emerging, stretching cramped limbs, and checking their rifles. Joshua couldn't help but feel sorry for the lone Chickamauga fisherman, who was being asked to betray his people. If the man was sufficiently honorable, he might not do it, even at the cost of his own life.

As it turned out, honor gave way to self-preservation. Glumly the Chickamauga nodded again. "I will guide you," he said.

* * *

For Cooper the sight brought excitement; for Joshua, a mix of pleasure at a goal achieved and sadness at the destruction of a town that put him in mind of the Cherokee towns he had lived in as a trader's son many years ago.

The town of Chickamauga was burning. Cabin after cabin sent great billows of smoke to the sky as flames licked them, destroying not only their structures, but their contents, most of which had been abandoned by the thoroughly surprised occupants. The captured guide had done his job, leading the army of troops through a swale and into the town itself. They had encountered virtually no resistance; Joshua had counted only two or three Indian deaths, though he did not know what others might have occurred out of his sight.

The approximately five hundred occupants of Chickamauga Town had fled to the hills upon the arrival of the invasion force. With great shouts the frontiersmen had rushed in, driving the Chickamaugas out, quickly putting down the meager and faltering resistance that answered them. There were few warriors in the town at the time of the attack, most of them being off in warfare for the British far away. Joshua had encountered an exultant Hugh Frost in the midst of the rout; Frost had waved his rifle above his head and said, "A bloody fine battle, eh, Joshua Colter?"

"This is no battle for a man to take much pride in," Joshua replied coldly. "This is women and children running from armed men."

Frost paid him no heed, rushing off to join in the torching of another rough Chickamauga cabin. Joshua was about to stride away when he heard a cry from inside a cabin already aflame. He darted at once to the door, rifle ready in case of danger.

There was no danger. Inside the smoke-filled cabin was an old woman lying on a pile of blankets. She was apparently sick and weak. When she saw Joshua's lean form in her doorway, she cried out again and put her arm across her eyes, obviously expecting to be killed.

"Don't be afraid, old woman. My name is Ayunini," he

said, using the Cherokee name the great chief Little Carpenter had given him as a boy at Fort Loudoun. "I'll carry you out."

He lifted her from her blankets and carried her out the door. Placing her on the ground, he returned to recover his rifle. When he emerged again, Hugh Frost was above the woman, rifle uplifted, about to club her with the butt of it.

"No!" Joshua yelled, lunging forward and knocking Frost to the ground.

Frost roared, "What the devil are you—"

Joshua kicked the young frontiersman once, twice, a third time. Frost grunted with each impact, then leaped to his feet to face Joshua. His face was wild with fury. He swore and demanded to know why Joshua had intervened to save a "savage."

"Savage? You squat sod, that's naught but an old woman too sick to sit up, much less be any danger to you!"

Frost said, "I'll not be deprived a scalp, Colter!"

"If you want a scalp, go kill a warrior and take his, if you think you're man enough! Or maybe you fancy you'd like to take mine! If so, come here and learn a lesson you sore need!"

Frost glared, picked up his rifle, muttered that Joshua was an "Indian lover," and stalked away through the burning town. Thus ended the superficial friendship between him and Joshua Colter, dying as rapidly as it had been born. Joshua could not have cared less.

Joshua went to the old woman's side and saw to his dismay that Frost had ironically succeeded in his lethal intent even without striking her. Her head rolled to the side just as Joshua reached her, her hands groped at her withered left breast, and she died with an expression of fright still on her face. Her old heart had not been able to endure the terror.

Joshua looked down at her sadly. She reminded him much of another old Indian woman he had known in childhood. Her name had been Kwali, and she had been kind to him while he was a frightened ten-year-old captive of the Overhills, vainly struggling to be brave and manly. Could this woman actually be Kwali? No, he decided. Kwali had been old nearly a score of years ago; she must have died long ago.

Joshua looked around. The "battle" was for all practical purposes no battle at all. Already torches aplenty were being applied to the town. There was no need for his further participation.

He bent down and scooped up the body of the old woman and carried her toward the edge of town. A strange but irresistible impulse had gripped him. He wanted to lay this old woman to rest, for the sake of the memory of Kwali, and as his private commemoration of all the innocents, white, black, and red, who had suffered and died in the endless warfare that characterized the frontier. Joshua knew and understood, far better than his wife back home realized, the victimization of innocents that is part and parcel of war. He had been so victimized himself as a boy and could not forget it.

He had nothing with which to dig but his belt axe and knife. The old woman's grave would be shallow out of necessity. He knew his efforts would seem foolish to anyone else. They did not seem foolish to him, and he had lost his stomach for the loud celebratorial destruction of Chickamauga Town now under way.

He thought he was unseen while he worked and sweated, but he was watched. Hidden only a few yards from him, Ayasta observed as he gouged out the burial place for a body she recognized as Atsina's. Ayasta was awed to see a white man doing this. Why would he bother with such a meaningless gesture?

Wasi was ill again and slept listlessly in her arms, making no sound to betray her. She watched in silence as the frontiersman finished his work and gently scooped armfuls of dirt over Atsina's corpse. Then she caught back a gasp of amazement when she noticed the object hanging from a cord about his neck.

A small coin.

Ayasta was awed. Could this be the unaka named Joshua Colter, the very man John Hawk had once befriended and whom she herself planned to seek out?

Should she reveal herself to him in the hope that he was indeed Joshua Colter? She badly wanted to, but was afraid. Whoever the man was, he was one of the destroyers who had swept out of the forest. He might kill her and Wasi.

Yet there was something gentle and touching in the way he buried Atsina. He did not look like a killer of women and children. She hovered between options, then found her opportunity taken from her when the man rose, knocked the dirt from his arms and clothing, and began walking back toward the town.

He stopped once, looking back toward the place where she hid. He seemed to be listening, and his nostrils moved like those of an animal sniffing the wind. Just when she thought he had detected her, he turned again and continued walking, leaving her alone with Wasi to ponder what she had seen.

The destruction was far from finished when the last cabin of Chickamauga Town crumbled into smoldering ashes. For many days thereafter, the frontiersmen moved in groups among the other Chickamauga towns, burning, looting, pillaging, forcing the evicted Indians homeless into the mountains. Eleven towns fell to the torch before it was done.

Joshua did his part, feeling it a duty to his people and the patriot cause, but he found no joy in it beyond the assurance that this devastation would certainly save the lives of many settlers who otherwise would have fallen victim in the anticipated springtime Chickamauga raids. It seemed tragic that so often destruction on one side could only be avoided by preemptive destruction on the other.

When the raids at last were done, the frontiersmen regrouped for a counting of heads and tallying of booty. Colonel Evan Shelby, the grand old man of the successful expedition, was thrilled to find not a single member of the American force had died. The Chickamaugas had fared little worse as far as fatalities, only a half dozen or so being recorded. Shelby was not overly disappointed by that. No wholesale killing of warriors had been expected in any case. The purpose of this venture had been physical destruction of towns and seizure of goods.

This had been well-achieved. Much peltry, crops, and livestock had been collected. Shelby calculated that a full twenty thousand bushels of corn had been taken, in addition to various other goods he estimated as worth about twenty-five thousand pounds.

Most cheering to the men themselves was the herd of captured horses, many of them fine animals. These were auctioned to the men. Joshua invested a hundred ten pounds in a fine black horse, almost the twin of one purchased for a slightly higher price by Colonel Shelby. Cooper had less money but did buy a decent mare. He and Joshua were glad to have mounts, for the homeward journey would be overland—much longer and more difficult than the downstream water excursion that brought them here.

The army had brought their boats to the north side of the Tennessee and dragged ashore all that were not needed by Montgomery's force, who continued on by river to join Clark. All other boats were piled and set ablaze in the most impressive bonfire Joshua had ever seen. He thought it a great waste to burn such sturdy watercraft, but there was no other option. Taking the boats upstream was out of the question, and leaving them behind would simply put them into Indian hands.

As the great fire blazed, the men ate, relaxed, and evaluated the booty they had seized. Hugh Frost, who now gave Joshua only bitter looks and silence, had been denied his coveted scalp souvenir and was very disappointed. Frost had a lot of growing up yet to do before he made for palatable company, in Joshua's estimation.

As the fire died and weariness overcame the generally jovial frontiersmen, Joshua spread a bearskin taken in the raid and lay down on it to sleep. Scarcely had he drifted off when a hand shook his shoulder and he looked up into the face of a man he had never met but had seen among Shelby's Virginia troops.

"You're Colter—Joshua Colter?" the man asked.

Joshua sat up. "I am."

"Thought so. Knew you by the coin. Famous man, you know."

Joshua wondered if this man had awakened him simply to meet him. If so, he was due a tongue-lashing fierce enough to draw blood. "What do you want?" Joshua asked gruffly.

"I want you to come with me. There's somebody asking after you."

"Who?"

"Come with me—you'll meet her."

"Her?"

"Aye, her. You coming or not?"

Joshua was intrigued. A woman, asking for him? No women had come on this journey, so who could it be?

He untied his moccasins from his rifle barrel—an old long hunter's habit—and in moments was ready to go. Cooper, who had fallen asleep nearby, had awakened by now and blinked in confusion.

"Come with me, Coop," Joshua said, figuring it might be wise to take company in case this stranger had some unknown antagonism he was hoping to vent when he had him away in private. He turned to the man. "Who are you?"

"Trent. Malachi Trent. I come from off the upper Holston."

"What's this about, Joshua?" Cooper asked sidewise as he walked.

"I don't know for sure. Reckon we'll see. He says there's a woman asking for me."

Leaving the circle of light cast by the dying fire of the heaped-up boats, Joshua followed Trent down to the river and along its bank. Trent led them in silence to a small inlet skirted by brush. Joshua sensed and smelled the presences there before he saw them—and it was so dark that even he could see little. He was surprised to hear the sound of a child's voice.

Trent said, "She's yonder. Says her name's Ayasta, from what I can understand of her. The boy's name is Wasi, or some such."

Joshua stepped forward toward a slim, dark figure that was arising in a little clearing fronting the brush. He could see it was a female, that she stood by a large boulder, and that she held a child. Then the boulder beside which the woman stood moved and rose. Joshua saw the vague outline of a man—a very big man—but of the face he could see nothing.

"That's Pont with her," Trent said from behind Joshua. "Pontius Pilate's his name. He's a Negro."

"Yours?"

"Well, he's with me, ain't he?"

Joshua took that for a yes. Now that he knew Pont's race he understood why he could not make out his features. His black skin blended in the black of the night so that he was like a ghost there in the darkness. Being so nearly invisible lent the man a mysterious aura. Joshua had been awed by only a few men in his life—Alphus, Daniel Boone, Little Carpenter, and the great war chief Oconostota among them. Now he was awed, unaccountably but instinctively, by a man whose face he could not even see and whose voice he had not heard.

"You are Ayunini . . . Colter?" said the woman haltingly.

"Yes. Who are you?"

"I am Ayasta. This one"—she held up her child—"this one is Wasi."

Had Joshua not been so bewildered by this unusual meeting, he would have thought to invite Ayasta to speak in her native tongue instead of the English she was struggling with. Later he would be angry with himself for not thinking of it, for Malachi Trent and Pont heard all she said, and what she would say in a few moments was something best unheard by all ears but Joshua's.

Ayasta stepped forward and looked at Joshua's face. "Are you the man who buried the old woman the day Chickamauga was burned?"

Joshua was amazed. "Yes. But how did you know?"

"I hid, I watched you. I have come looking for you, Colter. My husband, he talked of you much."

"Your husband knew me?"

Her answer was like a kick in the stomach to Joshua, bringing into his mind a stark memory he wished every day that he could forget: two sweating, fighting men, the thrust of a knife, and the unwanted death of a beloved friend turned enemy, yet still beloved.

"Yes," Ayasta said. "He knew you, and you knew him. He was John Hawk."

6

When the talking was done about twenty minutes later, Joshua descended alone to the river and stood there in the darkness, leaning on his rifle and looking across the water. Astonishment at what had just happened had momentarily erased his weariness. To think that the widow of John Hawk himself had sought him out, to think that she had just requested of him what she had . . . it was simply astonishing.

She had asked that Joshua take her and her son back to the settlements. And not just for a temporary visit, but permanently. She wanted refuge for herself and her son. She wanted her son to live a life radically different than the one his father had lived, for she feared that otherwise he would die. In effect, she had asked Joshua to adopt her and Wasi fully into white society, and raise her son as an unaka, a white.

The irony of being approached with such a request by the widow of John Hawk was overwhelming. Ayasta's talk had made Joshua's most sheltered secret burn in him like a coal; he feared that somehow she could look into him and know that here was the man who had slain her mate. His common sense told him, of course, that such was an irrational fear, but that didn't much change matters, for fears not born of common sense are also not easily killed by it.

When Joshua had left his home to join this expedition, his worry had been the usual one of warriors: that he would be killed or maimed. The last thing he would have expected was to have a Chickamauga widow throw herself and her child on his mercy. Did Ayasta not realize how much she was asking of him? And why him, of all people?

He knew the answer to that already. His friendship with John Hawk had been deep. At one time John Hawk had lived on Joshua's own land. They had hunted and explored together like brothers. Even after personal and political differences had forced them into antagonistic roles, Joshua's respect and affection for John Hawk had remained intact, and the same clearly had held true for the other. John Hawk must have said many good things about his old unaka friend to his wife for her to have the confidence in him that she obviously did.

But how could he agree to Ayasta's request? How could he ask Darcy to accept such a bizarre situation? He could imagine how shocked she would be to see her husband come back from war with an attractive young Indian woman tagging along behind, coming to join the family. It was simply inconceivable.

Yet he hadn't yet turned Ayasta down, and wasn't at all sure he could. She had been John Hawk's wife. To deny her help was to be untrue to the memory of his old friend. Further, denial would be equivalent to heaping more trouble upon a woman he had already made a widow. He couldn't simply abandon her now that she had specifically asked his aid.

Never before had Joshua faced such a dilemma. He could not say yes without feeling disloyal to Darcy; he could not say no without feeling disloyal to the memory of John Hawk.

He heard someone approaching and assumed it was Cooper. When he turned, however, he saw it was Malachi Trent. Instantly he tensed; something about Trent rubbed him wrong and made him distrustful.

"Hello, Colter. Quite a problem that Indian's give you, eh?"

"I've had problems before."

"So we all have, so we all have. I'll tell you this: If old Pont didn't have so keen an ear, you wouldn't have this problem now. That woman would be dead."

"What are talking about?"

"Pont saved her skin, that's what. Me and him were out by the river and he heard a ruckus, heard it before I did. It seems the woman had come ashore downriver in a Chickamauga dugout. Some of the others here had caught her and were about to, well, do what some men do when they come upon a squaw. Disgrace her, you know. Reckon they would have killed her after. Pont waded in and busted a few heads, and that changed their minds right fast. Quite a brave thing for a Negro to do, eh? Old Pont ain't scared of nothing or nobody."

Joshua had not known of this; hearing it made him furious. "Who were the ones who tried to hurt her?"

"Don't know. Didn't recognize them in the dark, and probably I wouldn't have known them anyway. I don't make a heap of friends most times. Keep to myself, you know. Just me and Pont."

Joshua said, "I'll have to pay my thanks to Pont."

"I'm sure he'd appreciate it. And I hope you appreciate what I'm about to offer you."

Joshua felt even more wary. "What?"

"You needn't worry about the woman . . . Ayasta? That's her name, ain't it?"

"Yes . . . but what do you mean?"

"That I'll take her off your hands. You're a family man, I hear. You can't very well go hauling a redskin woman back home with you. Me, I'm a lone-running wolf, except for Pont. She's a fine-looking squaw. I'll be glad to give her a home with me."

Joshua was so surprised that it took a moment for disgust to roll over him. He stepped forward and squarely faced Trent; it was so dark that even this close he could not clearly see his face.

"She's a woman, not a pelt or Indian rifle to be claimed for booty. She didn't ask you to take her—she asked me."

Joshua felt rather than saw Trent's smile. "Why, Captain Colter, I think that squaw has sunk her hooks in you already. What do you think the woman back home's going to say about this?"

Joshua knocked Trent to the ground, wheeled away, and walked back up to where Cooper was. He heard Trent laughing to himself as he got up, as if this were all a great joke he was much enjoying. It made Joshua rage inside, but he refused to turn around.

Ayasta remained with Wasi and Pont over by the river, somewhat away from Cooper. Joshua stalked up, face set like cold iron.

Cooper said, "Joshua, think we ought to talk about what—"

"Hush, Cooper. Come with me."

Cooper followed, a little awed by Joshua's intense manner. Joshua walked back to Ayasta and knelt. He spoke to her tersely in Cherokee, stood, and strode back toward the main camp. Ayasta rose with Wasi and began to follow. Cooper, now baffled, did the same. Pont fell in behind him.

They drew closer to the main camp; when some of the men still awake saw Ayasta, they reached toward their rifles. Joshua stopped and said, "There'll be no harm done this woman. She's in my care and is no danger to anyone."

The expressions visible in the red illumination of the charred boat fire ranged from confusion to carnal smiles. Joshua ignored them all. No one spoke.

Cooper felt a big hand on his shoulder. Turning, he faced Pont, whose face was visible to him now for the first time. It wasn't a handsome face, but impressive, somehow boyish despite its breadth and the bristled black beard that covered much of it. "What's he going to do with her?"

Cooper said, "I don't know. I don't talk Cherokee and couldn't understand what he said."

"You going to ask him?"

Cooper was as reluctant as anyone else to bother Joshua

right now, but he had to know what was going on.
"Reckon I will," he said to Pont. Over the big man's
shoulder he noticed Malachi Trent walking up from the
riverbank. Trent was rubbing his jaw and grinning. He
joined Pont as Cooper went to Joshua, who was occupied
in making a bed of blankets for Ayasta and her child.

"Joshua, if you don't care me asking, what did you say
to her back there?"

"What do you think I said, and what makes it your
business?"

"If I knew what you said I wouldn't have asked. And
the only business it is of mine is that you're my brother."

Joshua laid down the last blanket and motioned Ayasta
over. She walked over and placed Wasi on the blanket,
then lay down beside the child. By now a score of men
were watching the goings-on with much interest. Joshua
swept his gaze across their faces, and most quickly turned
away and lay down again. Those who didn't Joshua bored
into with longer stares until they also saw the better part
of discretion and ended their observations.

Joshua still didn't answer Cooper. He walked away,
toward the dying bonfire. He pulled out his pipe, loaded
it, and fired it with a burning splinter. Cooper hesitated,
then followed.

"You're taking her back home with us?"

Joshua nodded.

A pause. "What will Darcy say?"

Joshua didn't reply, and Cooper realized it was not a
well-taken question. He left Joshua alone, returned to
Pont, and told him and Trent what Joshua had indicated.

Pont nodded, and strode away, and Cooper went back
to his bedroll. Trent, however, remained where he was,
looking down at Joshua until the latter grew tired of the
gaze and stared back. Trent touched his cap, smiled, and
walked away, casting one lingering look at Ayasta, who
had already fallen asleep with her arm across her son.

The warrior who strode with Ulagu through the charred
ruins of Chickamauga was a man of fearsome appearance.
Head shaven but for the central scalp lock, he was pock-

marked, tattooed, and decorated. His earlobes, like those of his father, the famed Attakullakulla, stretched long and were hung with silver. The unaka settlers who had come to fear him often called him the "Dragon," a punning derivative of his actual name, Dragging Canoe.

It was ironic that the Chickamaugan leader whose name had become synonymous with militant resistance to every white intrusion was the son of Little Carpenter, who had often been friendly to the whites. There was little similarity between father and son beyond a common ability to move the souls of others. But where Little Carpenter had often moved souls toward peace and coexistence, Dragging Canoe moved them toward war.

It was his belief that to allow the whites to overtake the Indian lands could lead to nothing but the destruction of all Indians as a people. From the day in 1775 when he had walked away from treaty-making with the white settlers for the last time, he had seen nothing that made him change his mind. At about forty years of age now, Dragging Canoe was as battle-ready as he ever had been.

Ulagu found Dragging Canoe both an awe-inspiring figure and a devoted friend, as had his late brother-in-law, John Hawk, before him. In Ulagu's opinion, the former head warrior of Malaquo Town was hope incarnated for the native peoples of this country. Through cooperation with the British, perhaps the white settlers could even yet be driven back. Many a hard blow they had been dealt by Dragging Canoe, and by loyalists such as Elisha Brecht, who cooperated closely with him.

There was no denying, however, that this time the unakas had dealt a harsh blow to Dragging Canoe's people. The riverborne assault on the towns had taken the Chickamaugas by surprise at a time when Dragging Canoe and most of his warriors were far away. Though the Americans had taken few lives, they had destroyed countless homes, completely stripped and gutted the important commissary stores of John McDonald, and left the Indians in a poor position to respond. Furthermore, they had driven home a point Dragging Canoe was loath to admit: His towns were vulnerable to riverborne attack. Repopulating some of them might be feasible, but some would best be left abandoned.

Dragging Canoe had already assured Ulagu that they were far from defeated by this blow. Alexander Cameron, the British Indian representative to whom Dragging Canoe had pledged brotherhood and personal protection, had sent along fifty loyalist rangers and a pack train of goods to begin to replace what the Americans had confiscated. As they traveled through Chickamauga, then moved on to see several other of the ruined towns, Dragging Canoe talked to Ulagu about the future. The fight, he said, was not finished; the unakas who had dealt this fierce blow would feel one just as fierce in return.

Ulagu was heartened by Dragging Canoe's determination, but he could not enjoy it to the fullest, because of a personal concern that weighed on him. What had happened to Ayasta and Wasi? Many of the Chickamauga women and children who had fled as refugees to the hills had since reemerged, and Ulagu had tried to find his sister and nephew among them. So far he had not succeeded, nor found anyone who had seen what happened to them. He was beginning to fear they had been killed. The thought devastated him.

Some days later, Ulagu mentioned his worries to Dragging Canoe. The Chickamauga leader looked solemn and nodded. "I have thought of John Hawk's woman and her son myself," he said. "You know nothing of what happened to her?"

"No," Ulagu replied. "I have asked many people and received no answer."

Dragging Canoe laid a strong hand on Ulagu's shoulder. "You are a brother to me, Ulagu, and so Ayasta is my sister. If she is alive and can be found, we will find her, and the boy as well."

Ulagu nodded as if in thanks, but he was masking deep worries. He recalled Ayasta's earlier disturbing talk about Wasi, her foolish, ignoble chatter about not wanting him to become what his father had been. Maybe this disappearance was no coincidence. If Ayasta was not dead, she must have flown with Wasi. Where would she have gone?

If Ayasta and Wasi proved to be dead, Ulagu would grieve for them. But if this disappearance was a ploy to remove Wasi from his proper place and people, he would deal with that in whatever way was required. This was his duty—to Wasi, to the Chickamaugas, to Dragging Canoe, and most of all, to the memory of John Hawk.

"Stop it, Cooper—stop it before you crush me!"

Cooper laughed and eased his grip around Hannah just enough to stop her protesting. He buried his nose in her hair and nuzzled his face against hers, bringing a new round of protestation, this time about Cooper's scratchy whiskers. They were in their secret meeting place in the forest, about a mile from Hannah's cabin.

"Why, you're just brimming with complaints, Hannah Brecht!" Cooper teased. "If you don't stop fussing, I'll start thinking you don't care for me and didn't worry while I was gone fighting the Chickamaugas."

"I worried over you every moment, especially after I found out what it was you were doing," she said. Cooper began to nuzzle at her again, and tried to kiss her. She pushed him away, and this time there was less playfulness in the way she did it. "Cooper, why didn't you tell me before you left?" she asked, looking him in the eyes.

Cooper shrugged. "Well, we were supposed to keep our mouths shut about it, just in case . . . well, you know."

Hannah had no smile at all now. "Just in case some Tory spy—like my father—got word of it and managed to forewarn the Indians. Is that what you're saying?"

Cooper didn't like the subtle change in her tone. "Hannah, you know what everybody—"

"What everybody says? Indeed I do, and I'm so weary of it I want to scream sometimes. My uncle Elisha, if he's yet alive, is a Tory without question, and I take no pride in him. But my father says he is not a Tory, and I believe him. Just because he isn't as loud and vigorous as some in fighting the war doesn't make him a Tory!"

Cooper didn't know what to say. Hannah's words touched on subjects he didn't like thinking about. He was remembering the meeting he had witnessed between Elisha and Solomon Brecht back in the winter—a secret he still held. Though he still tried to rationalize around it, in his heart Cooper knew that meeting provided strong evidence that Hannah's father indeed was spying for his brother.

He wondered sometimes how much Hannah really knew about her father's mind and activities. She declared that she believed his declarations of American patriotism . . . but what if she herself was lying? Might Hannah be part of the same grand deception being foisted by her father? Doubting the honesty of the young woman he planned to marry was not pleasant for Cooper . . . but sometimes he couldn't help it. He would awaken in the night sometimes and wonder.

The worst aspect of that question lay below the surface. If Hannah was lying about her own war sentiments, she might lie about her other sentiments as well, Cooper reasoned. Maybe she really didn't love him, but hoped to use him as a source of information for her father. Or perhaps the old Carolina feud between the Brechts and Colters motivated her; maybe she was feigning love for him in order to maneuver him and the Colters into some sort of compromising, hurtful situation. Just how far could he trust Hannah, anyway? How well did he really know her?

"Cooper?" Hannah said, brows knitting. "Why are you looking at me that way?"

"Just listening, that's all."

To Cooper's surprise, Hannah suddenly kissed him. Her little outburst seemed to have relieved her mind, and she was her old self again. "That's one of the things I love about you, Cooper. You always listen. You don't look down on me the way so many men look down on women."

Cooper grinned. "Reckon I'm a fine gent."

Hannah laughed and kissed him again. Cooper held her close, looking into her eyes. "When are we going to be married, Hannah? I'm tired of waiting."

"Me too . . . but not yet. I can't."

"Why not? Now seems as good a time as any."

"No," she said. "Not with Father's troubles. He needs me."

"Don't take this wrong, Hannah, but what can you do to help your father? If folks think him a Tory, it's going to take his own doings to prove otherwise, not yours."

"It's not just that." She was growing solemn again. "It's Mother."

"Oh."

"She's worse than ever to him. Sometimes I think she really is . . ."

"Mad?"

Hannah winced. "That's such an ugly word!" She paused, then cautiously asked, "Cooper, do you think she really could be that way?"

"I don't know her well enough to say. I ain't received too many Sunday dinner invitations from your parents, you know. What do you think about it?"

"I don't know what to think . . . except that I know Father needs me right now. He can't bear up with Mother and all these Tory accusations as well. He needs someone in the house to support him."

"There's an easy answer to the Tory part," Cooper ventured. "If Solomon would take some active part for the cause, that would go a long way to ease people's minds. As long as he makes excuses and keeps things all talk and no doing, nobody's prone to believe him."

"Including you?"

"Hannah, you know I've always defended your father, even among my own, and even though he's got nothing good to say about me."

"Yes—but what do you really think?"

Cooper took a long, slow breath, then made a decision: It was time Hannah knew of what he had seen. "Back at the first of the year, Hannah, I saw your father and uncle together in the forest. There were some Chickamaugas and such with them. They talked, then parted."

Hannah's eyes were wide. "So Uncle Elisha is still alive! But why would Father be—" She stopped. "Cooper, do you think he might have been doing what people say?"

"I don't know what he was doing. I didn't hear anything that was said."

Hannah's body was tense now and she pulled free of Cooper's arms. "Well, whatever it was, you can be sure there was no treachery in it."

"Let's not fuss over such things . . . but do think for a moment. You didn't know until just now that your uncle was even still alive. But your father has known since January. Why wouldn't he have told you?"

"Because . . . because—I don't know . . . maybe he felt Uncle Elisha was safer if he is believed dead."

Cooper paused a long time before asking the next question. "Hannah, tell me this true: Do you truly love me? Truly?"

"Cooper! You know I do! How could you doubt it?"

"Because for months now you've believed, or said you have believed, that your uncle was dead because of a rifle ball that I myself put in him. How is it, believing that, that you haven't held bad feelings against me? Maybe you have held them. Maybe you've just pretended you didn't."

Hannah's face reddened and she exploded in anger. "Is this the man you are, Cooper Haverly? Not believing the word of the one you claim to love? What is it you really think of me? That I'm a liar?"

Cooper wished he had steered this conversation in a new direction many sentences before. "I love you, Hannah. I want to marry you . . . but I have to know you are being truthful with me, not using me for . . . " He faltered.

Hannah understood him clearly. "For what? To help my father learn Whig secrets to pass to his Tory brother? No wonder you didn't tell me you were going off to fight the Chickamaugas! You didn't think I could be trusted with that information!"

"I didn't want to put you in a bad position, having to decide whether to be true to me or your father."

"So you do believe my father is a Tory spy, don't you!"

Cooper was beginning to feel like a fly being web-wrapped by a spider. His temper surged. "Hang it all, Hannah, yes, I do believe it! After seeing what I saw, how could I not? But before you stomp off thinking ill of me, think about one more thing: I could have told Joshua or John Sevier or any one of a score of others about what I saw in the forest that day, and like as not your father would be strung up by now, or at best chased from the country. But I said not a word. I haven't told a soul, and the reason is you. I love you too much to betray your father, even though I'm full convinced he's betraying me and them I love to the Tories and Chickamaugas. Hannah, I've held back from doing the right thing, and all for your sake. I'll not be the man who puts Solomon Brecht's neck in a noose. Not when I love his daughter like I do." Cooper stopped, almost out of breath. "Likely they'd have me whipped at the pillory, or maybe worse, if they knew I'd been keeping it secret that Elisha Brecht is yet alive, and that his own brother really has been meeting him."

Hannah touched away one small tear, the only one she had shed in this tense exchange. She was a stoic young woman, much like her mother in appearance and strength of will, though not in mentality or personality. She swallowed and went back to Cooper.

"It's not going to be an easy life for us, is it?"

"No. I think not. There's too much tending to divide us. But one thing there is that there's no doubt of, and that's that I truly do love you, Hannah Brecht. I love you more than I love family or anything else I can think of."

She put her arms around him and laid her face against the beaded breastwork of his hunting shirt. "I understand why you couldn't tell me beforetime about going to fight the Chickamaugas. Forgive me for being so harsh with you about it."

"There's nothing to forgive." He wrapped her in his arms. "But Hannah, I must ask you: Do you still believe your father is not a Tory?"

He felt her tighten at the question. "Yes," she said. "I can't let myself believe otherwise, for it would be the same as calling my own father a liar."

Cooper once again found himself in the ironic position of defending a man he despised, and who despised him even more. "Maybe Solomon doesn't see it as lying," he said. "In time of war, men are forced sometimes to say things they don't really think. Keep in mind that I was raised by Peter Haverly, and he was as Tory as they come. I understand Tories better than some, Hannah, and I don't fault them as much as lots of folks."

Hannah smiled. "I love you, Cooper, but now I've got to go, or Father will start prowling for me."

"Will you be here tomorrow?"

"Not tomorrow . . . come back the next day, the same time, and if I can, I'll meet you here."

"Hannah, I been thinking . . . James Robertson, Callum McSwain, and heaps of others are likely to move to the Cumberland country soon. Maybe you and me could marry and be among them."

Hannah smiled. "Maybe we can . . . we'll see. Good-bye, Cooper."

"Good-bye, Hannah. I love you."

"I love you too."

When she was gone, Cooper stood alone, trying to determine just how a man was supposed to feel after a meeting like this one. His emotions, and Hannah's, had run the full gamut. Would it always be this way with them—so many difficulties to overcome?

Today was the first time since deciding that Hannah was the woman for him that he had experienced any sincere doubt about the wisdom of marrying her. Maybe he was going blind from love, like Sina Colter declared some people did. Already he was violating his own principles and withholding important war intelligence from his own people, and trying to excuse the behavior of a Tory spy he had the power and obligation to expose. What kind of a man was he, anyway? Was he willing to do wrong just to keep Hannah?

Indeed he was—and realizing it gave him the most peculiar and unpleasant feeling in the pit of his stomach. It was a familiar feeling, called guilt.

He decided to head for Thomas Colter's trading post. Even Thomas's hidden stock of fine whiskey wasn't powerful enough to wash the guilt out of a man, but it surely could warm his soul enough to make guilt easier to live with. Hefting his rifle, Cooper strode off.

7

The Reverend Israel Coffman knew as well as any sincere Christian the dangers of "glorying in the flesh," but as he rode through the crisp autumn air, rifle cradled over his arm, he couldn't help but feel he was a grand figure of a man.

Certainly he was a finer physical specimen than he had been when he first came to this wild region some years ago, even though his thick, sandy hair was now beginning to include streaks of gray, and what had been a youthful face was traced with unerasable lines of age and weathering. The frontier Presbyterian preacher was actually grateful for the scrimshawing time had done to his features; he had always looked slightly boyish and therefore had not been taken as seriously as he felt he should have been. Now that he was starting to show his years, people respected him more.

Coffman's horse plodded along the dirt path, the preacher letting it set its own pace. Autumn was a fine time of year in which to put aside hurry and enjoy the splendor of the colorful countryside and the rejuvenating nip of the wind. Today Coffman felt young and strong—and when he thought of his wife Virginia back home, her belly swelling with pregnancy, he felt virile as well. He liked the feeling. This, surely, was the way God intended a healthy man to feel on a beautiful fall day.

Life had brought many changes to Israel Coffman in the past several months, just as it had brought changes to the frontier on which he lived. When first he had come here, Coffman had been an exception among frontier preachers, for he had been under the full hire of the relatively wealthy would-be empire builder Peter Haverly, and had not been required to work a practical trade to make his daily living. Even after he and Haverly had parted ways over matters of theology, politics, and personality, Coffman had managed to live off the generosity of the people whom he served, along with long-distance financial support from his wife's father, the Reverend Uriah Blanton of New Jersey, his former theological tutor. As time passed, his eyes had opened to the fact that he was imposing too often upon too many kindnesses, and risked developing secret resentments toward him.

So Coffman had decided to make his own way. He had taken to farming and was now being taught farrier and blacksmithing skills by one of his flock at the recently founded Newberry Hill Church, where he was pastor. The smithy work had physically transformed the preacher more than any other endeavor. Though he was still on the small side, he was muscled, lean, and callused. No more was he the soft scholar that John Hawk, back before his warring days, had called a "funny little man."

Coffman had met John Hawk while the Cherokee was a guest of Joshua Colter back in 1772. Today Joshua's new home on Limestone Creek was first on Coffman's list of stops during what he anticipated to be a two- or three-day journey.

Coffman had heard some bewildering things about Joshua's family throughout the summer. Supposedly Joshua had come home from the Chickamauga raid in the spring with an Indian woman and child tagging after him. Now, the talebearers said, the pair were living on Joshua's own property in a little cabin he had built within sight of his own, so close it would be within the stockade wall once it was done.

The Indian woman was reportedly called Ayasta Hawkins, and her son, though also possessing an Indian name, was now called Judah Hawkins. How they came to have Christian surnames was part of the story Coffman hadn't yet heard.

A strange tale it all made for, but to Coffman here was the strangest part of all: Even though he had no memory of ever meeting an Indian woman such as the one supposedly at the Colters' place, she reportedly knew of him and talked about him.

It was all very mysterious. Coffman was eager to discover how much of the story was true. Virginia's pregnancy had made her deathly sick throughout the summer, and this had kept Coffman from visiting Joshua to clarify the mystery before now. Now Virginia was better, and at last he felt free to make the approximately twelve-mile jaunt to Limestone Creek. He thought it a shame that such a pitiful tally of miles between his home and Joshua's had proven such an obstacle to their seeing each other as often as old friends should.

When first he had come to this region, Coffman had lived at Colter's Fort when it was still called by its original name of Haverly's. The name had been changed after the loyalist Peter Haverly fell into disgrace in the summer of 1776. From Colter's Station, Coffman had moved to Watauga, but since had moved a third time and now lived on the eastern fringes of the watershed division of the Watauga and Nolichucky rivers.

Coffman had chosen the area because its location between the region's two main settlement areas would be convenient for a frequently traveling clergyman. Roughly that same geographic advantage had also led to the choice of a nearby tract to become a town to serve as the seat of Washington County. The town, the first one officially organized and chartered in the region, had been named Jonesborough in honor of Willie Jones, a North Carolina statesman from Halifax who was a consistent friend of the westerners.

Coffman, who had recently developed a fascination with ancient things, found it interesting that the place where Jonesborough stood had been a town of a far different type long ago. According to the Cherokees, the site once had been an ancient native town, called Nanathugunyi, meaning "spruce tree place." Some time long ago, for reasons unknown, the Cherokees had vacated that site, and had not established permanent villages in this vicinity since.

Back in May the Washington County Court had held its first meeting in a private residence within the bounds of Jonesborough, a courthouse as of yet lacking. Coffman had attended simply to witness the occasion. He saw the coming of a more stable government to the frontier as a great blessing.

A more personal blessing to Coffman had been the coming of his old friend, the Reverend Samuel Doak. He had met Doak when he and the native Virginian were students in Maryland's West Nottingham Academy. Later they had also studied together at the College of New Jersey. Though he and Doak differed greatly in personality, Doak being more stern and impassive, the two clergymen were good friends with a common goal of establishing Christianity and education on the frontier.

Doak and his wife, Elizabeth, had moved to the Holston River settlements late in 1777, when Doak was twenty-eight, then migrated down to Little Limestone Creek in Washington County, a few miles from Joshua Colter's residence. Already Doak had been actively preaching in the region, and was planning the establishment of an academy. Doak had found a great religious hunger in the Overmountain people, and had once been asked to preach on the spot by a band of frontier folk he happened to meet while traveling through the region. That incident, he had told Coffman, had helped confirm his decision to cast his lot with the frontier folk.

Coffman halted his horse and took his bearings. Another mile and he would be within sight of Joshua Colter's cabin. The trace shifted slightly southward across the rolling, forested hills. Coffman resettled himself in the saddle, checked the loading of his rifle and the brace of pistols thrust under his belt sash, and began whistling an Isaac Watts hymn as the horse again plodded forward.

Joshua watched sadly as Israel Coffman eyed Alphus, concern obvious in his expression. Alphus was seated outside Joshua's cabin, his back against the log wall and his arms crossed over his chest. As he stared off over the stockade wall toward the treetops, his lower lip moved slightly, as if he were talking silently to himself. His eyes were transfixed and did not blink as often as it seemed they should.

"How long has he been like this, Joshua?" Coffman asked too softly for Alphus to hear. The caution was polite but unnecessary. Alphus would not have reacted to the preacher's voice even if he had spoken right into his ear.

"A couple of hours now. Likely he'll remain that way at least a couple more, if not longer. I've seen him sit like that and stare most of a day. You can talk to him, yell at him, say anything you want, and he either doesn't hear or doesn't care to answer. He worries me when he's like that."

"Do you believe it's because of Gabriel?"

"Aye, I think that's most of it. I believe he sits there and pictures Gabe at the stake—goes over and over it in his mind."

"A sad thing. A man's private hell." Coffman shook his head. "I was surprised to see Alphus here at all, much less like this. Does he not stay much about his mill anymore?"

"Not as much as he should. I never know when I'm going to look down the road and see him riding up. He leaves most of the millwork to Cooper these days."

"Is Sina here?"

"No. He left her at home. He was fine when he arrived, then I was fool enough to make some passing mention of Gabriel for some reason or another, and he set to brooding. He's been sitting there since, his body here and his mind off in some other place nobody else can reach."

Coffman wished he knew what to say to comfort Joshua. One thing experience had taught him was that pious pronouncements seldom helped much. Worry, suffering, and growing old presented puzzles without human solutions, and Israel Coffman was not so presumptious as to think he could solve them.

"Alphus will be in my prayers every day, Joshua, and you and your own family as well," he said. "I didn't realize things stood so badly with the old gentleman. I don't think he even heard me when I spoke to him—and him once so sharp of sense that you couldn't come within a rifle's range of him without him knowing it. It's sad."

Joshua slapped Coffman on the shoulder, deliberately trying to break the gloom that had settled over them all. "Come inside and have a bite of food if you're hungry," he said. "It's good to see you again, and I'd like to share my table with you."

"Much thanks, but no. I ate on the path and I'm quite satisfied. I'll be truthful: I came to learn, not to eat. I've heard some queer stories, and I see"—he gestured toward the new log cabin—"that there seems to be at least some truth in them."

"Let's walk down to the river together," Joshua said. "It'll take me some time to explain it all, and it's easier done away from Darcy."

Joshua talked as they walked down the leafy path to the river, telling Coffman the details of the expedition, of the burning of the Chickamauga towns, and even of his burying of the old woman who had died. Coffman listened intently to it all, especially so when Joshua at last reached the portion describing how Ayasta came to him and asked him, in effect, to give an entirely new life to herself and her son.

"And as you might have heard, she has talked of you many times," Joshua told his friend. "Apparently John Hawk spoke highly of you to her; she came to believe that you and I were the only unakas she could trust for such a peculiar thing as she asked." Joshua grinned. "She calls you 'the God-man Coffman.' What do you think of that?"

"I hardly know what to think about any of it. John Hawk's widow . . . I can scarcely believe it."

"Nor can I. But it's true. Ayasta and I have talked about

John Hawk a lot since she came. There's no doubt she really was his wife."

"Does Darcy know whose wife she was?"

Joshua grimaced slightly at mention of Darcy. "Yes, she knows. I saw no way not to tell her, and in any case I wanted her to know it was for John Hawk's sake, and for no bad reason, that I took Ayasta in. Even so it's been deuced hard for Darcy to take kindly to all this. Darcy has been given lots of reasons in her life to fear Indians, you know."

"Is it fear alone that has her unhappy?"

Joshua knew from Coffman's look what he was getting at. "I think she has some jealousy, that maybe she thinks that I have some interest in Ayasta beyond simple kindness."

"And do you?" Coffman was as forthright with Joshua as ever. The frontiersman didn't mind it, not from Coffman.

"No, Israel. It's for the sake of good Christian charity and John Hawk's memory that I've helped her. She still grieves for him, by the way."

Coffman's next question came as a surprise. "Do you have any notion of how John Hawk was killed?"

Joshua looked deeply at Coffman, trying to see if he could read any suspicions behind the question. Coffman was an intelligent and perceptive man, not at all as gullible as some perceived. Joshua had long been of the opinion that if anyone ever deduced who John Hawk's slayer had been, it would be either Darcy or Coffman who did it. Joshua believed that Darcy already suspected the truth. But if Coffman's question betrayed a similar suspicion, Joshua could not tell it.

"John Hawk was killed fighting, I suppose," Joshua said. "The Indians say his corpse came back into his town tied to the back of his horse. You have to figure a man like John Hawk would go out fighting."

"Aye. And is that also what Ayasta thinks?"

"I don't know," Joshua replied tersely. He had so far avoided the subject of John Hawk's death when talking to

Ayasta. The subject probed far too close to the heart to be endurable. He was eager for Coffman to drop it.

"Joshua, I think you shouldn't reveal to anyone else that she is John Hawk's widow. John Hawk was as badly hated as Dragging Canoe. There might be those who would seek revenge on his family, if they knew of them."

"I've already considered the same thing, Israel."

"Ah! So that explains the 'Hawkins' last name I've heard."

"Yes. It seemed to me that if she and the boy were to take on white folks' way of life, they needed a proper-sounding white folks' last name. Hawkins seemed the natural choice, from Hawk, you know. Ayasta kept her own first name, but changed Wasi's name to Judah. She had Darcy read her names from the Bible and chose that one because she liked the sound of it." He grinned. "It was between that and Beelzebub. I managed to talk her out of that one."

Brief silence followed, during which Joshua picked up a stone and tossed it into the river. "There's one thing worrying me, Israel. This Trent who first took me to Ayasta—he heard her speak of being John Hawk's wife."

"I see. And you're afraid he'll spread the tale?"

"I'm not sure what I'm afraid of. I don't trust the man. Likely I'm fretting over nothing. He said he came from the upper Holston, and probably he's returned there and we'll see no more of him." He paused. "Yet there was something in his manner about Ayasta, the way he looked at her and acted toward her, that hasn't left my mind. He wanted her for his own, even offered to take her off my hands, as he put it."

"I see. Do you think his intentions were honorable or carnal?"

Joshua had to grin. "You can give a preachery sound to anything you talk about, Israel! Trent didn't look the type to be on the front bench in your church house come Sunday, let me put it that way."

"He did save her honor from the men who first found her, did he not? That would speak well of him in my mind."

"You sound as if you're saying I should have let him have her, Israel."

"Not really. I'm simply trying not to presume the worst of the man. It's one of my principles to believe the best of someone until they give me reason to think otherwise."

"Then that's a difference between you and me. I find that by the time you find there's reason to think the worst of somebody else, your horse has already been stolen. I didn't trust Trent. I couldn't risk letting harm come to Ayasta. Besides, she asked for me to help her, not Trent."

"You seem to feel a strong need to protect her."

Joshua frowned. "What are you digging for, Israel? You sound like Darcy. I'll tell you again what I've already told her a hundred times: It's for Christian decency and the sake of my old friendship with John Hawk that I took her in."

"You are sure?"

Joshua was starting to grow angry. "Are you saying there is something improper in me caring for the widow of an old friend?"

"No. But you must remember, Joshua, that your first loyalty must always be to Darcy and Will. Be careful in your dealings with Ayasta. I tell you that as a friend. Keep a tight rein on your feelings, or else they may bolt away with you. Sometimes a sense of duty to the past can endanger you in the present."

Joshua shook his head in exasperation. "Save your sermon for the pulpit, Israel. I'm doing only what I must."

Israel Coffman nodded. "I've got great confidence in you, Joshua Colter, whether you believe it or not. Now, take me to meet this Ayasta. By the way, out of curiosity, what does her name mean in translation?"

Joshua sorely wished Coffman hadn't asked that question, for the answer seemed terribly ironic in the context of this conversation. He looked away as he answered. " 'Spoiler,' " he mumbled. "Her name means 'spoiler.' "

Solomon Brecht knew now there was no mistake. He hadn't imagined the noises; someone was outside the cabin. He sat up on his bed. The pair of hounds outside sent up a chorus of bays, then one yelped as if in pain, whimpered, then fell silent. A moment later the other did the same.

Beside Solomon, Repentance stirred and sat up.

"Solomon, what—"

"Hush, wife! I think someone has killed the hounds."

This time there was none of Repentance Brecht's usual scorn. She, too, had heard the strange noise, then the silence, of the hounds. "Solomon, who could it be?"

"I'll know soon enough," he said grimly.

Quietly he slipped on his French-fly trousers and hunting shirt, which in his haste he left hanging open and sashless. His two loaded rifles leaned against the wall; he picked up both.

"Father?" The voice from above was Hannah's.

"Quiet, child," he whispered up into the loft. He could just make out her white face peering down at him over the loft's edge. "I'll be back in a moment."

"I'm going with you, Father." This time the speaker was Perrin. He and Andrew were looking down from their side of the loft.

"No, son. You boys look out for the womenfolk."

Solomon went to the rear of the cabin and looked out the little crack between the closed shutters. He saw nothing but darkness. He crept barefoot across the hard dirt floor to the front of the cabin. Slipping back the loophole slide, he peeped out and saw as little as he had before.

Now he was torn. Should he remain inside, or go outside to investigate? He wanted to do the latter but was hesitant, for it was quite possible that whoever was out there wanted him to do precisely that. So for a full minute he stood silently by the door. The white-gowned figure of his wife appeared beneath the loft.

"Well, are you going to stay here or go chase them off?" Now that Repentance was fully awake, she had adopted her usual harping attitude.

Anger welled up in the tense man. "If you want me outside, Repentance Brecht, then outside I'll go," he said rashly. He handed Repentance one of the rifles. "If aught happens to me, it'll be up to you to see to the safety of the children."

Repentance took the rifle hesitantly; now she looked uncertain. "Solomon, you needn't go out there," she said.

There was no turning him now. He was too angry at her, and at whoever was out there come to torment him, to stay inside now. "Hush," he said again, and lifted the bar of the door. "Close it behind me, and keep your ears open."

The sound of the bar thudding into place on the inside of the door made Solomon feel very alone and exposed outside the cabin. He looked around at the dark woods skirting the cabin's clearing. Nothing. He moved to the left, bare feet sliding quietly on cold earth, leaves rustling and crunching despite his efforts at silence.

What did silence matter, anyway? Surely he was even now being watched. He rounded the side of the cabin, scanned the woods in that direction—and then saw the dark form of one of the hounds at the edge of the woods.

He went to it. An arrow had pierced its midparts. That explained the yelp and sudden silence. He glanced around the clearing and quickly found the other hound, also arrow-pierced and dead.

Arrows . . . The implication was both frightening and confusing.

The silence of the night was disturbed by a faint sound like a hiss in the wind, then something thudded into a maple only half a rifle's length from Solomon. Another arrow. It was still quivering, buried deeply into the tree trunk.

Solomon felt a dreadful chill that rose from his feet to his head and made his scalp prickle. He dropped to the earth and rolled into the brush at the woods' edge. Thrusting out the rifle, he looked desperately for the source of the arrow.

"Brecht!"

The voice came from somewhere in the woods due across from him, and had a distinctly Indian sound. "Brecht! We have come to kill you!"

Panic rose in Solomon. He considered firing in the

direction of the voice, then dismissed that as futile. He thought of rising and running for the cabin, and gave up that as well. If he wasn't dropped in the clearing, he surely would find someone waiting for him on the other side. Why had he left the cabin? He might have thrown away his life tonight simply in anger over Repentance's taunting.

"Brecht! You will die, Brecht!"

There was something very bizarre in this. Solomon had expected his harassers would be Whigs. It made no sense for Indians, surely Chickamaugas, to be attacking him, for the Chickamaugas knew of his past aid to their ally Elisha Brecht. And this attack didn't stem from misidentification, for they knew his name.

"Why are you threatening me?" Solomon called out. "I'm a loyal follower of the king and a friend of the Chickamaugas!"

A pause, then an answer, in the same voice but minus the Indian inflections. "Glad to hear you finally confess it, you bloody Tory!"

God help me, Solomon thought. God help me, but what a fool I am!

It was obvious now. The arrows, the feigned Indian voice—these were mere deceptions designed to make him declare his true allegiance. The men hidden in the forest were not Chickamaugas—far from it. Probably they were the same ones who had been frustrated in court in attempting to prove him a Tory.

They had gotten their confession now, and Solomon Brecht knew full well that what would come of it would be far worse than anything the Washington County Court would have inflicted.

He rose and ran as hard as he could for the cabin, rounding to the front and pounding on the door. He called out for entry and heard someone inside fumbling with the bar.

From the forest came the sound of voices and running men. The door opened and admitted Solomon just as vague forms emerged from the forest into the clearing.

He slammed the door closed and rebarred it, the sweat of pure fear dripping off his trembling form.

"God help us," he said. "Oh, God, help us, save us!"

The boys, seeing their father in panic, began to cry and ask if they were about to die. Solomon was too distraught to answer them.

Repentance looked around the room as if it had become new and strange, and fainted to the floor. Hannah ran to her mother's side. She herself was too scared to cry.

She knew that as horrible as the moment was, what was to follow would be far worse. She had heard her father's shouted confession from the forest and been devastated by it. It was really true after all: Solomon Brecht was a secret Tory, just as so many said and Cooper himself had come to believe. Solomon had deceived her along with everyone else—no, deceived her far worse than everyone else, for she had truly believed his claims of innocence while others did not.

Hannah had loved her father all her life, but right now she despised him. She and her brothers had taken much abuse defending him to their peers. Now it all seemed a mocking sham. He was a Tory, and because of it his family was about to suffer the punishment that came to Tories on an unforgiving frontier.

God, she prayed, let me live to see Cooper again. Whatever happens, let me live to see Cooper again.

Then she heard them. They were at the door now—several of them, judging from the sound. Solomon Brecht stopped his wailed prayers, leaped to the door, pushed the slide off the loophole, and fired through the opening. The ball spit out into the night, sailing high above the heads of the assailants outside.

Hannah bit her lip and made not a sound until the shutter of the rear window burst open and the barrels of two long rifles probed in. She cried out and threw herself over her mother's fainted form.

8

Thomas Colter had seen a mystifying thing late in the afternoon, and it remained on his mind long after he had closed his trading post, finished his usual solitary supper in his nearby cabin, and settled down with his pipe. A band of seven riders, none of whom he recognized, had plodded past his store. There was nothing unusual in that in itself . . . but one horse had been pulling a narrow cart on which was a cask of tar and a large, well-stuffed sack. Even more striking, one of the riders had been carrying a Cherokee bow and quiver of arrows. Most peculiar.

Thomas puffed on his pipe and thought the matter over. The sight implied to him that some unfortunate Tory was on his way to the ignoble fate of riding a pole while covered with tar and feathers—the latter being the probable contents of the well-stuffed sack. But why the bow and arrows? He couldn't figure that part.

Living alone made it unnecessary for Thomas Colter to be orderly when it came to sleeping. Sometimes he undressed and crawled into his bed; other times he fell asleep in his fireside chair and remained there for half or more of the night, until at last he would rouse enough to stagger to his bed and drop in fully clothed. This night appeared destined to be one of the latter, for he fell asleep in his seat, dropping the pipe to the floor. Destiny, however, had a more interesting evening than usual planned for the aging merchant.

A pounding at his door startled Thomas awake so severely that he almost fell from the chair. His fire had died to embers and cast only a faint red glow across the hard-packed cabin floor. His first thought was of Indians, his second was of his rifle above the mantelpiece, and his third was of the fact that raiding Indians would not likely bother to knock on his door. He took down his rifle anyway, put his thumb on the lock hammer, and said loud and gruff: "Who's there?"

"Callum McSwain! Open the door, Thomas!"

"Callum! What are you . . . wait a moment, just a moment . . ." He removed the bar and slid out the latchstring. The door opened and Callum McSwain stepped in. He had his rifle and seemed very intense.

"Evening to you, Thomas. Sorry to bother you late."

The merchant ran his hands through his white hair. "What brings you here this time of night?"

"I've been hunting today—with blasted little luck, I might add—and was riding back to the cabin when I noticed the light."

"I don't have a light on."

"Not your light—a light in the forest. You'll have to step out to see it."

Thomas Colter wiped the bleariness from his eyes and followed McSwain out the door. They rounded the edge of the cabin, and McSwain pointed northeast. "See it?"

Thomas did not have the keen long hunter's vision of his brother Alphus, but even his slightly myopic merchant's eyes could see the distant yellow-orange glow through the treetops. Obviously a building was ablaze.

"Merciful saints!" Thomas declared. "Whose is it?"

"If I had to make suppositions, I'd say Solomon Brecht's," McSwain replied.

"Brecht's! Aye, it does lie that way, with no other place close by it," Thomas said. Suddenly he remembered the mounted young men who had passed in the afternoon with their tar and feathers and bow. "Callum, I think I saw the ones who did it," he said, and told of the riders.

McSwain nodded. "I'd wager those are the very ones. Now mind you, Thomas, I've got no love for Tories, but I'm going to have to ride out there and see how bad things have gone for sorry old Solomon Brecht, and I may have to butt in like the old goat I am."

"Because of his family?"

"Aye . . . particularly his daughter. Cooper Haverly's set on marrying her, you know." He paused. "And I would hate to see harm come to his wife."

Something in the tone of McSwain's last sentence struck Thomas. He recalled other times that McSwain had made offhand comments about Repentance Brecht. Not improper comments, though unquestionably admiring ones. Interesting—especially in that Repentance bore a close resemblance to McSwain's late wife, Jean. He wondered if maybe . . . then dropped the thought. "You want me to go with you?" he asked.

"If you will."

"You know the feelings of the Brechts toward the Colters . . ."

"I know. But I need a trusty man with me. I know none trustier than you."

"In that case, I'm ready as soon as I saddle my horse."

They rode through the dark forest together, drawing ever nearer the fiery light ahead. They had not gone far before it became evident that it was indeed Solomon Brecht's cabin ablaze. They listened for sounds of raiding and destruction, but heard none.

"We may be too late," McSwain said. "Brace yourself for whatever we find, Thomas."

All was strangely silent in the forest, and the ever brighter light ahead cast an eerie glow back toward them. Near the end of the path the two men dismounted, took rifles in hand, and advanced on foot.

"Solomon Brecht!" McSwain called as they approached. "It's Callum McSwain, come to help you."

A slender, dark figure darted from the clearing to the

edge of the forest. "Come quickly, Mr. McSwain!" Mc-Swain and Thomas Colter recognized Hannah's voice.

The sight that met them in the clearing was pitiful. The Brecht family huddled together, watching their home burning down. The boys were crying, Repentance was staring listlessly into the flames, and Solomon Brecht lay on the ground, covered with tar and feathers, tears streaming down his face. Even Thomas Colter, who despised the Brecht clan almost as much as the Brechts despised the Colters, felt sad for the humiliated man.

"I knew it would finally come to this," he murmured to McSwain.

"Aye—I'm surprised it's taken this long."

There was nothing to be done now except to comfort the afflicted family. McSwain went to Solomon's side and knelt. Thomas Colter hung back out of discretion.

"Are you hurt beyond the tar and feathers?" McSwain asked Solomon.

"No." Solomon's voice was broken and sad.

"That's good. Did you see their faces?"

"Masked. They were masked."

"Give thanks to God they didn't hang or shoot you," McSwain said. "Have they told you to leave the country?"

"Aye."

He stood, looking at the flaring cabin. "Then I think you should, Mr. Brecht, as soon as you are able."

Solomon sat up, looking ludicrous in his feathery coating. He plucked a feather from his face and tried to toss it away, but it stuck to his pitchy fingers. "We'll leave," he said. "I'll not stay in a place where a man is treated so." Solomon turned his head and saw Thomas Colter standing at the clearing's edge. "You dare to bring a Colter to my home tonight?" he said to McSwain. Then to Thomas: "Go ahead and fill your eyes, Colter! I'll wager you're not the first of your brood to be at this place this evening!"

"I doubt any Colter had a hand in this," McSwain said.

"Do you? Well, I don't. You give warning for me, McSwain. You tell the Colters that if ever I see aught of them again, my rifle will speak my mind for me!"

Hannah stood to the side, listening. So far tonight she

had not cried; now she burst into tears. Thomas Colter watched her and understood the reason for her tears. She was thinking of Cooper.

"We'd best get to peeling off this tar before it eats into his skin worse than it has," Thomas Colter said. "That is, if Mr. Brecht will let himself be touched by a Colter."

Solomon Brecht's expression was almost a snarl. "If you want to peel, then peel," he said. "A Colter may as well help fix what another Colter has done."

Thomas Colter did not bite at the chance to snipe back. He began carefully peeling away the stiffening tar—an essential task that had to be done with the greatest delicacy in order to keep from ripping away the skin beneath and subjecting the tarring victim to potentially fatal infection. Thomas wished there were a physician in the vicinity to oversee this process, but there was none.

Thomas glanced over and saw McSwain now at Repentance Brecht's side, comforting her. Again he wondered . . . Callum McSwain, after all, was a lonely man, and Thomas Colter knew how loneliness could turn a man's head. At the same time, he knew McSwain well enough to doubt the man would do anything unfitting.

McSwain came over and joined in the tar-stripping process. Solomon Brecht gritted his teeth and squeezed his eyes shut and managed to hold out for a full five minutes before giving in to the need to scream. When he did scream, Hannah put her hands over her ears.

Word spread quickly the next day of what had happened. All around Colter's Station people talked, and in many cases chortled, about the suspected Tory Solomon Brecht finally getting his due. Just as fascinating to most was the news that Callum McSwain, firm Whig that he was, had for some reason taken the Brechts under his wing and was letting them live for the present in his own cabin.

Had McSwain lost his senses? Why would he be kind to a Tory family—especially one with blood ties to Elisha Brecht himself? Some who had heard McSwain comment idly upon the beauty of Repentance Brecht were quick to assign improper motives to McSwain's action. Everyone knows McSwain is about to leave for the Cumberland country, they said. He must want to take Repentance Brecht along with him.

One gossip even suggested that McSwain had helped spark the cabin-burning simply so he could play the rescuer afterward and earn the favor of Repentance Brecht.

Then there was Cooper Haverly to speculate about. Though Cooper had tried to keep his desire to marry Hannah Brecht quiet, almost everyone knew about it. Before a day had passed, some were declaring that Cooper had led the masked raiders who burned the Brecht cabin, that indeed the event had been inspired by some rebuff from Hannah.

Others said that Joshua Colter may also have been involved. This claim was countered by those who knew him best; they declared authoritatively that cabin-burning and tarring and feathering were not Joshua's style of dealing with Tories.

Israel Coffman heard of Solomon Brecht's humiliation while still a guest of one Anthony Moore, a tall and impressive man who had settled in the area. Born of native Irish parents in Northampton County, Pennsylvania, Moore was a devout Presbyterian who had led his family in a prayer service even before unloading their wagons when they arrived at their new home the prior year. It was natural that such a man would become a good friend of Israel Coffman's. Moore had prevailed upon the preacher to spend the night at his home after Coffman rode up from Joshua Colter's home to see him.

As soon as he heard of the attack, Coffman departed from Moore's and rode toward Callum McSwain's house. On the way he saw a rider approaching from another direction, and reined up when he saw it was Cooper Haverly.

"Cooper!" he called. "Wait—let me speak to you!"

Cooper's face showed his distraught state. "Hello, preacher," the young man said glumly.

"Hello, Cooper. Are you off to McSwain's?"

"I am."

"So am I—let's ride together."

"My business there is private."

"I know of it, Cooper. Joshua told me of your marriage plans."

Cooper grew more visibly upset. "He'll not carry her off from me," he declared. "I'll see him dead first!"

"For heaven's sake, take a grip on your temper, Cooper! You think Hannah would marry a man who would talk of killing her father!"

"What about his talk of killing me? What about all his hate for my own kin? She stays true to her father through that! The time has come for her to make a choice."

"If you force her to a choice, you may not like what she chooses."

"We'll see about that."

Coffman was disturbed by Cooper's demeanor. He was glad he had come along when he had, and hoped his presence would restrain what could prove a fierce confrontation. "I'm coming with you," he said.

"I don't want you to. What I have to say to old Solomon may be less than Christian."

"Cooper, answer me straight. Were you among those who burned the Brecht cabin?"

"You think me a fool, preacher? I wouldn't put in danger the girl I intend to marry."

They rode together to McSwain's cabin. Callum McSwain came onto the porch as they approached. He nodded and smiled at Coffman and looked cautiously at Cooper.

"Hello, gentlemen. What brings you here?"

Cooper swung down from his horse. "Where is he?"

"If you're speaking of Solomon Brecht, he's inside, and you'd best stay away from him."

"And Hannah—"

"Inside as well. You'd best leave, Cooper. Tempers are already hot and there's nothing gained by rubbing them hotter."

"I want to see Hannah. I want to know she's well."

"She is well, take my word. I mean it when I say you'd best go. I think—"

Hannah Brecht came bursting out of the door behind McSwain, ran past him, and darted to Cooper. At the same time, Solomon Brecht's voice boomed out in protest from inside, and he appeared shirtless in the doorway, loaded pistol in hand. The feathers were off him now, but much tar still clung to his reddened skin.

Callum McSwain turned, grasped Solomon's arm and wrenched at the pistol. It went off, the powder flash burning McSwain's face and making him yell. The blacksmith McSwain was stronger than the farmer Brecht, and pulled the empty pistol free. In a burst of anger he pushed Brecht to the ground just outside the cabin.

Hannah, meanwhile, had reached Cooper, who put his arms around her, watching Solomon Brecht as intently as a nesting bird watches a tree snake.

"In the name of our holy God, stop this!" Coffman shouted, throwing his hands upward. "Cooper, please come away from here before someone is hurt, or worse!"

"If I come away, Hannah comes away with me." He fired his next words at Brecht like they were bullets. "I'm marrying your daughter, Solomon Brecht! You and all hell itself can't stop me from it!"

"Hell, you say? It's hell I'll send you to, you dung-fouled cur!" Solomon shouted back, trying to rise. McSwain put a foot on him and pushed him down again, and not at all gently.

"Please, gentlemen, please!" Coffman's urgings sounded feeble now.

"That Colter whelp will never give his name to my daughter!" Solomon declared.

"My name is Haverly—I'm no more Colter than you are!"

"You're brother to Joshua Colter—that makes you Colter in my eyes! Was it you who burned my home last night, you devil?"

"I'd nothing to do with it."

"You lie! You lie like Satan's brood!"

"This is terrible." Coffman said. "Terrible!"

"Come, Hannah, let's leave here," Cooper said.

"No."

He glared into her face. "What?"

"No!" She pulled free of Cooper's grasp. "Can't you see that this cannot be, that this cannot work?"

Cooper stared at her in disbelief. Meanwhile, Coffman and McSwain cast glances at each other.

Repentance Brecht, in the meantime, emerged from the cabin and crouched on the ground beside her husband. McSwain's foot still kept him pinned to the ground. "I'm sorry, Mrs. Brecht," McSwain said. "If I let him up, they'd fight like drooling dogs."

Hannah was struggling with her emotions. "If we were to marry now, there would be murder to come of it!"

Cooper was stunned. "Hannah! Do you not love me?"

"Of course I love you, and I love my father—and I hate the whole cursed world for forcing me to choose between you!"

Cooper felt he could explode. He waved a finger at Brecht. "You choose him—him!—above me?"

"I am his daughter. I can't abandon him when the world has turned against him."

Cooper could find no words. Solomon Brecht began to smile. "You hear that, whelp? She'll have nothing to do with the likes of you!"

Hannah wheeled. "Hush, Father!" she screamed. "Hear me: I despise the hate in you that makes me give up my own happiness because of your bitterness!"

Cooper suddenly remembered the woodland meeting he had witnessed and held secret. He would hold it secret no more. "Solomon Brecht, why not tell this good preacher about the forest meetings you've held with your murdering brother! And don't think you can lie your way out of it; I witnessed one such meeting with my own eyes!"

"He lies!" Solomon shouted.

"No—no lies. Not anymore," Cooper said. "I've been a liar up until now by holding my silence. Callum, Preacher Coffman, I saw that man meeting with Elisha Brecht in January of this very year, and held my peace about it for the sake of Hannah. Now there's naught to keep me quiet. Ask Hannah herself; I've talked to her about it before."

"Is this true, Solomon?" McSwain demanded.

"It's a damnable lie!" Solomon responded. There was fear beneath his defiance.

McSwain looked at Hannah. "Hannah, what of this?"

Hannah Brecht looked as frightened as any young woman Coffman had ever seen. He waited breathless for her answer. If Cooper had in fact witnessed such a meeting, Solomon Brecht would surely stand to face charges before the local court again under the strict anti-Tory laws of North Carolina, and this time he probably would not escape punishment.

Hannah stammered wordlessly for a few moments, looking from face to face. She was being forced again to choose between her father and her lover—to either brand the former a Tory or the latter a liar.

When she spoke, her voice was strangely shrill. "I know nothing of it—Cooper has never spoken of such a thing to me!"

Cooper stared at her a moment, then swore, wheeled, and stalked back to his horse, a young man knowing what he had lost. As of this moment Hannah was his no more, but her father's alone—a father who didn't deserve such a jewel as she. Cooper felt crushed in the gears of a great clockwork that operated beyond his control.

Cooper had known grief in his time. He had watched his adoptive mother, the only mother he had ever known, die during the siege of Colter's Fort. He had seen his foster father killed by Cherokees shortly thereafter. He knew what it was to wait for death at the fire stake—a fate he had most narrowly escaped. But no suffering had hurt him as badly as this day's grief over Hannah, and no loss had taken so much from him.

Cooper mounted and rode away. He didn't look back, and so did not see Solomon Brecht spit contemptuously in his direction as he disappeared around the bend.

Alphus Colter had snapped out of his brood as quickly as he had entered it. Less than an hour after Israel

Coffman's departure from Joshua's home, he had become talkative, almost chipper. Joshua noted privately that Alphus seemed unaware that the preacher had been there at all; it showed clearly how untouchable were the depths into which Alphus's mind descended when his "spells" were upon him. He departed Joshua's house well before suppertime in order not to arrive too late at his own cabin and worry Sina and Zach.

The following night Joshua sat with his pipe and whittling knife, carving out a toy soldier for little Will from a piece of hickory. Though he seemed to concentrate on his work, in truth he was more interested in watching Darcy as she taught Ayasta the skill of weaving rugs from rag strips. Darcy was good at that task despite her withered hand. She was a good teacher as well, for Ayasta picked up the knotting patterns with little difficulty. The little ones, meanwhile, slept side by side on a big paddock of cloth-covered flax within reach of the fire's heat, but safely out of reach of the occasional sparks.

It pleased Joshua to see Darcy and Ayasta seeming to get on well tonight. So far there had been hardly a trace of that. Darcy had tried to hide her harsh feelings toward the Cherokee intruder, but Joshua had been able to detect them.

As he watched the two together, hoping now that a corner had been turned, he thought about Israel Coffman's warning. The preacher's words had offended him. Could not even he understand the innocence, the positive rightness, of what he was trying to do for Ayasta?

Joshua turned the wood in his hand and carefully carved off a few tiny slivers, shaping the rear of the wooden soldier's uniform. This was to be a British soldier of the type Joshua had known back during his Fort Loudoun childhood, red-coated, tricorned, and gaitered. It was only too bad, he reflected, that it wasn't soldiers so obviously marked that were the foe on the border. Here the enemy looked like your neighbor—often was your neighbor. Either that or he was a marauding Chickamauga, far harder to kill than any redcoat Joshua had ever known.

Will murmured and moved. Darcy rose, looked at him to see that he was well, then returned to rug-making.

Joshua covertly studied Ayasta. She was a lovely woman indeed, though in a different way than most women of his own race. Her beauty was fully natural and unpampered, like the beauty of a deer. How out-of-place Ayasta looked here in this unaka cabin, clad in a white woman's dress Darcy had given her! The dress, homespun yet attractive, complimented Ayasta nicely but unnaturally. In fact, everything about seeing an Indian woman in this setting seemed unnatural.

Joshua had to wonder how Ayasta felt about this new life she had adopted for herself and her son. His mind was full of questions he didn't dare ask. Was it what she had expected? Did she sense Darcy's hostility and resentment? Would she really be able to abide this way of living forever? Would it give her the peace of mind she wanted so badly?

Joshua was pessimistic on the last question. The frontier was no more a safe haven for whites than for Indians. Ayasta, it seemed to him, wanted a life free of all threat, and she would not find it here any more than she had in Chickamauga Town. But that would be a lesson she would have to learn for herself.

Darcy stood up suddenly. "For God's sake, Ayasta, do you not see what you are doing? Now you've gone and ruined these rags!"

Ayasta looked up with an expression of innocent surprise. Joshua cleared his throat. "Now, Darcy, whatever she's done can surely be fixed."

"Oh, do you think so? How many rag rugs have you woven, husband?" Darcy cast down her own half-finished rug and walked to the water bucket, where she took a drink from the dipper, then sloshed it back into the water so hard it splashed onto the puncheon floor.

Ayasta wordlessly stood and went to where Judah slept. She picked him up, walked toward the door, paused there, and turned to Darcy. "I'm sorry," she said, then departed.

"Well, there's two words of English she's learned to

speak well indeed, as much as you give her cause to say them," Joshua said. "Need you be so critical of her?"

Darcy cast a cold stare at Joshua. "Need you always take her side?" She left the room.

Joshua filled his pipe and lit it, puffing out great white clouds and watching them disperse. At length he rose and went to bed. Darcy was already there, seemingly asleep. But when he lay down, she rolled over and looked at him.

"I'm sorry, Joshua," she said. "It's hard for me. She's so . . . different. So Indian. You know how I fear Indians."

"Yes, I know."

"She's of a race that was ready to take my life at one time. Every time I look at her I live through it all again."

Hearing that made Joshua feel guilty. He had no idea that Ayasta's presence revived in Darcy the tormenting memories of being an Indian prisoner. No wonder Darcy was so harsh with Ayasta. He could hardly blame her.

Joshua rolled onto his side and fell to thinking, and was silent for so long that Darcy thought he had gone to sleep. She herself was almost in slumber when he spoke next. "Darcy."

She opened her eyes. Joshua had moved to his side of the bed and was sitting up, back against the wall, eyes looking straight ahead. From his manner she could tell he wished to tell her something of importance. She sat up. "What is it, Joshua?"

He looked at her. "Do you remember back while we yet lived on Gone to God Creek, back in 'seventy-seven it was, the time that I packed my horse and went off alone looking for John Hawk?"

"Of course I remember. I prayed every day that you wouldn't find him. I feared that if you did, he would kill you."

"Aye—I remember well how happy you were when I came back and told you I hadn't found him."

"It was an answered prayer."

"No. It was a lie."

She said nothing, but even in the dark he could sense her confusion.

"I did find John Hawk. I offered him peace, if he would only stop his killing. He wouldn't take it. We fought with knives. I lived. He died."

Darcy was stunned. After a few moments she said, "You, Joshua? You killed John Hawk? Why didn't you tell me?"

"A man doesn't like telling what gives him no joy. John Hawk was my friend long before he was my enemy. The first time ever I laid eyes on him he was just a sickly ten-year-old Cherokee boy in his uncle's house in Tikwalitsi."

"Yes. You've told me many times."

"I suppose I have." He put his hand on Darcy's. "I'm sorry I kept the truth from you this long. It was a raw wound inside me, you see, the kind a man don't like to rub. The reason I've told you at last is that I want you to know why I'm so obliged to help Ayasta. It's because I'm the very one who put her into the situation she is. It was me who killed her husband."

Darcy remained silent, absorbing the astounding news.

"She must not know, Darcy," Joshua said. "If she knew, she would . . . I don't know what she would do."

No answer.

"Do you understand what I said, Darcy? She cannot know what I've told you tonight. No one must know."

"I understand," Darcy replied. She rolled over, back toward Joshua, and stared into the darkness for the next hour, until at last she was asleep.

The rider came from the east while the sun was yet behind him. The hounds set up a loud baying as he approached, and Joshua eyed him through a squint under a shading hand.

"My name is Eli Candle, Mr. Colter," the man said. "I've come looking for the Reverend Israel Coffman. He was planning to stop here, I believe."

"He did stop, two days ago. Like as not he'll be heading back through today or tomorrow."

"I must find him today. He's direly needed back at his home."

Darcy, who had been watching the interchange from the cabin, now came around and joined Joshua, slipping her hand into his.

"Is there sickness?" Joshua asked.

"Of a sort," Candle said. "I doubt there's harm in telling you: It's his wife."

"Virginia!" Darcy said. A pause. "Merciful God, is it the baby?"

Candle nodded. "Aye, it is. She had an early issue and travail, and the baby was stillborn. Mrs. Coffman still lives, thank God, but she's in deep grief. She needs her husband with her."

Joshua said, "Mr. Candle, with your permission, I'll join you and help you find him. It may be that I know the ways here better than you."

"I was hoping you'd make just that kind offer, sir."

As Darcy watched them ride away some minutes later, Ayasta approached her from behind. In her halting English she asked what had transpired, and Darcy told her.

Ayasta, who had been very happy to meet Coffman two days before, showed little reaction in her face. She was a stoic woman, accustomed to hiding her feelings.

"Reverend Coffman will blame himself," Darcy said, as much to herself as to Ayasta. "He'll hold it to his own fault that he was away from his wife when it happened. I wish I could understand why such tragedies happen, why there must be such sad things in this world."

Ayasta had listened closely to make sure she understood Darcy's words. Now she struggled to respond as best she could.

"There is the above world, the sky world. Light, goodness. There is the below world . . . darkness, death, evil things. There is our world, between them. Here there is above and also below. Here the above and the below touch each other. So we smile, laugh, and we cry too. Good from above, bad from below. That is why."

Ayasta gave the most sincere smile Darcy had ever received from anyone. Her explanation, couched in struggling English and reflecting the viewpoint of a world from which she had estranged herself, was unexpectedly touching to Darcy—not because she understood it, which she didn't, but because of the spirit in which it had been spoken.

For a moment Darcy almost saw Ayasta in a new way—then stubborn will and jealousy overcame her again. She would not, in any circumstance, allow herself to begin to accept this intruder, this self-invited threat to her very security and marriage.

"That's heathen talk," she said. "If you want to be like we are, you must put such foolish things behind you . . . if your kind can do that." And with that she walked away.

Ayasta watched her go and felt sad. Darcy Colter almost always made her sad, and she didn't understand why it had to be that way. Was this the way of all unaka women?

It was going to be hard indeed to become part of the unaka world, Ayasta decided. So far she could make no sense of it at all.

Joshua and his companion finally tracked down Israel Coffman at Alphus Colter's mill. Giving the tragic news to the preacher was hard, and, as Joshua had feared, Coffman took it badly.

"I should have never left her alone," he said. "It's my fault."

"No. No one's fault," Joshua said. "You had no way to know such a thing would happen."

"I should have stayed with her. I should have stayed."

Joshua didn't argue further, seeing it was pointless. Coffman joined him and Candle, and the three began the long, sad ride back to Coffman's home.

At last Coffman began talking about what had happened with Cooper and Solomon Brecht at McSwain's cabin, of Cooper's claim of seeing Solomon and Elisha Brecht conferring in the forest, and of Solomon's fierce denial. He also told Joshua of Hannah's refusal to back up Cooper's story, and his own suspicion that she might be

covering for her father. Coffman seemed eager to talk
about these things . . . probably, Joshua figured, to take
his mind off his own immediate tragedy.

Joshua was naturally intrigued and bothered by the
information. He had feared matters would eventually
come to this. He wished he were free to turn back and go
talk to McSwain about the matter, but with Coffman's
situation that didn't seem feasible.

One part of the situation was a puzzle: Why had Mc-
Swain made himself the rescuer of the Brecht family?
Never before had he expressed any interest in them—
except, Joshua abruptly recalled, to praise the beauty of
Repentance. Could that be what motivated McSwain? It
didn't seem the type of thing he woud do, but then, he
had changed much since his wife's death.

Another aspect of the matter bothered Joshua as well.
"If Cooper saw Elisha Brecht alive as early as January, he
was wrong to keep it hidden so long," Joshua said to
Coffman. "Why would he do such a thing?"

"Because of Hannah, he said."

"Well, that makes sense—though he was still in the
wrong. Do you believe he saw what he claimed, Israel?"

"I don't know what to believe."

"Callum McSwain must believe Solomon. Otherwise I
don't think he would take him under wing."

"I fear there are motives of the heart moving our friend
McSwain," the perceptive Coffman commented. Obviously he was drawing the same conclusion as Joshua.

They reached Coffman's home far too late for Joshua to
return to his own home, so he spent the night on a pallet
on the floor before Coffman's fire. The night brought little
rest; he could hear too clearly the sounds of sorrow from
the Coffmans' room—husband and wife grieving for the
loss of a child they had wanted badly. The baby had been
a boy, which only made the pain worse for Israel Coffman.
He had prayed for a son who would grow to become a
man of God, like his father.

The next morning Joshua stayed only long enough to
pay his respects at the side of the Coffman infant's tiny

grave, then returned home to tell Darcy all that had happened.

As sorrowful as Darcy was for the Coffmans, she seemed even more so for Cooper. Joshua understood why. Darcy, once married to a man she had tried to love but who had refused to love her in return, knew well the pain brought by wounds of the sort Cooper now suffered.

In the end Darcy's wounds had been healed and the bad in her life had turned to good. Joshua could only hope the same would come true for Cooper.

After the encounter with Cooper Haverly, Solomon Brecht, skin raw from the tar-stripping, had spent the rest of the day in deep conversation with Callum McSwain. In the moments when her grief subsided enough to allow thoughts of anything but what had happened, Hannah wondered what the two men could be discussing so intently.

The answer came that night when Solomon gathered his wife and children around him at McSwain's table. The Scotsman stood in the corner of the cabin, arms crossed, and watched in silence.

"We cannot remain here any longer," Solomon said. "To do so would invite nothing but treachery and suffering for us all. And so we will be leaving."

"Where will we go, Father?" Perrin asked.

"On a voyage, God willing," Solomon replied. "We will go tomorrow to the Long Island and seek a place in the fleet that is forming to travel to the Cumberland country. I don't know that we will be allowed a place . . . it will depend on what has been said about me, and to whom, and how much of it is believed."

Hannah blinked back the water from her eyes. The Cumberland country . . . she remembered Cooper talking about the Cumberland as one possible refuge for them when they were married, a place they could go and escape the venom of her father's hatred for Cooper and the Colters. The memory was brutally ironic.

Perrin's eyes were wide. "A voyage!" he said. "I've never been on a voyage before!"

"Like as not you'll never be on another like this one will be," his father said.

"Will Mr. McSwain be coming with us?" Repentance asked.

"Not on the boats. He will go ahead by land to help those who will prepare the country for the rest of us. I would do the same except that I cannot desert my family at so uncertain a time."

McSwain stepped forward. "The man we must see is named Donelson, John Donelson. I'll do all I can to secure you a place—though as Solomon has said, there's no assurances."

"I wish you would consider going with us by river, Callum," Solomon said.

McSwain lowered his head and shook it. "No. It would be best for me to go on by land." He glanced sidewise for half a moment at Repentance, then looked down again, and no one but Hannah noticed it.

THE
VOYAGERS

9

The autumn gave way to the coldest winter the frontier had known for a century.

For years thereafter folks would huddle by their hearths on snowy nights and comfort themselves with the reminder that as hard and harsh as the present winter was, it wasn't nearly as bad as the "Hard Winter." The bitter season closed its grip late in the fall of 1779 and refused to loosen it as one year passed into another.

Many months of 1780 would go by before either man or nature recovered from the effects of this terrible season. This was a lethal winter that killed game in the forests, a biting winter that iced the rivers from bank to bank and made water travel impossible. For those who had abandoned their cabins, sold their livestock, and pulled up all other roots in anticipation of traveling by river to the Cumberland country, the frozen rivers posed an unexpected and serious problem.

Hannah Brecht pulled the blanket more closely around her shoulders and scooted a little nearer to the fire. Her mother sat beside her beneath the same blanket. They were in a tiny hut built within sight of the icy Holston River and near the mouth of Reedy Creek. They had been ensconced here for about a month, waiting, shivering, hoping, and waiting some more, living like refugees in a farrago of crude log shelters built by those unfortunate enough, like the Brechts, to have found no harbor as guests of the permanent settlers around them.

The winter days were short, and there was lots of activity going on continually as the voyagers took advantage of the delay to better the fleet of covered pirogues and flatboats. It didn't matter to Hannah. For her the days were endlessly long and barren. She struggled almost continually to think of anything in the world but Cooper Haverly, and by so doing ensured she would think of nothing else.

Despite what had happened that day outside Callum McSwain's cabin, she still loved Cooper dearly. It wasn't loss of love that made her throw him off, but the fact he had forced her to choose between loyalty to him and loyalty to her father. She hadn't wanted to betray Cooper—but what choice had she? If she had verified the secret forest meeting between her father and uncle, Solomon Brecht might have been whipped and driven from the country in disgrace. Maybe even shot or hanged.

Solomon still denied to all around him that he was a Tory. That Hannah could understand; what she could not understand was his insistence on still denying it to her and her brothers as well. His denials carried no weight with Hannah. Solomon might not have lost his daughter's love, but he had lost her trust.

He excused the confession he had shouted during the raid against their cabin as a desperate lie contrived to save life and family. What man wouldn't call himself a Tory if he believed he could avert fatal disaster doing it? Didn't the Whig leaders themselves sometimes feign loyalty to the crown in correspondence and conversation, if it suited their momentary purpose?

Hannah pretended to accept the explanation; it was easier that way. Her brothers, less mature than she, seemed to still believe their father, and she did not try to dissuade them. What her mother knew and thought Hannah had no idea; Repentance held her silence, as she always had.

Though it grieved Hannah to know her father was a liar, it made no fundamental difference in her sense of duty to him. She was still his daughter, still his favorite child, and she would stand by him out of love and obligation. For his sake she had already cast aside the young man she loved, so why should she quail now at any future sacrifices? Nothing could compare to what she had already given up.

Hannah was well aware that Callum McSwain had managed to obtain her family's place in the flotilla only by the narrowest margin. Had James Robertson still been about when he and Solomon came asking, they might not have found a place at all, Robertson not being prone to give quarter to Tories. But Robertson wasn't there to make the decision; he had already departed with a party of Cumberland-bound overland travelers by the time Solomon and McSwain arrived at Fort Patrick Henry, seeking a refuge in the fleet for the beleaguered family.

Unfortunately for Solomon Brecht, those who had raided his cabin had spread whispers abroad. Word of his shouted confession had preceded him to the Long Island country. He and McSwain found Colonel John Donelson, flotilla leader, hesitant to accept a man so many believed to be a Tory and maybe a traitor.

Hannah was not allowed close by while McSwain and her father pleaded Solomon's case with Donelson, so she had no firsthand knowledge of how they managed to talk the Brechts into the expedition. She had since heard, however, that it was mostly Callum McSwain's good name and rather inexplicable assurances of confidence in Solomon that finally persuaded Donelson to accept the Brechts.

Callum McSwain . . . there was a mystery. Hannah could not understand why the Scotsman had been so kind. Why he, a firm Whig and even a member of Joshua Colter's rangers, was risking ostracism by being helpful to perceived Tories. Why had he done it?

Hannah had an unsettling suspicion of the answer. Since the evening Solomon had announced that they were joining the voyage, she had kept her eye on McSwain. She had seen how he looked at her mother when he thought no one else was watching, and detected his tension when Repentance was near him.

McSwain had fled the scene as soon as the Brechts were accepted into the flotilla, going on to catch up with James Robertson's overland party, which by then was already driving the livestock to the Cumberland country far in advance of the water travelers. McSwain had said his farewells and rushed off like a man on the run.

Having come into the flotilla late, Solomon had initially arranged to distribute his family over several of the already crowded flatboats. Then had come the hard freeze of the river and the temporary delaying of the expedition at Reedy Creek. Though bad for the overall expedition, the delay had proven fortuitous for the Brechts in one regard.

One of the families that had begun the voyage on a relatively small and poorly made flatboat had grown discouraged and withdrawn from the flotilla. Solomon obtained their small flatboat and was using this wait to enlarge and improve it. He had dubbed it the *Carolina*, and was doing so fine a job of its improvement that some other men in the flotilla were turning to him for advice and help in bettering their own craft. Gradually and unconsciously, some of the animosity toward Solomon Brecht was beginning to fade, ever so slightly. Hannah detected this and was glad for it. Solomon had even managed to obtain two oarsmen to help him navigate the *Carolina*. One was a widower farmer named Jesse Clinton, the other a former seaboard boatman named Zekle Holly. Hannah liked Clinton, but found Holly's probing stares disconcerting.

The fire had begun to die, so Hannah rose and refueled it. "We're nigh out of wood," she said to Andrew. "Come with me and we'll fetch some more."

Andrew grumbled about going into the cold, and Hannah chided him, reminding him that his brother and father, who were out roofing the nearly flat shelter that covered most of the rear of the *Carolina*, were certainly far colder than he.

Shivering, Hannah and her youngest brother gathered wood and carried it back to their hut, where they found the solemn and somnolent Repentance beginning to mix ground corn with water. The woman had been of grim demeanor since the postponement of the voyage. After placing some of the wood by the fire, the young people again left the hut. All around smoke rose from other huts and shelters of every conceivable type, as well as from several of the flatboats themselves.

"I wish we could either go on or go find a real cabin somewhere else to do our waiting in," grumbled Andrew as he looked over the crude and makeshift waterside village.

"You know we can't leave here," Hannah said. "The weather may warm at any time. We all must be here and ready to go on as soon as the river thaws. Besides, many of the people here have no empty cabins to go back to. They've sold their lands."

Hannah and Andrew descended to the shore, where Solomon and Perrin still labored on the *Carolina*. Zekle Holly was there, too, smoking but not working. Clinton was nowhere in view.

Other than being small, the *Carolina* was a typical broadhorn flatboat, its white oak gunnels and six-inch sleepers neatly hewn, fitted together tightly, coated beneath with tar and caulked with fibers of oakum. Its shelter was boxy and rough, but much better than its previous state thanks to the labors of Solomon and Perrin. It would double as a platform upon which Solomon would stand to man the great sweep that served as a rudder for the raftlike craft. Like all the flatboats in the fleet, the *Carolina* boasted a rough but serviceable stone hearth for cooking.

Flatboats, along with covered pirogues, were the most important watercraft on the border. Flatboats rode high in the water and were capable of becoming temporary floating homesteads for those who traveled the frontier rivers aboard them. Onto the raftlike flatboats went everything the settlers would require to begin new lives at their destinations. Often this included livestock, though not in this instance, Robertson's group having already taken the cattle and horses with them overland.

Hannah had never traveled by flatboat except for the brief three-mile stint on this expedition's aborted first attempt back before Christmas, and she was nervously anticipating the actual journey. Her father had some experience in flatboat travel and had warned his family that the voyage would be difficult. Hannah, like Andrew, was so restless that even the prospect of troubles roused little dread. Anything had to be better than this limbo of waiting in the cold.

And for Hannah there was another thing driving her eagerness to proceed. Now that her ties with Cooper were severed, she wanted to be away from this region where he lived. The longer she remained stranded here, the more she feared that Cooper would come and seek to regain her. It would hurt terribly to have to part from him a second time—in fact, she wasn't sure that she would be able to do it. If Cooper came, she might abandon her family instead, and that would be wrong. It was her duty to remain.

"Hello, Hannah!" Solomon said cheerfully. "What do you think of our roof?"

"It looks very fine, Father," Hannah said, eyeing the new hand-riven white oak boards atop the shelter.

"Well, she's not as fine or big as Donelson's *Adventure*," Solomon said, referring to the sail-bearing, swivel-gun-mounted flagship flatboat upon which Colonel Donelson would head the expedition, "but I do believe she'll carry us as far as we need her to—and not even leak! Perrin is quite the man with a roof board!" He reached out and playfully poked a fist toward his son.

"I'm hungry," Perrin said grumpily.

"Mother was starting to make corn cakes a minute ago," Hannah said.

"Ah, excellent! I can eat my weight in good corn cakes," Solomon said brightly. "Come, Perrin, let's go up and see how they're coming."

The interior of the riverbank hut was filled with the scent of the cooking cakes when they entered, bringing the cold in with them. Repentance had made the cakes with cornmeal, salt, water, with pumpkin added for flavoring and extension. The cakes cooked on a griddle placed over the coals. A small bit of salt pork sizzled beside the cakes. If it all made for a simple meal, the family was content with it. Already Solomon had predicted that even such basic fare might be harder to come by once they reached the Cumberland country. The cold winter would make springtime game scarce and freeze the ground so hard they might be delayed in planting the precious gourdfuls of seeds they would carry to their destination.

Hannah ate only a little, leaving more for Solomon and Perrin, whose labors, in her estimation, had earned them the right to extra food. She nibbled her own meal slowly and enjoyed watching her father happily talking of the day's work and of several conversations held today with other men of the party. Real conversations—no snapping exchanges of political accusations and defense. For the first time since the family's arrival on this frontier country, Solomon seemed to be developing an embryonic sense of comradery with his peers. Hannah went so far as to wonder if his political attitudes might be softening in the process . . . or was that too much to hope for?

The day waned and Hannah became restless in the little hut. Solomon and Perrin had run through their stock of roofboards and had not returned to their labors, for too little of the day remained for them to achieve anything significant.

Repentance moved around listlessly, saying little. Toward evening Hannah wrapped her cloak around her, set her teeth against the cold, and left the hut for a walk. She hoped that dark-eyed Rachel Donelson, daughter of John Donelson, was nearby. Though Rachel was younger than Hannah and they had talked only a little, Hannah liked Rachel and hoped to develop a friendship with her. The estrangement Solomon Brecht had brought to his family through his standoffish personality and perceived Toryism had left Hannah cut off from much fellowship with other girls, and she hungered for it.

The sun was riding the western horizon, obscured and nearly invisible behind a mantle of gray clouds. As the light fell, a soft snow set in, its white flecks clinging to Hannah's cloak. It was too cold and late for a walk after all, she quickly decided. Turning, she prepared to return to the hut.

Something in the forest attracted her eye. There was motion and the barking of a hound. Peering through the trees into the darkening woods, she saw a lone rider, seemingly a hunter, for he was followed by a hide-laden packhorse and surrounded by hounds. Though she couldn't clearly see his face, she knew at once that it was Cooper Haverly. He had come, just as she secretly feared—perhaps secretly hoped—he would.

Now that it had happened, the sight of him froze her in place. A wild burst of feelings rose: surprise, happiness, excitement, and a great sense of disturbance. The latter sensation was strongest of all. Cooper was not supposed to be here, in the same way a person dead and gone is not supposed to appear and walk again about among the living. He belonged to her past, to her old life.

A fear arose. What if her father emerged from the shelter and saw Cooper? She dreaded to think what would result from that. Hannah felt impelled to bolt back toward her family's shelter—but what if Cooper followed?

So she did not move. Cooper remained astride his horse, looking at her without gesture. Then he slowly began to ride toward her. She could see his face now, dirty and bearded, as if he had been in the forest for many days.

Cooper reached the edge of the clearing where the huts and shelters stood before Hannah turned and ran as hard as she could for the shelter, her breath steaming in the ear-reddening cold. Opening the rough door, she disappeared inside and closed out the outside world and Cooper Haverly.

For a full minute Cooper stayed where he was, poised between the forest in which he had hidden away most of the time since Hannah's rejection, and the hut-filled riverside clearing. He was stunned that Hannah had run from him, run like he was something repellent. The wound of his earlier rejection had healed substantially in the solitude of long, lonely winter hunting—healed so much that he had dared hope that he might find Hannah receptive to him again. Now that deception was swept away and his wound reopened. Blinking back tears that threatened to freeze in his eyes and lashes, he turned his horse and rode back into the forest, the packhorse following and the dogs trotting alongside.

The last mile to John Sevier's home was the hardest. Israel Coffman dreaded the task that awaited him: comforting a bereaved man. Since the premature birth and death of his own child, Coffman was an ironic specimen— a preacher who desired to give comfort and hope to others, but who had substantially lost comfort and hope himself.

The atmosphere in the Coffman household now was as overcast and gray as today's snow-spitting sky. Virginia Coffman grieved deeply for her lost child. Coffman himself grieved doubly, first for the child, second for his wife. Since the miscarriage Virginia had withdrawn from her husband, her friends, and even, Coffman feared, her faith. She no longer wanted to hear her husband's sermons come Sunday, and seldom read from the big leatherbound bible that stayed open perpetually on their wide hickory mantelpiece. And several times she had bitterly asked her husband why the God she had tried to serve would smite her with such a loss.

Coffman himself did not ask that question. Long ago he had struggled as best he could through the eternal problem of reconciling his belief in God's goodness with the undeniable reality of suffering. He had never fully settled the question, but at least took some satisfaction in knowing that no honest thinkers of any merit purported to have fully settled it either.

Life on the frontier had taught Israel Coffman how terrible and unrelenting human pain could be. He had

watched many frontier families suffer through the deaths
of innocent children by illness, accident, and, by far the
worst of all, Indian massacre. He had observed and tried
to share the grief of such as Alphus Colter, who had to
struggle with knowing a loved one had died in deliberately inflicted pain. He had seen uncounted people, white
and Indian, die in ways that seemed to mock the very
concepts of divine justice, goodness, and love, the very
precepts he believed and taught.

It seemed a rule of life that every person had a share of
suffering reserved for him. If so, Coffman thought, it
seemed his time had come, in the sad form of a stillborn
baby.

Coffman shook his head broodingly, remembering how
happy he had felt during that jaunt back in the autumn,
while unknown to him, Virginia was losing their child.
Life could turn grim on a man without warning. The drop
from the top of the world to the pit of hell was a far
shorter one than Israel Coffman had ever imagined.

He spoke aloud to his horse, like Balaam talking to the
ass in that curious biblical story that had roused Coffman's
laughter as a child. "What is your answer to this puzzle of
a world, Brother Horse? What am I to tell my friend
Sevier to comfort him in the death of his wife? How am I
expected to explain mysteries I can't hope to fathom?
Answer me, my four-legged friend!"

Unlike Balaam's donkey, Coffman's horse had nothing
to say. The preacher rode on a bit farther, listening to a
jay scold hungry sparrows away from some rare and choice
morsel in the woods. This harsh winter it seemed even
God's animal creation was receiving a special lesson in
suffering and deprivation.

A little frightened by his own mounting sense of doubt
and cynicism, and uncomfortable with the resurfacing of
questions he had wrestled into neatly labeled mental
boxes back in his days of theological schooling, Coffman
wrenchingly refocused his mind on the ministerial task
immediately ahead. What comfort indeed could he bring
John Sevier? What could he say?

After several minutes of thought, he nodded. "Brother

Horse, I may know few answers, but at least I do know one bit of comfort to give my friend Sevier. I will say, 'John, cry in grief for your Sarah if you must. But look around you when your crying is done and know that your dear wife has left you the treasure of ten living children to give you company and comfort. There are many men who would rejoice to have even one-tenth the treasure of offspring you possess . . . but who are denied it.' " He stopped the horse abruptly, swallowing with a tightening throat before continuing his make-believe counsel—but now the counsel was directed not to Sevier's situation, but to his own. "One such treasureless man stands before you, Mr. Sevier. In the losing of my child I have also lost my joy." Tears began streaming down the preacher's face. "Mr. Sevier, perhaps it isn't this smitten preacher who needs to give you comfort after all. Perhaps it's you who can give comfort to me."

Emotionally broken, Coffman guided his horse off the trail and into the forest, where he wept alone for a long time. Since his tragedy, he had tried not to cry very much, believing it unmanly and perhaps a little faithless.

When finally he stopped weeping he began a prayer both loving and bitter, reaching up to the God who had scourged him, like a child reaching out to seek comfort from the same parent whose hand is still white from gripping the whipping rod.

"God," he prayed, "God of heaven, have mercy on me, and mercy on all who suffer. We have the forms of men and women, mighty God, but we are yet children, all of us children who cry alone in the dark."

When he reached John Sevier's home an hour later, Israel Coffman attributed the redness of his eyes to the bitter cold.

Had Israel Coffman been able to see Elisha Brecht in the midst of his heart-ringing forest prayer, he might have revised his view somewhat: There were at least a few of the world's children who did not cry alone in the dark. Some rather enjoyed darkness, and Brecht was among them.

The Tory turned up the jug of rum and savored the taste and sensation of it on his broad tongue. Rarely anymore did he have the privilege of enjoying this, his favorite beverage, for the war had made it hard to come by. He took several swallows, sighed with contentment, and leaned back against the tree. A roaring fire blazed before him, casting off the cold. Brecht smiled, a man content.

"Ned, Ned, I'm deeply ashamed of you, holding out such fine rum from me, your good friend. I wish you could tell me where you came by it."

Elisha Brecht's companion, a scrawny wisp of a fellow who lay on the ground well away from the blaze, could say nothing, for he was dead.

Brecht filled and lit his pipe, savoring the rich smoke of the sot weed. The wind shifted slightly, blowing the heat of the fire away from him, so he rose, went to Ned's horse, and removed the blanket from behind the saddle.

"Ned, I'm half afraid to use your blanket, as lousy with nits as you are," Brecht said to his silent companion. "But I've got plenty of my own, so what does it matter, eh?" He took the blanket back to his resting spot and resettled himself beneath it. Glancing skyward, he estimated the time from the location of the sun behind the wintry clouds. Another hour, he guessed, and Ulagu would be here. Good. By then he would have finished most of the rum and wouldn't have to share much of it. Elisha Brecht was selfish when it came to liquor.

"I'm truly sorry you're dead, Ned," he said after taking another pull on the little jug. "You've been a fine friend and help to me for these two years. But the time comes when every man has to go."

Brecht pulled the dirty blanket up around his neck, kicked another piece of wood onto the fire, and soon was as warm and comfortable as if he were in a feather bed.

Brecht wondered exactly what had happened to Ned, who hadn't lived long enough after reaching this meeting point to explain just who had put the lethal rifle ball into him. Brecht had surmised it was some farmer who had caught Ned scrounging corn from his barn. Brecht doubted that was the whole story, for frontier folk were usually generous, even with strangers. Ned probably had tried to take more than just a handful of corn. Knowing Ned, Brecht figured he had made a play for the farmer's wife or daughter. He grinned at the thought.

"Well, you were a fiery man with the maids, I'll say that for you, Ned," Brecht said. "And I rightly admire how long you lingered before that bullet done you in. Here's to you, my friend, and here's hoping a better fate than yours awaits your old partner Elisha." He took another swallow of rum.

Brecht's thoughts drifted to a fragment of information Ned had managed to share before expiring. The implication of it was fascinating to Brecht, and would be even more so to Ulagu. Brecht closed his eyes and huddled lower. He was eager for Ulagu to get here—though not until he had finished a little more of the rum.

The effects of the rum and fire eventually put Brecht to sleep. He snored lightly, holding the rum jug against his broad belly beneath the blanket. Sometime later he stirred, sensing something had changed. When he opened his eyes, Ulagu was there, crouching beside the fire. Brecht sat up straighter, pulled out the jug, took a swallow, then without a word handed it to the Chickamauga warrior.

Ulagu took the jug and lifted it to his lips. Brecht studied him as he drank. A savagely handsome devil this Indian was, lean and dark. His arms were muscled, not with knotty muscles like Brecht's, but with graceful, curving muscles that rippled as he lifted the jug up and down.

Because of the cold, Ulagu wore a long sleeveless deerskin shirt that covered his chest and hid his intricate gunpowder tattoos and decorative scars. He also wore a breechcloth and deerskin leggins. Around his head and covering his oiled scalp lock was a colorful scarf that Ulagu had taken from a Whig's cabin during a raid the year before. Brecht had been with him at the time; it was his own hand that had killed the woman who had once owned and prized the beautiful English-made article.

The fire had died some and Brecht was cold again even under the blanket. Ulagu, though dressed more lightly, didn't seem to notice the cold at all. It had always secretly aggravated Brecht that Indians seemed so immune to cold while he himself found it tormenting. He had seen warriors stride heedlessly through snowstorms with hardly any clothing at all.

Ulagu waved the jug toward Ned's corpse. "What happened to him?" he asked in the dialect of the Overhill Cherokees.

"Some farmer put a ball into him," Brecht replied easily, having mastered the Cherokee tongue through long association with the Chickamaugas. "The rum was Ned's."

"He won't need it now," Ulagu commented, taking another swallow.

"Ned had some things to tell me before he died," Brecht said. "Things he found out while he was on the Watauga."

"What?"

"For one thing, my brother's cabin is burned and he is gone. Ned doesn't know where. He may even be dead."

"I hope he is alive," Ulagu said, though in fact it didn't matter to him.

"There's more, Ulagu. I think Ned may have found your sister and her boy. Old Ned gritted his teeth and kept himself alive long enough to get back and make sure you heard about it. A damned fine old bugger, Ned was."

Ulagu, like Ayasta, seldom showed visible reaction to much anything, but this news made him turn and look fiercely at Brecht. "Tell me!"

"Ned said that Joshua Colter has got him a couple of guests living in a cabin on his land. An Indian woman and a boy."

"Colter!" Ulagu tossed away the rum. Brecht watched in unspoken sadness as the jug broke open and the last couple of swallows drained out.

Ulagu knew well the name of Joshua Colter, the coin-wearer whom John Hawk had held in such esteem.

"Yes. It seems there is much talk about this woman

among the unakas. Ned said she came back with Colter
from the burning of Chickamauga, and the story told him
was that the woman asked Colter to take her in so her son
could be raised as white."

Ulagu's expression was almost frightening even to
Brecht. He kept his own expression somber, though secretly he was enjoying watching Ulagu's reaction.

"I don't believe it," Ulagu said after a few moments.
"Ayasta would not do such a thing."

Brecht shrugged. "Maybe it isn't her. Though it does
make sense that it would be. If Ayasta took a notion to do
such a thing, who among the unakas would she go to
except the man her husband talked so highly of?"

Ulagu did not answer, but Brecht could detect the
impact of his words. And his experience with Ulagu told
him that he had said enough for now.

The Chickamauga walked about restlessly for a few
minutes, going to his horse and taking from it a fresh
tenderloin he had brought. He spitted the meat on a stick
and began to roast it. Hardly a word passed between the
men until the meat was done. Ulagu knifed off a sizable
portion and passed it to Brecht, and they ate silently.

When he was finished with his meal, Ulagu wiped his
fingers on his breechcloth and sat on his haunches, staring
at Ned's body. Finally he spoke.

"I must find out if what Ned said is true," he said. "If it
is, then I will take Ayasta and Wasi back. I cannot allow
her to do this."

"I'll help you, then. You know I've been wanting to go
back to the Watauga and 'Chucky in any case. I've wasted
my time southward long enough. I've got matters of my
own to settle with the Colters, and it's due time I did it.
Hell, I would have had Joshua Colter's scalp in the fall of
'seventy-eight if not for that rutting whelp who shot me!
You know who he was, Ulagu?"

Ulagu did know; Brecht had harped on the matter until
Ulagu was ill of hearing about it.

Without a pause Brecht continued. "He was Joshua
Colter's own brother. It's a pox on my soul to have taken

a Colter rifle ball. But I'll have my satisfaction or be damned."

Ulagu was hardly listening. He cared nothing about Brecht's personal squabbles, and the subject of Solomon Brecht was particularly uninteresting since that last forest meeting in which Solomon had declared he could be a spy for his brother no longer.

Brecht had talked so long and wearyingly about the familial hatred between the Brechts and Colters, and his desire to begin raiding again about Colter's Station, that Ulagu no longer listened to him. He was uninterested in such unaka concerns, alien to him. As far as Ulagu was concerned, raiding farmsteads in South Carolina was just as satisfying as raiding in Brecht's favored regions along the Watauga and Nolichucky. Ulagu had as well been thoroughly uninterested when the Tory sent the dull-witted Ned Spratt up to the Watauga country to look over the situation there in anticipation of a new round of raids. Ulagu had certainly not expected Ned to bring back any news of interest. For once the warrior had been surprised—and now he was even more eager than Brecht to return to that region.

"Come, Elisha. We must gather the others," Ulagu said.

Elisha Brecht smiled, nodded, and rose, keeping the blanket around him. Snow began to fall, melting on the still-warm body of Ned Spratt. Before nightfall the corpse would be cold and the snow would cling to it. If enough of it fell, the body would be hidden.

As far as Elisha Brecht was concerned, that was burial enough for Ned Spratt. He had never liked him much anyway.

Callum McSwain was a strong man, his muscles made tough and sinewy by years of pounding hammer against anvil. Today they strained at a different task, that of cabin building. McSwain took pride in his relatively good skills at cabin-making; after all, a Scotsman such as himself, springing from a people who built mostly with stone, was somewhat out of his element working with wood.

McSwain stood straight and arched his back to alleviate the strain of having stood humped over too long. His back hadn't ached so in a long time, but given his labor, the pain was easily accounted for. Not so apparent was the reason for the ache in his elbows and knees. He wondered if he was on the brink of some infirmity. No, that couldn't happen. There just wasn't time enough for illness, with all the work that needed to be done.

He looked around him. Already several new cabins, crude but strong, stood along a cedar-covered hillside above the French Lick. McSwain didn't much enjoy the labor of construction for its own sake, but at least the exercise warmed a man in this biting cold, and filled

149

the gray winter days while the advance settlement party awaited the arrival of Donelson's river settlers.

Not that they were expected anytime soon. The cold winter had frozen rivers that had never been known to freeze before. The prospect of any river travelers reaching the French Lick before spring seemed highly unlikely. So sure was James Robertson that the flotilla had been delayed that he had already given up plans to journey overland to the Muscle Shoals. If that route had proved navigable by land, Robertson was to leave certain physical signs on the northern shore at the upper end of the shoals, and at that point the flatboats would be abandoned and the travelers would advance the balance of the distance to French Lick by land. All this was moot now, however. Obviously the flotilla could never set out in such cold weather.

In a way McSwain was glad. The coming of the river party would mean the arrival of the Brechts, and he was in no hurry for Repentance Brecht to be close at hand again—not until he got a better hold on the feelings that had overwhelmed him so unexpectedly the night he had come to their aid. What a fool he was, letting himself get snared like a fish on a hook by a woman already married and unobtainable, and who probably wouldn't have him even if she were free!

McSwain didn't know just what, other than her resemblance to his late wife, had so entranced him about Repentance Brecht, especially given the frequent whisperings that she was daft, bedeviled of mind. Any man with sense would be put off by such as that—but then, McSwain had to admit, he didn't seem to have much sense about anything lately.

His infatuation with Repentance had left McSwain feeling silly, foolish, and, most of all, guilty. He had always been a man who believed in leaving be the spouses of others. There were practical as well as moral reasons for his attitude. McSwain had observed Joshua Colter back in the days that Gabriel Colter was married to Darcy, and had seen how badly being in love with a claimed woman could tear up a man. He wanted no such torment for himself.

McSwain had hoped that by leaving the Brechts back with Donelson's flotilla on the Holston, he could escape Repentance's presence long enough for his unwanted infatuation to die. That had been in the fall of '79. Now it was January of '80 and Repentance Brecht was hundreds of miles away, and he still found himself thinking of her every other moment.

Having talked the Brechts into a place in the flotilla last fall, McSwain had taken to the frozen route already being traversed by Robertson and his overlanders. Their path to the Cumberland followed the familiar Kentucky route that led through Cumberland Gap. Traveling alone, McSwain had overtaken the advancing party quickly, coming first upon the sheep and goats that brought up the rear of the group. He had found one of Robertson's sons in charge of the flock, and having a difficult time of it because of a particularly hateful ram that kept butting him to the ground whenever his back was turned.

McSwain didn't remain in the rear with the sheep, but advanced up. He went past the squealing, grunting hogs, through the plodding cattle herd, and finally reached James Robertson and the some-thirty mares and additional packhorses that led up the processional. By that time he knew this journey would take its toll before it was finished, for already the animals were struggling to find sufficient forage in the frozen forest, and for the humans driving them there was little game to be shot at, much less devoured.

Nevertheless, the men went on with little complaint. They were woodsmen and used to deprivation. And along the way their numbers were bolstered when veteran long hunter John Rains, leading his own party of travelers to the Cumberland by prearrangement, joined that of Robertson. With difficulty, the hunters managed to bring in enough game to keep the combined groups fed.

Beyond Cumberland Gap they passed a variety of stations that had arisen along this pioneer highway, and kept up with their progress by counting the passing days and noting the waterway landmarks: Dick's River, Green River, the Little Barren and Big Barren rivers, Drake's Creek, the Red River. Last of all, after passing the station of Cumberland frontiersman Caspar Mansker, they finally arrived at the Cumberland River at the French Lick, or Big Salt Lick, as some called it, and saw their journey's end lying ahead across an expanse of frozen river.

By then 1779 was drawing to a close. The broad Cumberland was frozen so thoroughly that the drovers were able to drive the livestock across the ice with no difficulty. When at last his chilled feet stood on the soil of their destination, Callum McSwain had never felt so glad to be through with a journey. Nor had he ever felt so cold. By heaven, what a bitter winter this was! On the way here, McSwain had seen wild turkeys fall frozen to death from the treetops.

Arrival at French Lick brought no respite from either cold or labor to the advance men. There were cabins, stockades, corncribs and such to be built in anticipation of the arrival of Donelson's group, whenever that would be. McSwain was one of the few men at the French Lick who did not have relatives in Donelson's party, and he saw as he looked at the faces around him evidences of worry, each man wondering if his kin would be among those to make it all the way through whenever the water voyage got under way.

There were a thousand potential hazards along the way that could bring disaster to the river travelers, including the threat of the Chickamaugas. The human price for this settlement effort could easily be high. James Robertson knew that as well as any. His own wife, Charlotte, and their five chidren, were to travel on the *Adventure* at the head of the flotilla, accompanying Donelson and his own family.

Settling in for a long and uncertain wait, the French Lick advance men had thrown themselves into their labors, hampered though they were by the cold. McSwain had made himself a makeshift builders' level by filling a green glass bottle with water, leaving only one pocket of air for the leveling bubble, only to have the bottle crack when the water in it froze. McSwain simply laughed and tossed it aside; such problems were part and parcel with station-founding.

Fortunately for the builders, some preparatory improvements had been made during the summer and fall by members of the previous year's exploratory expedition, in which McSwain had taken part. A few of the men had remained on the Cumberland to begin clearing and cropping while Robertson, McSwain, and others proceeded into the Illinois region before returning home.

McSwain recalled that earlier eight-month exploration with pleasure. It had been a fascinating and exciting trip. In all there had been ten in the exploratory party: Robertson himself, McSwain, Robertson's son Mark, Zachariah Wells, Edward Swanson, George Freeland, William Neely, William Overall, James Hanley, and one of Robertson's slaves. Callum had stayed in the company of James Robertson throughout the excursion, riding at his side through Cumberland Gap, from where they had proceeded deep into the lower Cumberland country of Kentucky. On the Cumberland banks they used hatchets, axes, and fire to create dugout canoes, and descended by water all the way to the French Lick. There, after finding a well-stocked log warehouse, they located and met the explorer and trader Timothe Demunbreun, from the Illinois country, and a band of his French associates. The warehouse belonged to them.

From the Frenchmen, Robertson purchased fine skiffs for a guinea apiece, having it in mind to venture on to the Illinois region while he had so fine a chance. McSwain didn't fully understand Robertson's motivation, but was interested in seeing the Illinois country for himself and so accepted Robertson's invitation to come along.

Leaving behind some of the men at the lick to clear land and plant corn, Robertson, McSwain, and a few others had traveled on the skiffs to the mouth of the Illinois River and on to a well-known trading site called Oak Post. There they enjoyed interesting talks with one Jean du Charleville, who had traded with the Indians about French Lick as early as 1710. After one frightening but nonviolent round of trouble with some Indians about Oak Post who suspected Robertson of treacherous intent, the group had purchased fine Spanish horses, then went on to meet with George Rogers Clark, who was already a frontier military hero and western scourge of the British.

Clark himself had earlier obtained some rights through Virginia to French Lick lands, and he and Robertson worked out an agreement to avoid any potential later claims conflict. Now McSwain understood Robertson's motivation for venturing all the way to the Illinois country: He was seeking to ensure the legality of his holdings on the Cumberland, should Virginia rather than North Carolina finally be determined to control the Cumberland region.

After visiting Clark, the explorers had returned home, Robertson going to Big Creek on the Holston and McSwain back to his home and smithy north of Colter's Station—and straight into the troubles involving the Solomon Brecht family and his unwanted emotional entanglement with Repentance Brecht. Since then he had wished several times that he had remained at French Lick with the clearers and planters last year and not come back to Colter's Station at all.

He brought down the axe again; it bit off another slice of poplar, hewn right to the line. He stood back, examined the log, and decided it finished, even though it was hewn only on two sides so far. For a rough and ready cabin, two sides was sufficient. The other sides could be hewn off square after the cabin was built.

The wind wrapped around McSwain. Despite the cold, he had worked up a heavy sweat with his hewing. A chill that seemed to rise more from within than without sent him into a dreadful shiver. With his leaf-insulated, moccasined foot, he rolled aside the finished log, then dragged another into place, pinning it down with an iron "log dog" to keep it still as he hewed. He set to work again, going at it hard to work up some heat and knock off that inner cold. I'm wearying something fierce, he thought. I suppose I'm getting old.

By that night Callum McSwain knew it wasn't age that

was getting to him, but fever. He was deathly ill with an
aguelike affliction, shivering and moaning in his blankets
in a corner of one of the new cabins, drenched in a sweat
that only made him colder. Unable to sleep, he huddled
beneath his covers, feeling so bad that he actually began
wondering if the others would be able to gouge out a deep
enough grave in the frozen ground to bury him, or if his
interment would have to wait until the spring thaw. At
first his fevered mind fretted over the question, until at
last his illness was so distressing that he no longer cared
whether he lived or died, much less what they would do
with his corpse once he was gone.

Hannah Brecht felt the boat move beneath her and
could scarcely squelch the impulse to leap in joy. It was
the morning of February 28, 1780, a Monday, and at long
last the gaggle of flatboats and partially covered pirogues
that made up the Donelson flotilla were under way. The
river had become navigable at last. Zekle Holly, the young
but veteran boatman, set up a loud hoot of joy as he
manned the left broadhorn oar of the *Carolina*. Jesse
Clinton was at the opposite oar, and, atop the shelter,
Solomon Brecht stood at the rudder sweep, a broad grin
on his thin brown face.

An attempt had been made to begin the voyage the
previous day, and had brought frustratingly little success.
Upon reaching a place where the road into Poor Valley
reached the river, John Donelson's *Adventure* struck a
shoal. Two other flatboats hung up immediately thereafter
on the same shoal, and the day's voyage was at an abrupt
and disappointing end.

The men had labored throughout Sunday afternoon and
into the night to free the boats, and by this morning had
been ready to go on. Hannah exulted in the sight of the
riverbanks sliding past. She was leaving behind at last the
endless waiting in the cold, leaving behind the sense of
frustration and stalling, leaving behind the uncertainties
of being caught in a limbo between an old life and a new
one.

Only the thought of the increasing miles between herself and Cooper Haverly dampered her happiness. Even though she had avoided him the evening he came toward her from the forest, her feelings for him remained strong. She had not avoided him because she cared little for him, but because she cared much.

She put her arms around her middle, thrust out her chin, and as haughtily as she could, declared to herself that, whatever her feelings, she would look ever ahead, never behind. Hannah was an unconsciously fatalistic young woman, believing that what occured in life generally happened by design. If Cooper was snatched away from her, it was because such a thing had to be, in which case there was nothing gained by crying or dwelling on it. Maybe, if destiny was kind, whatever force that had taken Cooper from her would bring him back.

In the meantime there was a new life to be forged in the Cumberland country—if the flotilla made it that far.

Hannah had but little idea of what lay ahead. She knew the river would carry them near the towns of the Chickamaugas, the same towns that had been burned and emptied the previous year. The best reports were that the towns remained empty, but others declared at least some had been repopulated. If so, the danger could be significant.

The rivers themselves held many perils: ice, sawyers, shoals, rapids, rocks. But certainly the greatest natural hazard that would face this flotilla would be what was called the Whirl, or the Suck, of the Tennessee River. Hannah had heard it described as a place where rocky mountain walls pushed in on both sides of the river, compressing it and making it a whirling, rushing torrent that could pull a boat asunder or dash it against the rocks. To make it worse, the Whirl was in the Chickamauga country. To be stranded there on a ruined flatboat would be nightmarish beyond description.

Hannah tried not to dwell on such grim matters. The Whirl was far ahead, and "sufficient unto the day is the evil thereof." Her father quoted that verse a lot, usually rendering it in his own terse paraphrase: Worry about one deuced thing at a time.

At the front of the floating processional was the broadhorn *Adventure*, appropriately the largest of the flatboats. The Brechts' own *Carolina* rode only a short way back in the flotilla, close enough to the *Adventure* to allow the Brechts a view of the open, empty river ahead of it. Hannah found the scene exciting; truly Colonel Donelson had aptly named his flatboat, for this was, indeed, an adventure.

Among the thirty people aboard the *Adventure*, Hannah could see both the Robertsons and Donelsons, including the attractive young Rachel Donelson, named for her mother, Rachel Stokely Donelson, who sat nearby her daughter at the moment, the pair of them huddling for warmth. In addition to human passengers, the *Adventure* and all the other flatboats and pirogues carried virtually everything that would be needed to set up a working homestead. Most of the goods were carefully stowed and lashed; items that would be used frequently along the way were kept more readily available, but even they had to be carefully stored and handled to avoid loss due to overwashing river waters, sudden tilts of the boats, or other such potentialities.

Stored on the flatboats were harnesses, axes, bottles, bowls, trenchers, kegs, looms, shafts of blacksmithing iron, steel rods for rifle-making, tree-crotch pack saddles, lead, bullet molds, gluts, wedges, gimlets, augers, hammers, shovels, draw knives, plows, traces, keelers, bread trays, froes, washtubs, and gums. There were skillets and griddles, foot adzes and knives, piggens and churns, pails and grubbing hoes, rifle flints and Deckard locks, flax hackles and seed-filled gourds, chests of clothing and family Bibles . . . all the countless items of frontier farming and domestic life, the latter including individual family heirlooms and town-bought items from the East, these being among the few tangible links with seaboard civilization that frontier families possessed.

And there were rifles, lots of rifles, always loaded, for no one knew when they might be needed. And of all the materials stored on the boats, the most closely guarded from snow, rain, and river were the stores of precious gunpowder.

Hannah's father looked strong and tall at the steering sweep. The boys were right beside him. The wind lashed at Solomon Brecht's face and he shivered in the cold, but his smile was warm when he glanced at his daughter. He gave her a fatherly wink and she grinned back at him. Hannah knew her father was as glad as she to be on the move at last. She hoped their new home to the west would provide him happier circumstances than what he had known here.

From the shelter of the flatboat emerged Repentance Brecht. Hannah caught her mother's eye for a moment and smiled. Repentance did not smile back. She seemed particularly harsh and distant today, as cold as the wind. Hannah turned away from her, not wanting her own spirit to decline through her mother's influence.

Later in the day the flotilla encountered difficulty. Attempting to land on a river island, some of the flatboats struck hard and were damaged, and some goods were lost. At length the flotilla stopped on the south shore for the night's camp, and in the meantime a few new vessels joined them, for interest in Cumberland settlement was widespread throughout the frontier.

The next day was a noteworthy one, for this year February had twenty-nine days. For Hannah in particular it was a special day, for it was her birthday. Her brothers teased her, her parents congratulated her, and Solomon presented her a gift: a little toy raccoon he had whittled out of cedar. Beyond that there was no time or means to further mark the day, but Hannah was satisfied.

The afternoon brought rain but no calamities, and in the evening the flatboats steered to the north shore and there the travelers encamped for the night. The following day proved rainy as well, and also uneventful. For the first time since the flotilla embarked, Hannah experienced some boredom. As the afternoon waned she watched Andrew shooting make-believe Indians from the riverbank with a make-believe rifle made from a stalk of cane, until Repentance made him stop, telling him that

what he was now treating as a game might prove far more
than that before this venture was done.

On the following day, rainy throughout the morning,
Hannah began keeping a journal, writing on a smoothed,
wide white oak plank with a quill whittled from cane and
ink made from water and a handful of gunpowder reluctantly conceded to her by her father. The journal-keeping
idea was not original to Hannah; she had observed Colonel
Donelson writing brief journal entries each evening and
had become intrigued by the idea.

> March 2, 1780. Today is Tuesday. Many difficulties.
> One boat sunk after striking an island in the current.
> The fleet put ashore to help raise and bail the unfor-
> tunates, requiring the balance of the day. Meanwhile
> one Reuben Harrison has vanished in the forest, gone
> to hunt, and not returned. Much worry among us all.
> Passed the mouth of the French Broad River today
> before our travails began."

The next day was occupied not with travel, but
with searching for Harrison. On Donelson's *Adventure* the small swivel-mounted cannon was loaded
with powder and fired several times throughout the
day, both in hopes of guiding back Harrison by its
sound and to keep the various search parties scouring
the woods for him from getting lost themselves.

On Saturday, March 4, Hannah had the joy of
making a happy entry: "Reuben Harrison was found
safely upon the bank today, having been gone for two
nights. He had traveled far down the river in the fear
of having been left behind by us. Indeed we had
gone on, though some boats had been left behind us
to continue the search, which in the provision of God
is no more required. Have this day reached the
mouth of the Tennessee River.

The river they had reached was in fact the tributary
that in later years would be called the Little Tennessee
River. At present it was considered part of the main river.
Hannah's father pointed to it as they passed and told her

that along that stream were the Overhill towns of the Cherokees, towns with musical and eerie names such as Chota, Tallassee, Toqua, Settico, and Tuskegee. From those Overhill towns most of the Chickamaugas had seceded, including Dragging Canoe himself.

Hannah was disturbed by her father's talk, for it brought to her mind that the dreaded and brutal Chickamaugas were the very ones her uncle Elisha aided . . . and not only him, but Solomon as well, the times he had passed intelligence to his brother. She wondered if her father ever lay awake at night, wondering if his aid to his bloodthirsty brother had contributed to the death of some innocent frontier woman or child.

On the fifth the flotilla reached the mouth of the Clinch River and there joined with another flotilla in mid-afternoon. This was Captain John Blackmore's party, from Fort Blackmore to the northeast. With Blackmore's addition, the entire flotilla consisted of upward of thirty flatboats and pirogues carrying some fifty families, along with guards and slaves.

Spread across the water, the boats made for an impressive sight. Hannah felt a renewed thrill of excitement as she took in the scene. "Mother, it's beautiful, it's beautiful," she said when Repentance came to her side. Repentance said nothing, but slipped her arm around her daughter and drew her close. Hannah felt a great burst of happiness; for a moment all was as it should be.

It was to be the last real happiness she would know in a long time.

Solomon Brecht knelt beside Thomas Hutchings, son-in-law of Colonel Donelson. Before them was stretched the pitiful and unmoving form of a black man, eyes half open and fixed, hands going gray at the fingertips, and feet and lower legs horribly miscolored.

"Dead?" Brecht asked quietly.

Hutchings nodded. "Indeed. What a sad thing."

"Aye." Solomon Brecht rose, pulling his coat around him in the gathering dark. He walked down to the *Carolina*, which was tied up with the other boats in a long line along the north shore. Smoke rose all around from dozens of fires. The smell of cooking meat and corn cakes was delicious, but at the moment Solomon had no real stomach for food.

Repentance was kneeling beside the fire, adding new wood beneath a kettle of steaming mush. The children were huddled on the other side of the fire, hands extended to its welcome warmth. Perrin noted his father's grim expression. "What's happened, Father?"

Solomon kicked a piece of dead log over near the fire and sat down on it before answering. "We've had our first death of the voyage," he said.

Repentance looked up sharply at her husband; the children went pale. "Indians?" little Andrew asked fearfully.

Solomon smiled and reached out to tousle the hair of his son. "No, Andy. We've seen none of those yet, and if God wills, we'll see none at all. This was a death from the cold. It was Captain Hutchings's slave man; you've seen him about."

"Yes." Andrew lowered his head. "I liked him. I wish he hadn't died."

Repentance began dishing mush into trenchers and handing them to the children along with wooden spoons. The children dug ash cakes from the borders of the fire, brushed off all the ash they could, and laid these on the edges of their trenchers to supplement the mush.

"It was the river that killed him, I wager," Repentance said. "God curse this river—it's a cold and deathly thing."

"It's naught but a waterway—nothing deathly about it," Solomon replied. "But it was the river that did it. The poor Negro chilled his feet in it helping free the bogged-up boats today. It's the first time ever I've seen a man die of cold."

"Well, he won't be the last we lose," Repentance said. "Before this voyage is done there will be deaths aplenty. Fools we were to attempt this in such a winter! It's tempting God, that's what it is, and he'll smite us for it."

Andrew put down his trencher and looked glumly at his uneaten food. Hannah took a tasteless bit of ash cake and glanced at her father. From his expression she could tell he didn't like Repentance talking in such a way before the children.

"Repentance, would you rather have stayed at a place where masked men burn your home and threaten your life?"

"Aye, and have you not considered that some of the very ones who are with us now might have been among them?" she said. "Do you think there will be an end to our troubles at the French Lick?"

"I see changes already. The men here, they treat me as a friend now. This voyage will bring us good things, Repentance. I'm certain of it. I feel it in my soul."

"Suffering and death, that's what will come of it," she said. "Mark my words, Solomon Brecht. Mark my words."

Solomon cast down his trencher, rose, and stomped down to the riverbank and onto the *Carolina*. The family could hear him moving about loudly and roughly on the flatboat, securing ropes that were already secured, relashing bundles already sufficiently tied down.

Repentance sniffed and shook her head. "Your father is a good man, but difficult," she said to the children. "Mind you that you don't lose your patience with him."

For the rest of the meal no one spoke at all.

11

J oshua stood to the side of
the cluster of men, smoking his pipe and eyeing his friend
John Sevier with some amusement. Sevier was inevitably
an amusing man to observe in a crowd, not because there
was any hint of buffoonery about him—far from it—but
because he was a man who so obviously enjoyed the
attention of others. It was as Alphus sometimes said: John
Sevier always looks to be alone, for once he appears,
everyone else seems to disappear.

Indeed, Sevier was an impressive man. Five years
Joshua's senior, he sprang from an originally French Hu-
guenot family that had borne the name Xavier. His father,
born in London, had emigrated to America, settling in
Virginia. John Sevier was a native of Virginia's Shenan-
doah Valley who had migrated first to the Holston country,
then to the Watauga settlement, where he had made a
name and place for himself with due speed.

Like Joshua, he was lean, handsome, and brown-
haired, was a veteran of the Battle of Point Pleasant and
the Cherokee attacks of 1776, and possessed the fully
deserved reputation of being a capable Indian fighter and
leader of men.

Beyond that, similarities between the two were few. Joshua didn't much enjoy leadership, and preferred solitude to company as often as not. At cabin raisings and wedding feasts he stayed off to the side, taciturn and out-of-place. Sevier, on the other hand, loved to lead, craved the company and admiration of his fellow man, and enjoyed a party like no one else Joshua had ever known. Even now, as Washington County's militia officers crowded around Sevier in the Jonesborough street, extending their condolences in the recent death of his wife, Sevier seemed to relish being at the center of things. He adored a crowd. Joshua wondered wryly if Sevier had sired so many children just to make sure he was never alone.

Sevier, Joshua, and the other militia leaders had just emerged from a meeting of import, and thoughts of what had transpired weighed heavily on Joshua's mind. Once again it was going to be necessary to send men from the Overmountain country to fight in the east. The British were pressing the southern states, by land out of New York, and from the sea off the Atlantic coast, and help in the resistance was needed.

The previous month a call had come over the mountains for a full two thousand militiamen to be raised to defend North Carolina, and possibly South Carolina as well. Today the Washington County militia leaders had done their part in answering, agreeing to raise a hundred troops to be sent east for the aid of Brigadier General Griffith Rutherford of the Salisbury District, who had ordered the call-up from both Washington County and her new sister county of Sullivan, which had been formed the prior year.

Joshua felt vaguely depressed. He had awakened in dark spirits and had found nothing yet to lighten them. Certainly the prospect of seeing five-score frontiersmen march away from their homes for war was nothing to be happy about. Joshua had known war all his life and did not flinch from it, but as years passed he found it increasingly distasteful and tiring. Sometimes he wondered if the conflict with Britain would ever end.

Sevier at last broke away from the cluster of talking

men and strode broadly across the dirt street. Joshua fell
in behind and called him down.

"John, I've yet to express my sorrow to you about
Sarah's passing," Joshua said. "How are you faring?"

"Well enough for a widower," Sevier replied. "I've got
plenty of young ones to brighten my days and keep the
homeplace spirited. Your friend the Reverend Coffman
reminded me strongly of that when he came calling."

"Good, good. Well, good day to you, John."

"Good day, Joshua . . . say, isn't that young Cooper
yonder?"

Joshua spun to look. Cooper? He hadn't seen him for a
full three months, and had been unable to find anyone
else who had, either. He had been quite concerned about
Cooper's welfare, fearing that he had left the region in
despair over Hannah Brecht. "Where?"

"Yonder, at the tavern door."

"By heaven, John, it is Cooper!" Joshua reached out and
pumped Sevier's hand, grinning broadly. "Good day—
and again, my sympathies to you." His wide smile made
the final comment sound rather comical to Sevier, but the
latter held back his own smile until Joshua's back was
turned.

Sevier watched Joshua lope down the street toward the
little log tavern. His eagerness to see his long-missing
brother was obvious. Sevier chuckled, turned away, and
headed toward the stable.

Joshua almost knocked down the tavern door as he
entered. Three patrons were inside the little log building,
including Cooper, who had just seated himself at a table
in the farthest corner. He immediately stood when he saw
his brother, and grinned. Joshua grinned back and strode
up to meet him, hand extended.

"Cooper! Lord, I'm happy to see you!"

"Hello, Joshua. I'm surprised to see you in town—I
thought you'd be home."

"It's too early yet for corn planting, and I had militia
business," Joshua couldn't restrain his smile; he looked
Cooper up and down as if his brother had been transformed into a new person. And in one way he had. Since

Joshua had seen him last, Cooper had grown thinner, more whiskered, and brown from the winter wind. He seemed to have aged three years in as many months, yet he did not look unhealthy for it. In fact his gaze was bright and his expression spirited.

"Sit down with me, Joshua, and let me buy you some cider."

"You've got money?"

"I fancy I can spare at least two shillings."

Joshua accepted his cup of cider with thanks. "So where have you been?"

"In the woods. Here and there and all about. Hunting some. Most of the time just walking and riding and enjoying seeing no one."

Joshua nodded. He understood Cooper fully. Using the forest as a place of escape from personal problems was an old habit of his own. As a child he had frequently delved into the forests around the Overhill towns to escape his gruff natural father, the Carolina trader Jack Byrum. Together with Alphus Colter and the since-deceased Carolina hunter Levi Hampton, Joshua had trapped and hunted the Tennessee country as far back as the 1760s. As a slightly older young man he had explored this wilderness alone after losing to suicide the first girl he had loved. And after he was mistakenly thought killed at the Point Pleasant battle, Joshua had again taken to the woods for a time, letting solitude shield him from the troubles he knew in that portion of his life. Joshua knew how fine a balm the empty forest could be to a hurting man.

"How was the hunting?" he asked.

Cooper shook his head as he swallowed another mouthful. "Fair at the outset, poor by the end. I brought in enough skins to put a jingle in my pocket, though hunting is hardly what it used to be for you and Alphus. This year it's the cold that's made things so bad. I've seen birds dead on their roosts and belled cattle dead in thickets and frozen solid. Me, I stayed warm enough."

"A log shelter?"

"No. A cave. With a fire and windbreak at the door and

hounds beside me at night I kept warm as a drunken deacon."

"So now you're home—or have I found you sooner than you wanted?"

"No. No more hiding, no more secrets. I'm home."

Joshua smiled and raised his cup. "Here's to your homecoming, then." They drank deeply. Joshua swiped the back of his hand across his mouth. "I had thought maybe you had headed overland for the Cumberland country. Going after Hannah Brecht, you know."

He had hesitated before mentioning Hannah's name, confident it was Cooper's heartbreak over her that had driven him into the forests to begin with. He watched Cooper's reaction closely.

"I'll chase Hannah no more, Joshua. I've had time to think about matters, and what it comes down to is this: She made her choice, and I was the loser. She picked her blood kin above me." He smiled wanly. "I seem to recall that you predicted long ago that just such a thing might happen, and I scorned the notion."

"There's too much bad blood between the Brechts and Colters for me to have thought otherwise. Of course, at that time you didn't want to hear that."

"Well, my head's not so cloudy anymore. I was a fool to let myself fall in love with a Brecht to begin with, and even more a fool for keeping my yap shut so long about Solomon meeting with Elisha Brecht." Cooper glanced around as if the very subject made him feel an object of anger. "Is there ill will toward me over that?"

"Not on my part, though at the beginning I was none too happy to hear you had kept such a thing to yourself." He paused. "I understand why you did it, though. A pretty young woman can turn a man's head until he forgets which direction he's supposed to go. And the fact is, Coop, only a few ever heard of your accusation against Solomon, and most who did suspect you made it up in anger, just trying to hurt Solomon because of Hannah. And the fact does remain that Elisha Brecht hasn't burned a single cabin or killed a single soul in these parts since we fought him back in 'seventy-eight."

Cooper narrowed his eyes. "I half believe you think I made it up too, Joshua."

"No. If you say you saw the Brecht brothers meeting, then I believe it happened. You may be a hothead from time to time, Coop, but you're no liar."

Cooper nodded thanks for his brother's confidence. "So tell me, Joshua—did Donelson's fleet get afloat?"

"So I hear, but I've heard no particular facts. How the voyage is going is something we may be a long time in learning. It's a hard winter for river travel."

"I hope it goes well. If anything happened to Hannah . . ." He paused a moment, then his eyes flickered up to meet Joshua's. "Don't look at me like that, Joshua. Just because I've put Hannah aside hardly means I want to see harm come to her."

"I know."

There was a brief pause. More cider was consumed. Cooper asked, "Well, how are they all?"

Joshua replied, "All healthy and strong, for the most part. Alphus has spent much of the cold weather bettering his mill, with Zachariah helping. They've missed your shoulders down there, I'll tell you, and worried much about you too. Sina is as always: somber as a magistrate. Darcy is fine—and wondering if she is with child."

"Well! Congratulations to you, Joshua!"

"We don't yet know it's true . . . though I hope it is."

"What about the Indian woman?"

"Ayasta? She's well, and quite fetching in the dresses Darcy has given her, though she looks as Cherokee as ever despite them. Judah is healthy and lively; he and Will take on well with each other." Joshua became serious. "Having Ayasta about the place has caused much trouble, though. Darcy has been unable to grow used to her, and it has been terrible hard for her. Frankly, I don't know what will come of it."

"I want to see them all."

"Then we'll go there straightaway. Where are your hounds?"

"Penned out back, behind the tavern stable."

Cooper paid two shillings for the cider, plus a shilling

and four pence for the stabling of his horses. Then he proceeded with Joshua down the Jonesborough street to a second stable, where Joshua had placed the black he had bought in auction after the raid on Chickamauga. It had become his favorite mount.

As they rode west over the rolling hills toward Joshua's home, pausing at one spot to rest the horses and enjoy a beautiful northward view of the mountain-backed winter landscape, their conversation turned to the war. Joshua told Cooper about the militia officers' meeting and the plan to send men toward the seaboard to help in defense of the Carolinas. Cooper listened solemnly.

"When they go, I'll be among them," he said.

Joshua wasn't surprised to hear it. "So your homecoming isn't for long, eh?"

"I reckon not. Not with a war on, and me free to serve."

Joshua understood his brother's feelings. In similar circumstances he would be just as ready to answer the call. What was there holding Cooper to this particular countryside anymore? He had no wife and no prospect of one . . . perhaps, now that Hannah was gone, even no wish for one. In August, Cooper would be a full score of years old, a man by any standard, especially by the standard of the wartime frontier, where even mere boys were sometimes called upon to be mature beyond their years.

Joshua had no question that Cooper would leave. He did question whether he would ever return if he did. Likely he would find himself a place of his own to make a new life. Or perhaps Hannah still held his heart more tightly than he pretended.

If so, eventually Cooper would be drawn to the Cumberland and the girl who had put him aside. By then, of course, she might be married to another. Joshua badly wanted to tell Cooper not to wait if in fact he still did care for Hannah. Joshua had moved too slowly in courting twice in his life; both times he had suffered loss because of it.

But he couldn't say anything like that to Cooper. It didn't feel right for the moment. So all he said was,

"Darcy will be mighty surprised to see you, Coop. Surprised and happy. Likely she'll feed you till you beg for mercy."

"Then I'll be a happy sufferer," Cooper replied.

They rode together to where Limestone Creek made a southwesterly course toward the Nolichucky River, and turned toward Joshua's home. They heard the snorting of hogs rooting in the forest and the dull jangle of belled, free-roaming cattle seeking forage beneath the cold thatch, and smelled chimney smoke and cooking supper long before the cabin and half-finished stockade on the creek came into view.

All in all, Hannah Brecht did not think she had ever been in so ominous a place. She felt eyes upon her when there were no watchers there, and imagined she heard strange and almost human noises in the wind that swept across this barren and lifeless place.

This was a large Indian town, or had been one. Colonel Donelson had said the Chickamaugas had lived here but now were gone. In the heightening gloom at the end of the cold day, Hannah's skin prickled as her eyes probed the shadows where a feared people once had resided.

From among the cluster of women gathered in and around a quickly erected tent shelter, a pitiful cry of feminine pain arose, keened on the wind, then died away. Hannah shuddered, and Andrew stepped a few inches closer to her side.

"I heard Mr. Hutchings say that the Indians believe there are bad spirits and such in this country," he said softly, his eyes darting all about. "Do you think that's why they left?"

Hannah was not a superstitious young woman, but talk of spirits was not what she wanted to hear right now. "Of course not, you silly thing," she said in an artificial tone of confidence. Another wail rose and died behind her. When would it be over? The woman had been in such pain for the longest time. "I'm sure they left because of the raid last year. Don't you see the burned buildings? They didn't feel it was safe to stay after that."

Andrew shivered. "I don't feel safe either."

"Hush, Andrew, hush. You'll just give yourself bad dreams thinking such things."

"I don't want to sleep here."

"Well, you hardly have a choice, do you?"

The river had been choppy and windblown throughout the day, driving the flatboats ever closer to the shores and greatly endangering several of the smaller craft. By afternoon Donelson had sent back the call for a halt, and the fleet had tied up at the edge of the abandoned Chickamauga town to wait out the afternoon and night.

There had been reason beyond weather for the halt. Mrs. Ephraim Peyton, wife of one of the men who had gone ahead to the Cumberland with Robertson's land party and daughter of Jonathan Jennings, whose flatboat was in the flotilla, had gone into a hard and painful labor, and it quickly had become evident she would give birth tonight.

Hannah pitied the travailing woman, having to suffer through childbirth in so cold and dismal a situation. Mrs. Peyton, like the poor slave who had died the prior day, was a victim of the hard winter, for had the voyage been able to proceed as had been originally planned last year, she would be giving birth in a new home along the Cumberland, rather than on a cold riverbank in an abandoned Indian town, far from her husband. Surely, if the Peytons last year could have foreseen the delays and difficulties coming to them, they would have never attempted this passage at all. It didn't matter now. The time for changing minds was long past.

The edge of the town was lighted by fires as darkness came. Far down the bank one little cluster of fires burned alone. Hannah watched it and felt sad and frightened because of what it meant. One of the families in the flotilla, named Stuart, had become stricken with smallpox; now they rode far back from the rest of the boats, and camped alone. It seemed a cruel thing, in a way, but Hannah knew there was no other choice possible without risking the lives of all the other voyagers.

At last Mrs. Peyton delivered her child and the sounds

of her distress ceased. Hannah initially felt relief, until she sat down beside her mother near her family's fire for the evening meal.

"That poor baby will never survive," Repentance said. "There are too many terrible things ahead for any to hope for that. God pity the Peytons."

Solomon Brecht eyed his children quickly, then said, "Repentance, must everything you say be designed to frighten the young ones?"

"I say nothing but the truth. We should never have started this journey, none of us. Colonel Donelson was a fool. The danger is too great."

"I would never bring our family into any hopeless peril, wife. Don't put such notions into their heads!"

"You feel for the children, do you? Well, it's a mite late for that, my husband. You yourself been bringing trouble to your children far earlier than this. Do you think your young ones haven't endured more than their share of suffering simply because their last name is Brecht?"

Solomon opened his mouth to rebuff her, then said nothing. Picking up his trencher, he began eating rapidly, in silence.

Hannah dreamed an unsettling dream that night, dark and violent and full of portent. When she awakened she remembered few of the details, only the image of a white and red man battling each other, and blood flowing. Rolling over in her blankets, she shivered and attributed the nightmare to her presence in this former Indian town, and to her mother's grim predictions.

Then, as she began to drift off to sleep once more, she remembered one other thing that didn't seem to fit. The white man in her dream had been Cooper Haverly. Slumber that had been descending on her pulled away like a jerked blanket. This was the first time she had dreamed of Cooper since their separation. Why was it a dream of violence? What if her mother was right in her belief that dreams of battle meant danger coming to the individual dreamed of?

So Hannah hardly slept any more that night, worrying about Cooper.

They cast off the next morning at ten o'clock and continued down the river. "The next Indian towns we see are not likely to be unoccupied," Solomon warned his children. "We'll have to keep our wits about us."

"Will they hurt us, Father?" Andrew asked.

Solomon Brecht smiled reassuringly. "I'm certain we'll come through safe, if we keep a sharp eye."

"So they won't hurt us?"

The man paused uncertainly. "No, Andy. They won't hurt us."

Dudley Grubbins's face was ashen. Darcy Colter involuntarily shrank back from him as he leaned forward and spat another gruesome dollop of mixed blood and spittle toward the gourd bowl at his feet. The mess struck the edge of the bowl and part of it ran down and, to Darcy's distress, stained the puncheon floor.

Joshua put his hand on the small-framed man's bony shoulder. "It was Elisha Brecht, you say? Are you sure?"

"Aye, Captain Colter," the man said, his voice garbled from the blood in his mouth, flowing from the place where a tooth had been. He had knocked it loose somehow in the desperate battle he had just escaped from, and lost it completely after falling from his horse upon reaching the Colter farmstead after a wild woodland ride. It was a sad loss for him, for like many frontiersmen, Grubbins had few teeth to spare. He spat at the bowl again. "I saw him with my own eyes, and I've seen him before. It was Brecht, alive as you or me."

Cooper, still visiting with Joshua's family, stepped forward. "Did I hear you say Jim Birdwell was killed?"

"Yes, yes . . . poor dear Jim. I saw them hatchet him and take his scalp. Redskins they were, most of them, with Brecht and a few more white men amongst them."

"What would bring Brecht back to these parts after so long?" Cooper asked Joshua.

"God only knows," Joshua replied. "Only thing I know is we've got to go after him. Dudley, which way did they head?"

"I couldn't tell you, Joshua, sorry to say. I crawled off

and went dark for nigh an hour, and it's only by the grace of heaven they didn't find me."

"Or that you didn't freeze to death," Cooper added.

Ayasta had left her own cabin and come to the Colter house upon noticing the stir about the place after Grubbins's arrival. Grubbins had come in draped over the bare back of a wounded horse that had died right in Joshua's bare dirt front yard and still lay outside, its body steaming away its heat.

Ayasta stepped to Joshua's side and put her hand on his shoulder. Across the room, Darcy noted the touch and glared at the Indian woman. No one noticed her.

"I know this Elisha Brecht," Ayasta said in English. She had learned to speak much better now, struggling less with the harder words. "Three times, maybe four, in Chickamauga Town with Dragging Canoe and Ulagu, my brother."

"Who is she?" Grubbins asked in a tone of alarm.

"Her name is Ayasta—she's a friend of me and my family. Don't have any fear of her."

"She's a redskin!"

"By birth. By choice she lives as a white woman."

Another spit of blood. "But she just said her brother rode with Dragging Canoe, and—"

"You needn't fear her, take my word," Joshua said in an edged tone.

Joshua had turned to Ayasta and started to ask her a question, but Grubbins spoke again.

"Wait a minute—did you say the name was Ayasta?"

"Yes . . ."

"I be damned! One of them redskins said such a name as that!"

Joshua's eyes narrowed. "You heard one speak her name?"

"Yes. Mean looking redskin, tattoos, stretched ears. I heard him say the name while he talked to Brecht."

Ayasta closed her eyes. "Ulagu," she said.

Grubbins leaped to his feet and thrust a bloodied finger into Ayasta's face. "Damnation, Colter! This is the sister

of the very heathen who hatcheted Jim!" He moved as if
to grasp her throat.

Joshua shoved Grubbins back down in his chair, causing
blood to splatter across his lip. "You'll lay not a hand on
this woman—you hear me?"

Grubbins stared back, anger overtaken by awe. He
nodded.

"Darcy!" Joshua called sharply.

Darcy leaned the iron poker against the mantel but did
not turn.

"Darcy, have you lost your ears?" Joshua wheeled. He
was tense and spoke very harshly.

She turned slowly and aimed a flat, cold stare at her
husband.

"Darcy, if there's aught a rag to spare around, let
Grubbins have it to bite on until that blood stops. How
bad are you hurt elsewhere, Grubbins?"

The little frontiersman said, "A sore noggin, mostly,
and this wrenched shoulder."

"You can put up for the night by the fire yonder. Darcy
will lay you a place."

Darcy was moving too slowly to suit Joshua in getting
the rag he had ordered. He frowned at her. Grubbins spat
out more blood, a little less than before this time, and
eyed Ayasta cautiously, like a mouse watching a sleeping
cat.

Darcy produced a scrap of homespun from her sewing
basket and brought it to Joshua. "Here you are, Captain
Colter."

Joshua looked at her strangely, struck by her use of his
formal title. Only then did he realize she was angry with
him. At another time he might have been concerned;
right now it only added to his own tension and made him
angrier at her in turn. He snatched the cloth roughly from
her hand. Darcy turned away and walked slowly back to
the fireside.

Ayasta watched her, understanding what was happening. Darcy felt the Indian's eyes on her and despised it.

Some minutes later Grubbins was well-settled by the
hearth. His injured mouth was no longer bleeding, but

his eyes teared as he thought of his slain partner. Cooper was already out, carrying the alarm to the neighboring cabins and rounding up as many of Joshua's ranger company as could be safely spared from the settlement to pursue Brecht.

Ayasta had retreated to the far corner of the cabin and was seated on her haunches, further heightening her Cherokee appearance, which remained evident despite her bed gown, as the frontier people called the typical long dresses of their womenfolk, the decorative handkerchief about her neck, and the white bonnet covering her clubbed-up hair. Darcy busied about the cabin, casting ever lengthening glances at Ayasta. Finally she walked over to her.

"Do you think it's wise, leaving Judah alone in your cabin for so long?"

Ayasta rose and looked into Darcy's eyes. Darcy could easily have slapped that beautiful face. "You are right," Ayasta said. "I will go." She paused a moment, looking closely at Darcy. "You are like him, aren't you?" she said quietly, gesturing toward Grubbins. "You are afraid of me."

Darcy didn't want to hear it. "You'd best go to your child, Ayasta."

Ayasta walked across the cabin, glancing once at Grubbins, then left. Darcy, on the verge of losing control of her emotions, received an additional jolt when Joshua emerged from the adjacent room and also left the cabin, going after Ayasta. Unconsciously, Darcy hid her withered hand beneath a fold of her dress—a habit of hers when she felt threatened, uncertain, or inadequate. She had done it quite a lot since Ayasta had come into her life.

Up in the loft, young Will began to cry. Darcy, meanwhile, was staring at the door through which Ayasta and Joshua had just exited and trying to hold back tears.

"Missus Colter, I thank you for your kindness to me," Grubbins said. "If not for you and your husband, I don't think I would—"

"You must pardon me, Mr. Grubbins," Darcy said tightly. "My child needs me."

She walked to the loft ladder and climbed up, leaving Grubbins alone by the fire. When she came down again, Ayasta and Joshua were back in the cabin, and at Ayasta's side was Judah, bleary-eyed from interrupted sleep.

"Judah and Ayasta will sleep in the loft tonight," Joshua announced. "I want everyone under one roof, with Brecht about."

It was all Darcy could do to keep from crying.

Joshua lay in the bedroom adjacent to the main room, where Grubbins snored by the fireside. Darcy was at his side, but he was hardly mindful of her with so much on his mind.

He was still in a tense humor, sleep far out of reach as he thought about the unwelcome news of Brecht's return and of the task of tracking, and possibly fighting, that would come in the morning. He also listened carefully for any sounds of trouble outside the cabin. If Brecht and a band of Chickamaugas were about, there was no predicting where or when they might show up. What if they had followed Grubbins here? When the ground thawed, Joshua thought, he would finish the stockade and blockhouse as quickly as possible. He would sleep better at night within a good protective paling fence.

He rolled over, sighing loudly and restlessly. Darcy moved in turn beside him.

"Joshua?"

"What." He didn't realize how gruff he sounded.

"Why did you go out after Ayasta when she left the cabin tonight?"

Joshua rolled over. "What kind of question is that?"

"Can you not just answer me?"

"I went out to tell her to fetch Judah over to our house. I would think that's obvious. What else would I have gone for?"

"You'll have to answer that, not me."

Merciful heaven, why is it put upon a man to have to deal with a fretful wife when he's already got so much to mull over? Joshua was in no mood for this kind of discussion tonight.

"Go to sleep, Darcy. If you're saying what it sounds like you're saying, you'd best get some rest and clear your head."

She rolled over and faced him. "Do you love me, Joshua?"

The question had an undertone of desperation that softened Joshua's hard attitude. "You know I love you, Darcy," he said.

"How long will Ayasta be here?"

So that was it. Joshua had thought that question had been settled long ago.

"She'll be here as long as need be. I owe that much to—"

"Yes, I know. To the memory of John Hawk." She paused as anger rose in her and got the best of her restraint. "I despise John Hawk's memory, just as I despised him when he was alive. He was a murdering savage! I'm glad you killed him! I wish I was free to throw it up into that damned heathen woman's face that it was my husband who slew hers!"

Joshua sat up, amazed at the vehemence of his wife's words and angered at their content. "Darcy, I charge you not to speak so again! And keep your voice down—do you want Ayasta to hear you?"

"If it would make her go, if it would make her hate you and leave you alone with me, then yes, I would welcome her hearing it!"

Joshua began to tremble in anger. "I never knew such a mean spirit was in you, Darcy."

"Far better a mean spirit than an adulterous one!"

Joshua seemed to grow larger and rise higher, looming over his wife in the dark. "Are you accusing me of infidelity? For if you are, woman, you are a wretched and shameful creature!"

"At least I'm no heathen squaw who casts herself uninvited into the lives of decent Christian folk and takes away the heart of a good man!" Now Darcy began to cry.

Joshua hovered for an agonizingly long moment between two options: exploding in anger and quite possibly striking his own wife, or deliberately taking a grip on emotions that had become too uncontrolled on both sides. With a great wrenching of his will, he achieved the latter.

"Darcy, forgive me for what I've said to you. Wipe it from your mind, for I meant none of it." He paused, struggling for the right words. "I've told you before and I tell you again, it's you I love, not Ayasta. What I do for her I do because of John Hawk. Yes, he was a savage, as you call him, but also a man and a friend who wore the very coin I wear."

Darcy, still wrought up, reached over and jerked the coin-bearing thong from around her husband's neck, and flung it angrily against the bedroom wall.

"If John Hawk were alive I could call down a pox on him and perhaps feel the better for it. But how can I battle with a man already dead? Will you let your damned eternal loyalty to the memory of a dead Indian come between you and your wife, Joshua? I have opened my home to Ayasta and I've tried to open my heart to her as well, but now I know it can't be done. You must make a choice, Joshua. If loyalty to John Hawk's memory means keeping his squaw forever in our household, then you cannot keep that loyalty and your wife as well."

"What are you saying?"

"That you must tell her to go. And if you won't, I will."

Joshua was stunned. "I can't turn her away! My God, woman, I killed her very husband! I can't throw her out into the world alone with John Hawk's blood already on my hands!"

Darcy took a deep breath. "And so a heathen's shed blood buys your soul and your honor, and binds you more tightly than the love of your own mate."

"This is foolishness, Darcy. Stop it. Go to sleep and get some sense back into your noggin."

Joshua stood, reaching for his trousers.

"Where are you going?" Darcy asked.

"Outside, to keep watch until the rangers arrive in the morning. God knows I'll get no rest in here in any case."

He finished dressing with no more words. Darcy

watched him silently as he bound the sash around his
hunting shirt, put on his cloak and hat, and hefted up his
rifle, horn, and shot pouch. He strode to the door, and
the last thing he did before leaving the room was to stoop
and pick up the coin and thong from the floor. He took off
his hat for a moment, put the thong back around his neck,
lowered the hat again, and left the room.

Grubbins stirred and moaned at the fireside as the gust
of cold air generated by the opening of the door struck
him. The door closed and sent a burst of sparks spiraling
up the chimney. Grubbins murmured, groped at his
aching mouth, and then resumed his snoring.

In the loft above the main room, Ayasta crawled to the
single shuttered window, cracked it open silently, and
peered out at the figure of Joshua Colter striding across
the yard, rifle in hand. The hounds, excited to see him at
this unusual hour, yipped and bounded at his feet.

Ayasta closed the shutter and returned to her pallet
bed. She had heard the muffled sound of harsh words
coming from Joshua and Darcy's sleeping chamber. She
had made out almost none of it, except for her own name
and that of John Hawk. Even without knowing the content
of what was said, the tone of the dispute had come
through quite clearly.

She could feel the venom of Darcy Colter in this cabin
as if it were a spirit that traveled through the very walls.
It made Ayasta sad, and for the first time since she had
come here, she doubted the wisdom of her flight to a new
way of life.

And it wasn't merely Darcy's bitterness toward her that
roused her doubt. She had a new worry now that she
knew Ulagu was raiding in this region again.

What if he had heard of the Indian woman and child
living behind the Colter cabin? What if he came to find
them and take them back?

Ayasta was overwhelmed with dismay. For so long she
had dreamed that joining the world of the unakas would
bring an end to fear and dread, yet now she was filled
with both, as much, maybe more, than before.

T he Chickamaugas stood in
a line on the shore, waving and calling across the water.
Several men were among them, but most were women
and children. From their smiles and open manner, Hannah Brecht was almost persuaded that the Chickamaugas
were the most friendly people on the frontier.

"Hello! How do you do, brothers! Come ashore! Come
ashore and share our food!" The cries blended into a
warm hubbub of invitation.

This Chickamauga town, visible behind the line of
Indians on the south shore, had none of the atmosphere
of gloom that had so chilled Hannah in the deserted town.
Hannah smiled, feeling that her fear of encountering
Chickamaugas had been unnecessary. She turned to her
mother, who watched the Indians with a somber expression. "See, Mother? They're friendly."

"I don't trust them," Repentance said, slipping her arm
protectingly around Andrew's shoulder.

Ahead on the *Adventure*, Colonel Donelson and others
of his party were also closely watching the Chickamaugas
and talking among themselves. Solomon Brecht came to

Hannah's side. "I wonder if the colonel will go to shore?" he asked.

"Heaven forbid it," Repentance said.

"I see nothing to fear on that bank," Solomon commented. He glanced forward to the *Adventure*, then pointed. "Look!"

Aboard the flagship boat, John Donelson, Jr., son of the colonel, and a man Hannah recognized as a John Caffrey, were hauling up a canoe that had been in tow behind the flatboat. "Are they going ashore, Father?"

"It does appear so," Solomon replied.

Indeed the junior Donelson and Caffrey were climbing into the canoe. Zekle Holly swore and Repentance cast up her hands in disbelief. "God preserve us," she said. "We are guided by fools."

The Indians cheered loudly at the sight of the two white men advancing toward the shore, and a handful Chickamauga men on the shore climbed into a canoe of their on and began rowing out to meet them.

Solomon watched tensely but with an expression of approval. "Perhaps some friendliness today will give us peaceful passage until we are past these towns," he said.

Sound carried easily across the water, and Hannah was able to hear, though not completely understand, the voices of Donelson and Caffrey as they talked to each other. Their canoe snaked forward through the water, and by now the Chickamauga canoe was very close to them.

In moments that canoe came alongside that of Donelson and Caffrey, and Hannah saw one of the Indians talking intently to the two whites.

Caffrey turned and looked back at the *Adventure*, and Hannah caught a clear glimpse of his expression. Her excitement faded. Caffrey looked concerned. Hannah stepped closer to her father.

Caffrey and Donelson turned their canoe and returned to the *Adventure*, followed by the lone Chickamauga canoe. The white men climbed out of their craft and onto the flatboat, then helped the Indians do the same.

The *Carolina* had drifted close to the *Adventure* over

the last moments. Solomon patted Hannah's shoulder. "Stay here."

He went to the nearest point and stood listening to the conversation aboard the lead boat. Hannah made as if to join him, but he waved her back. Meanwhile, Donelson was handing various trinkets to the Indians, items he had brought along as peace presents for occasions such as this.

"Oh, children, oh, children . . ." Repentance pointed toward the shore.

Other Chickamauga men were mounting canoes and beginning to paddle toward the flotilla. "Perhaps they're coming for presents of their own," Perrin suggested.

"No, no," Repentance said. "Look at the paint on them!"

Hannah shuddered deeply as she looked closely at the approaching Chickamaugas. They were painted in red and black. Hannah knew only a little about Indians, but she was aware of their habit of painting themselves for war. Whatever displays of friendliness were taking place on the *Adventure*, it was clear the Chickamaugas now approaching had no friendly intentions.

She looked back to the *Adventure*. By now those aboard it had also noted the approach of the other canoes. One of the Indians, lighter skinned than the others, stepped to the edge of the flatboat and began making hand signals across the water. In a moment the advancing canoes stopped; an Indian in the foremost one signaled back.

"What are they telling each other?" Hannah asked her mother.

The question went unanswered, for Repentance knew no more of Indian signing than did Hannah. She pulled her children close to her and knelt among them in the attitude of a martyr awaiting the Roman lions.

"Oh, Mother," Andrew said, beginning to cry.

Hannah, for her part, was too frightened for tears. In a moment, however, her spirits leaped. The several canoes now in the water abruptly began to turn, and in moments the Chickamaugas were returning to shore. Obviously the lighter-skinned Indian had signaled them back.

"Oh, praise be to God!" Repentance said. "Praise be!"

Solomon came striding back to his family. "The colonel has given the signal to continue with all speed," he said in a serious tone.

"Amen to that!" Jesse Clinton said.

"What has happened, Father?" Hannah asked.

"Hush, child. There's no time for talking now."

Hannah was sobered anew at her father's intent manner. He returned to the steering oar as the fleet continued traveling. Meanwhile, the handful of Chickamaugas aboard the *Adventure* had returned to their own canoe, but had not gone back to the shore. They traveled alongside the lead flatboat, riding between it and the south shore, along which the long line of Chickamaugas moved, following the fleet on foot.

Hannah prayed more fervently than she had ever prayed in her life.

Members of Joshua Colter's ranger band had begun converging at his house by the middle of the morning. Joshua was pleased with the number that arrived, a full dozen, which was more than he had anticipated. Upon arrival at the nearest ranger cabin, Cooper had sent that ranger to fetch another while he went on to yet another homestead to repeat the process. The result was a relatively swift conveying of the call to arms.

Cooper was weary from a night without sleep and looked it, but he declared himself ready for the job ahead. "You look none too rested yourself, Joshua," he commented.

Joshua, still stung by last night's argument with Darcy, told Cooper only that he had spent the night outside at guard, keeping warm by sitting beneath a blanket over an earth-covered fire of smoldering coals. Many was the night he had spent that way during long hunts, but this was the first time he had ever done so right at his own house.

"I guess many were surprised to see Cooper Haverly at their door, after you being gone so long," Joshua said, changing the subject.

"Aye. And in a case or two I had trouble convincing

them that Elisha Brecht is still alive and raiding after so long an absence. Nobody was eager to believe it."

Joshua's parting from Darcy was clumsy and difficult. Cooper seemed to notice it but was sensitive enough to ask no questions.

With the bandaged Grubbins at the lead with Joshua, they rode down a forest trace to the Nolichucky, then turned in the upstream direction and followed the winding contours toward the mountains. It was cloudy, and occasional spits of snow freckled the ground and clung to the stiffened leaves that lay on the ground, the dead sloughings of a long-past summer.

The raiders had set fire to Grubbins's cabin, but it had not caught well and most of the structure still stood. Inside, the cold, scalpless body of James Birdwell was a sad thing to see. Grubbins refused to look at it.

Joshua ordered the body wrapped in a blanket and placed on the cabin table. The cold would preserve the corpse quite well until a proper funeral and burial could be performed.

They found clear evidence of the raiders' trail and followed it. Their route took them through dark forest, then the sign made an abrupt northward turn.

"Lord a'mighty, they headed for Miller's," Grubbins said. "And him with a wife and three boys."

Joshua knew better than to be optimistic, especially when only a few dozen yards of further travel brought him to a rise where, through a gap in the treetops, rising smoke could be clearly seen. There was too little smoke to indicate an active cabin fire, but too much for it to be accounted for by a regular chimney fire. Therefore no one was surprised when arrival at the Miller residence revealed a burned-out cabin. Miller's horse pen was broken down and his stock taken. In a gesture of mocking petulance, his slain hounds had been laid across his woodpile, which had then been set afire along with the cabin.

Inside the remains of the cabin were five charred bodies. The entire family had been killed and scalped.

"Damn Elisha Brecht and his murdering rabble!" Grubbins declared, fighting back tears. "I wish I could open hell's gate itself and toss in Brecht with my own hands!"

Joshua looked at the bodies for a long time, thinking the thought such a sight always roused: This could easily have been me and mine. Someday it might be.

Right then he wished he could return to Darcy and put his arms around her. There wasn't enough time in a man's life for him to waste a moment being divided from the one he loved most.

Maybe Darcy was right. Maybe he was too much devoted to his sense of duty to John Hawk's memory. He should have never allowed his efforts to help Ayasta to come between him and the wife he loved.

Such matters could not be dealt with here, in any case. "Wrap them and lay them out behind the thicket yonder before we go on," Joshua directed. "Pile some rocks on them and maybe we can keep the critters off them until we come back through."

They rode on, searching for Brecht.

The man's name was Coody, Arch Coody, Solomon Brecht told Hannah and Repentance as the *Carolina* continued on near the head of the flotilla. Half Indian and half white, he had come out to the *Adventure* to warn Donelson that it would be unsafe for any of the travelers to come ashore. Eyeing the half-breed, who with his Indian companions still rode beside the *Adventure* in the canoe, Solomon commented that from what he had heard and seen, Coody seemed a friendly enough fellow, intent on protecting the travelers.

"With my own ears I heard him say that the village back yonder was the only Chickamauga town we'll directly pass," Solomon said.

"Then why is Coody still with us?" Hannah asked.

"He possesses a helpful and friendly spirit, I suppose. He must feel a kinship with us through his white blood."

"I don't trust him," Holly said. "Red blood spoils the white."

The Chickamaugas who had lined the bank and tried to lure the boatmen ashore had followed for a great distance but had disappeared now, much to Hannah's relief. Riding the river with them hooting from the shore had felt unsettlingly like running a gauntlet. Coody's assurance of no more Indian towns ahead cheered her tremendously. Perhaps the voyage would go forth from here on with no Indian contact at all.

At length Coody shouted across to Colonel Donelson in a voice loud enough for Hannah to easily hear. "No more towns!" he assured again. "Now you will have safe passage!" And with that he and his companions pulled the canoe away from the fleet and began paddling toward the shore.

Hannah felt grateful to the helpful half-breed and watched as the canoe moved away. Coody chanced to turn his head and his eye fell on Hannah, who smiled her silent thanks at him.

Coody smiled back, and something in his expression made Hannah feel as if iced water had been tossed in her face. He held her gaze far too long as the canoe moved away, until at last she turned toward the front of the boat so as not to see him any longer.

At that same moment, she heard her father give an exclamation of dismay. When she saw what he had seen, she understood.

Ahead was an island, splitting the river into a south and north passage. But the island didn't matter; the sight that did, the sight that gave the lie to the half-breed Coody's assurances and caused Hannah's heart to sink, was the Chickamauga village clearly visible on the south side of the south passage, roughly opposite the island. And as before, the bank was lined with Indians, waving and calling and seeking to lure the flatboats southward and toward them.

Zekle Holly swore and declared he would never again be fool enough to ride a flatboat through hostile country.

The Chickamaugas shouted claims of friendship and assurances that the southern passage was far better for passage than the northern. "Oh, I hope Colonel Donelson doesn't listen," Hannah said to her mother. "They only want us near them so they can kill us."

Donelson, to her relief, began by signs to order the
fleet to bear for the northern passage. Solomon Brecht,
his face somber, nodded his understanding and agreement with the order. Hannah looked up at him.

"Go close to the north bank, Father," she said. "Take
us as far from them as you can."

"Don't you worry, my dear," he said. "I want the
broadest space I can have between us and those heathens."

The flatboats and pirogues proceeded steadily into the
north passage; Hannah felt safer for the moment when
the island came between the *Carolina* and the Chickamaugas on the south shore.

Then a strange thing happened. Repentance, usually
silent and stoically glum, suddenly became agitated. She
rushed to Solomon and took his arm. "Don't go so close
to the bank, Solomon, please!" she urged.

"Repentance, the Chickamaugas are on the far side."

"Please, Solomon, not so close! Don't you see that's
what they want us to do? They knew we would never
come near them on the south shore!"

Solomon paused, thinking, and a look of fear came over
his face. For once Repentance made perfect, chilling
sense.

It was a realization come too late. A shot sounded from
the northern bank, sounding like a flat slap. The sound
carried across the water so that every traveler of the flotilla
heard it. They also heard the feminine scream and wail
that followed: "They've shot him, oh God help me, they've
shot him!"

Holly set up a cacophony of cursing; Clinton began
praying aloud.

Hannah looked to her father. He was gazing back down
the line of boats, eyes wide. "That was from the Blackmore boat," he said. "They've shot someone aboard the
Blackmore boat."

Suddenly the north bank was alive, figures moving in
the woody, winter-bare brush. Gunfire sounded, mixed
with the whisking of arrows slicing air. One sailed past

Hannah, missing by no more than three inches. She screamed and dropped to her face.

"Get into the shelter!" Solomon shouted. Hannah heard but felt unable to obey. Following a panicked and irrational impulse, she clawed at the flatboat bottom as if to dig a hole in which she could hide.

"Hannah, into the shelter!" Solomon urged again, laying to the rudder oar with all his strength, trying to move the flatboat farther from the shore.

Holly and Clinton, meanwhile, continued cursing and praying, respectively.

Across the water the Chickamaugas were shouting triumphantly at the sound of the shots and commotion. All down the flotilla rifles cracked and bluish bursts of powder smoke filled the air. More shots came from the bank, and on the south shore Indians were mounting canoes and launching into the river to attack from the other side.

Hannah suddenly found her senses and darted toward the shelter. Repentance's hand grasped her wrist and dragged her forward even faster. Already Andrew was huddled and screaming in the shelter and Perrin was manfully dragging out a pair of rifles to defend his family. He took a position at the shelter door.

Then Hannah realized how precarious her father's position atop the shelter was. Pulling free from Repentance's wrist-whitening grip, she ran back onto the open deck. "Father, you must hide!"

"Hannah, in the name of heaven, get yourself inside!"

Perrin leveled one of the rifles and fired, the butt of the long weapon kicking his shoulder like the back hoof of an angered mule. As the noise faded, Hannah heard Solomon scream.

An arrow had struck his foot at almost a vertical angle, passing through it and into the wood of the shelter roof so that he was literally pinned in place. He staggered and almost fell, putting painful pressure against the piercing shaft, then caught himself and knelt, grimacing and pulling at the arrow. The effort brought wracking pain and he cried out, but did not stop what he was doing. Hannah screamed, again and then again, and then was finally pulled into the shelter by her mother.

Solomon wrenched the arrow free and stood just as a painted Chickamauga warrior rose from behind a deadfall high up the bank and fired another arrow. This one passed at a slight angle through Solomon's side, the head emerging on the right portion of the small of his back. He groped at the arrow and fell to his knees. Another arrow passed through his shoulder, and he pitched forward.

Perrin had stood to fire the second rifle about the time the first arrow struck Solomon. The terrible sight of his father pegged in place like a doll to a store shelf caused Perrin to hold his fire, in the shock of the moment literally forgetting what he was doing.

Now Perrin scrambled up to his father, tears streaming down his face. "I'll kill him for you, Father, I'll kill him!"

"Give me the rifle, son, and below and inside with you." Solomon's words had a tight, forced tone, edged in pain. He reached down, grasped the rifle by the barrel and pulled it from his son's hands, then shoved the boy, roughly but necessarily, down toward the shelter. Perrin began to sob, and scrambled to safety on his hands and knees.

Solomon Brecht, blood streaming down him, walked to the edge of the shelter roof and raised the rifle. The Indian who had shot him had ducked back to cover now, but Solomon, growing stupefied by descending shock, fired at the place he had been. The emptied, smoking long rifle clattered to his feet, and Solomon Brecht slowly leaned forward, like a tall poplar pushed by a mountain wind, and fell flatly into the water, face first. Clinton groped after him but could not reach him.

Inside the shelter, Repentance Brecht wailed and fainted. The two boys put their arms around each other and cried. Only Hannah held back her tears. She rose and clambered atop the shelter and looked for Solomon in the water, as if oblivious to the danger she was in. There— there he was, floating facedown in water which was pinkening around him as he drifted toward the bank.

"Get him! You must get him!" she screamed at Clinton.

"I'll try, I'll try with the oar," he said, "but you must go back inside!"

"No! No!"

Clinton wrapped his arms around her and dragged her kicking back down to the shelter. Her father's still body drifted toward the bank. She screamed until something like a hot iron scraped across her skull and she went limp, drooping in Clinton's arms like a great rag doll.

Miles away, across miles of wintry forests, mountains, waterways, and valleys, another battle was taking place. Joshua's rangers had tracked Brecht and his Tories, along with Ulagu and several Chickamaugas, deep into the rugged forest many miles from the nearest settlement. The rangers had gained the advantage of surprise in their attack, demanding immediate surrender. Brecht did not surrender; he would die before surrendering. And so it had begun.

The first half hour, which had sped past like a handful of seconds, had been confined to an exchange of rifle fire typical of such conflicts. Every man had taken to the trees, rocks, and ravines, and fought like a one-man army against skilled opponents similarly situated. At times the battle scene would be strangely silent as combatants reloaded or scrambled for more advantageous positions. Other times the forest would ring with rifle fire and shouts—Chickamaugas sending up ringing cries, and the rangers giving out the disconcerting battle yell of the borderers.

The day was cold, but Joshua Colter didn't feel it. Battle generated a heat all its own. He darted through a ravine, head low as he bulled through brush and branches, and placed himself securely behind a massive evergreen. There he stopped, set the stockpiece of his rifle against the ground, and poured a quantity of powder down the barrel from his powder horn. In a more casual situation he might have measured the powder carefully with the smaller measuring horn that also hung on the powder horn's strap, but in the pressure of the fight he relied on long experience and familiarity in judging the amount of powder he used. This was fine powder, not prone to burn wet and clog the barrel or touch hole.

Alphus Colter himself had manufactured this gunpowder—a skill he had developed back in his early Carolina days. Joshua was proud of his father's powder-making skills, and smiled to himself every time he heard some other borderman complain of his own poorer powder and declare enviously that he wished he had some "Alphus" in his powder horn.

After restopping his powder horn, Joshua produced a rifle ball from his shot pouch. This he wrapped quickly in a greased cloth patch and set into the end of the barrel. He slid the long hickory ramrod from its holder under the barrel and rammed the patched ball home. Resetting the ramrod, he then powdered the pan of his flintlock and was again ready to fight.

Peering around the tree, he caught a glimpse of movement beyond a thicket and recognized it as an Indian. Moving his head slightly, he detected that the Indian was aiming a rifle eastward; Joshua quickly sighted down on him and fired. The Indian spasmed and fell. Even as Joshua began to reload he saw one of his rangers run across for cover of his own, and knew that man had been the intended target of the unfortunate Chickamauga.

Elsewhere in the battle, Ulagu felt a burst of joy as his own rifle ball brought down a white man, who fell wounded on the earth. Ulagu advanced and used his war club to finish the job. He pulled out his scalping knife and took a trophy, then returned to his covered position, reloaded, and went looking for another victim.

Ulagu was a fierce warrior, almost as fierce as John Hawk had been. He held an advantage over many of his fellow warriors, for he possessed a fine Pennsylvania rifle he had stolen in a raid on the Watauga. Many other warriors had to rely on .75-caliber "Brown Bess" muskets, unrifled firearms of British origin that served well in the traditional British style of warfare—musketeers facing off in ranks and laying down volleys of fire—but which lacked the precision and accuracy of the frontiersmen's smaller-caliber rifled weapons. Though a trained musket fighter

could reload a Brown Bess up to four times in a minute—
obviously advantageous in a British massed formation—
he could not hope for accuracy beyond about a hundred
twenty-five yards. If that mattered little in British linear
warfare, it made a life-or-death difference in American
frontier fighting, especially when the enemy carried rifled
weapons that could pick off a musketeer who was still too
far away to hit any target with his own weapon. Furthermore, the Brown Bess weighed about eleven pounds and
could eventually tire a man from weight alone as he
carried it over rugged terrain in thick forests.

Brown Besses were in use by most of Ulagu's fellow
warriors in today's battle, but not all Indians possessed
even that clumsy firearm. Weapons supplies had always
been a problem for the Indians, and was even worse since
a huge store of Brown Bess muskets laid in by Dragging
Canoe had been taken by the unakas in the 1779 raid on
the Chickamauga towns. Ulagu had seen many warriors
still doing battle with such traditional weapons as war
clubs—such as the one Ulagu carried as a sort of side-
arm—knives, blow guns, and five-foot bows that fired
barbed arrows. Of course, even some of the unaka settlers
were insufficiently armed; back before the secession of
the Chickamaugas, Ulagu had once seen a settler vainly
trying to hold off a band of Cherokee raiders with nothing
but an old trade musket and a crude blunderbuss loaded
with rocks, metal scraps, and broken glass.

Ulagu was a keen-minded man with a great interest in
military affairs. He had often quizzed the British he knew
about their style of fighting, which he thought was illogi-
cal and wasteful of lives. Ulagu held the practical viewpoint traditional to the native people of the frontier, that
the point of warfare was to take as many enemy lives as
possible while preserving your own, to achieve the desired goal, and to withdraw until the next battle. He had
heard British officers talk of valor and fighting gloriously
to the end, and had made little sense of it. What glory
was there in defeat? The purpose of war was to win and
survive.

And Ulagu intended to survive today, and to take as

many lives and scalps as he could. He thrived on making war, loved the heat it put into his blood, loved the excitement of filing along secret war trails with a band of warriors who communicated to each other with hand signals alone, and who moved as silently as birds through the air, stepping in each other's tracks to hide their numbers.

Ulagu saw movement through the trees and advanced, believing he had detected another of the unaka rangers. When he drew closer, however, he saw it was Elisha Brecht, creeping through the woods like he was stalking a deer. He was disappointed for a moment, then turned his head to find Brecht's prey. There, barely visible from his angle, he saw a young rifleman, reloading desperately. Light filtering through the treetops revealed a flash of red on the unaka's chest. Blood. Either this young fighter had spilled the blood of his enemies on his own clothing or he had been badly hurt himself.

Either way, Ulagu decided, he would leave this one to Brecht. Brecht rather enjoyed killing a wounded foe; such were less a threat. There was little bravery in Elisha Brecht's soul.

Ulagu had no fondness for his Tory ally, even though Brecht insisted on calling them friends. His fellowship with Elisha Brecht was cemented not by affection but by mutual usefulness. Though Brecht feigned great devotion to crown and king, Ulagu had been with him long enough to see the man's true stripe. Brecht was merely a thief and outlier whose lack of scruples fit comfortably into the environment of war. When Brecht raided, it wasn't out of any philosophical loyalty beyond loyalty to himself.

Ulagu knelt as Brecht passed; the Tory saw him and nodded to indicate the enemy he was secretly approaching, and mouthed a name: "Colter."

Ulagu immediately gained a new interest in the bloodied young man who was even now finishing his reloading. Could this be Joshua Colter himself, the man to whom, he was sure, Ayasta had fled with Wasi? If so, in no way could he afford to let Brecht kill him, not until he had a chance to question him thoroughly. Ulagu began moving in the same direction as Brecht.

As soon as he was close enough to the bloodied frontiersman to see his face, Ulagu realized this could not be Joshua Colter. This man, bleeding from what appeared to be a musket ball wound to the lower part of his right shoulder, was young, hardly more than a boy. And he wore no coin about his neck. If this was a Colter, it was not Joshua. Perhaps he was the younger brother of Joshua Colter, the one who for reasons unknown to Ulagu bore a different surname. Ulagu had heard Elisha Brecht drunkenly cursing the name of Joshua Colter's brother several times. He had often said the brother—whose name was Haverly, Ulagu suddenly remembered—was the whelp who had wounded and driven him off when he was on the verge of killing Joshua Colter back in '78. Elisha had once said something else about young Haverly as well, something about the young man wishing to marry the daughter of his brother—an intolerable union Solomon Brecht was firmly and correctly against, Elisha had said.

If this was Haverly, he held no particular interest for Ulagu; Brecht could have him if he wanted. His presence here, however, did make Ulagu wonder if Joshua Colter himself might be about as well. He decided to look for him.

Ulagu stayed where he was long enough to watch Elisha Brecht level his rife and shoot down the wounded young man, who sent up a terrible cry as he fell. Then Brecht, laughing aloud, moved in with his rifle upraised, the butt of it ready to club his victim. Ulagu turned away before the blow fell, not out of squeamishness, but simple disinterest.

Fifteen minutes and several rife balls later, Ulagu was at the edge of the battle site, his war club upraised over a man who was pleading with a contemptible amount of cowardice for his life. Ulagu suddenly recognized him as a man who had deserted his own companion and fled from a cabin they had burned the night before. The companion had been killed and scalped, but this one had escaped. He would not escape this time.

As he was about to bring down the club, however, a thought stopped him. Looking into the white face, he said, "Colter! Joshua Colter!"

"No, no, my name is Grubbins—"

"Colter is here?"

"Yes, he led us—this is his doing, not mine . . ."

Ulagu had learned some English from Elisha Brecht and his white followers, but he still had to struggle with it. "The—The amulet, the coin—Colter wears this?"

"Yes, yes—I'll show him to you if only you'll—"

A swift blow and it was over. Ulagu took his usual trophy, then moved away from Grubbins's still form. Joshua Colter was here, the man who held the secret of Ayasta and Wasi's disappearance, and Ulagu was determined to find him.

13

Hannah felt as if she were being pulled up a dark, narrow well, with hands reaching out from the slimy walls to slap at her face. She moaned and tried to move, but could not. The slapping continued; now she felt her back scraping the side of the well itself. It was very cold here, cruelly cold.

Her eyes opened and made out vague forms. Faces. More slaps, and now urgent voices. Something red and liquid stained her vision. A hand descended and wiped the red haze away, and she saw that the closest face was that of her mother, and she was crying.

"Mother . . ."

"Hush, child, hush. You are safe now."

Hannah closed her eyes again. She heard screams, chilling screams, and imagined again she was in the dark shaft. Great fear arose. What if she should fall into whatever terrible place was below. It seemed the screams arose from there. A hand slapped her face again, lightly, and she heard her mother pleading for her to reawaken.

"Mother . . ." Hannah opened her eyes and this time kept them that way. "Mother, what is happening?" She was in the flatboat shelter. The boat was in motion. Her head ached, and again a red stain clouded her eyes. She wiped it away herself this time. It was blood.

Suddenly the image of her father's still form floating in the water returned to her mind. "Father . . . where is Father? Is he dead?"

Screams again, but more distant than before. They seemed to come from far back in the flotilla.

"Your father is gone," Repentance said. "He was shot by Chickamauga arrows and fell into the water. You were grazed by a rifle ball trying to go after him."

Hannah's voice trembled. "He is dead?"

"We didn't see him die . . . but Perrin saw the Indians dragging him from the water. They had tomahawks." She paused. "We must consider him dead."

Tears gushed up and Hannah cried.

"Hush, girl—we must be strong now," Repentance said. Her voice had a different, more imposing tone than usual. "Your father is no longer here to help us and protect us, and we must make our way on our own."

Hannah sat up, then sank down again from dizziness. "Who is screaming so, Mother? It's so terrible—am I dreaming it?"

Repentance shuddered visibly. "You are not dreaming. It is the poor pox-stricken people on the Stuart boat. The Indians saw it alone, back from the rest of the boats, and have . . . taken it."

Hannah's sorrow doubled. Already she had pitied the sad, smallpox-ridden family and crew, isolated at the rear of the flotilla. Now that very isolation had done them in. Like wolves downing the weakest and hindmost member of a herd, the Chickamaugas had fallen upon the unprotected Wataugan flatboat.

"Is there nothing to be done for them?" Hannah asked.

"Nothing but to pray for their souls"—Repentance's expression and voice went cold—"and that whatever justice there is in this world will see fit to let the pox itself avenge the lives of those poor murdered people. Oh, merciful God, if only we hadn't started on this hellish voyage!"

"Is the Indian danger behind us?"

"We are past the town, but the heathens still follow on
the banks." Repentance paused. "And ahead, Zekle says,
is the Whirl of the river."

Hannah touched her wounded head gingerly and
winced. "There are mountains there, they say. The Indians won't be able to follow us past the mountains—will
they?"

"We'll pray they cannot," Repentance replied.

As the flatboat moved on, Hannah tried to rest, but
whenever she closed her eyes, all she could see was the
floating body of her father, and all she could hear were
the death screams of the Stuart party, echoing fresh in
her memory.

Her mother was right. This voyage should have never
been undertaken. Hannah was very sure now that they
had not seen the last of troubles, and she wished intently
that right now she were miles away from here, safe in the
arms of Cooper Haverly.

But Cooper Haverly was deep in trouble of his own at
that moment. Completely unconscious, he lay on his back
on the cold forest floor. Beside him knelt two of his fellow
rangers, both looking down upon him with the attitude of
men anticipating the descent of death.

Cooper was a sad sight to behold. His chest was bloodied terribly. There were two rifle ball holes in him, one
in the lower right shoulder, the other in the outer part of
the neck. Even worse, a portion of the skin along the edge
of his brow was peeled back, well into the scalp area, the
result of a grazing blow struck by the butt plate of Elisha
Brecht's rifle.

Only the fortuitous arrival of the two rangers before
Brecht could render a second blow had kept Cooper
Haverly from being clubbed to death. Now the rangers
wondered if their salvation of the young man's life had
been any favor. A quick death would have been more
merciful than the slow one Cooper appeared destined for.

"Right strange, isn't it, that Elisha Brecht should be
the one to do him in," the first one, named Russell Proud,
said.

"Aye . . . but I pity Brecht for it," replied the other. He was the cousin of the first man, and named Jacob Proud. "Joshua Colter will go after him, and any man with the captain breathing down his neck has cause indeed to fear." He stood, looking around. "The fight seems mostly through. I'm going looking for Captain Colter."

Joshua, in the meantime, knew nothing of what had happened to Cooper. He was locked in hand-to-hand, knife-to-knife combat with a swarthy Chickamauga whose strength easily equaled his own. They had wrestled so for almost ten minutes, sweating despite the cold, slashing at each other with their knives until blood ran down both of them from myriad minor wounds.

Joshua had not fought in such a manner since that final bout with John Hawk—and this time he was not at all sure he would emerge the victor. His strength was ebbing more quickly than that of his foe.

At length he fell back, his hand numbingly struck a rock, and he lost his knife. The Chickamauga smiled and lifted his own blade, but Joshua's fist shot up and broke his nose. Though blood streamed over his mouth and chin, the swarthy fighter did no more than flinch. For a terrible moment Joshua was certain he was about to die.

A rifle cracked and the Chickamauga jerked backward. Joshua rolled and leaped up. Jacob Proud was already busily reloading his rifle. Joshua found his opponent dead. Proud's rifle ball had pierced his heart.

"I thank you, Jacob," Joshua said when Proud reached him.

"You'd best come fast, Joshua," Proud said. "Cooper's hurt bad."

Joshua closed his eyes a moment, then opened them. "Take me to him," he said.

The sound of battle had caught his ear from miles away, and he had turned his steps in that direction at once. His thoughts were with his partner, for the fighting came from the general direction of their riverside log cabin.

When the sound of the first echoing rifle blast reached

him, he had just finished skinning a deer, and it was a poor one, half starved and little. But meat was meat, and Pontius Pilate was glad to have it.

He had cut away the hams, saddle, and other choicest portions of meat with the skill of a trained butcher, for a butcher he once had been, back when he was treated as a piece of property in a Virginia city named Williamsburg. He spread the deer hide, skin side up, on the hard ground.

After placing a stout stick with two sharpened ends crossways across the skin near the area of the hind legs, he gouged the two sharpened points into the hide, then laid out the meat atop the stick and inside the skin. The entire thing folded and tied up into a neat and tidy package, the bottom strengthened and spread by the now-enclosed stick. An Indian pack, some folks called this sort of meat conveyance. Pont had made many Indian packs in his day, though fewer this winter than any season for a long time, given the weather-caused depletion in the game supply.

He abandoned the pack upon hearing the gunfire, but took time to hang it on a branch high above the ground, out of reach of any but the most determined forest denizens. With any luck it would still be there when he returned for it. Then he checked his rifle and began moving in a steady woodsman's lope through the leafless forest, heading for what was beginning to sound like a full-fledged battle.

The rifle fire had not abated but increased. In a little while Pont was cheered to determine that the fight, whatever it was about and whoever it involved, was not engaged near his and Trent's cabin after all. It was under way somewhere this side and slightly north of the cabin.

Pont slowed some, deciding that his partner was probably in no danger. Trent had been sick to his stomach this morning and had laid up in the cabin after a sleepless night; it was unlikely he had ventured out since Pont had left him to go hunting, and even if he had, clearly this fight didn't involve him. The amount of fire evidenced that this was not one man holding out against a party of

Chickamaugas or some other attackers; this was clearly a conflict between entire bands.

Pont slowed further, merely walking now, mulling the situation. At this place in these times, challenges between armed groups usually involved Tories, or Chickamaugas, or both, facing off against Whigs. Pont knew of the bands of Whig rangers who roamed the countryside, rousting out and punishing Tories wherever they found them, and of the occasional Tory raiders who inflicted so much woe on the rebellious settlers.

Just the day before, Pont had detected sign close by of a large band of riders on both Indian and American horses, and guessed them to be Tory marauders. He had warned Trent and kept his own eyes open for trouble, but beyond that he hadn't thought much about the matter. Disputes over politics and society and governments were not his concern and he seldom involved himself. He had gone along on Shelby's expedition against the Chickamauga towns, but that had been only because Trent wanted to go, and where Trent went, Pont went. Pont was not Whig or Tory, white or Indian. He was Pont, and that was all. He had no politics but freedom, no home but the wilderness, no friends but Malachi Trent, and no ambitions beyond never again being slave to any man.

Pont advanced up a slope. He was very close to the site of battle now, close enough that he decided to hole up and wait to see what part of it drifted his way. A snarled maple ahead looked climbable enough, so he made for it and clambered into the branches with ease, never losing his grip on his rifle. He climbed high enough to get a good view of the forest, but stayed low enough to be able to jump to the ground without injury. Then he waited.

At length he saw a Chickamauga warrior dart through the woods almost out of his sight; a moment later he caught a glimpse of a white woodsman about a hundred yards due east. Just as he had suspected, this was an engagement between Whigs, Tories, and Chickamaugas. Nothing for Pontius Pilate to get involved in. He remained still, his dark skin and earthen-hued clothing blending into the tree so that he was nearly part of it.

At first the fight was interesting, but then it began moving a little too close for comfort. Pont was about to swing down and move on when he witnessed a young frontiersman, already wounded, being felled by a rifle blast from a rotund, bald-pated fellow who surely must be a Tory, in that he was in the company of a fierce-looking tattooed Chickamauga. Pont wished he hadn't seen that, for he was naturally sympathetic toward downtrodden folk. He felt an unwanted impulse to help the gunshot young fellow, who was now being advanced upon by the bald-headed man, whose rifle was uplifted for a clubbing. Pont winced as the rifle butt descended.

He swore beneath his breath and impulsively raised his own rifle, aiming at the bald man as he brought up the rifle for the second stroke. Just then two other men broke into the clearing. Pont held his fire.

There were shouts, a shot fired, and confusion. The bald man fled into the forest, one of the others pursuing while the remaining man knelt beside the injured young fellow, examining him closely. The first man returned a few moments later; Pont made out some words about "that bloody sod Brecht" escaping.

Brecht . . . Pont knew the name. Elisha Brecht was a Tory renegade, widely feared by the Whig settlers. Pont was impressed to realize he had almost shot down quite an infamous fellow.

He watched a while longer, mostly to see if the wounded young man would die. Meanwhile, the battle was continuing elsewhere in the forest. One of the pair who had chased off Brecht left abruptly. Pont settled back against the tree, restless but more curious than ever. Where had the man gone?

Eventually the man returned, and he was not alone. Pont was truly interested now, for he recognized the newcomer: the man named Colter, whom the Chickamauga woman, Ayasta, had come to find that night on the river. Pont remembered Ayasta well—it was impossible not to, as much as Malachi Trent still talked about her. He was continually wondering aloud what had become of her, and if she was still in the company of Joshua Colter.

Pont had never heard Trent talk so much about any woman in all the time he had known him.

Pont watched as Joshua Colter knelt beside the wounded fellow. He had the impression the lad must be either a special friend or maybe a brother. Perhaps it was that tag-behind brother who had been with Colter the night Ayasta had come across the river.

Pont's mind worked busily. He had planned to watch this fight and then vanish unseen. Now that Joshua Colter was involved, he was developing a different notion. Trent had talked lately about going to find Colter and see what had become of the Chickamauga woman he couldn't forget. Well, perhaps Pont could make that unnecessary for his friend. Perhaps he could bring Joshua Colter right to Trent.

He slid down from his perch with the silent grace of a puma. Hefting his rifle, he began walking toward the clump of men in the clearing, and so silent was he that not even Joshua Colter detected his advance until he was within thirty feet.

"Free of them red heathen at last!" Jesse Clinton declared joyously as the country grew more mountainous and the Chickamaugas following on the bank were at last forced out of sight of the flatboats. Hannah, her head clearer, for her wound was minor and now neatly bandaged, had insisted upon leaving the shelter. She stood beside her mother on the flatboat deck and examined the river ahead. Perrin had taken his father's place at the sweep.

Even in the numbness of grief over Solomon Brecht's death, she was awed by the natural wonders she saw. Here the river was very wide and flowed through a valley. The current was swift from the sheer volume of water, fed by the innumerable rivers and smaller tributaries that drained the country for several hundred miles around. Ahead great mountains loomed, tall and fearsome and topped with bare rocks as much as a hundred feet tall. The river began to bear toward the right, pounding the base of the stony range.

For five or six miles the fleet followed the curve of the river. The water sped ever faster and challenged the skill of those steering the crude craft. Hannah and Repentance backed up to the shelter and sat down against it, their hearts pounding in anticipation of what lay ahead.

The gorge of the mountain was before them, compressing the river into a narrow channel about seventy yards wide. Hannah's heart was at her throat, and she wondered how the fleet could hope to make it through that swirling, roaring passage.

Untiguhi, the Cherokees had named this portion of the river: "pot in the water," so called for the swirling appearance of its rapids. According to the legends, in these parts had lived Untsaiyi, a great gambler and inventor of the gatayusti game, played with wheel and stick. Even now, the Cherokees claimed, the great flat stone where Untsaiyi played his game was visible and marked with the lines left by the rolling wheel. And the "pot" itself, their legends said, had come about after the wife of Thunder tossed into the river a boiling pot containing Thunder's scrofula-afflicted son, whom Untsaiyi had challenged to play with his "pretty spots" as the stake.

Hannah had heard such legends and thought little about them and the place that they concerned. They had seemed like the well-known old tales that had come over from Europe—steeped in mystery and age, but ultimately nothing but stories. Now, as the *Carolina* approached the rapids that flowed into the gorge at a rate so fast that two or three minutes would convey a boat a mile, the "pot in the water" was far more than an idle tale. She feared for her very life.

A canoe attached to one of the other flatboats suddenly overturned and dumped its cargo into the swift water, and at Donelson's direction the other travelers, seeking to help in the recovery of the goods, made for the northern shore and halted. Men from several flatboats stepped ashore and began talking over the best way to recover the dumped material.

Hannah was glad for the delay in trying to navigate the rapids. In the idle moments, though, she remembered anew her father's passing, and began grieving again, hoping that his death had mercifully come before the tomahawk-bearing Chickamaugas dragged him ashore.

On the opposite side of the water rose massive cliffs. Hannah, standing with her brothers, let her gaze idly crawl up the barren stones until she saw the top edged against the sky—and her eyes widened and a fearful shout welled up from inside.

"Look!" she yelled. "Look—above us!"

As if her cry was a prompting, rifle fire and arrows began raining down from the clifftop. A line of Chickamaugas was up there, having laid in wait for the arrival of the flotilla. Hannah screamed and darted with Andrew toward the shelter; Jesse Clinton and Zekle Holly, who had gone ashore with the other men, came darting riverward, splashing across to reach the flatboat. An arrow sliced into the water not a foot from Holly's right leg.

From the door of the shelter, Hannah took in a scene of great fright and confusion. Flatboats, canoes, and other craft were moving amidst a rain of musket balls and arrows out into the waterway and toward the gorge. There was no time to salvage lost cargo now, nor even to make mental or physical preparation for what was sure to be a perilous bound over rough water.

"This here's Satan's washpot sure as hell, so take a grip on your hind end and hang on tight!" Zekle Holly yelled.

Years later Hannah would wish she had kept her eyes open during the actual navigation through the gorge, for such an event comes but once in one lifetime. But those were the thoughts of reflection. When the passage took place, all Hannah did was lie down inside the shelter beside her mother, burying her face in her arms, and fight to hold down the contents of her stomach as the flatboat lurched, jerked, groaned, and shuddered through the passage. All she could hear, beyond the sounds of the boat seemingly trying to rip itself apart, was the roar of the water, the curses and yells of Clinton and Holly, and the weeping of Andrew.

And then they were through. Hannah knew it from the leveling and slowing of the boat and the relieved laughter

of the oarsmen. She laughed herself, a wonderful laugh of
eased tension, and hugged each member of her family
one by one. Andrew was still crying when she embraced
him, and when she released him, she was crying as well,
for her father was not there and would never be again.
Life was capable of particularly cruel jokes. How could
they celebrate even their own survival after what had
happened to Solomon Brecht?

They emerged onto the deck. The river grew wide and
placid; the *Adventure* sailed prettily just ahead. A look
and count behind revealed all the craft still in place,
except for one, a boat belonging to one John Jennings.

"The Jennings boat never made it past the cursed
Whirl," Zekle Holly explained in grim demeanor. "It ran
up on a north shore rock and stuck, and there was naught
to be done for them but to leave them for the bloody
savages."

The voyagers did not make camp that night; everyone
wished to put as much distance as possible between the
boats and the Chickamaugas. Hannah sat on the deck and
tried to write the day's tragic events onto her wooden
journal, until she realized she had lost all desire to record
anything further of a voyage she had grown to hate.
Disheartened and angry, she picked up her journal board
and cast it into the river. She would write no more until
the journey was done.

Malachi Trent's sun-browned face gleamed in the light
of the fire as he lifted bloodied fingers holding a misshapen lump of lead. "And there she is," he said with
satisfaction. "Out at last."

Joshua exhaled loudly, relieved that the terrible job of
extracting the rifle ball from Cooper's midsection was
behind. He had to admit that Trent had handled it as well
as could be expected. The ball had entered at a sharp
angle, cracking a rib and lodging just below it. Fortunately
it had not buried itself very deeply, and Trent had been
able to dig out the ball with his knife—a horrible ordeal
for Cooper even in his semiconscious state.

"You're a good man with a knife," Joshua said to Trent.

The compliment was sincere even if slightly grudging. Joshua still instinctively disliked Trent and had brought Cooper here to his cabin only because his injuries were too severe to allow him to ride home. Quite a surprise it had been to Joshua, seeing Pont striding toward him and the Proud cousins while they debated how best to deal with Cooper. Truly the black woodsman and Trent had been godsends—though in Trent's case, Joshua wouldn't have complained if God had seen fit to send someone else.

"I think your brother will come through well enough as far as the bullet wounds," Trent said as he washed his bloody hands in the cold contents of a water bucket in the corner of the cabin. This was the roughest of structures, made with unhewn logs that still retained the bark, and chinked with straw and mud rather than the more permanent lime and gypsum daubing used in cabins in the settlements. "The ball didn't lodge in his neck, so that should heal with no more than a scar for him to show off to the womenfolk. It's that blow to the head that worries me most."

"Aye." Joshua paced restlessly. "I wish I could get him home to care for him proper."

"He shouldn't be moved, not yet," Trent said. "Pont and me, we don't mind having him here until he's stronger. You stay too. You'll want to be close by him, eh?"

"I'm obliged to you, Trent." He paused. "Tell me, though, why're you here? I recall you saying you lived up on the Holston."

"So I did, until last fall. Pont and me, we get itchy in the feet from time to time. When the Holston got tiresome, we headed for the Nolichucky and threw up this cabin here before the winter set in."

"Trapping and hunting?"

"Yes, what little there is to find during this godforsaken winter."

Joshua looked around. "Where's Pont?"

"He said he had killed us a deer before he stumbled up on you and your fight. He's gone back to fetch it."

"Aye? Well, he looks big enough to carry a buck on each shoulder."

Joshua took out his pipe, frowned to find the clay stem had broken off short, then shrugged and filled the bowl anyway. Lighting the tobacco with a burning splinter from the fire, he went to Cooper's bedside and looked down at him in concern.

Elisha Brecht had dealt Cooper such a blow that it had all but scalped him in the process. Joshua had seen enough head injuries in his day to realize that one couldn't know at once what their full effects would be in the long run. The flesh and bone could heal nicely, yet leave a man weakened or childish or blind for the rest of his days.

After a while Joshua became aware of Trent's eyes upon him. Trent was seated on a log-section stool, back against the bark-covered wall. Joshua deliberately turned his back toward him, but still felt the gaze. Already tense, he wheeled. Even though Trent had done a kind act for him in taking in Cooper, Joshua couldn't abide being stared at. "Is there something on your mind, Trent?"

"Just thinking about that Chickamauga woman you took home with you."

Joshua had expected this subject to arise sooner or later, but it made him angry anyway now that it had. He still felt, inexplicably, that Trent was a threat to Ayasta, and it made him feel just as defensive as it had that first night he had met both of them. He began refilling his pipe. Trent continued to stare at him.

"Where is she now, anyhow?"

Joshua felt his face reddening with temper, but played ignorant. "Who?"

"That Indian woman, that Ayasta."

"She's where she wants to be," Joshua replied.

"Living among the white folk, eh?"

No answer.

"She was a fine sample of a woman. I had me an Indian woman once. Shawnee. I called her Kate. Spent two winters with her." He shook his head like a man thinking back on a particularly fine meal. "There ain't nothing like an Indian woman to keep a man warm at night. I wouldn't

mind having old Kate with me this winter, cold as it is."
He paused, still looking squarely at Joshua. "Or maybe
Ayasta. My, wouldn't she warm a man's bed!"

Joshua stepped toward Trent, curling up his fist. Only
one thing kept him from driving his knuckles into Trent's
nose: fear that Trent would decline to give any further
help and quarter to Cooper if he did. So Joshua stood,
helpless and fuming, his ignited temper burning the
inside of his stomach.

As for Trent, he hadn't even flinched at Joshua's approach, and this despite Joshua's widespread reputation
of being a man worth fearing. Joshua noticed Trent's lack
of response and felt all the angrier because of it.

"You'd be wise to put a rein on that tongue," Joshua
said coldly.

Trent arched one brow. "Hell, Colter, she's just a
squaw! That's all she is to you, ain't it? Just a squaw?"

Joshua detected the hidden meaning of the question.
"I'm a married man, Trent, and a faithful one—not that
my life and actions are any of your bloody affair."

"Sorry to have made you mad, Colter. I have a way to
doing that to folks. I speak my mind too free, I reckon."

"I reckon you do."

"I meant no disrespect for your squaw—"

"She's not my squaw, not anybody's squaw. She's a
friend of mine . . . and of my wife." Joshua could only
wish the last statement were true.

"She lives in your home?"

"She's got a place of her own behind mine."

"And your woman don't mind her being there, eh? A
pretty squaw like her close by her red-blooded husband?"

Joshua took another step toward Trent, lifting a long
finger and pointing it down at Trent's nose. "Trent, I
thank you for what you're doing for my brother, but
there's something that needs saying here. I didn't like you
from the first time I laid eyes on you, and I don't like you
now. Your tongue wags far too free and you've got a way
about you to rile a man. And I warn you, you don't want
to rile me, because when I get riled I don't always act like
the good Christian soul I try to be."

Trent rose slowly, his gaze locked on Joshua's and not faltering at all. He smiled slowly, lips tightly closed. "Colter, you have my apology if I've stirred you, for that wasn't my intent. But since you're talking straight to me, let me talk as straight to you. I've not stopped thinking about that woman since first I saw her. 'Twasn't my choice, it's just the way it's been. Now, if she's your squaw, then its no right of mine to covet what you've got. But if she ain't yours—and you just got through saying she's not— then it's no right of yours to tell me how I ought to think about her or talk about her or any other such thing. So don't be surprised if one day you see me ride through your gate. And it won't be you I've come to see. It'll be Ayasta . . . and I'll be obliged, when that time comes, if you'll stand aside and let a man tend his own business."

"You're one to talk about tending business, the way you've stuck your nose in mine today!"

"Don't forget that boy yonder on the bed, Colter. I'd think you might be glad I got involved in your family business today."

Joshua said no more. He stared at Trent in a way that would have sent any lesser man cowering to the corner.

At length he spoke. "Trent, it seems we weren't intended to share the same country, much less the same cabin. I'll put myself up a half-face camp outside, and stay close by until Cooper heals enough to go. Then I'll be glad to take my leave of you—and if ever you do come about my house, you'd best come when I'm in a real sweet humor, otherwise I won't be responsible. You understand me?"

"I understand you just fine. Maybe better than you understand yourself." Trent smiled again, almost smirking. "You're more like me than you know, Colter. That squaw has took hold of your heart like she's took mine. The only difference between us is that I'll admit it and you won't."

Joshua drew back his fist and hit Trent in the jaw so hard it should have knocked him down. It didn't. So he pulled back his fist again for another blow.

The cabin door opened and Pont walked in with the

deerskin Indian pack across his shoulder. One sweep of his eyes took in what was happening, and without a word he drew a knife from his sash. To Joshua he said, "You hit him, and I'll cut your throat clean to the neckbone."

Joshua glared at the black face, then lowered his fist. Stomping to the corner, he fetched up his rifle, slapped on his broad-brimmed hat, and pushed past Pont and out the door.

14

Darcy Colter moved about
the cabin quietly. Will had gone to sleep at last, and she
was determined not to waken him. Today the child had
gotten in the way of every task she had attempted and
undone every one she had completed. Now that he was
dozing she finally had the chance to put the kettle on to
boil at the fireplace.

Darcy had felt tangled like a knot since Joshua had gone
off yesterday morning with their dispute of the previous
night still hanging between them. It seemed a bad thing
to let your loved one go to battle with troubles lingering.

She went to the window made of real glass that Thomas
Colter had imported for their cabin from the East and
looked out. She scanned the barren forest for rangers
coming back from the search for Elisha Brecht, and was
disappointed to see no sign of any. A full night had passed
since their departure, and none had yet returned. It was
growing frightening.

Her view shifted to Ayasta's cabin. Smoke spilled out
the chimney. The door opened and Ayasta appeared,
tossing washwater out of a pan to the ground, where it
steamed. Judah came up behind his mother and tried to

push past her and outside, but Ayasta caught him and pushed him back. The Indian woman glanced toward Darcy's window before closing her door; Darcy pulled back into the shadows so Ayasta would not see she had been watching her.

"I hate you," Darcy said impulsively beneath her breath. "I hate you and your heathen child and I wish you both were dead."

Darcy was startled that such a dreadful thought had passed her lips, but now that it was out it gave her a dark satisfaction. She had heard Israel Coffman and Samuel Doak and other righteous folk say it was wrong to hate. But they also said it was wrong to be a liar, did they not, and wouldn't it be lying to herself and to God to deny the way she honestly felt? Besides, she rationalized, Ayasta was an Indian, part of the race that had killed her brother and mother, and almost killed her. Surely it wasn't as wrong to hate an Indian as it was to hate a white person.

Darcy went to the cupboard Joshua had built for her last winter, and from it removed an earthenware jug. She examined it, dusting it off and wiping it out with a rag. After setting it on the puncheon table, she turned to the three rabbits lying skinned and gutted on a cutting board close at hand. Darcy had snared these herself, and Joshua would surely be glad of it when he came home. Jugged hare was one of his favorite meals.

With a knife in her withered right hand, Darcy began cutting the meat into small pieces, pushing them to the edge of the board with the blade until she had a sizable pile.

Ayasta can't be allowed to stay. She must go. The thought came as unexpectedly and forcefully as the declaration of hatred that preceded it. Darcy began cutting the meat too rapidly, almost giving herself a sliced finger. She deliberately stopped for a few moments, and to her mind came the threat she had made in the night to Joshua: You must tell her to go—and if you won't, I will.

Darcy thought about what she had said. When she had made the threat she was angry, saying things she meant and things she probably didn't. The threat to drive off

FREE — MAGNIFICENT WALL CALENDAR!
FREE — PREVIEW OF SACKETT

- No Obligation!   • No Purchase Necessary!

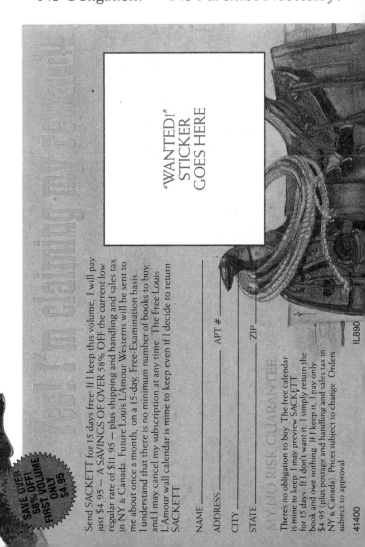

"WANTED!"
STICKER
GOES HERE

Yes! I'm claiming my reward!

Send SACKETT for 15 days free! If I keep this volume, I will pay just $4.95 — A SAVINGS OF OVER 58% OFF the current low regular rate of $11.95 — plus shipping and handling and sales tax in NY & Canada. Future Louis L'Amour Westerns will be sent to me about once a month, on a 15-day, Free-Examination basis. I understand that there is no minimum number of books to buy, and I may cancel my subscription at any time. The Free Louis L'Amour wall calendar is mine to keep even if I decide to return SACKETT.

NAME _____

ADDRESS _____ APT # _____

CITY _____

STATE _____ ZIP _____

MY NO RISK GUARANTEE:
There's no obligation to buy. The free calendar is mine to keep. I may preview SACKETT for 15 days. If I don't want it, I simply return the book and owe nothing. If I keep it, I pay only $4.95 (plus postage and handling and sales tax in NY & Canada). Prices subject to change. Orders subject to approval.

IL890

41400

SAVE OVER 58% OFF! FIRST VOLUME ONLY $4.95

Track down and capture exciting
western adventure from one of
America's foremost novelists!

• It's free! • No obligation! • Exclusive value!

Ayasta had fallen into the latter category—hadn't it? Or could she actually consider such a drastic thing, even though Joshua had forbidden it?

Darcy began rubbing a fatty chunk of bacon over the pieces of rabbit, her heart pounding too fast as she considered the unconsiderable. Dare she do it? Could she actually summon the courage and wifely defiance to send Ayasta away against Joshua's order?

Her shoulders gnarled with tension as she worked and worried. She felt guilty for her thoughts, and at the same time angry that she should have to feel guilty for them. Why should she feel badly about wanting to preserve her own marriage? Since Ayasta had come uninvited into the Colter family's lives, Darcy had felt she was no longer the mistress of her own home. Joshua had been so distracted by the beautiful Indian woman, so determined to do good by her, that Darcy now felt second place in his life. For the past week she had thought and dearly hoped she was with child, which she believed might have renewed her bond with Joshua. But only this morning her monthly issue had come in late arrival and her hope had been dashed, leaving her even more dejected.

She had so much to think about. Since learning the truth about John Hawk's death, Darcy had understood better why Joshua was so driven to befriend Ayasta. She had even tried, very sincerely, to accept his attitude in light of her new understanding—tried, and failed.

She couldn't escape the belief that Joshua's devotion to John Hawk's widow, even though understandable, was still not right. The cold fact was that John Hawk had brought his death upon himself by the murderous life he had lived. If Joshua hadn't killed him, someone else surely would have. Such deaths were simply a reality of war, and Darcy could see no reason that her own family's life should be so torn asunder because of the circumstances of one Chickamauga marauder's passing.

Joshua had sworn repeatedly that he felt no improper affection for Ayasta. Darcy had tried to accept that as well, and again had been unable to do so. And even if Joshua's devotion to Ayasta had not gone beyond proper limits, it seemed to Darcy that it would only be a matter of time before it did. Darcy knew something of the ways of the Cherokees, of the liberality of their attitude toward marriage and the intimate relationships between men and women. If Ayasta remained here, Joshua would eventually be seduced. Darcy could tell it, could anticipate it like a coming rain.

Working even faster now in tension, Darcy seasoned the meat with pepper and salt, then placed it in the jug, adding an onion and a mixture of sweet-tasting herbs dried from her summer garden. Picking up the jug, she carried it to the boiling kettle and set it slowly into the water, which bubbled around the jug almost to the rim. She laid a heavy pewter plate across the jug to serve as a lid, then sat down on a stool away from the fire, a thoughtful expression on her face.

This is my best opportunity, she thought. Joshua will be angry at me, but he's angry already. If she stays I will lose my husband, and I couldn't abide that. I mustn't let it happen, I mustn't.

She stood suddenly, chin thrust out firmly. Yes, by heaven, she would do it. She would march across the yard, face Ayasta in the very door of her cabin, and tell her to go.

But to simply order her away would infuriate Joshua. It would be better if Ayasta left of her own volition. Darcy knew only one way to achieve that: to tell Ayasta the truth about her husband's death. Then she surely would leave— and if Darcy was fortunate and Ayasta departed before Joshua returned, Joshua would never need know what had happened.

This indeed was a day of opportunity, and Darcy was not going to let it pass. She gathered her will.

Walking toward the door, she took her cloak from a wall peg and slipped it over her shoulders. Will moved and murmured on his pallet as she opened the door. Darcy was dismayed. No, Will, you mustn't awaken yet! She waited until he was quiet again, then walked into the yard and around toward the cabin of Ayasta Hawkins, hoping she could do what she planned to do before courage failed her or her heart pounded itself right out of her chest.

Jacob and Russell Proud rode together up the dirt trail that led to Joshua Colter's farmstead. They had come here upon Joshua's request, to give word to Darcy about what had happened to Cooper Haverly. After stopping here they would continue on to Colter's Station and there inform Alphus and Sina Colter about it as well. It was a lengthy ride and quite a lot of trouble for two tired men, but for Captain Colter the Proud cousins would do almost anything.

The farmstead looked peaceful and still as they approached. Smoke rose from the chimneys of the cabins of both the Colters and that of the squaw he had taken in— quite a peculiar situation, that matter of the squaw, both Prouds felt. But the captain's business was his own.

In her cabin Darcy heard the two riders approaching, quickly wiped away the tears that stained her face, and headed for the door, hoping it was Joshua, but also dreading his return if it was. Will was up now, scampering about playfully, and had asked his mother why she was crying.

"It's nothing, dear, nothing," she had answered. How could she tell such a small child his mother was crying because she had just cut another woman with words sharper than a blade, and now that she had done it, she was no longer sure it had been right to do it at all?

Ayasta had taken it, as usual, with stoicism, but Darcy had seen the pain in her dark eyes when she learned that the man who now protected her was the same who had killed John Hawk. Ayasta had turned away from her, gone and picked up her son, and sat down with him on a stool beside her window, rocking silently back and forth until Darcy turned and left. Where was the sense of satisfaction she had expected? She knew none of it.

Darcy opened the door and was surprised to see Jacob and Russell Proud riding around the corner of the stockade, serious expressions on their faces. It took only a second for panic to set in. Obviously they had come to tell her that Joshua had been killed, or else Joshua would be here himself. She gripped the frame of the doorway, her legs weakening beneath her.

"Howdy, Missus Colter," Russell Proud said, removing his hat. "We've come to bring you some bad news."

"Oh, God—Joshua is dead!" Darcy slumped to the side and looked as if she would faint. Jacob Proud leaped from his saddle, rushed up, and took hold of her to keep her from falling. Little Will, seeing his mother in distress, began to cry in confusion.

"Russell, you poxed fool, don't you ever give a thought to what you say?" Jacob scolded. "Missus Colter, you've been given the wrong idea. Joshua is fine, he's fine."

Darcy took several moments to recover. She looked in confusion at her visitors. "Then why is he not here?"

"He's with Cooper Haverly, down in a cabin by the Nolichucky. We fit with Brecht and some Chickamaugas, and Cooper got hurt right bad, shot twice. That's the bad news Russell was talking about." Jacob succinctly filled in the details of the battle up to Cooper's wounding. "Brecht got away clean again, him and most all the redskins."

Darcy felt both relief and concern, the former for Joshua and herself, the latter for Cooper. "Will Cooper live?"

"It appears so, though you can't know. There's a man tending him with Joshua, fellow name of Trent, and a big Negro named Pontius Pilate, like in the bible. They was kind to take Cooper in."

Darcy did not respond, for she had just seen Ayasta coming across the yard with Judah behind her. Darcy could hardly bear to look in the face of the woman she had just wounded so severely. Ayasta, however, kept her head high and did not falter as she looked back at Darcy.

The Proud cousins turned and nodded uncomfortable greetings to Ayasta. Judah came up behind his mother and gripped her long skirt, looking at the Prouds with the unabashed inquisitiveness typical of children.

"What has happened?" Ayasta asked. Darcy knew the woman had drawn the same conclusion as she when seeing Joshua was not one of the two incoming riders.

Darcy forced herself to hold Ayasta's gaze. The Prouds, meanwhile, were still looking at Ayasta uncomfortably, having heard Grubbins whisper before the battle that the Indian woman at the Colter farmstead was the sister of Elisha Brecht's feared Chickamauga cohort, Ulagu. "Cooper Haverly has been shot fighting Tories . . . and Indians," Darcy said. "Joshua is with him, and these men have come to bear the news."

Ayasta gave no answer. Her black eyes veiled many things as she looked at Darcy.

"Gentlemen, please come inside and have a meal. Hungry men deserve a feeding, and Joshua won't be here to eat what I've cooked," Darcy said to the cousins. Her omission of Ayasta from the invitation was deliberately blatant; she couldn't bear the thought of having the woman under her roof again after what had transpired today.

The scent of the cooking rabbit was enticing; Russell twitched his nose, appropriately enough, like a hare. "I wouldn't mind that at all, Missus Colter."

"No," Jacob said. "We've got to get on toward Colter's Station for the captain. If you've got a loaf and water to spare, though, we'd be obliged for it."

"No, no, you must eat better than that, and I want to hear more of the battle and Cooper," Darcy insisted.

In the end the Prouds relented and entered the cabin. Ayasta turned back to her own home, and once inside picked up her son and laid her cheek against his brow.

Ayasta's next hour was a time of reflections deeper even than those of the days when she was debating whether to abandon the life of the Chickamaugas. She knew one thing: She could no longer stay here now that she knew it was Joshua Colter who had killed her husband. She could not make her life with the slayer of the only man she had loved.

But was Darcy Colter's claim true? Ayasta was perceptive and knew the deep fear and animosity Darcy held for her. Ayasta had sensed long ago that Darcy's greatest desire was for her to be gone—and gone she might have already been, had she not so feared leaving the protection of Joshua Colter. Ayasta had not anticipated that acceptance into the unaka world would come easily, but it had proven even harder and slower than she had expected. If not for her protective association with the respected Joshua Colter, Ayasta "Hawkins" and her son would probably have come to harm by now at the hands of those who, like Darcy Colter, feared all the native race.

Ayasta could think of only one way to find out the truth about what Darcy had told her, and that was to ask Joshua Colter directly. She did not believe he would lie to her. And she hoped desperately that he would tell her that Darcy's words were false.

But the longer she thought about it, the more Ayasta began to feel Darcy had told her the truth. Joshua Colter had been so kind to her and her son, kind beyond expectation. Sometimes she had wondered why he was so excessively generous and protective. Until now she had attributed it to the natural kindness of the man. Now she had to consider the possibility that his kindness was driven by guilt.

Ayasta faced a great dilemma. If Joshua Colter denied being John Hawk's killer, Ayasta would be pleased; all would be well. If he confessed his guilt, then obviously Ayasta could not remain.

But what would she do with her son? If she left the Colters, where could she go and to whom could she turn? She would face either a forced return to the Chickamauga world she had abandoned and still felt was doomed, or life alone in a hostile white man's society, with no means to care for her son or protect herself, and him, from harm.

Ayasta thought over the matter, searching for answers, until at length she found the only possible one.

She rose and went to a rough chest in the corner and from it took the Indian clothing she had worn when she first came here. Stripping off her dress, she donned her original clothing, noting that it felt strange to be wearing it again after so long a time.

She went to her bed and from beneath it took a pouch filled with items specially collected and kept. She then led Judah across the yard to the Colter cabin, outside which the Prouds were already at their horses, preparing to depart for Colter's Station. Darcy Colter was outside the cabin with the men, and Ayasta could see the dread and discomfort in her expression as she approached, and her obvious bewilderment at seeing Ayasta in her native garb again.

"I must speak," Ayasta said haltingly to Russell Proud, who struck her as the most approachable of the three. Proud looked uncertain, but nodded. Darcy blanched, looking at Ayasta with wide, fear-filled eyes.

"I can help Cooper Haverly, with these," Ayasta said, lifting and opening the pouch she had brought. It was full of dried herbs, barks, berries, roots. "Take me to the place he is."

Russell looked even more unsure, glancing from his brother to Darcy and back to Ayasta. "Well, you see, we're ordered by our captain to go on to Colter's Station after this and—"

"One can go, one can take me to Cooper Haverly."

Darcy intervened. "You need not go to Cooper. You'd best leave him be."

Jacob Proud said, "Missus Colter, if you don't mind me speaking, it might not be a bad thing for her to go. These Indians, they've got healing ways about them. I've seen it myself."

Darcy felt like wilting away, and had no idea what Ayasta was up to. "But, you see, I . . ." She could find no words.

"I reckon it wouldn't take both of us to bear word to Colter's Station," Russell said.

"You go on, then, Russell," Jacob said. He turned to Ayasta. "I'll take you to Cooper if you want. I believe in Injun healing—seen quite a lot of it done."

"But what about Judah?" Darcy protested, looking for some flaw in the plan. She was growing afraid Ayasta was merely looking for a way to be near Joshua—perhaps to confront him with what she had told her. The prospect was tormenting.

"Reckon you could care for him a bit?" Jacob suggested to her.

"Me . . . I'm sure Ayasta wouldn't want me to do that . . ." she faltered clumsily.

"Yes, you keep Judah," Ayasta said, surprising Darcy. She spoke her next sentence slowly and carefully, obviously wanting to ensure it was understood clearly. "And if I do not return, then take him to the God-man Coffman. He and his woman will take him—they are lonely for a small one."

Darcy was certain now that something indeed was going on beneath the surface of this affair. Ayasta was talking like a person making final arrangements.

Darcy was utterly confused now, and out of argument. She didn't trust Ayasta and felt helpless to deal with her unexpected request. She nodded feebly. "Very well. I will take care of Judah."

"Ma'am, it would be wisest if you'd take up with a neighbor and not remain here alone—Brecht could still be about."

"Yes, yes," Darcy said. "I'll do that."

Russell Proud set off at once for Colter's Station. His cousin went to Joshua's stable and fetched out a horse for Ayasta. Within minutes he and the Chickamauga woman were riding out of the yard.

At the edge of the yard Ayasta stopped, looking back across at Darcy, who stood with the two children beside her. Ayasta stayed there for several moments, then turned her mount and rode on, catching up with Jacob Proud and disappearing around the bend into the forest.

It all gave Darcy the strangest feeling. Something beyond the obvious had just transpired here, and she had no idea what it was, or how it was going to affect her.

Joshua Colter was astounded to see Jacob Proud and Ayasta come riding back to Trent and Pont's cabin. Joshua had busied himself finishing a rough but sufficient half-faced camp shelter outside Trent's cabin, being unwilling to share the same roof with the man. Anyway, Joshua had never liked being crowded even in amicable settings.

He heard Trent swear in surprise when he, too, saw the approaching pair. Trent grinned at the sight of Ayasta. A ripple of anger ran up Joshua's spine.

He stepped forward. "Jacob, Ayasta . . . what is the meaning of this?"

"When she heard what happened to Cooper, the squaw wanted to come tend him," Jacob Proud replied. "It seemed wise to me, so I brought her back."

Joshua was not at all pleased to see Ayasta, not because he failed to appreciate her helpful intentions toward Cooper, but because he despised the idea of her being in the same place as Trent. He had not dreamed she might come back here.

Ayasta, strangely, would not look at Joshua. Even when he spoke his greeting to her, she ignored him, as if she hadn't heard. Her eyes swept the little cabin clearing, and when she saw Trent and immediately after noticed Pont coming around the other side of the cabin, she sparked with recognition of the men who had given her aid the night she had crossed the river from the destroyed Chickamauga towns.

She dismounted and unlashed her pouch from the saddle. "He is in the cabin?"

"Yes," Joshua replied. Ayasta looked at him directly for the first time since her arrival, and her eyes were the coldest things Joshua had ever seen.

Trent swept off his hat and spoke a hello to Ayasta as she passed him. She glanced at him only a moment, and nodded. It was little enough greeting, but far more than Joshua had received, and both Trent and Joshua noticed it. Trent looked at Joshua, smiled faintly, and followed Ayasta into the cabin.

"Well, do you need me longer?" Jacob Proud asked.

"No," Joshua said. "Go on with you." His tone was unfriendly.

"Did I do something to anger you, Captain?"

Joshua frowned up at him, realized his manner was improper, and forced out a grin. "Sorry, Jacob. I've just got Cooper on my mind. Thank you for bringing Ayasta— I'm sure she'll help Cooper much."

Jacob touched his hat in salute and nodded. "I'm off, then."

"Jacob—how is Darcy?"

"Fine, though she seemed rather wrought up. I'm supposing it's because you're gone off. I told her to go join some neighbors with the children, just for the sake of safety, you know."

"Thank you. I should have told her that myself."

Jacob Proud paused, then said, "That Indian woman in yonder seems to put your wife particularly on edge, Joshua."

"Aye, she does. Darcy's had a hard row to hoe with the redskins, you know. Good-bye, Jacob, and thank you again."

Joshua entered the cabin and found Ayasta examining Cooper's wounds. Cooper had remained in a deep stupor since his injuries, in a near-deathlike state that worried Joshua considerably. Thus he was glad to see Cooper much more responsive now, groaning and looking around as Ayasta gently removed his bandages and probed his injuries.

"Cold water," she said.

Trent was quick to respond. As Ayasta used the water to bathe Cooper's wounds, Joshua settled back to watch her work and to stew in his own wide-ranging mix of feelings about all this. For the next hour Ayasta treated Cooper's wounds with plasters made of beech, dogwood, and oak bark, then brewed an astringent tea of some of the further ingredients she had brought in her medicine pouch. This she gave to Cooper in small sips. Afterward he thanked her—the first words he had spoken since his wounding.

Cooper slept soundly after that, not in a stupor, but a state of true rest. Joshua was greatly relieved. Whether Cooper had naturally rounded a corner in his healing, or whether Ayasta's treatments had made the difference, Joshua did not know. It didn't matter; what mattered was that Cooper was getting better.

* * *

Joshua explored the area in the afternoon, for he was still concerned that Elisha Brecht and his followers might yet be about. The battle, as battles against Brecht always seemed to go, had achieved some results and scattered the foe, but left the main culprit alive. Brecht was harder to kill than a fighting dog. No one had seen Brecht after Jacob Proud drove him off, so Joshua had to assume he was reassembling with his force elsewhere in the forests.

Perhaps he would go elsewhere, as he had after that first engagement more than a year ago. Or perhaps he was even now sweeping down on some other farmstead.

He was beginning to want to see Darcy very badly. He missed her, and worried for her. He was ashamed that Jacob Proud had shown more concern for Darcy's safety than he had himself. What was wrong with him lately? Why was he so distracted and thoughtless?

And what if Darcy hadn't gone to a neighbor's, as she should? She was stubborn in that way, and slow to impose on anyone. Joshua decided that come first light, he would ride home and see if all was well. Cooper seemed destined to improve now, and Joshua didn't feel the need to be at his side.

Only two things made him not want to leave, and both involved Ayasta. The first was her peculiar manner toward him, her obvious coldness and distance. The second was the presence of Trent, who hovered over the Chickamauga woman like a vulture waiting to descend—which he surely would as soon as Joshua was gone.

Dozing in his shelter early in the evening, Joshua awakened suddenly and found Ayasta crouched beside the fire, looking at him. No one else was about. The daylight was dwindling.

"Ayasta . . ."

She spoke to him now in Cherokee, perhaps because she wanted a familiar language for the assurance of correctly expressing herself, perhaps because she wanted no one who might overhear to understand what she said. "I must ask you a hard question, Joshua Colter."

Joshua sat up. "Aye?"

Ayasta looked him directly in the eye, then asked a

question that jolted Joshua like a kick in the teeth. "Is it true that you killed my husband?"

The blood drained from Joshua's face. "Ayasta, why do you ask a question like that?"

"Your wife told me that you confessed to her that you killed my husband in battle. I must know: Is it true?"

A great rage flared inside Joshua. Darcy had betrayed him, had done the very thing he had told her not to do, had violated the trust he had placed in her as his wife.

He felt the impulsive urge to deny the charge, and opened his mouth to do so—then he looked into Ayasta's face and knew he could not.

"Yes," he said after a long pause. "I did kill your husband."

She stared silently at him, expressionless.

"I tried to avoid it, but there was no other way. John Hawk knew it as well as I did. We fought together where the town of Tikwalitsi once stood. If I had not killed him, he would have killed me."

Ayasta turned away and looked into the forest. Joshua said no more. At length Ayasta rose and walked away.

Darcy indeed had not taken refuge with any neighbor, Joshua discovered when he rode into his yard the next day. Smoke rose from the chimney; he heard the sound of the boys playing indoors.

He was putting his horse into the stable when Darcy came around the house, having seen him from the window. Her face was somber, her eyes weak and strained.

Joshua walked toward her silently. They did not embrace, did not even touch, as they came face-to-face in the windblown clearing.

"How is Cooper?" Darcy asked in a very soft, weary voice.

"Better. Ayasta treated his wounds with barks and had him imbibe a tea. He'll live."

"I'm glad." A long pause. "Joshua, I must tell you—"

"You needn't. I already know. She came to me, asked me if it was true."

Darcy's eyes began to moisten again. "What did you tell her?"

"The truth."

"I'm sorry, Joshua. I'm sorry for violating your word—but you have to know I didn't do it in spite or meanness. I did it for us, because if she stayed here I knew I would lose you."

Joshua said nothing.

"Hear me, Joshua: I have never loved another human being the way I love you. Without you there would be nothing, and with Ayasta here I saw you slipping from me. I had to send her away."

"Then why didn't you just tell her to go? Why did you feel you had to betray me?"

Darcy took a long, trembling breath. "Because if I told her to go without reason, you would have gone and fetched her back, and faulted me for cruelty. I had to make her go away on her own." She paused. "I had hoped she would say nothing to you of what I told her."

"You hoped in vain, then."

"Do you hate me, Joshua? I know I did wrong . . . yet a part of me even yet doesn't believe it was wrong. I'm sorry for it . . . but a part of me isn't sorry."

Joshua chuckled sardonically, without a smile. "You're honest about that, at least."

"Don't mock me, Joshua."

Silence. Husband and wife looked at each other and both knew a moment of import had come. This could be a time of turning away or turning toward.

Joshua was deeply angry at Darcy for her betrayal. A thousand bitter words that had rolled through his mind on the way home, all potential verbal whips with which to lash Darcy, remained on his tongue, ready to be unleashed. But he did not open his mouth, for as he looked at Darcy, he was remembering the first time he had seen her. She had still been Darcy Fiske at the time, and was traveling with her brother and parents to the fledgling settlement of Haverly Fort. She hadn't struck Joshua as all that pretty, and there was that withered hand to mar her, but something about her had touched a deep part of him.

And it was still that way. She was the woman he loved, the one too precious to lose. She was what no other woman could be: She was Darcy.

"Come here," he said, lifting his hand toward her.

She flinched back, and it stung Joshua to realize she had actually thought he was about to hit her. And that was enough to bring the water to his own eyes.

"No, Darcy, no, it's not like that. Come to me . . . I need you."

She came to him and he embraced her, holding her in a crushing hug. Then he put his hands on both sides of her face and looked into her eyes. The steam of their breath mixed in the cold air. Joshua kissed her, lightly at first, then with passion.

"You were wrong to do it, you know," he said, still holding her. He meant what he said, but the words bore no harsh edge.

"I know."

"But I was wrong too. Wrong to endanger what we have. But don't go thinking you pushed me to that conclusion by what you did—I was already becoming of that mind when I set out after Brecht."

Darcy laughed a laugh thoroughly healing. "I love you, Joshua Colter."

"And I love you too, Darcy Colter."

15

The voice came from the edge of Hannah's dreams, faint and weak.

"Help! Help me, please!"

She stirred against her mother, murmuring, coming half awake long enough to know a nightmare was coming.

"Help me, please!"

It was her father's voice, or so it seemed, pleading from behind in the darkness, a ghost bewailing its abandonment. Hannah shifted again. She tried to wake herself and make the dream go away, but still the voice sounded, closer this time.

Repentance Brecht sat up, and then Hannah did awaken. The Brechts and their fellow voyagers were settled for the night amid an array of cookfires. Hannah rubbed her eyes and wondered if it was Friday morning or still Thursday night.

"Help me . . . help me . . ."

Hannah heard it again. This was no dream. Repentance had heard it too, as had many others, for all over the camp people were rising, reaching for rifles, looking about in confusion.

"Father!" Perrin exclaimed, sitting up on the other side of his mother. "Father's alive!"

Wild hope stirred; Hannah leaped to her feet. "Oh, Mother, could it be?"

"Help me . . . help poor Jennings . . ."

Jennings. Hannah's heart sank. It wasn't Solomon Brecht back there at all, but Jonathon Jennings, whose boat had become lodged on the north shore rocks during the passage through the Whirl. Hannah sat down slowly and wrapped her blanket around herself, then buried her face in it.

"Don't cry, daughter . . . if Mr. Jennings came through alive, perhaps Father did too. Maybe he just hasn't caught up with us yet."

"No, Mother. Father is dead," Hannah said. "I know he is."

Saddened as the Brechts were that it was not their loved one who had survived miraculously, they proceeded to the place where Jonathon Jennings came stumbling up through the darkness toward the campfires. His boat was out on the river with his wife and others aboard it, including Mrs. Peyton, Jennings's daughter, who had given birth in the abandoned Chickamauga town.

Jennings's story was so remarkable that no one regretted the loss of sleep in sitting up to hear it. Hannah was so entranced she actually forgot her grief for a few minutes—at least grief over her own family's situation, for Jennings's tale was one of tragedy as well as near-miraculous survival.

As the Jennings survivors were given food and drink and warmed by the fires, Jennings described the adventure. When his boat had lodged on the rocks, Jennings had realized he and his would be left to fend for themselves, so had ordered at once that all cargo be thrown overboard in hope of lightening the boat enough to float it off the rocks. In the meantime the Chickamaugas had observed his situation and had concentrated their rifle and arrow fire upon his craft. A fine marksman, Jennings had returned fire as best one man could against a numerous enemy.

Jennings's son, a young male slave, and another young male passenger aboard the boat, had initially helped with dumping the cargo, but panic had gripped them and all three leaped into the water in a desperate attempt to swim to a safety that the shores could not actually provide. Jennings had seen the black youth drown, and saw one of the other young men injured by gunfire. He feared that both were taken captive when they reached the shore; whether they were now alive or dead he didn't know.

With the youths gone, the task of lightening the boat fell to the women aboard, and they worked at it with great vigor despite the rifle fire that peppered the water and boat and ripped at their very clothing. In the confusion, sadly, another tragedy occurred. Mrs. Peyton's infant child was accidentally tossed into the water in the scramble to unload the boat, and died before it could be recovered. Despite the shock of sudden bereavement and her weakness from recent childbirth, Mrs. Peyton had continued helping lighten the craft.

Jennings gave chief credit for their salvation, however, to his wife and a black woman aboard the boat, both of whom exposed themselves to withering fire while freeing the boat. Mrs. Jennings, in fact, had actually descended into the water to push the craft free, and when it launched off in a rush, she was almost left behind to become a victim, as Colonel Donelson would record it, "of her own intrepidity."

Fortunately, Mrs. Jennings had been pulled onto the boat at the last moment and now was safe, her clothing torn by an amazing number of bullet cuts, in evidence of how close to death she and her comrades had come.

Hannah and her family returned to their fire and blankets after the stories were told. Hannah snuggled close to her mother's warm body. "I miss Father especially bad tonight," she said.

"Yes," Repentance said. "So do I. But take heart, dear. For now we have the protection of Mr. Holly and Mr. Clinton. And when we reach the Cumberland country,

Mr. McSwain will be there. He will help us as he helped us before. He is a good man, I think."

"Yes," Hannah said. "He is a good man."

Joshua took Darcy and the two boys all the way to Israel Coffman's house before returning to Trent and Pont's cabin on the Nolichucky. The preacher and his wife were glad to see the visitors, though Coffman told Joshua, out of earshot of the women, that he hoped the presence of children in the house would not upset his wife.

"I hadn't thought of that, Israel," Joshua said. "Perhaps I should go on elsewhere with them."

"No," Coffman replied. "Virginia must become accustomed to normal life again. She can't bury herself in grief forever. Besides, the boys are a pleasure to watch. Now, tell me, do you want me to go with you back to Cooper?"

"No need for it, Israel. You stay here and keep good watch over the womenfolk in case of trouble."

As Joshua rode away he pondered that not long ago he would never have dreamed of trusting Israel Coffman to protect anyone. The preacher had been as green and unweathered a sprout as Joshua had ever seen when first he came to the frontier. Now he was far more seasoned, and not a bad shot, if he was firing a decent rifle.

Joshua had more reasons than protecting the women for Coffman not to go with him back to the river cabin. He had told Coffman nothing yet of what had happened between Darcy and Ayasta, and preferred to keep the preacher out of the situation for the moment.

When he reached the cabin, Pont was outside, building a half-faced shelter not far from Joshua's.

"For Ayasta?" Joshua asked him.

"No," Pont replied in his deep, rich voice. "For me."

"But you've slept in the cabin until now."

"There's another sleeping there now, and there ain't no room for me, none at all. A man and a woman together, they don't need no extra company."

Joshua understood. During his absence, obviously far more had happened between Trent and Ayasta than he would have guessed. He wondered if Ayasta had yielded to Trent's advances because she truly wanted to, or because she simply didn't have the will to resist him in a time of renewed grief over her lost husband.

Trent had hung an old blanket between Cooper's bed and the rest of the cabin to create at least a minimal privacy for himself and Ayasta. Cooper was stronger today than when Joshua had seen him last, and talking again. The others left Joshua alone in the cabin to talk to his brother.

"Thought I was going to die, Joshua," Cooper said. "Thought old Brecht had done me in proper."

"I knew better. It would take fifteen Brechts to do in Cooper Haverly."

Cooper pointed at the blanket. "You know why that's there?"

"Sure do. Trent's claimed the squaw he wanted. I admit it riles me . . ." He paused. "But I'm finished getting riled over the business of others. What Ayasta and Trent do is their affair, and my household has had enough trouble over that woman already without me bringing on more. I've learned my lesson."

Cooper's voice was a whisper; he lacked the strength yet for anything more. "What do you mean?"

"There's been some things happen with Ayasta and Darcy . . . and me too." He outlined what had occurred. Cooper, having never known until now that Joshua had killed John Hawk, was appropriately awed. Joshua pledged him to secrecy.

"Ayasta will never go back with you now," Cooper said.

"I know. I'll wager that's one reason she was so quick to take up with Trent. He can give her a home, you see. A place she can live without taking her boy back to the Chickamaugas . . . and without her having to live in the shadow of the man who killed her mate."

"Do you think she'll bring Judah out here? I can't see a child being raised in this place . . . especially not by Trent."

"Neither can I."

"Maybe she'll leave the boy to you and Darcy—have you thought of that?"

Joshua shook his head. "Give her son to the man who killed his father? I doubt it."

They talked awhile longer, and Cooper declared himself eager to return home as soon as he was able. Despite his woundings, he wanted to be up and battle-ready again, still having it in mind to join whatever force was sent east over the mountains to aid North Carolina in its resistance to the British advance.

Cooper quickly grew weary with talking, and Joshua left. Trent and Ayasta were nowhere in sight. Pont was still working on his shelter. Joshua walked over to him and looked the structure over. Pont was building himself a slab camp, a stronger and more permanent structure than the bark-and-brush-topped shelter Joshua had made. The leaning roof of Pont's shelter was topped by two layers of slabs he had split from small, straight logs, flat sides turned up on the lower run, down on the upper, with the top logs covering the gaps between the lower ones.

"Fine job," Joshua said.

"I've made aplenty in my day, and slept in the rain when I couldn't."

"You've got the look of the land about you, Pont. How long have you roamed?"

"Many a year, many a year."

"Is Trent a good master to you?"

Pont flashed Joshua a vague smile. "You believe he is my master?"

"What should I believe?"

Pont still had his smile, but his words came through as dead seriously as he intended them. "Colter, the only master of Pont is Pont. Trent and me, we let folks believe he owns me. Makes it easier."

Joshua quickly surmised that Pont was an escaped slave. How Trent figured into his history was a question that made Joshua curious, but he didn't ask. Joshua had also noted that Pont had not called him "Mister Colter," as was the custom when a black man addressed a white one. It clearly was no oversight. But it didn't rile Joshua, who for his time and place was a man remarkably free of bigotry.

"You talk your English better than Trent does. Where'd you learn it?" he asked Pont.

"In the place I used to live."

The vague answer made its point. "Reckon I shouldn't have asked such a direct question, Pont. I beg your pardon."

Pont studied Joshua a moment. "There's something I like about you, Colter. I think I'll get on fine with you— but there's some things you need to hear right off."

"I'm listening."

"First is, I'm a man. Just as much a man as you, and just as proud. Just as free too, and I'll die free. Second thing is, don't never lift a hand or say a bad word against Malachi Trent." He lifted a muscled right arm, fist clenched. "See that arm? That's a part of me. You break it, burn it, skin it, and it's me that feels it. It's that way with Trent. You cut him and I bleed. You hurt him, and you've hurt me."

"Trent must have done some fine things for you, for you to feel that strong."

"That he has, and I won't forget it. I'm a man that don't forget anything, good or bad."

Pont fell to working again, and Joshua pitched in to help. Pont hadn't asked for aid, but neither did he decline it. In a few minutes the shelter was finished.

"I'm going off into the woods for a spell," Pont said. "Come with me if you want."

"Where's Trent?"

"With the woman. Out gathering barks to poultice your brother again." He set his eye on Joshua. "What did you do to that squaw, Colter?"

"Why do you ask a thing like that?"

"Because that first night across from Chickamauga Town, I was beside her at the river, waiting for you to come. When she first saw you it was like she was pulled toward you. But it ain't like that now. You walk by, and she pulls the other way."

Joshua was not happy with the topic. Pont was too perceptive to suit him. "I'll strike a bargain with you, Pont: I'll mind my own affairs, and you can mind yours."

"That woman is my affair, now that she's Trent's. He loves his squaw."

"There's love and there's craving, and the two ain't the same."

Despite his reformed attitude about Ayasta and his own relationship to her, Joshua was angered to hear her referred to as if she were Trent's possession. In fact, there was much about Pont's defiant, almost pompous attitude to anger Joshua Colter. The strange thing was that even as his temper grew ruffled, he found himself liking Pont all the more, and growing more curious about him.

"You've got ways that remind me of a certain Cherokee I once knew," Joshua said. "His name was John Hawk, and likely you've heard of him."

"So I have." Pont picked up his rifle. "Come on, Colter, if you want to."

They set off together, plodding through the forest in the natural, rolling style of the woodsman. There was a fluid motion in the movement of an experienced man of the forest, a flat-soled step and rolling of the hip joint that was distinctive and particularly noticeable to those new to the wilderness. Joshua, a woodsman since early childhood, had walked that way all his life. Pont had adopted the gait naturally after putting behind his former bondage and taking to the wilderness.

Joshua asked no more questions of Pont as they proceeded on their informal reconnaissance through the hills and hollows along the Nolichucky. At length, however, as Pont's trust in Joshua grew, he began talking about himself, and bit by bit his past and Trent's were unveiled.

Pontius Pilate's name had been given him by his father, who stabbed a finger into an open bible and took the first thing he found. When the boy had grown old enough to learn that his biblical namesake had been a ruler, he had been proud, for Pont had believed from his youngest days that he was destined for greater things than his fellow slaves in Williamsburg, Virginia. That the biblical Pilate's name was sullied by the condemnation of Jesus didn't bother Pont. The important thing was that Pilate had been a man to be reckoned with, a man of importance and strength.

Pont learned quickly that a young black man in slavery was not allowed either importance or strength in any realm beyond his dreams. Just be thankful and accept your lot, his mother had counseled him. Be thankful you are a house slave, not a field laborer. Be thankful you're learning a skill that makes you valuable.

The skill was meat-cutting, but if that gave Pont value, it was only in the monetary sense. Be thankful? Pont had not an ounce of gratitude in his heart for any aspect of his forced servitude. By the time he passed into his thirteenth year, he was determined that someday he would be a free man, and once free, would never know bondage again.

His mother was a brilliant woman who defied the mores of her time, secretly taught herself to read, and began a sporadic but effective process of self-education through books she stole from the shelves of her master's house. The master never missed them; he kept his volumes for show, not reading. To his mother's tutelage and cajoling, Pont owed his own literacy and better-than-average vocabulary. But his mother died when he was sixteen, leaving him alone. His father had preceded her when Pont was just a baby.

When Pont was nineteen, financial problems had embroiled the household that possessed him. Pont heard rumors from the other slaves that the master was in financial distress and that he had fallen so low that he was suspected of having hired a professional thief to steal livestock for him in hopes of covering some of his debts.

Pont hadn't believed the tales until the day he found the thief himself hidden in the master's cellar while colonial authorities searched for him. Men with stern faces had come to the house and asked Pont if he had seen such a man as they described—obviously the very man in the cellar—and Pont sincerely shook his head. No sir, no. No one like that has come here, sir, but if he does, I'll be sure to raise a yell, sir.

When they were gone, Pont descended to the cellar again. The thief emerged and clasped his arm across the shoulder of the slave who had saved him. From that point on there was a bond forged between Malachi Trent, thief, and Pontius Pilate, slave. Soon the bond would be made even stronger.

Two weeks later a notice was hung on the taverns and in the square: "By virtue of a Decree of the Honorable General Court, obtained by Mess. Davenport and Wales of New York, against Mr. Philip Peales, Debtor, seven Negroes of value will be sold, for ready Money, in Williamsburg, on the 14th day of March, before the Raleigh Tavern."

Pont, having just turned twenty years old, stood on the block and watched his world being taken from him. A few waves of the auctioneer's hand, a few shouts from the crowd, and suddenly Pontius Pilate was property of a visiting South Carolina landsman, destined to be hauled away within the week to a place and people he had never seen.

He laid awake most of the first night, thinking of what was about to happen. The second night he got up, put on his clothes, stole food, a rifle, shot, and a pair of knives, and declared himself free from that moment on.

The slave-catchers pursued him the next day, through forests and swamps, at one point drawing so close he had hidden in the only place possible—the inside of a great hollow tree, in a space so small he was wedged against his own rifle. He heard footsteps drawing near and believed himself discovered. He wrenched the rifle around, clicked back the flintlock against the inside of the tree, set the muzzle beneath his chin, closed his eyes, and with difficulty strained to reach the trigger.

The face that peered in at him was that of the thief he had protected. "Keep quiet," the thief said, "and I'll lead them away from you. Keep quiet and you'll stay free."

Pont laid his finger on the trigger but did not push it.

He waited, hoping, praying. For three hours he held the painful position inside the tree, until once again the thief was back, laughing and talking of how he led them for miles before letting them discover it was a white man they were chasing, not the runaway slave they wanted.

Pont knew what a risk the thief had taken on his behalf. He himself was wanted by the authorities, but had risked identification and capture to repay the protection Pont had given him in the cellar.

The thief and the runaway took up with each other. They made their way through life together, and a rugged way it was, inevitably leading them to the only place such men could hope to be left alone: the wilderness across the mountains.

"Wherever Malachi Trent goes, you'll find Pontius Pilate following," the former slave said to Joshua. "I'd follow that man into hell itself . . . someday I likely will. I'd die for that man in a moment. To me there's only two things in this world worth dying for, and that's freedom, and Malachi Trent."

The two frontiersmen walked in a great circling route through the forest, and now worked back down to the river again. There they found human sign, relatively fresh. "Brecht's men," Joshua said. "Hang it all—I had hoped they'd be gone."

A rifle shot echoed through the forest, coming from upriver, from whence they had set out. Joshua and Pont glanced at each other, turned, and loped off through the forest, heading back to the cabin.

They were almost fired upon by Trent when they emerged from the forest. Trent, recognizing them at the last instant, came out of the cabin with his rifle in hand and a wild expression on his face. Ayasta appeared in the doorway behind him.

"What was it?" Pont asked his partner.

"I seen a redskin," Trent replied. "Me and her, we had just come back in. I heard something, turned around, and seen him scampering off. I shot at the sorry coon, but missed."

"One of Brecht's?"

"I figure it was."

Ayasta stepped up to the men. She talked to Trent, refusing to look at Joshua. "I recognized him," she said in English. "The unakas who would come to Chickamauga Town called him Bark. He is a friend of my brother."

Joshua asked, "Did he see you?"

She did not look at him when she answered. "Yes," she said. "He saw me."

Jesse Clinton walked back down to the Brechts' campfire on the northern bank of the Tennessee River. The roaring of the water was greater here than at any place along the way so far, except for the Whirl. This was Muscle Shoals, a perilous, rocky waterway that roused the dread of the finest boatman.

Even so, the voyagers had reached this place with a great sense of expectation and excitement. Here, along the northern shore where they now camped, James Robertson was to have left signs for the water travelers, indications that he had traveled to this spot overland from the French Lick and had blazed a route for them to follow. If the signs were there, the voyagers knew, then the difficult river journey was over, and the challenges of the shoals and hundreds of miles of farther river travel would not have to be met.

"From here to the lick it's but a hundred miles and twenty, traveling like an arrow or bird," Clinton had said as they neared the shore. "Of course, it will be farther for us by land, maybe a couple of hundred miles. But I'm for it, I surely am. I've had my fill of river travel, with God as my witness."

After setting up temporary camp, he had gone off with Colonel Donelson and some others in search of Robertson's markers. Zekle Holly took off toward the rear of the flotilla to join a friend who was willing to share a few pulls from a jug of whiskey he had stashed in his pirogue.

As Clinton now returned, the Brecht family awaited his word expectantly. His face told the story before he spoke. "Not a thing," he said, settling himself by the fire and extending his hands to it. "No sign that Robertson has been here at all."

Hannah was gravely disappointed. "But why? Did he not give word he would come here?"

"Who can say what might have happened? Likely as not he just figured we wouldn't be reckless enough to set out on a river voyage in the midst of a winter like this one has been." He pulled a burning twig from the blaze and watched the wind blow it down to a glowing-line red cinder. "I guess we were greater fools than Robertson gave us credit for."

"What will we do now, Mr. Clinton?"

"That's a decision for the colonel, not me." Clinton flipped the cinder off the stick. "I doubt we'll turn back, after coming this close. I daresay it will be back to the river again for us."

"Across the shoals?" Perrin asked. "Can we make it?"

"I'd rather brave the shoals than pole back through the Chickamaugas," Clinton replied. Even now the Indian threat remained strong; that very morning, the fleet had been subjected to another gauntlet of gunfire as they passed another Chickamauga village. This time the shots had struck no one, but had done nothing to help anyone's nerves.

The word that soon came back from Donelson was just as Clinton had predicted: Passage by land would not be attempted in absence of positive indications from Robertson. The flotilla would attempt to pass the shoals before nightfall, and go on the rest of the way by water. The danger in lingering was too great to allow any other option.

Everyone in the party understood the import of the decision. To proceed by water would eventually mean poling, sailing, or dragging the boats against the current of both the Ohio and Cumberland rivers. It would delay arrival at the French Lick by too many weeks to be foreseen. It would mean untold exertion, deprivation, suffering, and quite possibly more deaths.

The only respite the situation provided was that there was no time for anyone to dwell long on any discouragements beyond the immediate challenge of the shoals themselves. Readying their boats as best they could, they began their advance into the roaring caldron.

Hannah would recall in later years that the passage of the shoals nearly equaled in intensity the passage of the Whirl, and at least to the extent that it lasted longer, was even worse. Bumping, turning, rocking in the water, the fleet raced over the shoals at occasionally breathtaking speeds.

Rachel Donelson would later show Hannah the journal entry made by her father at the end of the passage:

> After trimming our boats in the best manner possible, we ran through the shoals before night. When we approached them they had a dreadful appearance to those who had never seen them before. The water being high made a terrible roaring, which could be heard at some distance among the drift-wood heaped frightfully upon the points of the islands, the current running in every possible direction. Here we did not know how soon we would be dashed to pieces, and all our troubles ended at once.
>
> Our boats frequently dragged on the bottom, and appeared constantly in danger of striking: they warped as much as if in a rough sea. But, by the hand of Providence, we are now preserved from this danger also. I know not the length of this wonderful shoal: it had been represented to me to be twenty-five or thirty miles; if so, we must have descended very rapidly, as indeed we did, for we passed it in about three hours. Came to, and encamped on the northern shore, not far below the shoals, for the night.

Ulagu reached out and put his hand on the shoulder of the warrior named Bark, who stood panting from the exertion of his run. "You are sure you have seen Ayasta?"

"Yes. It was Ayasta—I thought at first my eyes deceived me."

"Did you see a child with her?"

"No—she was with a man, the same man who fired at me."

"Was there an amulet on a cord about his neck?"

"If there was, I did not see it."

Ulagu nodded his appreciation to his friend for the startling but welcome information just provided. He did not know how Ayasta had come to be at this place, when according to the late Ned Spratt she was at Joshua Colter's, somewhere on Limestone Creek. While raiding along the Nolichucky, Ulagu had searched for the Colter cabin but had not found it.

Now, finding the Colter place would not be necessary, if Bark was right. Ayasta was within his reach—and surely Wasi would be there too. That Bark hadn't seen the child might mean nothing except that Wasi had been inside the cabin and out of view.

Brecht, half drunk, came rambling up and inquired what was happening. The Tory had been drinking steadily since the battle, which had scattered the Tory/Chickamauga forces rather badly. Only now were they fully regrouped here in a little valley so deep and narrow that it might have been made by the blow of a giant axe.

"We must talk, Brecht," Ulagu said. "We have found Ayasta."

16

"Colter! Joshua Colter!"

The call came a second time from the forest. It was twilight. Joshua, Pont, and Trent were stationed at the cabin rifle ports, while Ayasta stood by in the corner, stoic and dark, and Cooper fretted on his bed, frustrated at his inability to join the riflemen and nearly hurting himself in his thrashing. Already he had yanked down the blanket Trent had hung beside his bed.

Pont and Joshua had left their shelters and taken to the cabin about ten minutes before, prompted by sign of human presences in the forests around—scents, movements in the brush, stirrings among the birds. Joshua, sure the intruders were Brecht and his cohorts, had expected a quick attack. So far nothing had happened, except the twice-shouted cry from the forest.

"Colter!" The cry resounded again. "You hear, you answer!"

"Recognize the voice?" Trent asked.

"No," Joshua said. "It's for certain not Brecht—sounds Indian to me."

Ayasta said, "It is Ulagu."

Joshua turned to her; her gaze instantly flickered away

from him. There was a wall of ice between them. "You're certain?"

"I know the voice of my brother."

Joshua called back out through the gun port. "This is Colter! What do you want?"

A pause, then: "I have come for Ayasta and her son. Send them out and you all will live."

Trent bristled and swore. Ayasta stared at the wall as if she could bore a hole through it.

"There is no Ayasta here, and no child," Joshua said. "You have come to the wrong place. Go away and let's keep the peace between us."

"You lie, Colter. Ayasta is there."

Trent, wrought up, shouted back this time. "You'll not lay your paw on her, redskin!"

Joshua wheeled. "You bloody fool, you've ruined any chance of deceiving them now!"

Trent glowered and spat back sharply, "You think you could run them away from here yelling pea-turkey lies out a rifle hole? If they've seen her they've seen her. There's nothing to do but stand our ground."

Ayasta said, "I will not allow this to happen because of me."

Trent waved a finger at her. "Hold your peace, woman. This won't be decided by you."

A new voice called from outside. "Joshua Colter! You hear me, Captain?"

Cooper made a sudden, vain effort to sit up. "Joshua— that's Elisha Brecht!"

"So it is," Joshua replied. Then, out the port, "I hear you, Brecht!"

"So you know me, eh? Colter, you can believe the word of my friend. Send out the squaw, and you can go home safe to your kin. You spite us, and you'll not live to see your own again. I give my word on both counts."

"Your word is so much dung, Brecht. No one is coming out of this cabin."

Ayasta's eyes snapped. She advanced to Joshua and spoke to him in Cherokee. "Do you make my choices for me, Joshua Colter? I am not atsi nahsa'i to you, for you to decide my life. If I go to them, they will go away. No one here has to die."

"What's she saying, Colter?" Trent asked desperately.

"Shut your flap, Trent." Joshua responded to Ayasta in her own tongue: "You would not save any lives by going to them. Once Ulagu had you he would still attack this cabin."

"No. My brother keeps his word."

"Maybe he does. But Elisha Brecht doesn't. His family and mine are old enemies, and not even your brother's word would stop him from killing me, or Cooper, or anyone else he sees as a Colter, if he has the chance. Ulagu may be satisfied to have you, but Brecht won't go until he has my scalp, no matter what he says."

Ayasta's eyes held a deep fire. "So you are trying to save yourself, Colter?"

"Trying to save us all."

"If I go, Ulagu won't allow this Brecht to violate his pledge. You will be safe. But I tell you this, it's not for you I'm doing this. It's not your life I want to save."

Joshua understood. "So you really are Trent's squaw! You find a thief is a suitable replacement for John Hawk?"

"Why you calling my name, Colter?" Trent demanded, having picked out Joshua's reference from amid what was to him the meaningless noise of the Cherokee tongue.

Trent's question went unanswered. "He is good to me, and a strong man. And what do I care if he is a thief? All unakas are thieves," Ayasta said. "What I do today is not for you to decide. I have no wish to return to my brother, but I will do it to keep Malachi safe."

"Damn it, what are you saying about me!" Trent bleated, thoroughly frustrated.

Joshua continued to ignore Trent. He looked at Ayasta closely and saw in her eyes the firmness of her determination. "Very well, Ayasta. Do what you will, and I won't stand in your way."

"I'm waiting for an answer, Colter!" Brecht called from outside.

"Here's your damned answer!" the agitated Trent yelled back abruptly. He thrust his rifle barrel out the port and fired a blind shot into the forest. It was a foolish move, done in anger and on impulse.

"Now you've fouled it proper, fool!" Joshua declared. And indeed several rifles did speak in answer to Trent's. Weak mud chinking burst in chunks back into the cabin as a ball penetrated between two logs. Abrupt silence followed.

"It's not too late to change your course, Colter!" Brecht shouted. "Send the squaw out, and the boy! You don't want to die today!"

Ayasta headed for the door. Trent came to her, grabbed her arm. "No!"

She looked at him with determination on her face. "Let me go, Malachi."

"You go out there, and like as not I'll never see you again."

"I have no choice."

"We have the choice, all of us! We can fight! They can't best us in this cabin!"

"They will burn this cabin with you in it," Ayasta said.

Pont approached Trent from behind. "Malachi," he said.

"What the hell you want, Pont?" Trent barked impatiently, without turning.

"Let her go."

Trent wheeled, looked into the steady black eyes. "What?"

"Let her go, my friend. She wants to go . . . so let her do it."

"You trying to save your own neck, Pont? What's the matter with you? It's never been your way to duck a fight!"

"We would not win this fight. If we resist, she likely would die with the rest of us. If she goes to her brother, she will be safe, and you might stay alive to get her back again."

"Hell, they'll kill us as soon as they've got her!"

"Maybe they will . . . but maybe not."

"Pont is right, Trent," Joshua said. "It's her decision, and the only wise one."

Trent looked from face to face, then spat between his feet in contempt. "Cowards, both of you!"

Hearing that, Cooper swore and almost came out of the bed, then fell back, groaning.

Joshua shook his head. "I'm no coward. I'll fight here until I die if Ayasta doesn't want to go back. But Pont's right; if we fight, either Ayasta will die with the rest of us or she will be taken anyway. And the truth is she wants to do this—for you. To keep you alive."

Joshua could look in Trent's desperate face and see him mentally scrambling for a way to change what was happening. "It's no good, Colter—they want her boy as well as her, and we don't have him to give them. When they see that, all pledges will be forgotten."

Joshua turned to Ayasta. "Ayasta, you must tell Ulagu your son is dead, and make him believe it. Otherwise he will continue to look for him until he finds him. Innocent ones will die, and all you've done for your son will have come to nothing."

Another call from Brecht came, warning of draining patience. Trent looked helpless; he argued no more. He went to Ayasta and put his arms around her. "I'll come after you, Ayasta. Your brother may take you now, but I'll find you, and I'll bring you back again."

"You must not try," she said. "It would be death for you to follow me. It may be that I will come looking for you this time." She turned to Joshua. "When you are gone from here, tell the God-man Coffman that Judah is now his son. Tell him the Great Man Above has given him a son in place of the one taken from him. Have him raise him as he would have raised his own." A tear formed on the edge of Ayasta's eye and trickled down her face. "Tell him to treat my son as his, to raise him in the unaka language and the spirit-ways of his big book. Tell him that as an unaka, my son will live. In the ways of his father, he would die. I don't know how I know this, but I do know. Perhaps the Great Man Above has revealed it to me."

"I will tell him," Joshua replied solemnly.

Ayasta looked Joshua up and down. "I don't think I will see you anymore," she said.

She turned away from him and back to Trent. Joshua and Pont withdrew and did not watch or listen as man and woman spoke words of parting. Ayasta walked to the door, opened it slightly, and called out the name of Ulagu. He answered. In their native tongue she told him she was coming to him to talk. Then she opened the door and stepped out.

"Ayasta, wait—" Trent said, stepping toward the door. Pont put out a great hand and stopped him.

All was silent as she walked across the little clearing and into the forest. Trent's face was ashen.

"I love that woman," he said in a choking voice, and this time Joshua could no longer deride the idea or attribute Trent's devotion to lust. He still disliked Trent deeply, but one thing was now clear: The man truly loved the Cherokee woman who was now forced to leave him.

Ayasta disappeared into the forest. Joshua thought of how she had changed since coming to him. Her experiences in the white settlements had made their mark on her. She now spoke English almost as well as her late husband had. She understood the daily life, the feelings, the mind of an alien people. But even so, she had never really achieved what she had set out to do. She had never really become part of the white man's world.

The light faded. The men waited. Ayasta returned after the last light was gone. The cabin was intensely dark inside, for the frontiersmen dared not build a fire or light a lamp. Even a feeble light in a besieged cabin at night would betray holes in the daubing, or cracks in the shutters, and endanger the occupants.

Ayasta spoke in a quiet voice: "I have told Ulagu that my son is dead, and he now believes it. He has said again that you all will live, as he had pledged. But none of you can safely remain here any longer. The man Brecht wants to betray his word and kill you all. Ulagu has stopped him for now, but he will not be able to stop him for long. You must leave in the morning. I go now."

She turned away.

"Ayasta," Joshua said.

She looked back at him.

"God go with you."

Silently, Ayasta turned back toward the forest and walked into the darkness and a life she had shunned, but which had come to reclaim her.

As the first light of dawn spilled into the forest, Joshua Colter left the cabin and with axe and knife began making a tandem litter strong enough to bear Cooper's weight. He felt he was in danger every moment he worked, and would remain in danger until out of the forest entirely, for there were unseen eyes that missed nothing. Back in the cabin, Pont and Trent stood watch at the rifle ports, eyes on a forest that looked empty but that surely was not.

Cooper was not yet sufficiently healed and fit for safe travel, in Joshua's estimation, but it mattered no more. There was no choice but to go. To remain here would be to invite and doubtless receive an attack from Elisha Brecht. Joshua worked swiftly, completing his task.

They traveled with few words, feeling they were being watched. One impulse on the part of some hidden Chickamauga or Tory, and their lives could end without warning.

Pont was cautious and somber, Trent sullen but fiery-eyed. Cooper made no complaint as he rode along the trackless route on the tandem litter, which hung between two horses, its support poles on either side of both animals. "Easy, brother," Joshua would whisper to him occasionally, when the horses jolted him. "Bear up until we're safe again."

They made it out of the forest without attack and reached the road that led to Joshua's home. The farmstead was still empty when the men reached it. By now Cooper was pallid and ill, his wounds hurting terribly from the jolting of the litter. Joshua and Pont carried him into the cabin and put him on Joshua and Darcy's bed. Pont built a fire as Joshua made Cooper as comfortable as possible. Then Joshua went to the window and peered out.

"Brecht?" Pont asked.

"Yes. He may have followed us. He surely watched us leave your cabin."

"Reckon we can stay around long enough to see if trouble's coming," Trent said.

"I'm obliged," Joshua replied.

There was little talk between the men. Joshua and Trent remained tense with each other; Trent in particular was on edge. In his movements, his expressions, his silence, Joshua saw the marks of a man with something weighing heavily on his mind. He wondered if Trent would really go after Ayasta, as he had said.

The day passed and no sign of threat appeared. Pont and Trent remained the night in the cabin, then rose and departed the next morning. Cooper was awake again and very sore, but none too bad off for the stresses of the previous day. Trent was as somber as ever, but with an expression of determination on his face. He rode his horse out onto the trail and sat astride it, watching the jays and squirrels in the treetops and looking restless while Pont was still finishing his own saddling. Joshua came to him.

"Thank you for the help you've given my brother and me," he said. He thrust out his hand. Pont looked at the extended hand and smiled with the corners of his lips. It wasn't often a white man extended a hand of friendship to him. He reached out and shook it.

"Good-bye, Joshua Colter," Pont said. "Your brother will be well. There's health in his eye now."

"Where will you be going?"

"With Trent."

"After Ayasta?"

"I expect so."

"It's death to do it. One man, trying to track one woman among the Chickamaugas—"

"Won't be one man. There'll be two."

"No difference. It's the same danger for both of you."

Pont grinned slowly. "Every man has to die some way or another, Joshua Colter." He touched his thick, long fingers to his hat. "Good-bye."

"Good-bye, Pont."

* * *

Hannah stood with her brothers on the bank of the Ohio River, her attention going back and forth between two interesting scenes. To the left was a large cluster of people, mostly men, with Colonel Donelson at the center. They were talking with alternating agitation and solemnity. To the right was her mother, seated upon a cask from the flatboat. Before her was Jesse Clinton, squatted like an Indian with hat in hand and thin hair blowing in the breeze. He was talking quietly to Repentance with a somber, gentle expression.

Hannah did not know what Clinton and her mother were talking about. There was no mystery, however, about the larger group's subject: They were deciding the future of the expedition, whether to go on to the French Lick or to drastically alter the original plan.

The flotilla had arrived just today at the mouth of the Tennessee. The last five days had been tiring but peaceful, with no further Chickamauga harassment. For the Brechts it had been a time for replacing the sharp pain of immediate fear with the full ache of grief. Hannah had cried many tears these five days for her father, cried so many she had none left to shed.

Repentance, strangely, had not cried, though she had been even quieter than usual, and more deeply withdrawn. Then, two days ago, a great change had come over her and she had seemed to toss off her brooding like an unwanted shawl. Yesterday Hannah had even heard her mother singing to herself. It had seemed unnatural to see such a recently widowed woman acting so carefree. It had made Hannah feel all the sadder, and a little disturbed.

Hannah looked across the water. The broad Ohio River was high and rapid, and flowing in the direction opposite to the one the fleet would have to travel to reach the mouth of the Cumberland. So far the boats had been riding along with the current; now they would have to work against it with poles and oars and even sails, though many of the boats did not possess these. The venture would be a terrible ordeal even for rested, strong folk. But the flotilla members were already exhausted, and what was worse, their provisions were almost gone. The talk under way right now was of abandoning the expedition and descending the Mississippi to Natchez, or heading into the Illinois country. Some seemed ready to do that, while those with family members awaiting them at French Lick were naturally against it.

Donelson and those around him were almost violently debating the issue. Hannah noticed Rachel Donelson meandering around the fringes of the group. When Rachel's eye drifted toward Hannah, she smiled and came toward her.

"Hello, Hannah."

"Hello, Rachel." Hannah nodded toward the clump of people. "What is going to happen?"

"I don't know—except I do know that my father will go on to the lick, just as planned. Others, though . . ." She shrugged prettily. Rachel Donelson had an enviable way of doing everything prettily. The girl's dark eyes flickered to Repentance and Clinton, then took on a playful sparkle. "Hannah, is your boatman asking your mother to marry him? He looks just like a dog pleading for a bone!"

The idea of Clinton marrying her mother struck Hannah so ludicrously that she laughed. "Mr. Clinton? What a thought, Rachel!"

That evening Hannah was surprised to learn from her mother that Rachel's insight was correct. Clinton had indeed proposed marriage to her.

Hannah's eyes widened. "What did you tell him?"

Repentance gave a light laugh. "Why, what do you think, Hannah? I told him no. But it was a dear thing of him to do."

"Yes, I suppose so . . ."

"Mr. Clinton believes we will be in a bad way upon reaching the lick, without Solomon." Her brows made subtle motions indicating mild disdain. "It's foolishness, of course. There will be Mr. McSwain there, and I'm sure he will help us until your father comes again."

Hannah thought she had misheard, and when she realized she hadn't, impulsively withdrew a step from her mother and stared at her like she had leper's spots. "What do you mean, until Father comes again?"

Repentance pursed her lips. "Your father brings no end of aggravation to me, Hannah." She leaned forward and spoke in a conspiratorial whisper. "Did you know he is a Tory, like everyone says? He's even passed secrets to your uncle Elisha. He's insisted I keep this from you children, but you are old enough to know, my dear, and if Solomon thinks so little of us to simply run off like this, I'll be thrashed before I'll keep guarding his precious deceptions for him." She nodded brusquely. "So there you have it, dear. When Solomon returns, I'm going to tell him myself that you know the truth. That will surely make him howl, don't you know!" She smiled with satisfaction.

Hannah was devastated. Now she understood her mother's recent abrupt change of mood. The strains and ordeals she had suffered in silence had proven too much for an already unstable mind to endure. Straining under the weight of her loss, she had broken.

Hannah remained to herself the rest of the day, wondering how to deal with this new situation. Should she go to Colonel Donelson, seeking advice? She considered it, but in the end didn't. Donelson was an intimidating figure to her, and was fully distracted already with worries of his own. He would have no time to help, nor any means to do so. And Hannah began to worry that if knowledge of her mother's mental state became widespread, her entire family might be shunned.

So she kept her thoughts to herself, feeling as if she would burst. The worse she felt, the more she longed for Cooper and regretted her decision to leave him.

Meanwhile, she felt sorry for Jesse Clinton, who moved about with a sad expression. Hannah had not had a prior clue that the taciturn old widower had been smitten by her mother. The idea of him becoming her stepfather had initially seemed ridiculous. In light of Repentance's new mental state, Hannah was beginning to think again. Soon she might be glad for any man, even so plain and simple a one as Jesse Clinton, to be willing to see to her mother's care.

In the night, Hannah was awakened by a terrible cry. Sitting up, she discovered Repentance wailing, face buried in her blankets. "He's gone, he's gone, he's gone!" she said over and over again. Hannah knew then that her mother's mind had awakened to the truth about Solomon Brecht once again. Even though it made her sad to see Repentance in such anguish, she was glad her mother's self-deception was over.

But not for good. In the morning, Repentance cooked an extra serving of food, "just in case Solomon returns hungry today." She said it in full hearing of all the children and the two boatmen. Andrew and Perrin rejoiced at their mother's words, thinking their father, incredibly, must be alive. The boatmen gaped at Repentance in astonishment. Holly swore beneath his breath, and Clinton surely thought it was a good thing after all that this woman had turned down his marriage proposal, for she clearly was mad, fit for a barred stone room and bed of rags on the floor.

Hannah called her brothers aside after breakfast and explained the situation. Both boys cried as their newfound, irrational hope was erased, though Perrin tried hard to hide his tears. He was the man of the family now, and ashamed ever to cry.

On March 21, a Tuesday, the fleet set out again for the French Lick, though with a somewhat reduced number. Some had left for Natchez, including one of Colonel Donelson's daughters and her husband. Hannah envied them; this voyage had become so tragic that the very idea of life at the French Lick had become distasteful. As far as Hannah was concerned, the French Lick would have to be as marvelous as heaven itself to make worthwhile such a sad expedition as this one.

The boats went on, propelled by wind and tired, starved muscles. All along the way Repentance Brecht kept her eyes on the shore, a madwoman waiting for her dead husband to appear, and complaining loudly about his thoughtlessness each evening after he failed to do so.

There was no keeping news of Repentance's mental condition from spreading among the voyagers, and before long Hannah found her fears of ostracism being fulfilled. Repentance made people edgy and afraid, like a bewitched woman would, and before long few others had much to do with the passengers and crew of the *Carolina*.

Only Rachel Donelson tried to give comfort to Hannah. She failed, for she spoke too frankly of what she was hearing others say. "They say it's only to be expected that a bastard woman would come to such a state," Rachel said. "They say she was the fruit of sin, and sin destroys the mind."

The voyage went on, days passing in drudgery, each of them ending with the sound of Colonel Donelson's horn as he signaled the halt. They reached the mouth of the Cumberland and turned up it. The final stretch this was, but a long one indeed. The last of the meat was eaten, and Donelson began sending out hunters who brought back mostly buffalo, the meat of which was hard for Hannah to ingest and even harder to digest. She longed for vegetable food, but such was scarce indeed, except for some early growing greens found along the bottoms of the river. "Shawnee Salad," Donelson and others called it, for the Cumberland was sometimes called the Shawnee River.

And so it went, from day to day, and all the while Hannah missed Cooper Haverly more than ever, thinking about him until soon she was hardly thinking of anyone or anything else, as the flatboats pushed on, fighting the current for passage.

The hard winter died at last and spring began to creep across the Overmountain country. The streams ran high and fresh and cold, and in the forests the half-starved wildlife that had survived the bitterest season foraged on new growth and slowly grew stronger and fatter.

In the household of Joshua Colter the spring brought healing and change. Cooper Haverly rallied under the care and feeding of Darcy, soon was on his feet again, and at length was his former self, strong and as determined as ever to join the riflemen who soon would cross the high ridges to help their eastern counterparts in the besieged Carolinas. Cooper never returned to his old home near Colter's Mill; instead he built a half-faced camp in the forests along the Great Limestone.

Cooper had special reason for remaining at the Limestone. As the winter ended, Alphus Colter fell ill, so agued and weak that Sina pleaded and cajoled him into selling out the mill to his brother Thomas and moving onto Joshua's farmstead. The cabin Ayasta had occupied became home to him, Sina, and Zachariah. Zach was ecstatic about the move, for he idolized Joshua and was proud to live on his land.

Thus it was that Alphus Colter finally left the region of the two places that bore his name: Colter's Station and Colter's Mill. Many saw it as symbolic of decline and declared that the old long hunter was about to pass on, that age had finally gotten the best of him. Even Joshua secretly believed his foster father was living his last days. So he and many others were happily surprised when the warming weather brought new strength to Alphus.

Alphus and Cooper began building a powder mill near the river. Meanwhile, Alphus started talking to Joshua of a new dream of his: a joint long hunt, as in the old days. "Just like we used to do it, Josh," he declared. "You, me, horses, dogs, and God's wilderness, where a man can live as he was intended. Coop can come too."

It made Joshua sad to hear Alphus talk that way, for the times were too uncertain to even consider a long hunt. Still, he couldn't bring himself to outright deny the old man, so he hedged and made half promises and hoped that somehow he could fulfill them before Alphus was too old, or perhaps dead.

Despite all this, Joshua was not unhappy. He was glad to have Alphus closer by, glad to have Cooper healthy again, and most of all, glad to fall in love with his wife all over again. He could see, in hindsight, how much Ayasta's presence had harmed his domestic life, and that he had

in fact been on the verge of coming to care too deeply for
the beautiful Indian woman. Israel Coffman's concerns for
him had been more on the mark than he had admitted.
He had come close to falling in love with the woman.

Now it was Joshua's turn to be concerned about Coffman. All was not right in the preacher's life; Joshua knew
his friend well enough to see it.

Coffman had been moved to tears when he learned that
Ayasta had given Judah to him and his wife. He had been
so joyous that he had given Judah a new, meaningful
middle name: Seth. He explained the name to Joshua.
"After Abel's murder by Cain, a second son was born to
Adam. He gave him the name Seth. Judah is to me what
Seth was to Adam: a graceful compensation for a great
loss. I'm thankful for my Seth. But I will call him Judah,
as his mother did."

Despite the happiness Judah Seth Hawkins Coffman
brought to the preacher's home, sorrows visibly haunted
the clergyman. At least Joshua had to assume they were
sorrows. The preacher had always been friendly, talkative,
jovial; now he was withdrawn, somber, and taciturn—this
even after the advent of Judah. Clearly whatever was on
the preacher's mind went beyond grief over the mere lack
of a male child in the family. Joshua knew he was not
imagining the change in Coffman; Virginia Coffman herself talked about it to Darcy, hinting that Israel had
entered some deep personal struggle, the nature of which
she seemed afraid to divulge.

From time to time Joshua would think of the Cumberland voyagers and wonder how they had fared through
their long winter journey. It had been a hard season for
such travel, no question. Had he been in Donelson's
shoes, he never would have permitted the voyage to start.
Of course, there was no way to know the outcome yet; it
would be some months later before Joshua would learn
that on April 24 the flotilla had at last reached the French
Lick, where families were reunited and the weary voyagers settled in for new struggles. The winter had depleted
the forest game, the angry eye of Dragging Canoe re-

mained on the fledgling settlements, and the neighboring Chickasaws were growing concerned as well.

The April 24 date would be an easy one for Joshua to remember, for on that same day Darcy informed him that she was with child, news that both thrilled and sobered him. In a time of war a man could not take lightly the responsibility of a new life.

Especially not with the war taking the bad turn it was. Distressing news came across the mountains. In May came word that Charleston, after a month of siege, had been surrendered to the British by American General Benjamin Lincoln. Reportedly upward of five thousand troops had been captured, seven being generals and almost three hundred being lower officers. Add to that the military supplies seized, and the blow was all the more crushing.

As troubling as news of the Charleston surrender was, another incident soon followed that saddened and angered the Whig frontiersmen even more. Near the end of May, British Colonel Banastre Tarleton, fiery-haired and brash commander of Sir Henry Clinton's Light Cavalry, attacked and sorely defeated a group of cavalrymen and Virginia Continentals in the Waxhaws region of North Carolina. Defeat the frontiersmen could swallow, but Tarleton's actions went far beyond those proper to a victorious military leader.

A hundred thirteen American patriots died brutally at the Waxhaws, hacked, shot, bayoneted, and crushed by Tarleton's men in the most fierce fashion, and this despite pleas for quarter.

The Americans would not forget Tarleton's cruelty, and their cry of "Give them Tarleton's Quarter!" would chill the blood of British regulars and Tory enlistees in battles thereafter, for Tarleton's Quarter meant no quarter at all.

As the British sought to strangle the South, where they hoped to find and arm large bodies of loyalists ready to drive the rebels from their home regions, the rearguard work of backwoods guerrillas and militiamen would only grow more important, and every Overmountain frontiersman knew it. Hopes of peace were, for the moment, to be in vain.

The war would continue, and it would become more than ever a border war, fought by border men.

III

FIRE
AND
SWORD

17

Cooper Haverly wiped the sweat from his brow and tried by will to still the pounding of his heart. His hand was gritty and moist on the stock of his long rifle, and his body was soaked with a perspiration brought on partly by the summer morning heat, partly by the exertion of a twenty-mile nocturnal ride that had begun at sundown the previous day, but mostly by the awareness that death could be one rifle's blast away.

It was July 30, 1780, a Sunday morning, but Cooper had little hope of a sabbath of rest for himself and his fellow soldiers, who stood in a great circle around a fort on the Pacolet River of South Carolina. Cooper studied the fort in the morning light and thought it looked as sturdy as any he had seen in a long time. Built in 1776 as a bastion against the Cherokees, the fort now was in the hands of Colonel Patrick Moore, who commanded a body of loyalists. Thicketty Fort this place was called, named after nearby Thicketty Creek.

Cooper looked around at the circle of riflemen that stretched all around the stockade. A full six hundred of them there were, comprised of patriots under Major Charles Robertson, under whom Cooper had come into service, Colonels Isaac Shelby and Andrew Hampton, and Georgia's Colonel Elijah Clarke. Their combined forces had come to take Thicketty Fort.

Cooper swallowed with a thick and sluggish throat and wished he had a cold flask of water handy. This waiting was agonizing, and even though the patriot force was significantly larger than the loyalist band inside the stockade, a siege of the fort could be bloody, especially if the loyalists were well-supplied.

Colonel Shelby reportedly was hoping that Thicketty Fort could be taken without a battle. But so far the situation seemed to still be moving toward conflict. Earlier Captain William Cocke, a veteran warrior of the Overmountain region, had entered the fort voluntarily to carry Shelby's demand for surrender. Moore had sent him back out with word that the fort would not be surrendered, not even if it meant fighting to the last defender. Moore obviously had more than his share of grit—or so it seemed at the moment.

Colonel Shelby, a man of keen military instincts, smelled a bluff in Moore's defiant pledge. He and his officers had conferred, then surrounded the fort even more completely, tightening the circle slowly until every rifleman was within firing distance of the walls. By now the morning light had risen sufficiently to allow Moore and the loyalists to get a good look at the fearsome backwoods army surrounding them—and, with any luck, change their minds about resistance.

Lord above, make them afraid enough to surrender, Cooper prayed. Let there not be a fight here today, if it can be helped.

Cooper smiled to himself. Here it was, Sunday morning, and he was praying. That was appropriate, he supposed. Most likely there were lots of other men here who were praying harder than they had on many a Sunday morning before this one. Like him, these weren't fearful men, but they were men who loved life and were in no hurry to give it up unnecessarily.

It went on like this for the longest time, until Cooper's muscles ached from holding his position and he began to fidget. He glanced rightward to the man closest to him and started to grumble about the delay, when a stirring among the officers caught his eye.

The fort's gate swung open a short way and a man exited beneath a flag of truce. To Cooper's surprise, the man wore the uniform of a British officer. Might this be Moore himself? The man strode toward the patriot officers, one of whom went out to meet him, bearing no weapon. The officer was taken into the group, words were exchanged, and Cooper saw Shelby nod curtly.

"Lord a'mercy, that's Moore!" someone near Cooper said.

"Are you certain?"

"Indeed. That's the man, and it appears to me he's giving it up already!"

His hopes high, Cooper waited anxiously. Some of the lesser officers fanned out and spoke to the soldiers closest to them. Word quickly passed down the line.

Cooper's neighbor had been right: Thicketty Fort was being surrendered. The frontier riflemen had taken the post without a shot. Cooper joined the others as they advanced forward, lining in behind the officers. They moved toward the gate, which opened to them. The patriots surged in and took prisoners, all of whom seemed thoroughly surprised to see their strong fortress so quickly infiltrated.

Later study of the fort would reveal that Moore's surrender had been unnecessary. Though the defending force was smaller than the attacking one, the fort was so well-stocked with loaded arms that Moore could have held his own with relative ease. In fact, the officers under Moore had wanted to fight instead of surrender, and when Moore had left the fort, that was the message he had been expected to deliver. Instead he had yielded and led in the rebels. No one inside the stockade had expected to see their leader return with the enemy, much less allow its army to march right in.

The final tally would reveal nearly a hundred loyalists had become prisoners upon the surrender, and more importantly, valuable supplies, powder, and ammunition had been taken, along with some two hundred fifty stands of arms loaded with ball or shot.

For Cooper Haverly, however, the most valued thing brought away from Thicketty Fort was his own hide, unpunctured, unbleeding, and still healthy. He had known enough of woundings in his time already—the wounds inflicted by Elisha Brecht in the spring, though healed, still hurt occasionally—and Cooper hoped to make it through to the war's end without further damage to his person.

But he wouldn't run from danger, even to save his own skin. He had volunteered to come across the mountains to fight the British, and fight them he would. He didn't mind admitting, however, that he would be plenty pleased if all the efforts he was involved in resolved themselves as neatly and safely as the taking of Thicketty Fort.

A pleasant dream—but surely no more than that. Cooper was a realist; he knew that today's event was in the realm of exception and not rule. Moore, perhaps, was a coward, but most British officers were not. There were challenges against far more able foes still ahead, and these would not be so easily and bloodlessly met as the challenge of Thicketty Fort.

Cooper had crossed the mountains with Charles Robertson's men, some two hundred strong and taken from the Washington County militia. John Sevier himself had not come; he, like Joshua, had remained behind to defend the Overmountain country against further Chickamauga and Tory depredations. About the time Cooper had left, Joshua had at last completed the stockade around his home, and even had the blockhouse well along, with the help of Alphus and Zachariah. The very day Cooper had ridden out to join Robertson's militiamen, in fact, Alphus had been laboring at the stockade and talking of his anticipated long hunt with Joshua. Joshua had been trying diplomatically to convince Alphus that such a thing couldn't possibly happen soon.

Cooper and about two hundred other Washington

County riflemen had ridden with Charles Robertson to the camp of North Carolina's Colonel Charles McDowell, located on the Broad River at the Cherokee Ford. It was mid-July when they arrived, and near the end of the month, Isaac Shelby and two hundred Sullivan County riflemen had shown up. Major Robertson had yielded command of his own men to the higher-ranking Colonel Shelby.

Every man in the combined forces knew the importance of what they were about. The British, under their new commander-in-chief, Henry Clinton, were in the midst of a major assault on the South, a change of strategy from their earlier plan for overthrowing the rebellion.

That earlier idea had been to divide New England from the middle colonies; this effort had gone awry. Now the British were taking a whole new tack and pinning their hopes on a perceived huge number of secret loyalists in the South, loyalists who King George and his Secretary of State for the Colonies, Lord George Germain, believed could be persuaded to rise and join in a great overthrow of the rebellion. South Carolina, once restored to its proper place as a loyal royal colony, would become the center from which North Carolina, Virginia, and the Chesapeake Bay could be firmly reensconced in British hands.

On June 3, General Clinton had declared South Carolina back under British subjection. For the rebel backwoodsmen, it had been a distressing proclamation.

But for delays caused by Shelby being inconveniently away doing surveying work in Kentucky earlier in the year, the Overmountain militiamen would have probably been on the march far earlier. By the time Shelby was notified and able to return, Charleston had already fallen and the British seemed to be gaining a new advantage in the South.

One of the key British officers in the South was a major whom Cooper had heard extensive talk about. His name was Patrick Ferguson, a Scotsman like Callum McSwain. Unlike McSwain, however, Ferguson came out of the landed gentry class around Aberdeenshire in the Highlands.

Cooper knew little of Ferguson's military career beyond the fact he had been trained as a soldier since boyhood and had been active in battle as early as age sixteen. Supposedly he was a fearless man, a determined aggressor, though not brutal like Tarleton, and an effective maker of the case for loyalism, willing to sit and talk quietly for hours with common American folk, persuading them bit by bit to turn their backs on rebellion. One of Ferguson's main purposes in the South, in fact, was to rally loyalists to arms and train them in warfare.

Cooper was intrigued by all he heard of Ferguson, just as he was intrigued by Dragging Canoe. Capable enemies, he found, were interesting folk. And the thing about Patrick Ferguson that was the most interesting was the remarkable rifle he had developed. The day after the Thicketty Fort surrender, Cooper had learned about the Ferguson rifle from a talkative captured Tory who had heard Ferguson personally discussing the weapon.

The innovative aspect of the rifle was its breech. A plug, attached to the trigger guard, was threaded through the barrel at the breech with a thread that allowed it to be lowered, opening the breech. The trigger guard worked as a swiveling handle for the plug; one quick twist and the breech was opened. Powder and bullet could be loaded quickly—and most time-saving of all, use of a ramrod was unnecessary.

Ferguson, according to the Tory, didn't claim to have originated the concept of the breechloader, but had greatly improved on the work of an earlier French gun maker. In 1776 Ferguson had demonstrated his new weapon before the British Master General of Ordnance, and had proven the rifle's accuracy at two hundred yards. He laid down a steady fire of from four to six shots a minute, sometimes walking while he reloaded.

Some Ferguson rifles had been employed in the war, but had been withdrawn after use at Brandywine, where Ferguson had been wounded, resulting in the loss of most of the use of his right arm. The Tory speaking to Cooper didn't know if the rifle had revealed some flaw, or if the British military had simply been too stubborn to see the usefulness of anything beyond the standard and familiar Brown Bess. Whatever the reason, Cooper was glad the Ferguson rifle wasn't a common British arm; even the best frontier long rifleman wouldn't want to face off with a weapon that could fire accurately at two hundred yards up to six times a minute.

Thicketty Fort's fall was scarcely past before Cooper and his fellow soldiers were once again sent out with Colonel Clarke's Georgia troops. Interestingly, their task was to keep an eye on the forces under Patrick Ferguson himself, headquartered at Fort Ninety-six, so named because of its location ninety-six miles from the Cherokee town of Keowee, which was across from Fort Prince George. In this new assignment, Clarke and Shelby led their men throughout the countryside, looking not only for Ferguson, but also for Tory bands on their way to join him.

On the afternoon of Monday, August 7, Shelby and Clarke halted to rest their men near Fairforest Creek, when intelligence was received indicating an enemy force close at hand. The patriots removed toward nearby Cedar Spring, a better position for battle, and such was soon engaged when British Major James Dunlap assailed the patriots with mounted riflemen and dragoons.

The fighting was fierce and close; Cooper, like many others, became embroiled in hand-to-hand combat. It was a fight he would not forget, for in it he had the first experience in his life of killing a man who was close enough to look him in the eye as he died.

After a half hour of pitched battle, the patriots were forced into retreat, which became a series of small, running fights. Ferguson himself came to Dunlap's assistance and pursued the fleeing Americans, hoping to free the more than two-score British prisoners taken. But Ferguson was to find that pursuing such experienced woodsmen in their own environment was a nearly useless endeavor, and eventually he gave up the chase as the patriots laughed and taunted him from the forests. The patriots regrouped and returned to camp, having lost only four men, but suffering from widespread woundings among their number. Cooper was among these, but his wound was slight: a bayonet slash across the left shoulder. When this was neatly bandaged, Cooper found it little more than a source of irritation.

That night he dreamed of Hannah. They were together in a hillside cabin he had never seen before. A new cabin, built by his own hands, and Hannah was his wife. He awoke the next morning feeling very sad and wondering if Hannah was even alive. Rumor had it the flotilla to the Cumberland country had reached its destination, but not without deaths along the way. It was a terrible thing, not knowing who had died.

The time would come, Cooper thought, when he would just have to go to the Cumberland settlements and find out for himself.

Hannah dreamed of Cooper that same night, but this was to be expected, for she dreamed of him nightly and thought about him almost constantly every day.

Life had not eased much for the Brecht family at the French Lick. Upon arrival, Hannah had felt some relief at finally being free of the flatboat she had come to despise, but the sight of the few meager cabins standing on a cedar-covered bluff overlooking the lick was nothing to generate much excitement.

Hannah had hardly recognized Callum McSwain when she saw him. Thin and wasted, he looked like a man who had been imprisoned and starved for weeks. He had fallen ill back in the cold weather, he informed the Brechts; for a time he was sure he would die. Somehow he had managed to cling to life, and now his strength was returning.

He expressed sorrow upon learning from Hannah of Solomon Brecht's death, then was promptly confused by Repentance's denial of the same. Hannah was faced with the distasteful job of informing McSwain that her mother's mind had become "clouded," as she put it. She expected

McSwain to turn his back on her family at that point, as almost everyone else had. Even Jesse Clinton, once so eager to marry Repentance, stayed far away from her once they reached the lick. But McSwain surprised Hannah. "What's become clouded can become clear again," he said. "She's been through a devil of a time. I'll see to it you all are cared for."

What a wonderful man Callum McSwain was! Hannah was more grateful to him than she knew how to express. Truly he was a godsend.

McSwain befriended the Brecht boys, almost becoming a father to them. And he did the best he could to keep the Brechts sheltered and fed. Without him, Hannah felt sure, the family might have died of exposure or outright starvation.

McSwain built the Brechts a rough but secure cabin on land of his own possession in view of the main fort, which was named Nashborough in memory of General Francis Nash of North Carolina, a fatality of the 1777 Battle of Germantown. Nash had been a close friend of and court clerk to fellow North Carolinian Colonel Richard Henderson, whose 1775 land purchase from the Cherokees had led to this settlement of the Cumberland.

There was a government of sorts for the Cumberland settlements, thanks to the work mostly of James Robertson and Richard Henderson. Adopted in May, by which time the settlements had a population of about three hundred, the Cumberland Compact set the basic rules of government and was similar in content to the document approved by the Watauga-area settlers some years before in their own first days. The compact established a twelve-member court with tremendous authority, obligated all males age sixteen and older to military service, and provided representation for all the eight Cumberland settlements: Nashborough, Mansker's Lick, Fort Union, Bledsoe's, Asher's, Baton's, Freeland's, and Stone's River.

Being a farmer's daughter, Hannah could see why the Cumberland country held such appeal to people of the soil. The land was rich, lined with creeks and rivers, and far more level than the country around the Holston,

Watauga, and Nolichucky. The forests, broken only by occasional Indian-cleared fields or fire-ravaged regions, stretched for miles, but these were fairly easily dealt with either by simply felling the trees or girdling them all around so they died and produced no foliage; and therefore there was no significant shade, allowing for planting around them.

Forests were of the highest quality. Hardwoods abounded: maple, oak, walnut, elm, cherry, beech, and sweet gums that dropped prickly brown balls on the earth, threatening the comfort of any who dared tread on them barefoot. Vast canebrakes lined the rivers. Game included the usual squirrels, bobcats, foxes, raccoons, deer, skunks, weasels, wolves, bears, and the like, along with rich-pelted otter and beaver making their homes in the rapid streams. Around the Great Salt Lick itself roamed buffalo, elk, and other game.

The settlers took advantage of the lick to kill game, particularly buffalo. These died in such great numbers that their bones were heaped at the boundaries of the lick, cane growing among them. Hunters also ranged into the forests for game, but found it rapidly growing scarce because of the population-diminishing effect of the hard winter—and, as they would finally realize, because it was being deliberately driven away from the region by forest natives who were not happy to see the white-skinned newcomers encroaching on their hunting lands.

It was not long after the flotilla reached its destination that Indian trouble began to manifest itself. About forty of the flotilla members had settled at the mouth of the Red River, some forty miles from Nashborough. The settlement became known as Renfro's. In June one of the settlers, Nathan Turpin, died at the hands of Indians, frightening the other residents toward the main settlements of Nashborough and Freeland's. One group of about a dozen, which lagged behind to recover items left in haste, was attacked while still a score of miles out from Freeland's, and all but one of the number were killed. The lone survivor, a woman, wandered several days in the forests and finally arrived in horrid condition at Eaton's, a fort on the Kentucky Road north of the main settlements of Nashborough and Freeland's. A party returned to bury the massacred people at what thereafter was known as Battle Creek. Sometime later, two brothers out looking for good building sites were also attacked; one was killed, and the other chased three miles to safety at Eaton's.

Such events put the settlers on edge and wiped out the early optimism that had derived from reports of no Indian residents within scores of miles. Ironically, the success of such efforts as Shelby's 1779 burning of the Chickamauga towns had actually worsened the situation for the Cumberland settlements. Falling back deeper into safer country, Dragging Canoe and his fellows were now situated where important Indian war paths came together—including the Nickajack Trail, which led straight to the Cumberland country. The more perceptive residents in the Cumberland settlements realized soon that the Chickamaugas could easily isolate them from their counterparts farther east. And as Callum McSwain was quick to point out, the Chickamaugas had every reason to concentrate heavily on the Cumberland country. The Overmountain settlements to the east were old enough to be firmly rooted; the Cumberland settlements, however, were like fresh sprouts that could be more easily destroyed. Dragging Canoe had watched one region be overrun by whites while the Indians faltered, argued, and acquiesced. He would not be willing to do the same again.

Spring had brought a further instigation of the Cumberland region's Indians when Virginia Governor Thomas Jefferson, incorrectly thinking the western Kentucky country was the possession of the Cherokees, ordered the building of a fort on the Mississippi a few miles south of the Ohio River mouth. The country was not the Cherokees' at all, but the Chickasaws', and the construction of Fort Jefferson, as the new structure was dubbed, angered that tribe. Up until then the Chickasaws had been basically friendly to the whites. Now they became hostile, striking the settlers and sending them fearfully into their stockades. Chickasaws had launched the attack on Renfro's and done the Battle Creek killings, but the settlers, harassed by two tribes, often did not know exactly who their enemy was.

Fort Jefferson itself, the settlers would learn in time, suffered a siege that called to mind the 1760 Cherokee siege of Fort Loudoun. For six days the fort was besieged, and when a Chickasaw chief was wounded while bringing a surrender demand to the fort, a massive night attack was instigated. Only the Fort Jefferson swivel guns saved the fort from being overrun, but even so, it was no real victory. The fort was abandoned thereafter, with the aid of the same John Montgomery who had aided Shelby in the Chickamauga expedition of 1779.

On the Cumberland, times were hard and growing harder. Food grew scarce and hunting expeditions dangerous. Grumbling set in, and many talked of fleeing to Kentucky. Hannah herself spoke longingly of that possibility, thinking that from Kentucky it would be no difficult journey to return to Cooper, but McSwain would hear nothing of the idea. "Too dangerous, dear lassie," he said to her. "The Indians are watching the trails, and we can't go into the forests long enough to get sufficient wood for boats. We've got no choice but to remain where we are."

As the summer advanced, the unstable Repentance Brecht continued waiting for the return of her lost husband. Hannah saw her stare out the cabin door sometimes for two hours at a time.

But there was a subtle, most faintly hopeful difference in Repentance now. No longer did she talk about what she was doing when she watched for Solomon; no longer did she declare what a fierce tongue-lashing she was going to give her long-absent husband when at last he returned.

Hannah dared to develop the notion that Repentance Brecht was ever so slowly beginning to realize that Solomon would never return. She prayed it was so, for it hurt deeply to see her mother so lost in delusion.

Hannah was developing another notion as well: Callum McSwain was still strongly attracted to her mother, even in her current mental state. And Repentance, when she responded at all to McSwain, responded tenderly. Hannah even allowed herself to hope that Repentance would agree to marry McSwain—if ever he asked her.

Days rolled by, filled with labor, fear, hunger, and new accounts of Indian forays. Hunters went out only in sizable groups, field workers took turns standing guard, and families trained their mixed-blood dogs, part hound and part mastiff, to smell out and attack Indians.

Through it all Hannah thought more and more of Cooper, and sometimes, almost like her mother, she watched the forests and trails, hoping for the unexpected appearance of one gone from her. She fantasized about seeing him come riding out of the woods, as he had that winter day beside the Holston when she had fled from him. How she wished now she hadn't run!

But someday, Hannah told herself, these troubled times will end. Someday maybe Cooper really will come riding out of the forest, and I will be with him again, never to be parted.

It had been a fine victory, no doubt, and Cooper Haverly was proud of it.

The place was Musgrove's Mill, some two-score miles from McDowell's camp. Intelligence had come that revealed the presence of about two hundred loyalist troops placed there to guard an important river ford—and between them and the Americans was camped none other than Patrick Ferguson himself.

The Overmountain riflemen had volunteered to deal with the situation. Colonel Clarke's Georgians again joined them, and a combined group of about three hundred mounted soldiers set out late in the August day toward the mill, passing in the night within four miles of Ferguson. Cooper had found that passage both frightening and exhilarating, and tried to imagine how the Scotsman would react when he learned his camp had been brushed so closely by the American riflemen.

A small gunfire exchange between scouts made up the first action of what would come to be known as the Battle of Musgrove's Mill. The Overmountain men soon discovered that the anticipated two hundred loyalists at the mill had been reinforced by several hundred others only the night before. The patriots found themselves virtually caught between Ferguson and the loyalists at the mill.

Taking cover along a ridge behind breastworks thrown up from available timber, rocks, and brush, the patriots prepared for battle. As was often the case, there was little time for anything more than rough-and-ready strategy—but this time that proved to be enough.

A portion of the patriot force advanced toward the loyalists, shooting and luring them into crossing the ford to attack. Meanwhile, the remainder of the Americans waited behind the breastworks—waited, as ordered, until they could count the buttons on the uniforms of the loyalists. When they opened fire, the loyalist ranks, which had been advancing to the beating of drums, chanting cheers for King George, felt the results sharply. Cheers turned to cries as red-coated men fell like pins tumbled by a ball.

The battle went on, and though the loyalists suffered under the keen rifle fire of the rebels, they didn't fall back. At one point Shelby's men, Cooper among them, found themselves being driven back by a fierce bayonet charge—and then, by good fortune, British Colonel Alexander Innis, a one-time underling of British Indian agent Alexander Cameron, was felled by a rifle ball. He was merely wounded, but the patriots thought him killed, and this led to a great rally.

Cooper would never forget the nearly animalistic feelings that ran through him as he joined the wild surge of mountaineer patriots as they advanced upon the loyalists, raising the wild Indian-style yell that had panicked many a redcoat. The effect was the same now. Fear struck the loyalists, and when their British officers began falling, wounded or dead, under the patriot advance, the loyalists turned and ran for their lives.

Hundreds of hooves and feet splashed across the river ford. Patriot swords slashed, and rifle balls sang through the air, thinning the fleeing loyalists' ranks even as they crossed the water. By the end of the hour-long battle, the British forces were depleted by sixty-three killed, almost a hundred wounded, and about seventy captured—this compared with only four patriots dead and fewer than ten wounded.

When the fighting was done, Cooper was exhausted but still flushed with excitement. When word came that their force would continue on and attack Fort Ninety-six, he lifted his rifle and cheered hoarsely.

The officers had mounted and were about to lead their forces out when a messenger raced in, bearing a letter. Cooper was close enough to watch him deliver it to Shelby, who read it and took on a most somber expression. He dismounted, and the advance to Ninety-six was halted without immediate explanation.

At length the troops learned the reason. The messenger had been dispatched by McDowell and had brought a letter written by North Carolina's governor, Richard Caswell. In Caswell's own handwriting the letter revealed that General Horatio Gates had suffered a dismal defeat to Cornwallis on the sixteenth in Camden. McDowell was advised to move his position at once, for the British were sure to advance upon him.

The messenger told Shelby that upon receiving the letter, McDowell had started at once toward Gilbert Town, North Carolina; thus the forces from across the mountains were left to decide for themselves the best course of escape.

Shelby stood before his men and announced the decision of the officers. Their force would head immediately into the mountains and, by the most remote route possible, work their way to Gilbert Town and McDowell. "Ferguson will follow and seek to cut us to pieces and regain his prisoners," Shelby said. "We must be swift and stop for nothing."

The wilderness flight was an ordeal Cooper Haverly would never forget. Heading northwest, their prisoners in tow, the patriots moved toward the familiar mountains, all but feeling Patrick Ferguson's breath down their collars. As Shelby had predicted, Ferguson did pursue closely, at one point reaching a point the patriots had been only half an hour before.

There was no time for rest, and hardly any food for beast or man. The fleeing troops subsisted on green corn and peaches, which painfully bound their stomachs. For Cooper, fatigue, heat, and humidity became so intense that his body began to bloat and his face to swell, so that he could barely force open his eyes to see ahead of him. The only consolation he could find was that almost every other soldier around him suffered in the identical way.

Groups of three soldiers were put in charge of one prisoner each. The prisoners were allowed to ride for a time on the horse of each of his three guards. To save further burdening the patriots, the Tory prisoners were required to carry their weapons—minus the flints—through the hot and muggy August weather.

There was scarcely any life left in the patriot army when at last it reached Gilbert Town and rejoined McDowell, who greeted Shelby with relief and happiness. Ferguson had dropped off his pursuit long before, but the patriots had no way to know that. Now that they were safe again, at least for the moment, all they could think of was rest.

Cooper slept the sleep of the exhausted. He felt ill and aged and aching in every joint. The old wounds he had suffered from Brecht and his men throbbed as if they had never healed, and when he awakened again, he felt he had tasted enough warfare to last him the rest of his life.

But it wasn't over yet, and would not be for a long time to come.

18

The Reverend Israel Coffman rode slowly across the flats along the Watauga River, studying the dugout shelters, half-faced camps, tents, and crude cabins that had sprung up here among the more substantial permanent cabins like mushrooms on fertile forest floor. The refugees who occupied these sad shelters were pitiful to see. Ragged, thin, poorly dressed, these people from the eastern side of the mountains had little but their lives and souls to claim as their own. And more came every week, driven here by the war deprivations on the other side of the ridges. And here they were welcomed. The people of the Watauga and Nolichucky opened themselves to the refugees, sometimes taking them into their own cabins, or building them shelters of their own, such as these that Coffman now rode among.

Some of the refugees stared openly at the clergyman as he rode past; these he nodded to, touching his hat. Others would not look at him at all, either staring blankly into the sky or gazing at the ground. These were the broken ones. The ones who had yielded to despair.

I understand despair, Coffman thought. I know the feeling well these days.

He shook his head, unhappy to find himself thinking along those lines yet again. What right did he have to despair over anything? Had not God been good to him, sending Judah to the Coffman family to soothe their grief over the death of their infant? Coffman had a dear and loving wife, a congregation of kind Christian people who showed him every kindness, and a healthy son. What more grounds for happiness did he demand?

Despite such arguments, presented to himself frequently these days, Coffman still knew an unexplainable despair that lingered and even grew. He had suffered low times before, but never one such as this. He wondered from time to time if he was losing his mind. In the silence of night he even wondered sometimes if a demonic force was trying to destroy him.

A ragged man with hollow eyes strode from one of the refugee cabins and up to Coffman, who stopped his horse upon the man's approach. Something about the man put Coffman on edge. He gave a cautious greeting, but the man said nothing, looking him up and down and eyeing the flapped leather pouch on the side of Coffman's saddle. The cover flap was unfastened and had been moving up and down with the motion of the horse, making visible the thick leather-bound Bible the pouch contained.

The man cocked his head, squinted at Coffman, and said, "You a preacher?"

"Yes, sir, I am."

"Aye, I can always tell your kind when I see 'em." The comment bore no tone of compliment. "Tell me, preacher, where is God, anyway?"

"He's present in all places, yet limited by none."

"Do tell! Do tell! You know, I got cause to doubt that, for God sure wasn't there when my son of fifteen years was roasted alive by the damned Injuns across them mountains yonder! If he had been, he'd have stopped it from happening. So you tell me, preacher, where was this God of yours when my son was dying in pain?"

Coffman could only stare at the man. How could he answer such a question?

"I believed in your good and holy God at one time,

preacher, but I believe it no more. If God there be, he's no good one by any terms I know. I don't love no God like that. I despise him."

Coffman wasn't easily shocked by blasphemy; by now he had encountered such in almost every imaginable form. Nor did he usually allow himself to become angered by those who challenged the faith he sought to perpetuate. But Israel Coffman as he was of late was not Israel Coffman as he had been before. Normally he would have felt deep compassion for this tragedy-stricken man. Today he felt only irritation bordering on anger. He didn't want to talk to this fellow, only to get rid of him. And he knew how to do it.

Looking down his nose, Coffman said, "Sir, by what standard do you judge our Creator?" He used the tone of a lecturer in a theological school. "Obviously, by some standard resident in your own mind. But if God is evil, as you charge, then your mind is the creation of an evil being, and you are compelled by logic to reject any standards you discover in it. So you see, my good man, that you have sawed off the limb you stand on when you condemn our maker. You have refuted your own claim. You have built a house only to remove its foundation. You have turned your own words into nonsense, and have wasted both your time and mine."

The man stared at Coffman blankly, as if he had spoken a different language. Obviously intimidated by a manner of speaking that was beyond his scope, he sputtered a little, waved his hand disdainfully, then swore and stomped away. Coffman watched him go and felt satisfied to have rid himself of a nettling pest.

He rode on, and it did not take long for satisfaction to turn to deep regret. What had he done just then, and why? He hadn't even tried to counsel and comfort a man who obviously was in deep sorrow. He had taken advantage of his own trained mind and verbal agility to brush him off as if he were no more than a troublesome fly. A man made in God's image had exposed the most bitter wound of his heart, and he had answered in theological paradoxes that twisted like the riflings in a gun barrel.

It was shameful. Such argumentation as he had given was part and parcel of his private philosophy, but he had never deemed it proper as part of his daily counsel. The frontier people typically were not educated or sophisticated folk; they wanted straight answers they could make sense of, not conundrums that intimidated them away. Grief-wounded people needed love far more than sermons and philosophical play-puzzles. Coffman sighed, marked another failure to his growing list of personal discredits, and rode on.

He had come here today partly to inspect the growing refugee community, and partly to visit parishioners in the settlement. Virginia and Judah were at the cabin of one such family at the moment; Coffman had ridden off alone, wanting time to think.

He approached the property of John Carter, who with his son Landon was building the finest house on the frontier. Tall and double-chimneyed, it stood near the junctures of the Doe and Watauga rivers. Coffman rode nearby, admiring the building, then went on to the river, where he dismounted and sat down on the bank, determined to think and pray through the feeling of despair that was his continual companion of late.

For an hour he sat in total silence, staring into the water. When he stood again, he felt the time had been worthwhile. He was beginning to understand what had him so depressed.

All about him was suffering and discontent—not only among the refugees here, but all across the frontier upon which he had been called to serve. Suffering and discontent were common to those of all races and political persuasions in these warring times. Ayasta had been unhappy and fearful in her life among the Chickamaugas, only to find new troubles among the white people. Alphus Colter was suffering the throes of age, the memory of his own lost son, and the knowledge that his days were passing like water through his fingers. Then there was Joshua Colter, bearing the hard responsibility of leadership and frequent personal danger. Solomon Brecht and his family provided another example, Solomon having suffered much abuse for his suspected Toryism. And all across the frontier, Tories suffered under the lash of patriots, and patriots suffered the torments inflicted by Tory ravagers, British soldiers, and Indians.

And at the root of virtually all of it was the war, the cursed, never-ending, bloody war. It dragged on, dividing people among themselves, making daily life uncertain and dangerous for everyone, and holding no immediate prospect of ending. Coffman thought of all the many militiamen and soldiers who had thrown themselves into danger across the mountains to try to move the war toward an end. Strangely, he envied them in one way. They faced great danger, to be sure, but at least they were actively trying to bring the conflict to a close. They waged war, but their goal was to earn peace.

As a clergyman, Coffman had always seen it his place to be a peaceful man and not to take an active part in violence, unless unavoidable. His primary role was to provide counsel, comfort, and prayer. Though he had fought alongside John Sevier and the other inhabitants of Fort Caswell in 1776, since then he had remained a noncombatant. Like Samuel Doak, he sometimes preached with a rifle within easy reach, but so far he had not actually used that rifle to further the American cause he believed in.

Coffman stood, locked hands behind his back, scuffed his foot in the mud beside the river, and thought about the war and his relative noninvolvement. Surely there was more he could do. But would it be right to actually take up arms? He had a church to serve, spiritual needs to attend to, and suffering people needing comfort. If he were away at war, these would be neglected. He didn't know what to do.

He walked back to his horse, which had wandered off in grazing, and mounted. Riding back through the cabins and refugee shelters of Sycamore Shoals, he felt somewhat better. Even though he hadn't yet found a solution to his despair, at least he had pegged down its source.

He rode back through the refugee hovels, this time not seeing the man he had encountered earlier, and neared the cabin where his family awaited. They were all in the yard and waved as he approached. Virginia was talking to her hosts; Judah, now five years old, was playing spiritedly with a puppy.

Coffman proudly observed the happy boy. Judah had cried much for his mother at the beginning, but now he seemed very content in his new home. Judah was a loving child, handsome of feature but still of delicate health. So gentle and frail was he that it took a great and deliberate effort now for Coffman to remember this child was the son of the fierce, strong John Hawk.

But no longer, he corrected himself. Now he was Judah Seth Coffman, the son, by the gift of God and Ayasta Hawkins, of himself and Virginia. Coffman was fiercely proud of the boy and determined to raise him as best he could.

"Papa!" Judah called, running toward Coffman. "Take me to see the big house, Papa!"

Coffman grinned; he reveled in hearing Judah call him "Papa." The boy was talking about the new Carter house, apparently a subject of conversation in Coffman's absence. "Judah, I just came from there, and I'm not prone to go riding back right away."

"But I want to see it, Papa!"

Virginia looked up, slightly sheepish. "I'm sorry, Israel. I suggested the idea to him . . . and I admit to wanting to see it myself."

Coffman knew he was defeated. "The truth is, I didn't get a close look myself," he said. "Come, climb up behind me. We'll go pay a call on the Carters."

They bade good-bye to their hosts and headed toward the Carter place.

It happened quickly and unexpectedly while they were passing through the refugee camp. A barking dog, a shying horse, and Virginia Coffman was bucked off onto the ground, landing with a loud thump and frightening Israel Coffman terribly.

"Virginia!" He leaped off his horse, leaving Judah in the saddle, and went to her. She had been riding sidesaddle on the horse—Virginia Blanton Coffman always insisted on ladylike propriety in her riding style—and so had been easily knocked from her perch.

Coffman grew even more frightened when he saw that Virginia was straining vainly for breath. Had she crushed her throat or collapsed a lung in the fall? In a moment she began gasping in little struggling breaths, and Coffman realized she had simply knocked the breath out of herself.

For over a minute he gently rubbed her back with one hand and held one of her muddied hands in the other. "You're fine, my dear, fine," he said. "Just let the breath get back in you."

"Not very . . . much a . . . lady," she gasped out.

Coffman smiled. "You're always a lady, my dear. It was the most graceful fall I've ever seen."

Virginia looked around. "Where's . . . Judah?"

Coffman looked back to where he had left the horse and found it and Judah gone. The boy had earlier begged his foster father for the privilege of actually guiding the horse. Coffman, of course, had refused.

Clearly Judah had taken advantage of the distraction to ride off on the horse—and none too trustworthy a horse it was. In fact, Coffman himself occasionally had trouble controlling the beast.

"Judah!" Coffman yelled in great worry. "Judah, where are you?"

"Oh, Israel . . . look . . ."

Coffman followed his wife's indication and saw the horse, riderless now, wandering between two refugee cabins. Around the back corner of one he saw movement. A man exited one of the huts and rounded the corner, joining whoever was back there.

An intuitive wave of dread washed over Coffman. Some of these refugees had come over the mountains with Indians fast on their heels; Coffman had heard dreadful stories of old men being caught by Indians and flayed alive, and boys being burned to death between two fires while their captors danced. These were the kind of happenings that roused such fierce hatred of all Indians in some elements of the frontier, and sometimes made it hard even for a clergyman to maintain a charitable perspective.

And Judah, even dressed as he was, was unmistakably an Indian.

"Please God, no . . ." Coffman ran toward the refugee hovels, his wife staring after him with a look of terror.

Judah was behind the cabin, on his back on the ground, wriggling like a bug on a pin. A man held him there, and another—the same man who had talked so bitterly of losing his son to the Indians—knelt beside him, a scalping knife in hand.

"No!" Coffman roared. He lunged forward, kicking out. The man who held Judah took Coffman's heel flat on his ear. Grunting, he let go of the boy and grabbed the side of his head. Judah wriggled free at once; the man with the knife swore and reached for him, catching him by the tail of his shirt.

"Get back here, you red-bottomed little—"

Coffman was on him in a moment, fists pounding into his face. The man swore vigorously and rolled back, trying to shield himself. The Israel Coffman that acted now was no longer the gentle preacher who had come to the frontier bearing a rifle he barely knew how to use and a mind ignorant of life outside the towns and cities. This was a hardened Israel Coffman, a man whose muscles had become strengthened at hammer and forge. Most of all, this was a primal Israel Coffman who was a father defending his son.

He struck blindly, thoughtlessly, fully intent on killing the man. Blood stained his fists and he kept on hitting. Then others grabbed him from behind and pulled him off. The beaten refugee, whimpering and battered, crawled to his feet and staggered away. Through a buzzing in his ears Coffman heard voices and the sound of his wife in tears. She had come around the cabin in time to see her husband at the height of his fury.

Coffman pulled free of those who held them, pivoted, and faced them down. No one held his gaze; they backed away from him as if he was the reaper himself. He stood glaring at them several moments, panting and covered with sweat, then looked down at his bloody hands. He sobbed out abruptly, loudly, wheeled, and walked clumsily back to his horse. He led it toward the road, his wife and adopted son following. Judah was silent, not even crying, but his faced showed his fear.

The Coffmans rode out of Watauga without stopping, and said not a word to any they passed, or to each other.

Joshua Colter knocked the ashes from his pipe bowl and tucked the pipe back inside his fringed hunting shirt. "It sounds like something I would have done, Israel," he said. "I don't fault you for it, nor do any who have heard about it, from what I know."

"I suppose the word has spread far and wide by now," the preacher said. He was seated on a stump outside his cabin near Jonesborough. It was the second day after the "terrible incident," as Coffman called it, and Joshua had ridden out to see the preacher as soon as he had heard the remarkable story.

"Aye, I think most have heard about it," Joshua replied.

Coffman nodded. "That seals my decision, then. Sunday morning I will resign my position in the church."

"Great day of judgment, Israel! Why do you think you should do that?"

"I almost killed a man. And I would have killed him had the others not stopped me."

"Had it been me instead of you, I don't think any others would have been able to stop me," Joshua replied. "That's no boast of strength, just the truth."

"The point is that I'm a man of God, a man of Christian leadership. What I did was wrong, especially for one who is supposed to present an example of forgiveness."

"Wrong? You think it wrong to defend your own?"

"What I did went far beyond defense. Judah was already freed when I went into that man so fierce. I was trying to punish him. It wasn't protection at that point, but vengeance. And vengeance is not ours, Joshua, but the Lord's."

"You're not an angel incarnated in the flesh, Israel. You're a man, and what you did was what most any man would have done. If you believe you did wrong, admit it to your people and the good Lord, ask pardon, and go on from there."

"There can be no going on, not now. I've sacrificed my right to be a spokesman of the gospel."

Joshua pursed his lips. "I see your mind is made up."

"Yes."

"Will you give up your calling entirely?"

"Not yet—only my activity. For now, to stay active in my work would only bring shame to it, and to my Lord. I need time, Joshua. Time to think and determine what I must do from here on. Perhaps someday I'll feel able to return to the pulpit . . . but not for now."

"How will you support yourself in the meantime?"

"My work in the church brings me little in way of this world's goods in any case," the preacher replied. "I'll keep tilling my fields and working my forge, and make my way like any man among us does."

"I can't see it, you not being a preacher. It doesn't sit right in my mind."

"Nor mine. But perhaps I can yet do good in a different way." He spoke eagerly. "I want to join the militia, Joshua . . . not as a chaplain, but as a fighting man. Not an hour before the incident happened, the conviction had come to me that I needed to be harder at work on behalf of the cause. Who can say? Maybe this was in part the working of God, to allow me to do just that. He uses evil for good ends, you know."

"I'm still not convinced there was any evil in what happened other than the evil that man was trying to do to Judah."

Coffman laughed without mirth. "You know, Joshua, the strangest thing in all this is that I understand how that man was feeling. Indians had killed his son in a fierce way, and the ache of it was so much the poor fellow could think of nothing but harming the first Indian he could find. That happened to be Judah. He was acting out of the same anger that was in me when I nearly beat him to death."

"Israel, you amaze me. I've never seen anybody so bent

on trying to find good in every sorry devil you run up against."

"There's good and bad in us all, Joshua. Which prevails depends on what we choose . . . and now the time has come for me to choose the rifle over the pulpit."

"If you're confident, Israel, you have my best wishes." He extended his hand.

Coffman shook Joshua's hand, and the two men walked back through the cooling September day to Coffman's house.

Joshua thought about what had happened as he rode home. He had known Israel Coffman for several years now, in the capacities both of friend and preacher. Coffman was still his friend, but it would be difficult to grow accustomed to him outside the latter context too. And whether Coffman would really be a feasible militiaman remained to be seen. Though he was full of much more grit than he had been when he first came to the region, Coffman even yet had not been much tested under fire. And fire aplenty he would have to endure as a militiaman, given the turn of the war in the past months.

Cooper and the others under Shelby had returned home cross the mountains sometime after reuniting with McDowell at Gilbert Town. Their brief enrollment of active duty had ended, but the situation east of the mountains remained perilous. Now that Camden had fallen, Ferguson was a greater threat than ever, with his Provincial Corps and Tory militia.

Recently Ferguson had marched his men into Gilbert Town and made it his headquarters. From there he had begun a combination of smooth diplomacy and threat, seeking to strengthen the Tory resistance in the region while sapping the courage of the stubborn rebels. Reports were that men were flocking to him in large numbers to take the loyalty oath. Joshua could only hope most were insincere, seeking to save their necks and property until they could more safely rejoin the rebellion. Lord Cornwallis himself had sent orders to Ninety-six, demanding the imprisonment and property confiscation of all unre-

pentant rebels caught in the subdued districts, and the
hanging of any Tory who was known to have turned coat
and fought against the motherland.

Meanwhile, McDowell's flower was wilting even as
Ferguson's bloomed. After leaving Gilbert Town and suffering a hard blow in battle at Bickerstaffs, he, along with
his one hundred sixty remaining men, had been driven
over the mountains to the Watauga country. McDowell's
stories of wartime horrors on the eastern side of the
mountains were spreading widely, having both bad and
good effects. The bad effect was the terror they struck
into the women, children, and aged; the good effect was
the strength they gave the Overmountain men's determination never to let the British overrun their own region.
Only by men with such determination could the British
be held back, Joshua believed.

South Carolina was again the possession of the British,
and North Carolina appeared doomed to the same fate
unless some major advance could be made. Charles Robertson had told Joshua of the conclusions he, Shelby, and
McDowell had reached prior to the return of the Overmountain men. Whenever the British launched their invasion, almost certainly with Patrick Ferguson at the helm
of it, volunteer forces from east and west of the mountains
would be required to answer it. So Joshua stood ready to
be called out for war at any moment. If Israel Coffman
wanted to become involved militarily in the war, he had
picked a ripe time to do it.

In the meantime there were some happier aspects of
life to momentarily distract the frontier folk from their
worries. One was the marriage of John Sevier to "Bonnie
Kate" Sherrill, a woman he had once saved from Cherokee
captivity, and possibly death, when he pulled her over
the stockade wall at Fort Caswell at the beginning of the
Cherokee onslaught of 1776. True to form, Sevier was still
celebrating the wedding, even though it had taken place
the previous month. A standing invitation was out to all
his friends to come by his Nolichucky River home and
enjoy food, horse races, conversation, and liquor. Joshua

had it in mind to answer that invitation very soon. He needed a good celebration.

At times like these a man needed diversion—and on all the frontier there was no one better suited to provide it, nor more enthusiastic in doing so, than the sparkling John Sevier.

Joshua had invited Cooper to accompany him to visit Sevier, but Cooper had declined with vague excuses. He had things to do, and things to think about.

A certain female to think about, more likely, Joshua had thought. He was convinced that Cooper had not forgotten Hannah Brecht, as much as he pretended he had. Cooper was too moody anymore for Joshua to believe otherwise. If anything, Joshua had it figured, Cooper's battle experience in Carolina had made him think more seriously than ever about his life and future, and how he wanted to spend it. War had a way of doing that to a man.

Alphus hadn't declined the invitation. The old long hunter had fairly leaped from his chair when Joshua had winkingly asked him to come along for some manly celebration with Sevier. Now foster father and foster son rode side by side along the road to Sevier's home on the river.

"They say the Chickasaws are fretful in the Cumberland country," Alphus said. "If not for that, we'd take out for that hunt of ours this very winter—just me and you."

Joshua replied, "Alphus, I don't reckon I could go this year, Chickasaws or no Chickasaws. It's likely to come to fighting before the new year comes."

"By Joseph, Joshua, you take the sour side of everything. This Ferguson, he won't cross them mountains for a ragtag bunch like us."

"This ragtag bunch might be of more interest to him than you give credit for," Joshua replied. "Over in the east they're pledging loyalty to King George as quick as they can queue them up. Over on this side we're still rebellious. Ferguson won't sit still for it."

"Well, if it comes to fighting, I hope it comes soon and gets done with," Alphus said. "I'm set on us making that long hunt together, and every year that passes these old bones get stiffer. Lately the winter wind cuts through me like a fish through the water. Give me another year or two and I might not want to do anything more than sit by the fire, like Sina wants. And you'll have missed your chance for a ripping good hunt with old Alphus, by Joseph."

Joshua grinned. "I wouldn't want that to happen. But I'm not worried. There'll be ice in July before you take to the fireside and the whittling knife, Alphus."

The old man smiled, but said nothing. Joshua wondered if Alphus had found his last statement patronizing. The truth that both men knew was that Alphus indeed was getting more feeble, and in another few months might not be physically able to go on any lengthy kind of hunt at all. It was terrible to think of, and made Joshua feel helpless. Curse the war, and the way it fouled the things a man needed to do, even things as simple as going on one final hunt with an old man whose happiness seemed to depend on it!

They rode until they were within a mile of Sevier's on the Nolichucky, when Joshua halted and turned his head. "Hear it?"

Alphus's hearing wasn't what it used to be, but in a couple of moments he picked out what Joshua had: hoofbeats on the dirt road behind them. A lone rider, from the sound of it, and moving swiftly.

Joshua and Alphus turned their horses to face the oncoming rider, not wanting any unhappy surprises. Both were amazed when around the bend came a familiar but unexpected figure astride a big black mount. The rider saw them, reined in, and stopped. Joshua advanced toward him.

"Isaac Shelby, what in blazes brings you all the way down to the 'Chucky?" Joshua asked.

Shelby smiled and stuck out his hand for Joshua to shake when he was close enough, but his smile didn't linger. From the look, manner, and smell of Shelby and his mount, Joshua could tell he had been riding hard for a long way.

"I've got important business with Sevier, and I hope to

high heaven he's not away from home," he said. He glanced past Joshua. "Hello, Alphus."

"Hello, Isaac. How's your father?"

"Well enough, under the circumstances."

"What's wrong, Isaac?" Joshua asked.

The man looked solemn, then glanced around. "Here is not the place to discuss it. Come with me to Sevier's, and I'll tell you there. You'll be among the first to know something that very soon will be the talk of this country all around."

Joshua had a suspicion already of the nature of what Shelby was going to reveal. He nodded curtly. The three men rode together toward Sevier's house, from which came the sounds of merriment and celebration.

"Listen to that now, while it lasts," Shelby said grimly.

"What do you mean by that, Isaac?" Alphus asked.

But Shelby would say no more.

19

Sevier was in an expansive, smiling mood, and welcomed his three visitors into the yard of his home with typically graceful enthusiasm. Joshua and Alphus gave their greetings and congratulations on his marriage; Isaac Shelby did the same, but in a most sober and distracted attitude.

"Come aside, John," he said. "There's something we must discuss." He glanced around at the revelry of Sevier's ongoing celebration. At the moment a horse race was in progress, drawing whoops and cheers from the several gathered to watch it. "This jollification is hardly proper in light of what I have to present."

Sevier studied Shelby, then summoned one of his sons. "When the race is ended, thank all who came, give word that I've come upon pressing business, and declare the celebration over . . . for now," he said.

Sevier and his visitors retired to the interior of the house; there "Bonnie Kate" Sevier was busy, the very queen of domesticity, repairing a tear in one of her husband's many hunting shirts. Like Joshua, he wore such rustic garb almost continually—and, unlike Joshua, had a way of making it look absolutely elegant.

A few quiet words from her husband, and Katherine Sevier retired from the room, leaving the men alone. Sevier was about to offer refreshment, but Shelby was in such a rush to speak he gave him no time.

"I've ridden forty miles with no rest to speak of to deliver my message," he said. "It came to me at Sapling Grove, borne by Sam Phillips—he's a kinsman of mine, and recently a prisoner of Ferguson."

"Ferguson? By Joseph!" Alphus said, anticipating what came next.

"Ferguson has sent us a direct threat," Shelby went on. "He paroled Sam to bring it to me. In short, he's ordering us to lay down our arms, swear allegiance to the king, and resist the British no more—else he'll march across the mountains, lay the land waste, burn our homes, seize our crops, and hang every last mother's son of those of us who have led in the rebellion. He would strike us with 'fire and sword'—his very words."

A few moments of silence followed, a time for hot rage to rise inside each man. Sevier swore beneath his breath, and Joshua said, "It would seem the time has come for something to be done by us before it's done to us."

"Exactly so," Sevier said. "We've anticipated just such an event as this—the only question was when it would occur."

"So what's to be done?" Alphus asked. Joshua could detect how angry Ferguson's threat had made the old man.

"It seems clear enough to me," Sevier replied. "We gather every available man from as many quarters as possible, march over the mountains, and surprise Ferguson at Gilbert Town. We'll need not only our own men from hereabouts, but those off the Clinch under Colonel Campbell, McDowell's force as well, and any others we can muster up."

"I agree, but such a thing will take money," Shelby said.

"Then we'll obtain it."

"How? Every bit of ready money in the region has gone into lands."

"Then I suggest we pay a call on the entry-taker and obtain a loan."

"I doubt such a loan is legal."

"The law was made for our service, was it not? We'll do what must be done."

"And what if our surprise should fail?" Alphus asked.

"We can't consider failure."

"I've lived many a year, John, and have learned you must consider all possibilities.

Sevier smiled. "Very well, Alphus. If we failed, and I remained alive, I think I would build myself a boat, float down the rivers until I reached the Mississippi, and from there head into Louisiana to cast my lot with the Spanish. I'll not live under the British thumb, come what may."

For a long time the conference continued, every aspect of the needed campaign coming under discussion. Powder would be required, and Alphus Colter quickly volunteered to do his part in providing it, estimating he could generate at least four hundred pounds of high-quality gunpowder from his new powder mill, to be provided at cost and on credit to Colonel Sevier. Other similar mills across the region could be counted on to produce a good share as well, the men felt sure.

When Joshua, Alphus, and Shelby left Sevier's, plans were firmly afoot, but with uncertainties remaining. Despite Sevier's confidence, the question of financing the expedition still loomed. Further, it was not clear whether military leaders from Virginia would be willing to furnish troops and leave their own frontier more vulnerable. A similar problem would be faced along the Watauga and Nolichucky, for to remove a substantial number of fighting men might tempt the Chickamaugas to strike. Even the subdued Overhill Cherokees might become warlike in the face of such an opportunity.

Uncertainties there were, but also one certainty: If Ferguson was left unanswered, there would be a dear price paid for it. Joshua had no doubt the Scottish major meant what he said, and under no circumstances could the Overmountain people run the risk of Ferguson's "fire and sword."

* * *

The days following were busy ones across the Overmountain country. Word of the coming expedition against Ferguson spread through the regular channels and from neighbor to farflung neighbor. Mills began grinding the new harvests of corn to provide food for the outgoing army. Over in Colter's Station, Thomas Colter was so busy with milling and Colter's Mill that he had to close his store temporarily.

One date was frequently on the lips and minds of the Overmountain people: September 25. On that day the great muster would occur at the Sycamore Shoals of the Watauga, in the vicinity of the camps of Colonel Charles McDowell and his refugees. McDowell himself would not be there; after receiving word of the approaching campaign, he headed back over the mountains to seek intelligence of Ferguson's recent movements, to spread word of the campaign, and to help gather in a force of men under strapping Colonel Ben Cleveland, of Wilkes County, North Carolina, Cleveland already having been notified by an express of the plans. For reasons of practicality, Cleveland's men would not join the troops at Sycamore Shoals, but farther along in the march.

Colonel William Campbell, of Washington County, Virginia, was also contacted and asked to participate in the campaign. At first he demurred, not thinking the plan the best option, but upon later urging changed his mind and agreed to unite half his county militia with Sevier and Shelby's force. Concurring in the decision was Colonel Arthur Campbell, brother-in-law and cousin of William Campbell.

A great spirit of aggression spread throughout the settlements, largely because of the pitiful stories told by refugees, and the frequently mentioned atrocities that had occurred under Tarleton at Waxhaws. Even Darcy Colter, ever fearful of being widowed through battle, seemed relatively agreeable to this campaign—especially after Sina Colter told her she had dreamed of Joshua and Cooper walking together over a hillside and returning home, a portent that the two would be kept safe, in her interpretation. Darcy trusted Sina's dreams, which had seemed remarkably revelatory at various times in the past.

Sevier, meanwhile, found money hard to come by. John Adair, the entry-taker who represented North Carolina in sales of the state's lands, proved, as hoped, to be the financial salvation of the mission. Informing Sevier that he had no legal right to turn over such treasury monies for any purpose, he nevertheless did it. "I dare not appropriate a cent of it to any purpose, but if the country is overrun by the British, our liberty is gone. Let the money go too. Take it. If this money helps drive the enemy from the country, I trust that will vindicate what I've done," he said. Sevier walked away with more than twelve thousand dollars.

Meanwhile, Alphus Colter was so busy with powder-making that it seemed to strip the years from him. Joshua rejoiced at seeing such activity and purpose in a man who had been expected to die mere weeks before. "He knows he can't go into the fight himself, so he's sending the powder to represent him," Sina told Joshua. "He swears this will be the finest powder he has ever made."

Alphus had located his mill near the river and not far from a well-hidden cavern Cooper had stumbled across the previous year. High on a bluff overlooking the river, the cave had been the abode of bats "since the days Adam run bare-bottomed through Eden," as Alphus colorfully put it. Its floor was therefore heaped with droppings from which saltpeter could be derived. Alphus, helped by Zachariah, spent several days gathering soil from the cave floor and hauling it back to the mill. There it was mixed with ash and washed through with water. The same water went through the mix time and again until at last it was rich with nitrate and salt. When it was boiled down, the crystalline leavings were a highly impure saltpeter.

Alphus refined this by carefully regulated boiling in several large iron kettles. The boiling resulted in some impurities rising to the top and others settling to the bottom of the kettles. Skimming the floating layers and

scooping out the bottom ones left a purified solution of
saltpeter, and this, when boiled down, deposited the
desired compound pure and crystallized in the kettles.

Along with saltpeter, the required elements of gunpowder were sulfur and charcoal. Alphus drafted Cooper and
several locals into charcoal-making service, an activity as
undesirable as it was necessary. Joshua begged off by
citing the necessities of preparing the militiamen—an
honest excuse he was glad to have available, for he hated
charcoal-making even more than he hated harvest.

Alphus ruled over the process with the authority of
experience. All around his mill huge stacks of timber were
placed in rounded, peaked mounds, which were covered
carefully with sod, leaving a single smokehole at the top.
Burning coals were dropped into this hole, and the coal
makers settled into the drudgery of watching the smoking
mounds, and heaping dirt onto them whenever fire broke
through the sod. The job was dangerous, especially if the
fire came through high on the stack, for this would require
the repairer to climb onto the mound itself and risk falling
through into the hellish heat below. Alphus generally
insisted on making the repairs himself. "I'm old," he
would say. "If I get roasted it's not nearly the loss it would
be if one of you young ones went through."

The third ingredient, sulfur, was conveniently obtained
by Alphus from his brother. In Carolina, Thomas Colter
had managed through a seaboard connection to obtain a
large supply of French-refined sulfur that had come in by
importation after the outbreak of the Revolution. He had
brought the sulfur with him when he migrated over the
mountains to Colter's Station. Alphus had been drawing
on that supply in piecemeal fashion in a smaller powder
mill near his grist mill; now he had Cooper obtain every
grain that Thomas possessed and haul it by horse cart to
the new and larger mill on the Nolichucky.

Alphus mixed his gunpowder with three-quarters saltpeter and twelve and a half percent each of charcoal and
sulfur. After the powder was mixed, a small amount of

water was added, and the powder was stamped with an ingenious water-driven pestle that operated on the lever principle. On one end of the lever, which rocked in a frame rooted in the ground, was a free-swinging pestle that was lined up to drop into a mortar hollowed from a log section. On the other end of the lever was a water box beneath a flume. As water filled the box it descended, dumping its contents and rising again, thus causing the pestle on the other end of the lever to descend heavily into the powder mortar. Under Alphus's tutelage, Zachariah became adept at keeping the powder just wet enough to be safe, and at judging when the several hours of stamping had done the job.

Alphus himself handled the next and final step of graining. Taking the moistened powder from the mortar, he forced the powder through a mesh-bottomed container atop a tub, using a stone roller to grind the powder through the mesh, which created a powder of the proper grain size for use in long rifles. Cannon powder was of larger grain, pistol powder smaller.

Lacking a drying house, Alphus relied on a simple drying table to remove the water from the powder. The large table was built in a sunny area and covered with cloth upon which the wet powder was poured. Alphus kept a close eye on the weather for any hint of rain or high wind that could blow the powder away, and watched his product until it reached the perfect stage of dryness. Then the powder was placed in barrels and delivered to Joshua, who stored it carefully for later distribution to the militiamen.

Joshua was proud of his foster father's work, which exceeded even his promise. In the end Alphus produced just over five hundred pounds of powder, which though "rough," or unglazed, was of high quality and would serve the Overmountain riflemen well when they reached Ferguson.

Completion of the task brought a change to Alphus, however. He seemed to age again, and to grow sad with the realization that his involvement in the effort was over.

Joshua tried to cheer him by reminding him of the importance of keeping good riflemen on the homefront, to
guard against attack by Indians who might take advantage
of the absence of high numbers of militiamen, but it had
little effect.

Darcy, well along in her pregnancy now, put up a good
front of courage as September 25 drew nearer. Only the
last nights before the muster did she shed any tears, and
these she hid. Joshua saw them but pretended not to, for
Darcy was easily embarrassed.

Joshua's relationship with his wife had grown much
more loving and intense since the departure of Ayasta,
and he included a word of thanks for that in his nightly
prayers. Still, he thought about Ayasta sometimes, wondering how and where she was. Somewhere in what had
come to be called the Five Lower Towns of the Chickamaugas, most likely. These towns, lower on the river and
more remote than Dragging Canoe's previous refuges,
were surely a world far from the one Ayasta had been
living in here on the Limestone. He wondered if she
regretted trying to become part of the unaka world. Or
maybe she regretted having been forced to leave it. Most
likely he would never know. He would probably not see
Ayasta again, as she had predicted.

Joshua, Cooper, Alphus, Darcy, Will, Sina, and Zachariah set out for Sycamore Shoals the day before the muster.
As they traveled, their party joined with those of others
also bound for the Watauga country. The gathering before
the departure of the soldiers would be the largest congregation on the Watauga flats since the great festival and
negotiation surrounding Richard Henderson's 1775 land
purchase from the Overhill Cherokees. Despite the battle
that loomed ahead, a certain levity marked the journey to
the muster site. At Sycamore Shoals, Overmountain people who seldom saw each other would be briefly united.
There would be time for talk and laughter and horseplay,
maybe even a horse race, a wrestling match, or a tomahawk throw competition or two. If nothing else, it would
be a fine day for children and dogs, the two classes of
creatures most excited by big gatherings.

Passing through Jonesborough, Joshua's party headed on to Israel Coffman's house. The former preacher, whose congregation had been stunned and saddened by his abrupt recent resignation, awaited the travelers. Gathering up his rifle, food wallet, powder horn, and horn cup, he kissed Virginia good-bye and gave Judah a long hug. Then he mounted and rode to Joshua's side. Tears glimmered in his eyes.

"There's no need for you to go, if you don't want," Joshua said. "Colonel Sevier, quite honestly, is reluctant to have you along as a fighting man in any case. He believes you'd best serve as a chaplain."

"No. If I go, I fight."

They rode on, and where the road bent to take them out of view of the house, Coffman turned and waved to his wife and adopted son. They waved back. Coffman looked at them a long time, then faced forward again and rode out of their sight.

"I'm never going to see them again," he said to Joshua in a tightening voice.

"Don't talk that way," Joshua said sharply. "It brings ill luck."

"I'm a man of faith, not superstition," Coffman replied.

"Then you don't know you won't see them again, do you?"

Coffman wiped his sleeve across his eyes. "No, I suppose I don't." He paused. "But I feel in my bones that . . . never mind. Never mind."

They went on in silence broken only by the noise of travel, and Alphus humming an old English tune behind them. Joshua and Coffman pulled up ahead of the rest, out of easy earshot, and Joshua ventured a question: "Virginia didn't want to come with you to the muster?"

"No. She doesn't favor what I've done in leaving the pulpit . . . and especially in taking up arms. She says nothing good will come of it."

Joshua replied, "It's common for the women to fret."

"I suppose it is."

They neared Sycamore Shoals by dark and made their

camp. All around, the light of dozens of cookfires lit the countryside—the fires of other travelers on their way to the muster. Darcy complained of not feeling well because of her unborn one, and ate little supper. Joshua figured it was more worry than anything else that had her distressed.

The next day the party rode into a scene so remarkable that none of them would ever forget it. All over the flats were men in broad hats and militiamen's fringed hunting frocks, carrying their long rifles and outfitted with pouches full of parched corn and maple sugar, the most common, filling, and nourishing repast of those going on long hunts or frontier military expeditions. Parched corn, which would expand in the stomach and create a lasting feeling of fullness, had kept many a man alive in the wilderness for weeks at a time.

Joshua hadn't seen so many horses in one place in many a year, for horses were becoming precious commodities on the frontier because of Indian raids. He, Coffman, and Alphus moved through the gathering, admiring the best of the horses and shaking their heads when they saw some of the sadder animals that a few had to make do with.

Most of the gathered frontiersmen carried a cup—in many cases made from a horn, like Coffman's—that hung either from their belts or saddles. To the man they carried belt axes, knives, and powder horns, in addition to their provision pouches. On the saddle of each horse a rolled blanket was tied. Beyond these goods the Overmountain men would carry little, for excess baggage would be nothing but an encumbrance once in the mountains. And many of the men had no horses. These in particular could not afford to be heavily burdened.

A herd of beeves was to accompany the men to provide fresh meat along the way; other meat would come from the wild game of the forests. Joshua had his doubts about the beeves, knowing the rugged terrain the Overmountain men would have to trek across.

The twenty-fifth passed with conversation and the rallying of spirits. Overall the mood was bright, declining only about sunset, when all present began to consider that it was all but certain that some who set out into the wilderness the next day would not return. Coffman seemed particularly somber, and Joshua remembered the preacher's prediction that he would never see his family again. Joshua could only hope Coffman wouldn't brood so that he unconsciously caused his own prophecy to be fulfilled.

The next morning the army gathered, surrounded by the civilians, and watched as the Reverend Samuel Doak mounted a stump to give a final word to the men before they departed. The stern-faced Presbyterian's voice was easily heard by all the sizable group: two hundred forty men from Washington County under John Sevier, the same number under Shelby from Sullivan County, and a full four hundred under William Campbell out of Virginia, along with the hundred sixty members of Charles McDowell's band, who had been already on the Watauga. Others were anticipated to join along the way.

Doak's speech was both lofty and direct. "My countrymen, you are about to set out on an expedition which is full of hardships and dangers, but one in which the Almighty will attend you," Doak declared. "The Mother Country has her hands upon you, and takes that for which our fathers planted their homes in the wilderness, our liberty."

Doak went on to decry the familiar realities of taxation without representation and the forced quartering of soldiers as evidence of the crown's determination to remove the "last vestige of freedom" from the Americans. Carolinians across the mountains were "crying like Macedonia unto your help," Doak told the men. "God forbid that you shall refuse to hear and answer their call."

But the oppression already under way across the ridges was not the sole factor drawing the Overmountain men to battle, Doak declared. "The enemy is marching hither to destroy your own homes." The reminder brought a murmur of martial anger from the assembled riflemen. Doak was doing a fine job of rallying the fighting spirit that would be essential for victory.

Citing the bravery of the assembled warriors, Doak noted they had "wrested these beautiful valleys of the Holston and Watauga from the savage hand." There surely could be no shirking from going forth now to fight the new challenger across the mountains.

Doak then called the assembly into prayer, asking divine protection upon the rough-hewn army that would in minutes set forth, and protection from both "savage" and "tyrant" for the homes they would leave behind.

"Thou, who promised to protect the sparrow in its flight, keep ceaseless watch, by day and by night, over our loved ones. The helpless women and little children, we commit to Thy care."

His voice rose as Doak continued: "O God of battle, arise in thy might. Avenge the slaughter of thy people. Confound those who plot for our destruction. Crown this mighty effort with victory, and smite those who exalt themselves against liberty and justice and truth."

Doak lifted his head and opened his eyes. "Help us as good soldiers to wield the sword of the Lord and of Gideon."

From hundreds of throats the cry returned to the preacher: "The sword of the Lord and of Gideon!"

When the Overmountain men rode out in the rising light of morning, Alphus Colter cried like a child.

The cattle proved as much a burden as Joshua had expected. The army had hardly made it a mile before it became apparent the beeves were in no mood to be rushed. "Reckon I'd lag too if I was being took along to be et," Joshua wryly told Coffman and Cooper.

By the middle of the day they had gotten no farther than Matthew Talbot's mill, which stood on Gap Creek about three miles from the shoals. Crossing the Little Doe River after their meal, they finally reached Shelving Rock on the Big Doe River, having now covered twenty miles in the first day. Wearied, the men made camp for the night. A few had horses shod by a nearby resident eager to lend his help to the expedition.

By the next morning it was evident that the cattle would

do nothing but hamper the journey. Some of the cattle were therefore promptly slaughtered and the meat packed up for hauling. The supply wouldn't last long, but would be welcome fare as long as it did.

Upon reaching Bright's Trace, which passed between two looming mountains, the Overmountain men ascended into a cold and snow-covered mountain country of wild beauty. Atop the range was a bald upon which the men paraded and fired off their rifles, their reports remarkably weak in the thin mountain air.

Coffman had brightened considerably since actually starting the journey, and laughed and joked readily as night fell and the men made camp on the cold mountain. "I'm not so dour about my prospects now," he told Joshua. "In fact, I'm somewhat embarrassed by the way I spoke before . . . the talk about not seeing my own again. I have a better feeling about this effort now, and fully plan to return from it alive."

"A good ambition," Joshua said, puffing his pipe. "Keep it in mind all the way through and it will serve you well."

The next morning, the Washington County troops found their colonel pacing about, face set in anger. Joshua approached Sevier and asked what was wrong.

"Treason, I fear," Sevier said. "Two of our number, Sam Chambers and James Crawford, are gone. They've been sought high and low and there's no mistake—they aren't here."

Israel Coffman had strode up in time to hear what Sevier had said.

"What does it mean, John . . . pardon me—Colonel Sevier? Might they have deserted to go back home?"

"I'd like to think it was only that, but I'd bet my immortal soul—now it's your turn to pardon me, Preacher—that they've betrayed us."

"Tories?" Joshua asked.

"Indeed," Sevier replied. "I'm convinced the pair of them have gone ahead to warn Ferguson."

20

The desertion and suspected treachery of Sevier's two men caused a change of plans for the traveling army. With Sevier at the lead, the force made its own trail and took a new route off the mountain, fearing spies might already have been sent to watch the originally planned route of descent. It was crucial that the patriot army not be intercepted before they connected with the reinforcements they were scheduled to take on along the way.

The descent was difficult for both men and horses, and took up most of the day. That night the army posted guards and camped on a tributary of Roaring Creek, and the next day continued through wildly scenic, autumn-painted mountain country down to the North Toe River. Along the Toe they found a cool spring, beside which they rested and ate a midday meal. Their advance continued thereafter until they reached Cathey's Mill at the mouth of a North Toe tributary called Grassy Creek. After a meal of parched corn and beef, they slept.

September 29, a Friday, found the army moving up the Grassy Creek valley, through Gillespie's Gap, and into view of the headwater region of the Upper Catawba River, where settlements were visible in the wild and tangled country. The force divided, the six-foot-six Campbell taking his men to camp at the homeplace of one Henry Gillespie, an Irishman after whom the gap was named. Gillespie, suspected of loyalism, was held in camp and questioned about any movements of the British in the area, but knew nothing worth the telling and was released the next day.

The rest of the troops had proceeded east to the North Cove above the mouth of Hunnycut's Creek. Colonel Charles McDowell rejoined the group there, from his Quaker Meadows home on the route ahead. He reported that since leaving the Watauga he had made extensive contact with regional military bodies about the campaign against Ferguson, but had gained only a little intelligence about Ferguson's position and strength. He knew only that Ferguson remained about Gilbert Town.

The most welcome news brought by McDowell was that Colonel Ben Cleveland and Major Joseph Winston were en route to join the Overmountain men with more North Carolina troops. Additionally, troops from South Carolina were also on their way. It would be a sizable fist indeed that would smite Patrick Ferguson.

Cheered by prospects of reinforcement, the troops at North Cove moved on the next day and reunited with those who had diverted to Gillespie's. The combined force was near Quaker Meadows at this point, where both the McDowells, colonel and major, resided. They moved on eagerly.

Exhausted upon reaching Quaker Meadows, the troops camped on the McDowell property, burning fence posts in their campfires with the full permission of the McDowells. Some of the men had traveled more than thirty miles that day, so the McDowells' generosity was particularly welcome.

Cleveland's and Winston's troops arrived to join the patriots at Quaker Meadows. Almost fourteen hundred strong now and close enough to Ferguson to smell him, the army anticipated action soon.

The first day of October fell on a Sunday and began

with the clear sparkle of a beautiful autumn dawn. In the afternoon, however, rain clouds rolled in over the hills. By the time heavy showers set in, the combined forces had advanced to the landmark Pilot Mountain, which they passed before making a soggy camp for the night.

Rain continued the next day, muddying the land and keeping the army motionless. The officers took advantage of the delay to settle a question that had been pending from the outset: the overall leadership of the campaign. This was no single, unified army, but a collection of individual units with loyalties to different regions and officers. It seemed prudent, for the sake of cohesion, to bring the command to a head before actually engaging Ferguson.

After extensive discussion, Virginia's Colonel Campbell was selected on the logic that he was the only feasible candidate who was not from North Carolina. To select one of the Carolina officers would likely cause bickering and jealousy between the Carolina troops, who already were restless and crotchety after a day of waiting in the rain.

Technically, the selection of a main officer was only a temporary expedient. To fill the command properly would require an appointment by the chief commander, General Horatio Gates. Colonel McDowell, who might have been the choice for the temporary command if not for the private view of several other officers that he was too slow and tactless for the job, was sent off promptly toward the headquarters of Gates to confer about the overall battle plan and to bear a letter making the request for a permanent chief officer.

The army was poised now a mere sixteen miles from Gilbert Town. When the troops bedded down for the night, they fell asleep sure that the time for marching would soon be past, and the time for fighting at hand.

Joshua awoke before dawn the next morning and lay still, watching the sky grow light above him until others were awake. With few words the troops arose and had their breakfasts, then rolled up their blankets and made ready for the day's march.

Before they set off, however, the hefty Colonel Cleveland called them to assemble in a large circle, each separate command together. He stood, hat in hand, within the circle. Campbell, Shelby, Sevier, and other officers stood close behind him.

"Now, my brave fellows, I've come to tell you the news," Cleveland said. "The time has come for every one of you to do a great service for his country, one that will have your children bragging that you have overcome the famous Ferguson. Now, my friends, when the pinch comes, you'll find me with you. But if there's a man among you who can abide to pull back from the battle glory soon to be ours, you now have the opportunity to do it. I'll give you a few minutes to think about it, and if you wish to go, you may."

Cleveland stopped speaking, and Major Joseph McDowell, who had been left in charge of the troops previously led by his colonel brother, stepped up with a big grin on his face. "Those of you who might be thinking of withdrawing, listen to me and think of something else before you do. When you return to your homes, what story will you give? Will you say that you turned your tails while your braver fellows went on to the victory?"

Joshua glanced sidewise at the faces of those around him. On most he saw a stony, stoic look. On the faces of those younger and more inexperienced, he saw either fear or eagerness. Cooper, by now an experienced warrior and no longer a boy, looked unfaltering and strong. Israel Coffman, on the other hand, looked like a man scared to death but determined to hide it.

Colonel Shelby stepped up and spoke. "You have all heard the offer given by Colonel Cleveland," he said. "If any of you wish to take advantage of it, you will be asked, after one more minute of consideration, to take three steps to the rear, and there stand."

The minute passed, and the individual officers went to their separate commands. Sevier passed by his men, looking a moment into each face, pausing longer at Coffman. "Preacher, if you wish to go—"

"No, sir," Coffman said. "When the pinch comes, I'll be there too."

Sevier smiled slowly. "Very well, my friend. And while you're there, be sure to bring the good Lord along with you. We'll likely need him."

Sevier took two steps, and to his men said, "Now is the time. If you wish to leave us, step back."

Joshua looked around. Not a man moved. His eyes swept over to Shelby's men, to Campbell's, to those of all the commands present.

Not one man had accepted the offer. Right then Joshua felt prouder than ever before to be a man of the frontier.

Somewhere in the ranks a soldier clapped. Others began doing the same, until a swelling round of applause and cheers rose to the sky. These were men proud of themselves and their comrades.

The officers glanced at each other and smiled subtly. What had just happened had done more to unify this army of independent-minded frontiersmen than anything that had happened yet. When the battle came, what had happened this morning would make a tangible difference.

Shelby waved his hands to quiet the applause. "I'm glad to see you to the last man determined to meet and defeat the enemy of your country," he said. "When we encounter the foe, don't wait for the word of your commander. Each of you will be his own officer, fighting as best you can, taking care of yourself and taking advantage of every opportunity you receive. If you are in the woods, hide yourself in the trees and give them Indian play. Move from tree to tree, pressing the enemy, killing or disabling any you can. I pledge that your officers will shrink from nothing and be constantly with you. And the moment the enemy gives way to us, listen sharp and obey the orders you are given."

The men were ordered to put provisions enough for two meals in their pouches and to ready themselves for a march that would begin in three hours. Before they began, the officers surprised them with a treat, liquor brought in by Cleveland and McDowell.

The day's advance covered little ground. The following

day they proceeded toward Gilbert Town with the anticipation of battle very high. Thus it was quite anticlimactic to find through local intelligence that Ferguson had already fled Gilbert Town, having learned from Sevier's two deserters of the approach of the Americans. Ferguson had pulled his army out on September 27, and was believed to be notifying his superiors of a need for immediate reinforcements. Rumors had it that bloody Tarleton himself might advance to join Ferguson.

Joshua was deeply disheartened by the news. He had hoped the element of surprise could be preserved, and that Ferguson could be struck before he strengthened his command. If Ferguson obtained reinforcements, the battle, whenever and wherever it came, could be bloody indeed.

It would be a long time before the patriots who pursued Patrick Ferguson would understand the reason for his military movements after he fled Gilbert Town. There was something uncertain and haphazard in them, something that suggested indecision, and perhaps a waffling between the desire to avoid encounter and the desire to attract it.

Several factors had to be considered by the Scottish major in reacting to the threat. Upon learning of the approach of the backwoodsmen he despised as human specimens but admired as marksmen, Ferguson had obtained word that Colonel Elijah Clarke's Georgians were on the march to join the advancing Overmountain men and their reinforcement forces. He was eager to intercept Clarke. Further, he was expecting loyalist reinforcements for his own band, feared a patriot cavalry attack from the east, and expected the arrival at any time of a wagon train of supplies.

He had camped on the Broad River on October 1, from where he sent a plea for a hundred reinforcement troops. Receiving the communication was Colonel J. H. Cruger, stationed at Ninety-six; Cruger would reply that with only fifty men holding Ninety-six itself, he obviously did not have any help to offer Ferguson.

Ferguson sent a similar plea for reinforcements to Cornwallis himself. The messengers bearing the letter, however, would face trouble from rebels who became wise to their mission, and would not arrive at the British commander's post until October 7, too late to help.

From his Broad River camp Ferguson dictated a third letter, full of fear-mongering fiction and addressed to the public at large as a loyalist recruitment notice:

> Denard's Ford, Broad River
> Tyron County, October 1, 1780
>
> Gentlemen: Unless you wish to be eat up by an inundation of barbarians, who have begun by murdering an unarmed son before his aged father, and afterwards lopped off his arms, and who by their shocking cruelties and irregularities give the best proof of their cowardice and want of discipline; I say, if you want to be pinioned, robbed, and murdered, and see your wives and daughters, in four days, abused by the dregs of mankind—in short, if you wish to deserve to live, and bear the name of men, grasp your arms in a moment and run to camp.

The letter went on to warn of the approach of the "Back Water men," calling its leaders by name, and then closed with a harsh and goading invitation: "If you choose to be degraded and spat upon by a set of mongrels, say so at once, and let your women turn their backs upon you, and look out for real men to protect them."

Ferguson signed the proclamation with his own hand: "Pat. Ferguson, Major, 71st Regiment."

From Denard's Ford, Ferguson proceeded on October 2 for four miles, then camped. At four the next morning his loyalist army arose and advanced in the darkness. Their twenty-mile, river-fording march took them to the plantation of a loyalist named Tate, where they remained for two days, vainly waiting for reinforcements.

On October 5, from Tate's plantation, Ferguson sent one final appeal for help to his commander-in-chief. He informed Cornwallis that the patriot force had been swol-

len by new additions from Clarke and General Thomas
Sumter. The intelligence was correct; a small group of
Clarke's men, and a force from Sumter, but directly under
Colonel William Lacey, had in fact joined the Overmoun-
tain force. Ferguson wrote to Cornwallis: "I am on my
march towards you, by a road leading from Cherokee
Ford, north of King's Mountain. Three or four hundred
good soldiers, part dragoons, would finish the business.
Something must be done soon. This is their last push in
this quarter."

On Friday, October 6, Ferguson put his men on an
early morning march, crossing fords and creeks, passing
between mountains, and at last reaching the vicinity of
the mountain Ferguson had mentioned in his communi--
cation with Cornwallis, King's Mountain. Wooded on the
sides, rocky and relatively level on the top, the mountain
drew Ferguson's attention, presenting to his mind an
option other than continuing on the remaining thirty-five
miles to Cornwallis's army and safety.

The place Ferguson had reached was a spurred mountain range some sixteen miles long, its upper portions
within North Carolina and its lower portions stretching
across the line in South Carolina. Ignoring the highest
peaks, Ferguson made for the flatter, lower spurs across
the South Carolina border.

About a mile and a half over the line, he led his force
up the sides of a six-hundred-yard-long, timber-sided
spur of the main mountain range. Tapering upward to a
height of sixty feet, the top ridge was no more than a
hundred twenty feet wide at its broadest portions, and
half that at the narrowest. On the summit, Ferguson
believed, his group could make a stand, if fate brought
their pursuers to them before reinforcements arrived.
There was water, natural cover, altitude. Here they could
fight if it came to it. Fight, and retreat no more. Patrick
Ferguson despised retreat.

Though Ferguson instinctively felt sure of the defensi-
bility of his low, narrow ridge, his second-in-command,
Captain Abraham DePeyster, did not. DePeyster worried
deeply, but kept his thoughts to himself.

Once situated upon the rocky spur, Ferguson declared his army unshakable by any force. Then he issued more communications, sat back, and waited for reinforcements, so confident that he didn't even order breastworks built from the abundant timber around him.

After Gilbert Town the activity of the patriot army was a tiring, somewhat confusing, and occasionally discouraging flurry of movement. The discouragement was mostly initial, brought about by the disappointment of not finding Ferguson where anticipated.

They learned that Ferguson had fled south, and so determined to make for Ninety-six. Having come this far, no one was eager to turn home without engaging the enemy.

Reinforcements continued to come. From the command of Georgia's Clarke came Major William Candler and thirty men, joining the group at Gilbert Town. After the army advanced to the Broad River area, Major William Chronicle and a band of twenty from Lincoln County, North Carolina, arrived. Joshua happened to meet some of these men. One of them, surnamed Crockett, seemed interested in his talk about his home on Limestone Creek.

Across Mountain Creek they moved, then over the Broad River, and at last to Alexander's Ford on the Green River, camping on a nearby farm. Here the army's leaders were forced to face the hard fact that their men and mounts were becoming exhausted. Some of the foot soldiers could scarcely be expected to keep up much longer, and some of the horsemen, on poorer mounts, were hardly better off.

It was evident that so large and wearied a force would have trouble in following Ferguson swiftly enough. So the force was divided, those with good horses being sent in advance of foot soldiers and horsemen with lame or slow animals.

Joshua Colter was privately glad for the division of men. He believed it would send Israel Coffman toward the rear, for the preacher's horse was poorly broken and unreliable. He was surprised when Coffman rode up to him on an entirely new and better mount—and refused to say where he had obtained it.

Joshua would learn later that Coffman had traded his poor horse for a good one, making the exchange with a younger soldier who was not really all that eager to be part of the advance force. Joshua never learned who the young soldier was, for Coffman had been sworn to keep that secret, and in all the hundreds present, Joshua was never able to pick out who was mounted on Coffman's old horse.

"I've not come this far to lag behind while others do the job," Coffman said.

Joshua grinned and nodded, but the gestures gave the lie to his true feelings. Try as he might, he just couldn't feel comfortable about Israel Coffman entering this battle. Coffman seemed as out-of-place as a warrior as Saint Peter would as a bet-taker at a dogfight.

During the division of the force, which took most of the night, a stroke of fortune occurred. Colonel Edward Lacey, who had been visited earlier by Colonel McDowell and informed of the campaign against Ferguson, arrived to inform the officers of Ferguson's general location, the size of his force, and other such intelligence obtained from a spy who had been directly inside a Tory camp. Further, Lacey promised, he would bring his own force to join the patriot army; he should be able to intersect them easily at Cowpens.

In the morning light, the soldiers moved out from Green River, going first to Sandy Plains, then southeast toward the border between the Carolinas. The mounted riflemen, a force of about seven hundred, quickly moved out ahead of the foot soldiers. Crossing the Carolina border, the horsemen came to Cowpens, named for the large cattle pens built by a wealthy Tory of the area. They discovered Ferguson had not come this way, but did have the recompense of slaughtering several of the Tory's cattle, stripping his fields of corn, and feasting by the light of their cookfires.

A crippled patriot spy named Joseph Kerr arrived at the camp at Cowpens with the most certain news yet of

Ferguson. He had learned that Ferguson had talked of making camp on King's Mountain; there, he was sure, the patriots would find him.

Meanwhile Lacey came again, as promised, with a force of South Carolinians, from whose ranks more well-mounted horsemen were selected, bringing the total number of mounted troops to just over nine hundred. When the horsemen, including Joshua, Cooper, and Coffman, pulled out of Cowpens on the rainy Friday night, every man in that number knew he would almost certainly be among the first to actually engage Ferguson.

They crossed the Broad River the next morning, then went on. Encountering and capturing some Tories, they confirmed Ferguson's presence on King's Mountain. When informed that they would pilot the patriots to the mountain, the Tories nodded, having no choice.

"So now we know where it will happen, eh?" Coffman asked Joshua, trying to hide the edge of nervousness in his voice.

"So now we know," Joshua replied.

Coffman smiled a very weak smile, and looked back over his shoulder in the direction of the distant Overmountain country. Joshua wondered what he was thinking, but had the courtesy not to ask.

The man's name was Gilmer, and the meal he was devouring was the finest he had put away in a long time. Fine company too—female and attractive. He smiled as he took another bite of chicken, and washed it down with a swallow of tea made from sassafras.

The tea went all over his lap when the front door of the house burst open and a handful of ragged, dirty, trail-gaunt men burst in, rifles up and cocked. The two women screamed and fell back; one dropped a bowl that shattered across the floor.

The first man who entered was tall and fierce of expression. "You damned rascal!" he shouted into Gilmer's face. "We've got you now!"

Gilmer, still seated, pushed back his chair. "A true king's man, I am!" he swore, punctuating it with an oath.

"Bring me the noose," the tall man said. One of the others with him put a looped rope into his hand, and this was roughly thrown around the neck of Gilmer and tightened.

"You'll hang on the bow of yonder gate, you sod," the tall man said.

"No, oh no, not there," said one of the man's companions. "Look at these poor women, all in tears . . . if we hang him there, he's sure to haunt this place. Let's at least have the decency to take him out of sight before we swing him."

The tall fellow looked none too happy for the suggestion, but nodded. "Very well, but let's be swift about it. The sooner this Tory's feet swing above the earth, the better earth it will be."

With the women crying pitifully, Gilmer was yanked from his chair by the rope and hauled without dignity out of the house. Led like a dog by the neck, he stumbled after his captors down the road and around the bend. The one who had urged that the hanging be done farther down the road paused long enough to unhitch Gilmer's horse from the front fence and take it with him. The women followed no farther than the gate, then turned and ran back inside, wailing loudly.

Once out of view of the house, the men stopped. Gilmer yanked the rope from around his neck and tossed it to the ground. "Did you have to yank so hard on the bloody thing, Colonel?" he demanded of the tall man.

Colonel William Campbell laughed heartily, making his normally ruddy complexion all the ruddier. He put a hand on Gilmer's shoulder. "God help us, I thought I'd laugh aloud before we could get out of sight!" he declared. "My good scout Gilmer, if I gave your neck too harsh a treatment, please forgive me. I had to make a good show of it, you know."

"And a deuced good job you did of it, sir," Gilmer muttered. "And what would you have done if Major Chronicle hadn't spoken up about sparing the women— would you have gone ahead and hung me from the gate, Colonel, just to keep up your good show?"

Colonel Campbell forced down his laughter and apologized again to the scout, assuring him the scenario had been thoroughly planned out and in no case would they have actually hanged so capable a patriot and scout as he.

"Now, tell us what you have learned," Colonel Campbell said as Gilmer mounted his horse.

Rubbing his neck as he spoke, Gilmer said, "I rode ahead, as ordered, and stopped when I saw the house. My heart thumped like a drum when them two pretty women came to the door. From the questions they gave me, I figured them for Tories, and declared myself a good and true follower of the king, looking for Ferguson's camp so I could join him.

"Well, that seemed to please them to no end, and they invited me in and fixed me that fine meal you interrupted so unkindly. They were big talkers, them wenches. The one that dropped the bowl, Colonel, she told me she had been in Ferguson's camp herself, carrying chickens for the major's meal. She says he's on a ridge of King's Mountain, between two creeks where some deer hunters camped a year ago."

"By Zeus, I know precisely the place, then!" Major William Chronicle declared. "I was one of those very deer hunters!"

Colonel Campbell smiled broadly at the generosity of fortune. "Then you know the lay of the land quite well, Major?"

"Know it? I know it like the rump of my plow horse!" Chronicle replied.

Campbell nodded, a man utterly gratified. "Gentlemen, let's return to camp and withdraw the officers into counsel," he said. "We're ready at last to settle our account with Major Ferguson."

21

The boy's name was John Ponder and he looked far too scared to attempt any deception. One of his captors, German-born Colonel Frederick Hambright, a veteran warrior who had served alongside Colonel McDowell in campaigns throughout the year and now would fight with him against Ferguson, looked closely at the fourteen-year-old boy and nodded.

"I know dis poy," the thickly accented officer said to the men of his command who had brought in Ponder, captured riding through a nearby field. "He got a brutter mit Ferguson." He spoke directly to the boy: "Dat right, poy?"

"Yes, sir."

Hambright noted the lad was standing in a rather strange posture, right arm clamped tightly to his side. "What you got dere, poy?"

"Nothing, sir!"

"Nutting, eh? We'll see, we'll see!"

Hambright thrust his hand against the boy's side and felt a packet there, clamped against his body under his arm. "Ah!" he said. "Give dat to me!"

Ponder didn't resist. Hambright tore open the packet

and produced a letter. Unfolding it, he squinted at it and read, his lips moving slightly in silence. "From Ferguson to Cornwallis!" he said, lifting the paper. "Asking for more solchiers!"

John Ponder looked like he might cry. Hambright turned a dark eye on him. "Poy, you want us to hang you for a Tory?"

The boy's face went pale and he began to tremble. "No, sir."

"You don't want to hang, den all you got to do is tell me one tink: How will we know de Major Ferguson when we see him?"

"He's wearing a shirt over his uniform, sir. A checked shirt, like a duster. No one else on the mountain has a shirt like it."

"Ah!" Hambright exulted, grinning. "Good, young Ponder! No noose for you!" He turned to his men. "Spread word, poys: When you see dot man on de mountain mit a checked shirt over him clothes, you will know who him is, and may mark him mit your rifles!"

The men nodded, and word of the new information spread through the ranks and out to the patriot army at large. When Joshua Colter heard it, he passed it on to Cooper and Coffman.

"Will they try to capture Ferguson?" Coffman asked.

"I doubt it, Israel," Joshua replied. "We've come a long way and through some hard country to get a man who threatened our homes and families. There's plenty of men here who won't consider the battle a victory unless Patrick Ferguson dies." He gazed off in the direction of King's Mountain. "And I reckon I'm one of them."

The capture of Ponder was just one of several such interceptions that aided the advancing patriots. Prior to snaring Ponder, a handful of Tories had been captured by Sevier's men; Joshua and Coffman had shared the honor of bringing in one of these. Joshua was amused by Coffman's obvious pride in the capture, pride he struggled in vain to hide. The captives had all confirmed Ferguson's presence on the mountain spur, and told the Whigs that the major had posted pickets all along the crest. A further confirmation had come when a Whig was overtaken; his name was George Watkins and he had been a prisoner of Ferguson, but now was paroled and going home. He verified the intelligence already obtained from the Tories. But Ponder's information was assuredly the best of all. Now undoubting of their destination and the status of the foe, the patriot army drew nearer King's Mountain.

Already the officers had set their strategy, and about a mile from their destination began its workings. Most of the so-far formless army was divided into two generally equal divisions, which were lined up in neat double columns. Colonel Campbell took the right double column and Colonel Cleveland the left. Major Joseph Winston was sent off with a third troop detachment to approach the mountain from yet another angle to cut off any possible retreat route for Ferguson.

Cleveland's column, including the troops under Williams and Chronicle, bore left; Campbell's column, flanked by the men of McDowell, Winston, and Sevier, veered to the right. An order of silence was given, and a surreal quiet fell upon the dividing army as it headed for the mountain spur. This was now an army of phantoms, unspeaking and grim, riding in silence that for many would remain unbroken until they gave out the wild frontier battle cry at the outset of battle.

Joshua knew, both logically and intuitively, that this would be a battle of import, and most likely the biggest he had been involved in since the Battle of Point Pleasant some years before. In that fight he had been wounded, and for some time thereafter was thought dead by his own kin. How would he fare today? No way to know. Only the battle itself would tell.

The soldiers abandoned their horses in the thickets at the base of the ridge, tying their blankets, cloaks, and other momentarily unneeded personal effects to their saddles. Joshua left his wide-brimmed hat there as well, tying a kerchief around his head in replacement, for the sides of King's Mountain were thick with brush that would snatch the hat from a man's head as he rushed up, and Joshua wanted no such distractions.

The soldiers checked their rifles, repriming pans, cleaning touch holes, making sure all was in order. Joshua was glad for the fine powder Alphus had made.

The thought of Alphus brought to mind his kin back home. He pictured Darcy at her spinning wheel at the fireside, Will playing with his whittled toy soldier, and Alphus, Sina, and Zachariah in the cabin behind the main house. Would he come through safe and see them again? Were they safe themselves, with so many of their men off across the mountains? He prayed for them, and for himself.

Sevier approached. "Well, my boys, the time has come. Let's give them all we can—and if your will fails you, remember Tarleton's Quarter and go on."

They moved forward, an army now on foot, treading rain-sodden autumn leaves in silence. Joshua patted Israel Coffman on the shoulder and shook Cooper's hand.

"It will be a devil of a fight," Cooper whispered.

"Aye," Joshua replied. "So it will."

They went on. From here there was no turning back. The onset of the Battle of King's Mountain was only minutes away.

The battle lasted only about an hour—an hour no man who survived would ever forget.

It began on the southwestern end of the ridge, which was heavily guarded as it was the most vulnerable to attack. Tories stationed along that ridge fired the first shots, peppering rifle balls toward Shelby's men as they advanced up the slope of the oblong mountain spur. The phantom army had moved so silently that no one on the mountain knew of their approach until they were within a quarter mile. The Tory fire hailed about the men, but Colonel Shelby urged them to hold their return fire until they were close enough to make every shot count. With straining patience the backwoodsmen continued their advance. When they did open fire, that patience paid off. Loyalists fell in great numbers.

Meanwhile Campbell's men were coming in from the southwest, sweeping up to press the Tories from the opposite side, while Joshua and the rest of Sevier's command came in between Shelby and Campbell.

Campbell, eager for battle, was the first to sound the cry for attack. He pulled off his coat in a dramatic sweep, then exclaimed: "Shout like hell and fight like devils!"

The cry that followed was exhilarating to the attackers and fear-inspiring to the defenders. This was the trademark yell of the mountain men, a ringing descendant of war cries heard across Europe in centuries past, mixed with elements of the scalping cry of Indians. Some of those defending the mountain had heard this yell before, at Musgrove's Mill and elsewhere. One of them was Captain DePeyster, who had faced Shelby at Musgrove's. DePeyster heard the battle cry, and turned to Ferguson, whose face clearly betrayed his surprise at the swiftness of this attack. "That's an ominous sound, sir," DePeyster said. "These are the damned yelling boys!"

Ferguson had heard much talk of these "yelling boys" and had been involved in their pursuit in Carolina, but, unlike DePeyster, had never personally faced them in direct battle. For a moment the major showed evidence of doubt, but his expression quickly became resolute and strong, and he stepped forward to direct his defense.

The patriots on the southwestern slopes advanced up the mountain, hiding behind trees and rocks and firing carefully. Joshua struggled against impatience as he made his own slow climb, firing and reloading, advancing another couple of yards, then firing and reloading again. He glanced over at Cooper and Coffman. Both were making about even progress with him, though they were gradually moving farther from each other laterally.

The attackers soon realized that Ferguson's plan was to use the bayonet as his key defensive weapon. Those Tories who possessed no standard issue bayonets had been outfitted with specially made knives with handles whittled down to fit into the muzzles of their long arms—subgrade, makeshift bayonets, but just as potentially lethal.

The first bayonet charge was directed at Campbell's Virginians, and had quite a telling effect. The Virginians were pushed back down the slope before the red-coated provincial Rangers, Ferguson's best-trained troops, experts in bayonet and sword warfare.

Campbell, seeing the demoralizing effect of the bayonet charge, sought to rally his men. "Remember liberty, boys, and come on!"

Meanwhile Shelby had led his men against the Rangers from the other side. His men, like Campbell's, were pushed back with the bayonets, but even as this happened, Campbell's forces were coming up again for their second offensive, forcing the Rangers to turn their attention in that direction. In the meantime every patriot rifleman was pouring down a rain of fire at every opportunity.

When Shelby's troops came to the base of the hill, Shelby rallied them just as Campbell had done. "Reload, boys, and let's advance and give them one more hell of a fire!" he yelled. Then it was back up the slopes for Shelby even as Campbell was again pushed back. Thus was established a style of fighting that would characterize much of the hour-long battle. With two sides of a mountain to defend, Ferguson's forces would be pushed from one side, then the other, then the other again, a rocking onslaught designed to wear them down like the back-and-forth raspings of a file.

Joshua and his fellow fighters under Sevier continued their upward creep. So far their flank had been spared any direct bayonet charges, and the musketeers and riflemen firing back at them were overshooting badly, sending balls into the treetops. Joshua grinned. How many times in his boyhood hunting days had he shot at a deer downslope from him and overshot in just the same way? It was easy to misplace shots in that way when firing downward, as any good rifleman knew. Surely some of the loyalists above knew it too; but in the panic of battle, they obviously were failing to make the needed compensation.

Blinking against the stinging, thickening powder smoke that hung in the trees and bushes, Joshua aimed through a wind-cleared hole in the haze and brought down a red-coated figure. Reloading, he moved up a few more yards.

The top of the hill was close now. He looked around for Cooper and Coffman, but the smoke was too thick to let him find them.

At last Sevier's men reached the crest of the hill, let out another fearsome war whoop, and advanced into a close-quarters fray. Now each man truly was his own officer. The various commands were intermixing in the confusion and drifting rifle smoke.

Only later would these fighters on the southwestern crest learn the details of what had transpired on the other fronts of battle.

Slightly northeast of Shelby's force and eventually intermingling with it, Williams's men advanced up the center stretch of the north slope. Soldiers under Lacey, Cleveland, and Colonel James Hawthorne, the latter Irish-born and a prisoner in his boyhood of Indians in South Carolina, swung in from the northeast. Chronicle's men advanced from a due east position, while below him, coming in from southeastern and southern positions, respectively, were the troops of Winston and McDowell.

The battle continued noisy, flashy, and bloody; across the rocky ridge rifles cracked, smoke drifted skyward, wounded men screamed in pain, and the Whig troops gave out again and again the yell that had become their signature. And through all the din a high, piercing sound was continually heard: Ferguson blowing a silver whistle he used to signal and rally his troops. All told, there were about two thousand men locked in battle on the two hundred fifty acre mountaintop. Yet despite the close quarters, this was not truly one battle at all, but a conglomeration of many smaller-scale fights.

Throughout the brutal hour, carnage was abundant. Increasing numbers of bodies, many of them clad in red coats, piled up amid the rocks and timber. Tories in plain clothing fell as well; these had put sprigs of pine into their caps to distinguish themselves from their rebel attackers, some of whom had followed a similar expedient by thrusting scraps of paper into their hatbands as their identifying mark.

Though the loyalists suffered the most, casualties also

came to the patriots. Major Chronicle, spurring his men forward at one point in the battle, shouted, "Face the hill! Face the hill!" A moment later a fusillade of Tory gunfire sounded and he fell dead, three others beside him dying at almost the same moment.

Colonel Hambright and others immediately took charge in place of Chronicle, and the attack continued. Tories rushed them, armed with the makeshift, muzzle-held bayonets, and the patriots fell back, but following the pattern of their cohorts on the other side of the hill, charged forward as soon as the Tories headed back up the slope. Colonel Hambright took a wound and kept going, blood streaming down his leg and filling his boot so that his foot made a squashing, wet sound with every step. "Huzza, brave poys, huzza!" he shouted, ignoring his injury. "A few minutes more, de fight be over!"

Williams also fell wounded in the battle; his horse already had been shot under him. "For God's sake, boys, don't give up the hill!" he urged those who came to his aid.

Burly Ben Cleveland was almost shot down himself, but his horse took the charge instead and fell beneath him. The big colonel leaped to his feet and continued advancing on foot, keeping pace with men half his weight.

It was growing evident that Ferguson and his loyalists were losing this battle—evident, at least, to all but Ferguson himself. The Scottish major, still blowing his whistle, brandishing his sword with his one good arm, and shouting orders, declared he would not yield to "banditti." One of his troops passed nearby, waving a surrender flag. Swearing in fury, Ferguson slashed it down with his sword. The battle progressed; Ferguson's horse was shot from under him. He obtained another, only to have it also killed. Mounting a third horse, he went on fighting even then, sword slashing, whistle shrilling.

Meanwhile, Joshua and Sevier's other troops were busily fighting their way across the mountain. Joshua had just seen Cooper through the haze, fighting energetically and apparently unscathed. Coffman's status was unknown. Though Joshua looked furtively for him when circumstances allowed, he could not find him. He hoped Coffman was alive—and wondered, if in fact he was living, what he now thought of warfare. Would he have been so quick to offer his services as a rifleman had he foreseen this hellish scene?

Another Whig soldier came to Joshua and shouted something at him; Joshua didn't understand it all, but heard the name of Tarleton, the hated Waxhaws butcher. Some minutes later he heard the name called again, and this time picked up the context. Tarleton supposedly was here, even now, reinforcing Ferguson.

Joshua hoped the word was false; Tarleton could turn the tide for Ferguson. He was encouraged some minutes later when Sevier, bravely mounted on a horse in the midst of the battle, rode among his advancing men, shouting that Tarleton was in fact not here at all, and that if he showed up, it would be merely to receive the same humiliation now being given Ferguson.

All in all, Sevier's troops seemed to be faring relatively well. Of Sevier's men, Joshua had seen only two killed so far, one being an Irishman named Michael Mahoney, who lived on the Nolichucky, the other a man named John Brown, who had died early in the fight.

Other commands had suffered higher casualties than Sevier's. As Joshua moved through the battlefield, he occasionally noted fallen Whig riflemen whose dead faces wore the familiar marksman's expression: one eye open, one eye shut. These men had fallen while taking aim on their foe—in some cases, the same foe who had killed them by firing more quickly.

One such case elsewhere on the battlefield bore a particular irony and would be much talked about among the troops afterward. Preston Goforth, a patriot from Rutherford County, North Carolina, faced off with a Tory; the two fired upon each other simultaneously, and both died. The ironic aspect was that the Tory had been none other than John Goforth, Preston's brother. John was one of three Tories of the Goforth family in the battle. Before the hour was done, all the Goforths were dead.

There were other such ironic stories that would make

the rounds and become part of the folklore of the battle. Residing near King's Mountain was a family named Patterson. Arthur, the father, received news the day before the fight that his three sons had been captured by some of Ferguson's men. He went to the mountain to seek their release, and while he was there, the fight began. The sons escaped their captors in the confusion and took up arms with the attacking army, one of them fighting with part of the rope that had bound him still around his neck. When the battle was done, the young Pattersons were all alive, but the father who had come to rescue them was not. He too had joined the fight, only to fall its victim.

From certain families the battle exacted a heavy toll. A Whig family well-represented and significantly bereaved in the battle was that of the Edmondsons, Virginians of Irish descent. Eight of that name were in the fight, serving under Campbell. Three of these fell dead, and one was wounded. Three of the family Laird also were serving under Campbell; two of these died in the battle.

As the battle advanced, all continued to be endless confusion and tumult. Joshua's ears rang from the constant clatter of the rifles and his shoulder grew bruised and sore from the recoil of his own rifle. He was carrying rifle balls in his mouth now, both for quick dispensing and to fight thirst.

Then a remarkable thing happened. Through the haze of the fight three horsemen came racing right toward Joshua—and the central one wore a checked duster. He was slashing at all who came near him, using a sword held in his left hand. The sword struck the barrel of a rifle in the hands of a nearby Whig and snapped off near the hilt as Joshua watched. The Whig screamed; obviously Ferguson's broken blade had struck flesh as well as metal.

"By Joseph," Joshua muttered to himself, borrowing Alphus's favorite expression. "By Joseph, if it ain't Ferguson himself!"

He darted aside to avoid being overrun, then raised his rifle to aim. It was no good; Ferguson and those with him had dashed past too quickly. Near Joshua was another of Sevier's men, named John Gilleland, who had been wounded but still fought. Gilleland raised his rifle and pulled the trigger, but the rifle, too hurriedly primed, did not fire. "That's Ferguson—shoot him!" Gilleland called out to another rifleman near him.

That rifleman, Robert Young, also of Sevier's command, stepped up. Joshua, darting in the direction Ferguson had gone, was close enough to hear his shout: "Let's see what Sweet Lips can do!"

Young pulled the trigger, and "Sweet Lips" sent out a gout of fire and smoke, simultaneous with the blasts of several other Whig rifles. At that moment Ferguson spasmed, dropped his broken sword, rode limply a short distance, then fell from the saddle. His foot hung up in his stirrup, and his body, still wearing its checked duster, was dragged over the rocky terrain. His head was bloody and gruesome, pierced by a rifle ball, and his arms were like loose strips of rag, broken by bullets.

Whigs all around sent up a cheer and fired at Ferguson's pitiful form as it was dragged past them. All wanted to say they had put a bullet into the hated Scotsman, and when the battle was over, there would be many arguments about who had fired the shot that had first wounded Ferguson. Young would claim that merit, as would others; the issue would never be settled.

The two riders with Ferguson, Colonel Vezey Husband and Major Daniel Plummer, had also fallen in the volley that brought down their commander. But it was Ferguson who was considered the real prize.

Even with Ferguson gone, the battle went on for nearly another half hour. Campbell's cry—"Remember liberty, boys! Another gun will do it!"—resounded again and again, rallying his men into the close-quarters combat of the final fray.

The loyalists were being forced steadily back. Ferguson's Rangers in particular were suffering, falling in great numbers. DePeyster, seeking to fulfill the wishes of his fallen commander, continued to press his defense, though at a great cost of men. At length surrender became the required course, and white flags rose among the cornered loyalists.

Yet the fight continued. Whigs continued gunning down the Tories even as they tried to surrender, partly because a returning band of foragers earlier sent out by Ferguson came upon the scene and, not knowing of the surrender of their fellows, opened fire on the patriots. Many of the patriots, misunderstanding what had happened, thought the Tories had merely feigned surrender to set a trap, and thus ignored the white flags. After all, they had seen these flags raised earlier, only to be hacked down by Ferguson's sword. How could they be sure the surrenders were not feigned?

Yet others who lacked the excuse of honest misunderstanding were just as deliberate in ignoring the surrenders. "Give them Buford's play!" some shouted, referring to the lack of mercy exhibited to the surrendering Colonel Buford by "Bloody Tarleton" at Waxhaws.

Joseph Sevier, son of John, was firing one shot after another into the mass of Tories; Joshua went to him and sternly told him to stop.

When Joseph looked up at him, tears were streaming down his face. "The damned rascals have killed my father, and I'll keep loading and shooting until I've killed every son of a bitch of them!" he declared.

"No, Joseph, no," Joshua said, firm but gentle. "Look there."

Joseph turned and saw his father riding up behind him. The tears came harder now, but they were tears of relief. "I thought you were dead," he said to his father.

"Not a bit of it, son. It's your uncle Robert who has fallen, not me, and I fear he's mortally hurt, though he's yet alive."

Sevier had no time for further talk. He quickly moved past his son and Joshua to join Shelby. Both officers began vigorously urging their men to stop shooting those surrendering. The Tories were pleading pitifully for quarter by now. Shelby advanced toward them and said, "Damn you, if you want quarter, throw down your arms!"

Colonel Campbell appeared, moving among his men. One Andrew Evins leveled his rifle to kill another pleading Tory, but Campbell pushed up his rifle with his arm.

"For God's sake, Evins, don't shoot! It's murder to kill them now that they've raised the flag!" Campbell waded into the midst of the Tories themselves, shouting for the fire to cease, which at last it did.

The New Yorker, Captain DePeyster, had survived the fight, his life saved at one point when a rifle ball glanced off a coin in his pocket. Still mounted, he advanced to Campbell, whom he recognized. Fuming over the shooting of so many trying to surrender, he declared, "Colonel Campbell, it was damned unfair! Damned unfair!"

Campbell looked up at him coldly. Unfair it might have seemed, but he knew of patriot men hanged by Tories in front of their families, and of women whose bellies had been knifed open when they refused to betray their patriot husbands to the loyalists. His sympathy was limited.

"Captain DePeyster, dismount your horse, arrange your officers by rank, and have the prisoners doff their hats and sit down."

And then for several moments all was strangely still. Smoke rose above the bloody scene as patriots crowded in around the huddle of seated Tories and provincials, examining the men they had defeated as if they were exotic creatures in a display cage. Then Campbell slowly smiled.

"Boys, I think the time's ripe for a cheer, eh?"

Together the patriots shouted, three times in succession: "Huzza for liberty!"

Joshua felt a hand touch his shoulder. He turned. It was Cooper. Brother smiled silently at brother, each glad to see the other safe. Hands clasped and shook, and there was no need to say a thing.

With scores of others, Joshua and Cooper went to see Ferguson's corpse, feeling strangely drawn to it.

Joshua had to respect the slain officer to large measure. Ferguson had died bravely, fighting for what he thought right in the best way he knew to do it. Joshua took no pleasure in seeing that a handful of the rougher patriot victors had crudely insulted the corpse of the fallen

Scotsman by evacuating their bladders on it and committing other atrocities.

Most were not so demonstrative. They filed past the corpse, pocked with at least eight bullet holes, looking down on it with great curiosity. These men were no newcomers to the aftermath of violent death, and there were other corpses aplenty for them to stare upon, but all seemed to need to see Ferguson himself, to verify with their own eyes that the man who had threatened them was dead. Even wounded Whigs demanded to be carried to the site, to view in death the man in whose defeat they had suffered.

Finally the body was wrapped in the raw hide of a beef—the only burial shroud that would be afforded the brave but imprudent Ferguson. He was buried near the spot on which he died, and interred with him was the corpse of a female camp cook who was, it was rumored, one of Ferguson's two mistresses. She had died early in the fighting.

Ferguson's silver whistle, about a foot long, was picked up by Shelby and would be kept as a lifelong memento. Colonel Sevier claimed Ferguson's broken sword, and DePeyster ceremonially surrendered his own to Campbell. Many of the other lesser officers had already turned their swords over to the tall Virginian.

Various other battle relics also were divided. Joseph McDowell obtained a portion of Ferguson's official china service, while Sevier claimed his silk sash. Some quick-snatching soldiers made off with Ferguson's pistol and pocket watch, which were exposed when the corpse was rolled over.

Joshua and Cooper made no scramble for souvenirs; they were searching for something more important: Israel Coffman. Neither had seen him since early in the battle. Joshua felt a great weight inside his chest as he scanned the white faces of the dead. Please, God, not Israel. He must not be dead.

"Joshua," Cooper said. He had stopped and was pointing toward a nearby cluster of rocks, amid which something moved. The brothers went forward, knelt. The moving thing was a man, his legs curled beneath him as he bent over, hands across his face.

"Israel?"

Indeed it was. "Joshua, Joshua . . . is that you?"

"What's happened to you, Israel?" Joshua grasped the preacher's shoulder and pulled him to an upright, seated posture.

"Israel—oh, God . . ."

He had taken a savage cut, apparently a saber blow, across the eyes and bridge of his nose, the latter being gapped terribly and bleeding both down the outside of his nose and through the nostrils. The eyes were cut and blind beyond all healing.

Joshua recalled the dramatic scene of Ferguson riding between his officers in a vain dash for freedom, slashing with his sword in the din and smoke . . .

Now it was clear who had screamed as Ferguson made his final, sword-breaking slash.

"I can't see, Joshua," Israel Coffman said in a tone of disbelief. He groped at his face. "I was right after all . . . never see them again, never again."

"Come, Israel, let's get you to a better place," Joshua said, fighting emotion. "We'll clean you and bind you up."

"Yes, yes . . . I thank you for that, Joshua. Thank you so much." Coffman's voice was strange. "Did I hear Cooper's voice?"

"I'm here, Preacher," Cooper said.

"Thank God," Coffman said. "We are all alive. Let's all bow our heads and say thanks . . . to . . ." Then he passed out.

Joshua and Cooper carried him through the camp and laid him in a shaded spot on a stray blanket they scavenged from the seized Tory supplies. They waited for a surgeon, but there were only a handful on the entire mountain, serving both the patriot and Tory wounded. At last the brothers realized that any tending of their blind comrade would have to be done by themselves.

As delicately as they could, they cleansed the blood from Coffman's face and bound a rag around his eyes, and all the time they did it Cooper cried without shame.

* * *

Joshua shed no tears until the following morning. It was Sunday, beautiful and bright.

Despite the soothing weather, the mountaintop was a terrible place of gloom. From the countryside around, the families of the fallen Tories came, searching the gory dead for their kin and wailing sadly each time one was found. Some rejoiced in finding their loved ones still alive, though wounded, only to have them die in their arms.

Burials were under way, but many of these were hardly worthy of the name. In some cases heaps of bodies were piled into deep pits and covered over. But all that was done in other situations was to heap bodies into shallow holes and cover them with logs, bark, rocks—anything the terrain offered. It was an effort scarcely worth the doing. Already great numbers of carrion birds circled in the sky above the mountain, and as soon as the human activity on the ridgetop ceased, they would descend to feast. By night wolves would come. Even the free-roaming hogs of the region were drawn by the smell of dead humanity. Around King's Mountain, folks would recount for a long time thereafter, few people had the stomach to eat the meat of their own hogs for months after the fight, knowing they had fattened themselves partially on human flesh.

Joshua Colter moved through all the carnage, feeling strangely distanced from it, his emotions having numbed since the previous day. Despite his near exhaustion, sleep had not come to him the night before; whenever he'd closed his eyes, he was in the battle again, rifle butt slamming into his sore shoulder, body tense, tingling with the expectation of being punctured by a bullet at any moment. And all night as he lay awake the wounded had groaned and cried and begged, sometimes for water, sometimes for the mercy of death that was too slow coming.

Joshua trudged pointlessly and listlessly, feeling driven to keep in motion. He made his way toward the edge of the battlefield near the north slope, and there something caught his bleary eye.

It was a wounded man, sitting up and staring silently ahead so unswervingly that for a moment Joshua thought he was dead where he sat. Then he saw the heaving chest; the man was breathing, slowly but steadily. On the ground beside him lay his hat, its band marked with a sprig of evergreen. This was a Tory.

Joshua, weakened and somber already, felt pity for the poor fellow. What did it matter now who was Tory and who was patriot? This man needed help, and Joshua would offer it. He went to the man, spoke to him, and received no answer.

Then, with a shock, he saw why. The man had been shot through the head, the bullet entering the brow and coming out the side, dragging out fragments of brain with it. Amazed, Joshua knelt and looked into the face. How could this man be breathing? It seemed impossible, yet breathing he was. Joshua looked closer. The man's eyes were open, staring back at him, but they obviously saw nothing. There was nothing of life left in this poor fellow beyond a thumping heart and a lingering ability to draw breath. He was alive yet not alive. Whatever had been rational and human about him had been destroyed by the rifle ball.

For a full minute Joshua stared into the face of the living corpse, wondering what kind of man this had been, whether he had a wife and family, and what kind of life he had led. Was this any way for a man to be, dead yet breathing, a mere thing, yet also a man? Joshua wondered who had shot him. He thought: Might it have been me? I shot so many men yesterday, shot them and watched them fall. I hope I left none of them like this.

The aura of despair that hung over the mountain grew heavier. Joshua prayed: Heavenly God, Father of Christ, please take this man on. Don't make him linger, not like this. A man ought to be alive or dead. He ought not have to be trapped between life and death like this poor wretch.

"Let me lay you down, friend," Joshua said softly to the unresponding Tory. "I'll do it gentle, I promise you."

And he did do it gently, moving to the man's side and with great care easing him back until he was on his back, the eyes staring upward. A trace of blood leaked out the exit wound on the side of his head.

"There," Joshua said. "Now you're down, now you're down." He paused, feeling mounting emotion. Leaning forward, he whispered into the man's ear, "Let go now. It's your time. Just let go and go on."

The man surely could not hear, much less understand, but right after Joshua spoke to him, he took one deep, shuddering breath, and died.

Joshua stood, blinked rapidly, and walked over the crest and part of the way down the mountain. God above, what kind of life do we lead on this cursed world, ever fighting and killing and dying and maiming and blinding each other? Why does it have to be that way? Why do we have to be what we are?

Joshua entered a thicket, looked around to make sure he was not seen, put his arms against a tree, leaned his head into them, and wept.

The trek back home from King's Mountain was long and difficult and marked with more death. The victors, carrying booty, and many wearing the captured swords that had been the most coveted of all the spoils, rode or trudged wearily along. The badly wounded Colonel James Williams died a few hours after the march began. Captain Robert Sevier, wounded by buckshot in a kidney, had been warned by the surgeon not to attempt the journey home. He ignored the directive, and the ninth day into the march, expired as predicted. The other Seviers were deeply saddened.

The foot soldiers who had been left behind by the horsemen prior to the battle had not arrived in time to participate in the fight, so these rejoined their battle-weary companions simply to make another tiring march back the way they had just come. With the reunited patriot army were the wounded, walking if they could, riding if they couldn't, and being carried on tandem horse litters if they were unable to hold themselves in the saddle.

And then there were the prisoners, nearly eight hundred of them, bearing flintless firearms and fearful expressions. There was much talk among the weary, short-tempered patriot victors of hanging at least some of the prisoners, talk enough to thoroughly frighten the captives. At one point along the way, one Tory escaped into the forest. He was recaptured soon, and one of the patriots who did it drew the sword he had taken as booty and with it hacked the man to death. Even Joshua, who had seen enough in his time to harden him to gore, was repelled by the sight of the dismembered body, and was actually glad, for that moment, that tender-hearted Israel Coffman was blind and spared the sight of it.

The officers tried to stop such brutality against the prisoners, but were hard-pressed to do it. Even now the army was finding Whig refugees in the most pitiful conditions, hiding in the forests for fear of Tories.

By the time the army reached Bickerstaffs, northeast of Gilbert Town, Colonel Campbell, seeing that some condescension must be given if the men were not to rebel against their own leaders, approved a military trial for several of the captured Tories. Thirty-six Tories were tried and convicted to death by hanging. A few received unexpected mercies. Even the two deserters who had left Sevier's force to warn Ferguson of the coming attack were spared death—this at the request of Sevier himself.

The condemned Tories died in threes, swinging from three ropes strung onto a huge oak after their horses were driven from beneath them. After nine had been hanged, a Tory named Baldwin, who was about to follow them, managed a remarkable escape when his small brother, crying and screaming out a pitiful good-bye with his arms around his condemned brother's waist, secretly cut the bonds that held Baldwin's wrists. The prisoner was placed upon the horse for the hanging, but pulled his hands around and raced off on the horse before the noose could be put over his head. Stunned patriots, though frustrated by the escape, would thereafter talk admiringly of Baldwin's daring. He was never recaptured.

The officers put a stop to the hangings after Baldwin's escape, and pardoned the rest of the condemned prisoners in hope that the deaths already witnessed had been enough to slake the blood-thirst of the patriots and stifle any thought of attempted escape on the part of the remaining Tories.

On the returning army progressed, Joshua and Cooper taking turns leading the horse upon which the blinded Israel Coffman rode. At long last they passed through the mountains and came again to the Overmountain country and home, and there had the sad task of delivering Coffman to his family. Virginia Coffman cried to see her husband's condition, but rejoiced to have him alive with her. As for Judah, he only stared at his adoptive father. Stared as if Israel Coffman, with the rags around his eyes, was a stranger.

Joshua was deeply shocked by the news.

Sina Colter was dead and already buried in a grave within the little family stockade. Only two nights ago she had retired early, complaining of weakness and a sense of unsettledness. The next morning Alphus had awakened to find her dead beside him. Since then he had been in a terrible state, deeply depressed and lost almost continually in the deepest yet of his silent broods.

Joshua tried to talk to Alphus, but it was as if the old man didn't hear him. He stared straight ahead and showed no reaction to anything Joshua said. Only when Joshua talked of the King's Mountain battle did Alphus give any reaction, and that was only a flickering one.

That night Cooper called Joshua aside. "I feel I should stay near Alphus, but—"

"I think I know what you're going to say," Joshua interrupted. "You're bound for the Cumberland country and Hannah."

Cooper was surprised. "How did you know?"

"Just a feeling. Likely the same one you've got—that you need to do it sooner instead of later."

"Yes. That's it."

"It's a fool thing, you know. You'll be risking your life and scalp the whole way."

"I've been risking my life this entire bloody year. Besides, she's worth risking it for. I've got to see her— and marry her, if I'm not too late."

"Godspeed to you, brother. And best wishes."

"And what will you do, Joshua?"

"For now, stay with Alphus. He needs me with him, I think."

"That he does." Cooper put out his hand. "Good-bye, Joshua."

"Good-bye, Cooper."

He left the next morning, and Joshua watched him until he was out of sight, for he knew the odds were good that he would never lay eyes on Cooper Haverly again.

IV

THE
PILGRIMS

22

Despite the great success at King's Mountain, the remainder of 1780 brought new danger to the Overmountain country. The British had seized upon the absence of the King's Mountain soldiers from their homesteads to encourage the dormant Overhill Cherokees to stir again to warfare. Now is the time for swift action, their agents told the war chief Oconostota and the other Overhill leaders. Patrick Ferguson and his troops are trained fighters who will destroy the ragtag unakas. Strike now against their settlements and you will prevail.

But the effort against Ferguson moved too quickly and the Cherokees too slowly. Before anything more than sporadic raids could be performed, John Sevier and his fellows were back from King's Mountain, victorious instead of defeated. Furthermore, the war plans of the Cherokees had been betrayed to the unakas. Nancy Ward, the Beloved Woman of the Overhills, had sent two Cherokee traders, Isaac Thomas and Ellis Harlin, to warn the settlers of the danger. This was the second time the Beloved Woman had sent such a warning to the Overmountain settlements; in 1776 she had done the same just before the Cherokee attacks.

Despite this unexpected turn of events, the British continued into December to press the Overhills to take up arms. Diplomatic counterefforts were made by Virginia and North Carolina, but these came too late.

Thus, not long after returning from King's Mountain to his home on the Nolichucky, John Sevier found himself again on the road toward war, traveling with a company under Captain George Russell, another under Captain Thomas Gist, and still others who joined the band at a rendezvous along Lick Creek. They promptly headed toward the French Broad River. On December 16, after crossing the river, they engaged an Indian force on Boyd's Creek. Sevier, though slightly wounded, came out the victor in the well-fought battle.

This was John Sevier's first direct offensive against Indian foes; it would not be his last. In coming years "Nolichucky Jack" Sevier, as both whites and Indians would come to call him, would build his fame as a capable Indian fighter.

Joshua Colter was not with Sevier at Boyd's Creek; he had remained home with Alphus. Though not physically ill, Alphus was in such a state of depression after Sina's death that Joshua feared he would die of despair alone. For long hours Joshua remained at his father's bedside, talking to him about that last long hunt he so wanted, hoping that keeping alive a bright future prospect would snap the old hunter out of his present state.

It didn't seem to be making much difference. Alphus hardly ate, hardly spoke, hardly did anything but lie on his bed and stare at the underside of the loft above him. Young Zachariah found his stepfather's condition so upsetting that he spent little time in his own home, preferring to sleep by the fireside in Joshua's cabin.

On the night of December 14, two days before Sevier would find himself fighting at Boyd's Creek, Joshua was seated by Alphus's bedside in Ayasta's former residence. The cabin was empty except for him and his foster father.

Joshua puffed on his pipe and remembered a story frequently told him by his late mother while they lived near Fort Loudoun in the late 1750s. He related it to Alphus.

"My mother told me more than once of something I said to her as a small child, Alphus," he said. "I had fallen into a creek near our home in Charles Town and got myself soaked and scratched up too. I was all in tears until Mother took me back into the house and dried me off and changed my clothes and cut up a big sweet apple for me to eat. I don't recall it myself, but she told me I looked at her and said, 'Mother, now I'm little and you're big and you take care of me. Someday when I'm big and you're little, I'll take care of you.' "

Joshua paused, drawing on the pipe. "I never understood why Mother always got a tear in her eye when she told that tale. Now I do. I reckon the way I saw it as a little child is the way it really is. It's the way it is with you and me, Alphus. I came to you a little boy, and you took care of me until I was a man. Now it's you who need taking care of. It's me who's big, you who's little."

Alphus showed no more immediate reaction to those words than to any others Joshua had spoken to him over the past many days. But an hour later, as Joshua dozed in his chair, Alphus stirred and sat up.

"Joshua."

Joshua blinked awake and stared at Alphus with no less amazement than he would have if a corpse had reanimated before his eyes.

"Alphus!" He stopped abruptly, partly out of amazement, partly out of surprise, for by the light of the fire he saw tears on Alphus's face.

"It should have been me, Joshua," Alphus said.

"What should have . . . I don't understand."

"It should have been me who died, not Sina."

Joshua didn't know what to say. He wanted to leap up and dance and laugh and cry at the same time. But Alphus's somber manner dampered those impulses.

"She had another of her dreams," Alphus said. "The day before she died she told me of it. A great buck falling in the forest . . . that was the dream. She said she knew it was a sign of my death. She said she couldn't bear the thought of it, and so she prayed it would be her and not me who died." Alphus wiped his face. "I didn't pay it all much heed. Didn't think there was much sense in it, until she was gone. It should have been me, not her."

Then the old man cried. Joshua let him be, saying nothing, but inwardly thinking that, heaven forgive him, he was glad it had not been Alphus who died. Sina had never really been a mother to him, Alphus having married her after he was already grown. Joshua wasn't glad she was gone, but he could endure her passing much more easily than if he had lost Alphus.

Over the next two days Alphus rallied remarkably. His grief, though still present, had thawed and broken. Joshua wondered if the story he had told had somehow made the difference, but never really determined the answer, for Alphus never made reference to it. Even so, Joshua felt his words had brought the old man out of his spell of grief.

Joshua scarcely had time to enjoy the improved circumstances, however, for with Alphus better, there was nothing to keep him any longer from joining Sevier. Darcy begged him to stay with her, citing her advancing pregnancy and every other reason she could to keep him home, but Joshua was as much as ever a slave to his sense of duty. On December 17, the day after Boyd's Creek, he set out to join Sevier, figuring he could easily enough pick up information of the army's route along the way.

Inquiring of a gaggle of nervous settlers he encountered along the way, he learned of the engagement at Boyd's Creek and headed toward the French Broad. He had also been told of a rumor that Colonel Arthur Campbell, a relative of William Campbell, was on his way to join Sevier with another force of men. And then it would be on to the Cherokee towns themselves.

That prospect filled Joshua with trepidation. He had spent his boyhood in the Overhill towns—and now he was on his way to become part of the force that would destroy them.

Could he do it, if it became necessary? Could he put the torch to the towns that had once been his home?

Usually Joshua had no such qualms; he could do almost anything that was militarily required in any given situation. Now he wasn't nearly so sure of himself, and it was a most uncomfortable feeling.

The town was called Amo-Gayunyi, or Running Water. It lay on the south side of the Tennessee River, along the Great War Path, below the treacherous Untiguhi that had imperiled the flatboat travelers at the beginning of the year, and just upriver from its neighboring sister town of Ani-Kusati-yi, or Nickajack. This was one of the Five Lower Towns of the Chickamaugas and the home now of Dragging Canoe himself. And tonight it was the place where, in the menstrual hut, Ayasta had just given painful birth to a girl-child fathered by Malachi Trent in his cabin on the Nolichucky back in the waning winter.

She had been as stoic as ever, even in the pain of childbirth. The baby had been slow to "jump down," as the Indians termed it, and sometimes during the ordeal Ayasta had wondered if either she or the infant would survive. Old women had gathered around her, one of them chanting an old formula: "Sge! Hisga'ya Ts'sdi'ga hana gwa da'tulehu gu kilu-gwu . . ." And they had blown a concoction made of yellow root on her head, breasts, and palms. At last the formulas and medicine had done their work, and in a wrench of pain Ayasta had been able to push the child from her body.

Then, in spite of her weakness, she had risen. Holding her child, she had been led by the old women to a nearby creek and there sprinkled the infant with the icy cold water. Returning to the menstrual hut, Ayasta had covered the little body with bear's oil and let the child begin to nurse.

Now she studied the new little life in her arms. Like Ayasta, the child was dark in hair and skin, but in the face and eyes was a clear impression of Malachi Trent. A great longing arose in Ayasta. Since leaving Trent earlier in the year, not a day had passed that she hadn't thought of him. He was not a good man, she knew. He was an outcast of his own people because of what he was. But to Ayasta he had seemed good. He had been kind and cared sincerely for her; that she had clearly seen.

She thought also of her son, now almost a year older than when she had last seen him. Was he well? How much did he remember of her? Surely he was now thoroughly unaka in his dress and manner and thought. No doubt he believed what the unakas believed, and lived entirely as they lived. He had been so young when she had been parted from him.

Sometimes she regretted having left him. She longed to touch him, to see him play and grow—yet she didn't really feel she had done the wrong thing toward him. Never once had she faltered in her conviction that to have failed to remove the child from his native way of life would have been the death of him.

And now she had a daughter. What would become of her? It seemed notably strange to Ayasta that she again was back where she had been in 1778, faced with the responsibility of a little life while living in a world that still seemed doomed. Would she yet again have to find an escape, or should this girl-child remain in the life she was born to?

Ayasta didn't know, but she refused to despair about it. Now was a time for happiness at this marvelous gift of life, this little living reminder of the man she had unexpectedly come to love. Perhaps, someday and somehow, he would be with her again.

When Joshua caught up with Sevier's force, he found them still camped at Boyd's Creek, and in none too good a condition. Sevier, wearing a bandage on his wounded temple, greeted Joshua with enthusiasm, outlined the Boyd's Creek battle, and discussed the current situation.

As Joshua had heard, Colonel Arthur Campbell indeed was expected to arrive, but so far had not done so. After the battle, Sevier had moved his force to a camp on the nearby Big Island of the French Broad to await Campbell, then had returned to Boyd's Creek to obtain better hunting after Campbell failed to appear. At the moment food was nigh nonexistent in the camp—so scarce the place had already been dubbed "Hungry Camp"—and the men were grumbling.

Joshua was not happy about the scarce provisions, for he was hungry after his journey. But he was no complainer and had seen far worse situations than this, so he made do with a skimpy meal of parched acorns and dried beef, and slept through the night like a worn-out child.

The next day Campbell arrived, bringing with him a hundred Virginians; about the same time Major Joseph Martin, the Virginia Cherokee agent, came in with a full three hundred Sullivan Countians to bolster the army even further. With more than seven hundred men now in the force, and bellies full from Campbell's provisions, the soldiers began their march.

They crossed the river at Tomatly Town and split up, part of the group heading for the lower Overhill towns, with the remaining group, of which Joshua was a part, making for Chota. They saw occasional Cherokees, all heading for the hills. By now Joshua wished he hadn't come here at all. This was no mission for him, not with his personal links to these Overhill towns. At Chota he had sat with John Hawk at the feet of Little Carpenter and heard the great chief tell of his youthful journey across the ocean to England. He had known and loved the people of Chota and revered the town almost as much as they.

It seemed terribly ironic to Joshua that the army reached Chota on Christmas Day. It made for a peculiar juxtaposition of time and place. Here geographically was the locale that more than any other represented a way of existence in which he had lived in his past, and here chronologically was the day that more than any other symbolized the life and religion of the white society in which he lived in his present. Both worlds, with all their differences, were part of him. He hardly knew how to feel, how to think, here in the Overhill country. He moved among the cabins and winter houses with a great sense of contradiction and unreality.

At Chota, which had been deserted in advance of the coming army, the soldiers found food and supplies that they gladly raided for their own use. Meanwhile, parties of scouts were sent out in pursuit of the fleeing Overhills, and to raid some of the neighboring towns. Joshua, however, was not assigned to any of these groups, and remained at Chota.

He was especially happy to have done so when the army was visited by an unexpected guest: Nanye-hi, or Nancy Ward. A striking woman in her early forties, she was a native of Chota and a Beloved Woman, or Agigaue, of the Cherokees, possessing many powers in that role. Among these was the authority to pardon condemned prisoners, and in this capacity Nancy Ward had saved the lives, in 1776, of both a woman captive named Lydia Bean, and Darcy Colter.

Joshua was initially so awed by the beautiful woman that he hesitated to approach her. He watched from a distance as she conferred with Campbell and made him a gift of cattle from her private herd. The sight of the cattle made Joshua smile, for Darcy had told him it was to learn the raising and use of these "white men's buffalo" that Nancy Ward had spared the lives of the female captives back in '76.

The arrival of the cattle created an unusual problem that might have been humorous except for the hidden jealousies it revealed. Colonel Elijah Clarke had come along on the expedition with some of his Georgians under Sevier, and ordered that the cattle be slaughtered. Major Martin, son-in-law of Nancy Ward, took offense to this, for he felt sure his presence there was what had prompted the Beloved Woman's gift of the cattle in the first place. He found Clarke's attitude of superiority and authority offensive in this context. Words were passed, and then the men broke into an open fistfight that Joshua found rather entertaining. Humorous or not, the incident showed a growing resentment between the troops of Sevier from Washington County, and the Virginians and Sullivan Countians. And at the heart of it was a mounting jealousy, on the part of many, of the dashing and widely admired John Sevier.

Sometime later Joshua gathered the courage to go

present himself to Nancy Ward and to thank her for sparing Darcy's life all those years ago. He found that the Beloved Woman remembered Darcy fondly and knew much of Joshua himself. "My uncle, Attakullakulla, spoke many times of his friend Ayunini," she said, using Joshua's Cherokee designation. "He saw greatness in you."

"Then I am honored," Joshua said. "I have heard that Little Carpenter is dead. Is this true?"

"Yes," Nancy Ward replied sadly. "He is gone, and it falls even more to me to try to keep peace between our peoples. But it is difficult to do. Your Colonel Campbell has given me no clear answer on my request for peace today." She looked around. "I am afraid he plans to destroy this town."

"No," Joshua said. "The Cherokees who have become troublesome to us are in Hiwassee and Chistowee, not Chota. I hope and believe the sacred city will be spared."

But Chota wasn't spared. Three days later, despite Nancy Ward's pleas for peace and despite her kinship by marriage to Major Martin, Chota was set ablaze. Nancy Ward, obviously saddened, was made a prisoner of sorts, but because of what Campbell called her "good offices," was treated more as guest than captive. Joshua protested the burning of the town, but to no avail.

He was told that various papers had been found here among the possessions of the absent war chief Oconostota; the papers indicated clearly that the chief had been dealing with British agents. "He's like all the rest—double-tongued and two-faced, pretending to live at peace with us while turning on us at first opportunity," one of the officers grumbled to Joshua. "The town must be burned to teach the old devil a lesson."

Towns other than Chota were burned as well, including Tellico and Tuskegee. There was sporadic fighting here and there; at the town of Kaiatee, Captain James Elliot was killed and buried beneath one of the cabins, which was then burned—to prevent the desecration of his corpse.

Joshua found the destruction of the towns sorrowful and distasteful; more than ever he was growing to despise the constant destruction and warfare that seemed to govern life on the border. Someday, he hoped, there would be peace here, for Indian and unaka alike. More and more, however, that seemed to be a vain hope.

Ulagu rode with a great sense of satisfaction, keeping his rifle ready and his eye on the unaka prisoner riding on the horse in front of him. Quite a fighter, this one had been; he had managed to kill two of Ulagu's band before being taken captive. He had richly earned the fiery fate that awaited him in Running Water Town.

Ulagu had been away from the Five Lower Towns for several weeks, raiding farmsteads in the valley of the Powell River near Cumberland Gap. Returning, he and his fellow warriors had detected this white man hiding in a briar thicket near the Whirl of the river. Why a white man would be so close to the Five Lower Towns mystified Ulagu. Might this man have been attempting to navigate the river and lost his canoe or flatboat? Possibly—but it seemed unlikely any unaka would attempt such a dangerous passage alone. Whatever the case, he was now a prisoner of the Chickamaugas, and his life was forfeit.

With great eagerness Ulagu rode on. By now, he was sure, Ayasta would have given birth to the child she had been carrying—a child whose father she had refused to reveal. Ulagu believed it likely the child had been sired by a white man, which galled him, but he had already decided that such would make no real difference. If the child was a male, he would be raised as a Chickamauga, whatever the color of his skin. He would be the replacement for Wasi, who according to Ayasta had died while among the unakas. Ulagu had been deeply sorrowful over Wasi's death, but it came as no great surprise, for the boy had always been sickly, and life among the unakas could only have made him weaker.

He eyed the prisoner before him. Quite a battered man he was, his face marred with a deep, fresh scar that ran down his brow toward his nose. It had the look of a healed tomahawk wound. Perhaps this man had encountered other Chickamaugas before, but somehow escaped. He would not escape this time.

Ulagu's excitement mounted as he neared Running Water Town. He would be welcomed there by Dragging Canoe, and would proudly display to him the seven scalps that he had taken in Powell's Valley. Ulagu had particularly enjoyed his raids there, largely because of the absence of Elisha Brecht. Brecht and Ulagu had parted company early in the year, shortly after the recovery of Ayasta on the Nolichucky. After Ayasta was safely with her brother again, Brecht had been ready to burn the cabin in which she had been found and kill the occupants, particularly Joshua Colter. Ulagu had promised safety to the occupants in exchange for Ayasta's return, and intervened to stop him. Brecht had grown furious. Even before reaching the Chickamauga towns, he had departed with his Tory raiders, declaring his association with Ulagu forever dissolved. He would leave the Chickamaugas and return to North Carolina, where Tories were abundant and the British were, at the time, preparing to rally the loyalists against their rebel neighbors. It seemed a good place to be for a man such as Elisha Brecht.

For his part, Ulagu was glad to see Brecht go, had not seen him since, and hoped never to see him again.

Unwittingly, Brecht had picked a good time to depart the Chickamauga towns, for a dread contagion had begun ravaging them. Smallpox, the unakas called this disease. The disease had killed many scores of Chickamaugas this year, ever since the capture of a flatboat bearing whites suffering from the contagion. Ulagu and Ayasta had not fallen victim, but many others had not been so fortunate. Riding with Ulagu even now were three warriors whose handsome faces were permanently marred by the scars of the pox.

Ulagu's arrival at Running Water Town was greeted with enthusiasm. Ulagu did not linger long to enjoy the welcome; he strode straight to Ayasta's cabin.

He found her with an infant at her breast. She looked up at him in momentary surprise as he entered the door, then greeted him.

"I am glad you are well, brother. Come and see my daughter," she said.

Ulagu said nothing and did not move for a moment. Then he stepped forward and knelt beside his sister. Ayasta removed the child from her breast and held her out for Ulagu to see. The baby's features clearly betrayed the race of her father.

"Her name is Walini," Ayasta said. "She is beautiful."

Ulagu examined the baby closely, without expression, then stood and walked back out the door, having not said a word to his sister.

Ayasta smiled sardonically to herself. Her brother's disappointment had been evident; she knew he had hoped she would have a boy-child to replace Wasi, to become the warrior Ulagu had hoped Wasi would be.

Ayasta put Walini to her breast again, more happy than ever that she had given birth to a daughter and not a son. Cuddling the tiny girl in her arms, she sang softly to her.

Meanwhile, on the other side of Running Water Town, the white prisoner Ulagu had captured was being roughly shoved into an empty cabin. His hands were bound behind him, and so he could not catch himself when he fell. The force of the fall drove the wind from his lungs and left him gasping as he was tied to a spike that had been driven into one of the logs of the cabin wall. Once he was secured, his imprisoners left him alone, closing and barring the door behind them.

He sat up, overwhelmed with despair. Was this how it was all to end for him: imprisoned by the Chickamaugas and doomed to death at the stake? No, he thought defiantly. Not me. Perhaps I will die in these towns, but I won't be toyed with atop a pile of burning wood for the pleasure of savages. I'll either find a way of escape or force them to kill me in flight. Whatever happens, I refuse to go to the stake.

He sat against the wall, straining at his bonds to no avail. An hour passed, and he heard movement outside the door. It swung open, spilling light and making him blink at the tall figure silhouetted in the opening. The prisoner caught the scent of food.

The figure strode forward, bearing a gourd bowl containing fish and dried pumpkin. He knelt and set it beside the prisoner, and in the process moved into a position that allowed the bound man to see him clearly.

The prisoner's eyes grew wide. "You're a white man!" he said.

"Yes," the tall man whispered. "I'm a prisoner, as you are."

"And they've let you live?"

"Yes, though I'm little more than a slave here. I'm afraid they have worse in mind for you, my friend. But at least they have been merciful enough to let me bring you food."

"Aye—and you can do more than that. Untie these bonds and give me a fighting chance to escape this place."

"I can untie only one hand, just long enough to allow you to eat. And you wouldn't escape even if I completely freed you. They are guarding this house closely." The tall man leaned closer, and the prisoner saw that his face was deeply pitted and scarred; the man obviously had survived a dire case of smallpox. "I will do what I can for you, but you must understand that for me to be caught helping you would be death for me."

"What is your name?" the prisoner asked.

"Brecht. Solomon Brecht."

"Brecht!"

"You know the name, I see. I'm not surprised; my brother Elisha has made it quite infamous. But my brother's association with these savages is what saved my life." Solomon Brecht began freeing the left hand of the prisoner. "I was wounded and captured off a flatboat bound for the Cumberland settlements early in the year. I would have been tomahawked to death on the spot had I not had the good fortune of being recognized as Elisha Brecht's brother by the Indian who captured me. He had ridden with Elisha in the past and had seen us together . . . but

I can talk no longer. I must go or they will grow suspicious. Tell me, my friend, what is your name?"

The prisoner stretched out his freed left hand, wriggling the fingers. He reached into the bowl and pulled out a chunk of fish. "My name," he said, "is Malachi Trent."

23

When Elisha Brecht had
angrily parted with Ulagu and left the company of the
Chickamaugas earlier in the year, he had done so with no
intention of returning to them. Two developments had
since intervened to change his mind.

The first was the surprising success of the Whig army
at King's Mountain. Brecht knew of the loyalist defeat
firsthand, for he had been there.

He hadn't wanted to be and wouldn't have been except
for a case of mistaken identity. Some of Ferguson's loyalists had heard rumors of a small band of advance patriot
scouts in the region and had mistaken Brecht's group for
them. The confusion had not been cleared up before the
battle abruptly started. Brecht and four of his men managed to melt into the tumult, and in the end made it
entirely away from the mountain by putting paper slips in
their hats to falsely mark themselves as Whigs. They
vanished into the forest undetected, leaving several of
their fellows behind, dead or captives of the patriots.

Now Brecht was all but alone, only a small fraction of
his original band of outliers still with him. And he was not
comfortable in this condition; he missed the feeling of

protective numbers around him. Returning to the Chickamauga country seemed a desirable option on that score.
Besides, time had passed and his anger at Ulagu had
cooled. So he had been denied his chance to take Joshua
Colter's scalp on the Nolichucky. What of it? There would
be other opportunities to draw Colter blood.

Changing feelings and circumstances weren't the only
factors driving Brecht to the Five Lower Towns. Another
prompting was a remarkable rumor he had heard shortly
before the King's Mountain fight. The source had been a
former member of his own marauder band, a man who
had been in more recent contact with the Chickamaugas
than had Brecht himself. He told a most startling tale:
Elisha's own brother Solomon reportedly was a prisoner
of the Chickamaugas in Running Water Town, captured
from the flatboat flotilla that had headed to the Cumberland country in the past winter and early spring. Now he
was atsi nahsa'i—a slave to his captor.

Elisha Brecht could hardly believe the tale . . . yet it
could be true. He knew that Solomon had left the Overmountain country earlier in the year. If in fact he had
made for the Cumberland region, he could have been
captured where the river passed through the Indian villages.

Night fell, and Brecht and his handful of cohorts
camped. There was danger in Brecht's being in this region
again. Having been gone so long, it was possible that he
might be cut down by some overeager warrior before he
was recognized. The prospect remained continually on
his mind.

He slept lightly, feeling on edge. Sometime after midnight he awakened. As he sat up, two of his companions
did as well.

"You hear that?" one of them whispered.

"Aye," Brecht replied. "Something moving out
there . . ."

The men rose and gathered rifles. The night was moonlit, bright. Into the forest they edged, looking about.
They heard no other suspicious sounds, saw no sign of
anyone. Perhaps it had merely been some forest creature

passing by. At last they retired again, but Brecht posted one man as guard. The sentinel sat nervously at the edge of the camp, eyes ever scanning, until finally weariness overcame caution and he slumped back against a tree, asleep.

In the forest a shadow moved and a figure darker than the night around him slid into the brush. Pontius Pilate had seen enough to know that Malachi Trent was not among the men camped here, whoever they were.

He would have to look elsewhere for his missing partner, even if it meant probing into the Chickamauga towns themselves.

Malachi Trent had heard of men who died for love, and had always thought of such as fools. There wasn't much beneath the stars worth a man's life, in his estimation, and certainly not any woman. Or so he had thought before he fell in love with the Cherokee widow named Ayasta.

He sat musing in the dark cabin, which he surmised had either been built by a white trader or British agent, or maybe had been made specifically to confine prisoners. He judged this from the fact it possessed a heavy barred door, whereas many of the Indian residential cabins had no closable doors at all. He knew that at any time he might be dragged out of this place to die at the stake—and all because he had been reckless enough to come looking for the woman he couldn't get out of his mind.

·Trent wondered if ever there had been as great a fool as he. If only he had let himself forget that woman, had let her melt back into the forests from which she had come—then he wouldn't be here, a condemned prisoner. He would be off somewhere enjoying a jug of whiskey, the brotherly companionship of Pont, and most of all, his precious freedom.

He grinned sardonically. Even if he had kept freedom on those terms, what would it have mattered? Life had foisted one fine jest on Malachi Trent, putting him into a situation in which even freedom didn't seem worth having if it meant being without the woman he loved. He never would have thought such a state could ever come upon a free-roaming old tomcat such as himself.

The day she had ridden off with her brother, Ayasta had warned Trent not to follow her. Trent, of course, had ignored the warning, tracking her almost all the way to the Chickamauga towns, Pont right beside him even though it wasn't his situation and didn't have to be his risk. Pont was like that, loyal to the furthest degree. Trent was glad Pont hadn't been captured along with him. He had been away two or three ridges over, setting a rabbit snare, when the Chickamaugas unexpectedly appeared, so Trent alone had fallen captive.

Trent shifted, sighed, and wondered where Ayasta was. For all he knew, she was in this very town. In fact, he was almost sure he had overheard one of the Chickamaugas address his captor by the name Ulagu—the name of Ayasta's brother, who had borne her away from the cabin on the Nolichucky. If this was the same Ulagu, there seemed more than an even chance Ayasta also lived in this place.

What a hard thing that was to think of! To be so close to her, yet locked away from her and the rest of the world, with the prospect of a torturous death ahead . . . it was the ultimate cruelty.

Trent had come close to finding Ayasta once earlier in the year, only to be driven away. When he had first trailed her brother's Chickamauga band, he and Pont had reached the vicinity of Dragging Canoe's towns before being detected. They had come under attack by a handful of Chickamauga hunters. They had scarcely held them off, and one had managed to lay open Trent's brow with a tomahawk blow. Pont had killed the Indian at once, then took Trent far away to tend him. The wound was fearsome and took months to fully heal, but once mended, Trent, bearing a broad facial scar, had again set out for the Chickamauga towns, still looking for his lost squaw. And again Pont had come with him.

Trent stood and stretched. Yesterday morning he had been freed of his bonds and allowed to walk about the cabin—a single, meager mercy for a doomed man. Yesterday afternoon he had been taken out and paraded around the town by Ulagu, being mocked and tormented all the way, during which time he had looked around for Ayasta. He had not seen her. In one way he was relieved. What if she had seen him and done nothing to gain his freedom? That would be a worse torture than any execution fire.

The door rattled and Solomon Brecht entered the cabin again, bearing more food. Trent took it and began gnawing at it like a hungry wolf.

"How long till they roast me?" he asked.

Solomon blanched at the blunt question. "Soon, I fear," he replied. "Dragging Canoe has been gone; I'm told your execution awaits his return, so he can enjoy it with the rest." Solomon shuddered. "A brutal race, this one. More brutal than I can understand."

"You've got to help me, Solomon." It was perhaps the twentieth time Trent had made that plea to his feeder.

And as many times, Solomon Brecht had given the same answer: "I can't—if I do, and they detect it, it will be me who dies at that stake."

"We'll escape together. You want to spend the rest of your days walking around being some redskin's living scalp? That's what a redskin's slave is, you know: a trophy. A living scalp on legs who's kept to be laughed at and mocked and humiliated with women's work."

Solomon looked offended. "At least I'm alive, and not condemned to die."

"For how long? There's no certainty in the life of a redskin's slave. Any minute now your owner could put his club through your skull and nobody would even blink over it. It's his right. What's wrong with you, Brecht? Ain't you got no kin awaiting you? Don't you ever think it might be worth trying to get free from here and see them again? Do they even know you're alive?"

Solomon Brecht, clearly disturbed, would not answer. Trent ate silently, staring unswervingly at the tall man. When he was done he pushed the bowl aside. "Wonder if that was my last one?" he asked, still keeping his eyes on Solomon.

The tall man left as quickly as he could, and did not

come again until the next morning. This time he brought more than food.

Beneath the victuals, at the bottom of the bowl, was a broken knife blade, about six inches long and very rusty. Trent did not acknowledge it when he saw it, but he quietly removed it and thrust it into a crack between the cabin logs.

When Solomon Brecht went to the door, he stopped and looked back at the prisoner. "Dragging Canoe has returned," he said. "Move swiftly, with God's speed, or it will be too late." And then he was gone.

Solomon Brecht's captor was named Diga-tiski, and all in all he had been quite kind to his prisoner. Diga-tiski, to Solomon's good fortune, had once been part of Ulagu's band when he had ridden with Elisha Brecht, and had even been present at the final woodland meeting between the Brecht brothers. It was Diga-tiski, in fact, who had almost detected Cooper Haverly watching in the nearby brush, only to be misled by a scampering rabbit.

Diga-tiski's own hand had given Solomon the wound that dropped him into the Tennessee River the day Donelson's flotilla was attacked from the north bank. If not for the warrior's last-moment recognition of Solomon's face, he would have killed his victim as soon as he was dragged from the waters. Instead Diga-tiski had declared Solomon his prisoner and taken him back to his own cabin, expecting that Elisha Brecht would soon be back from the Nolichucky, where he was at that time, and be pleased to see his brother's life spared. Diga-tiski was a mercenary fellow and hoped for some reward.

But Elisha Brecht, to Diga-tiski's surprise, hadn't returned. Ulagu had come back without Brecht, bringing his long-missing sister Ayasta with him and saying that Elisha Brecht had departed from him after a dispute. At that point Diga-tiski considered clubbing Solomon Brecht to death and being done with having to feed him, but he was beginning to grow fond of the lanky unaka and kept delaying the execution. By now Diga-tiski perceived Solomon as something like a pet or mascot, and appreciated

Solomon because the capture had earned him the war title of Ahu'tsi-di-ski', or Slave Catcher.

Then Diga-tiski had taken sick with the smallpox—known to his people as unu-da-kwa'la, "holes in face"—that had spread to the Chickamaugas from the infected family aboard the intercepted flatboat. Solomon had nursed his keeper well during his illness, and Diga-tiski had survived. When Solomon himself came down with the pox, Diga-tiski returned the kindness Solomon had shown him, and Solomon as well had survived the illness. Now both captor and captive were quite scarred. Diga-tiski seemed more fond than ever of Solomon, proudly sharing his slave's services with his friend Ulagu. Solomon feigned appreciation of Diga-tiski, but in truth remained deeply fearful of him, for his very life remained bound to the Indian's whim.

Tonight Solomon was more fearful than ever. He had actually done a forbidden thing—he had given a weapon to a condemned prisoner. Solomon had found the broken knife blade several weeks before and had hidden it for his own possible use later—the one possible use being the taking of his own life, if ever it appeared Diga-tiski lost his affection for him and planned to do him in. Now Solomon was afraid that his act of betrayal would be discovered. In trying to help Malachi Trent, he might have sacrificed his own life.

His fear roused a second form of distress: disgust at himself for his cowardice. Malachi Trent, a man bravely determined to do all in his power to gain his freedom or die trying, put Solomon to shame. Diga-tiski had given Solomon much freedom, not even maiming him to keep him from fleeing, and through his laxness provided many opportunities for him to attempt escape. Yet Solomon never took advantage of these, simply because he was too afraid. If he was half a man, he told himself, he would have tried by now to reach his family. But it seemed he wasn't half a man. He was nothing but a coward, lingering in servitude to a savage because he was afraid to make a break for freedom.

Solomon walked through Running Water Town, think-

ing about his family. What had become of them? Had
they made it to the Cumberland settlements? Were they
safe? He looked at the wilderness beyond the edge of
town and wished he had the courage to simply walk into
it, disappear, and go find the answers to those questions.
He could steal a horse, a gun, and ride away, and if
providence was with him, he might make it to the settlements and then on to the French Lick. Or perhaps he
could take a canoe and escape by river as far as the Muscle
Shoals, and from there go overland to the Cumberland
forts.

But he was still too afraid. Too afraid to do anything but
stay here and hope Diga-tiski continued to keep him alive.

He saw the stake then, standing in a clear area in the
midst of town. Malachi Trent's stake. The sight made him
feel ill. How could he remain among a people who took
delight in roasting a man alive? Was he no better than his
brother, who had made himself as savage as the Indians?

Dejected and ashamed, Solomon turned on his heel
and strode back to the house of Diga-tiski, his head low.
Thus he didn't see the band of unakas who rode into the
opposite side of town, Elisha Brecht at their lead.

Solomon Brecht did not know it, but great changes
were about to come to his life.

No one ever knew how Malachi Trent managed to break
free from his cabin prison in the night, but the speculation
was that he had managed to jam some sharp object
between the edge of the door and the frame of the
doorway and lift the bar from the inside.

He wasn't seen until he had already stolen a horse and
was riding out of Running Water Town. A Chickamauga
boy, coming in late from harvesting a fish trap in the
river, was the first to spot him, and sent up a shout of
alarm that brought warriors scrambling out of their
houses.

Elisha Brecht was in a drunken stupor when the commotion began, and heard none of it. Upon arriving in
town, he had planned to seek out his brother, if in fact he
was here, but an offer from a friend of a jug of whiskey in

a nearby sweat house had intervened to change his plans, and so far Solomon remained ignorant of Elisha's presence here.

Solomon was still awake when the escape happened, and suspected at once what the noise and tumult meant. He rolled over on his blankets, buried his face, and prayed fervently.

In the cabin, Ayasta was also awake at the time, nursing her daughter. She rose and went to her door—and was amazed to catch a fleeting sight of what appeared to be a white man racing past on a bare-backed horse. Something about him caught her attention and took her breath. She knew that Ulagu had brought in a white prisoner, and supposed this surely must be him . . . but why did the sight of him speed her heart? He was gone too quickly for her to obtain a close look, and he never glanced her way at all.

A large number of mounted Chickamaugas followed moments after, many of them barefoot and unkempt and obviously freshly roused from their beds. Ayasta hugged Walini close as they passed her house.

Less than an hour later they returned, and long before they reentered the town the success of their pursuit was clearly evidenced by their elated whoops and cries. Ayasta felt an inexplicable sadness.

In Diga-tiski's house, Solomon Brecht buried his face deeper in his blankets and thought to himself that if he still had his blade, he would bury it in his own heart.

And Elisha Brecht, oblivious to it all, gave another drunken snore and rolled over on the sweat house floor, his arm across the whiskey jug.

Walini was asleep, so Ayasta was alone when she emerged from her house to see the slain prisoner's body returned to the town. The warrior who had caught and killed him had tied a rope around the man's feet and dragged the limp, scalped body behind his mount. The people of Running Water Town gathered around to examine the slain man. Ayasta waited on the back fringe of the crowd until they dispersed, then stepped forward.

She looked into the dead face of Malachi Trent for a

long time, her own features as expressionless as those of the corpse. She turned slowly and walked back to her house, feeling as if the sky had just caved in upon her with a crushing weight.

The failed escape attempt of the unaka prisoner was the talk of Running Water Town all the next day. Solomon Brecht listened as Diga-tiski described what had happened, and felt immensely relieved to hear no mention of a broken blade having been found in Trent's possession. Solomon could only guess Trent must have lost the blade in his flight. Or maybe he had been noble enough to toss it away when his recapture became inevitable, to spare Solomon any suspicion and reprisal. Whatever had happened, the blade's absence was a stroke of good fortune for Solomon. If it had been found, someone would quickly have deduced it had passed to Trent—and Solomon, as the food bearer, would have been the obvious suspect.

The prisoner had died fighting, Diga-tiski said with unveiled admiration. For an unaka in particular he had been a brave man, and had earned the respect of every warrior who had pursued him to his death. Had he lived to be taken to the stake, Diga-tiski was sure, this prisoner would have made a courageous and defiant showing for himself. Such men, even though condemned, merited a special kind of respect.

Later in the day, Solomon walked alone through the town, thinking deeply about Malachi Trent, and about himself. Until now Trent's determination to escape had made Solomon feel ashamed of his own cowardly acquiescence to his captors. Now it was making him feel something else besides—something like inspiration, a sparking of his courage.

Malachi Trent had possessed the courage to escape. Perhaps Solomon Brecht could possess it too . . . and perhaps Solomon Brecht could succeed where Trent had not. By the eternal, it was his duty to himself and family at least to try!

"Solomon!"

The voice, familiar and utterly unexpected, came from behind him. He wheeled.

Striding toward him, red-eyed, wild-haired, and dressed like a Chickamauga from head to toe, was none other than his own brother, Elisha. Solomon was so stunned he staggered. Elisha stepped forward and steadied him with his hand.

"Brother, what's wrong with you? It's me who ought to be staggering, for I drank the night away!"

"Elisha—how, where . . ."

"I heard talk that you were a captive here, Solomon. I had to come see for myself. Damn, man, but you're pitted bad in the face! Was it the pox?"

"Elisha . . ." Solomon staggered again. This was too much to take. Suddenly he felt as weak as he had when the pox had seized him. The world made a quick spin, and he fainted to the ground.

When he came around he was in Diga-tiski's house again, lying on his blanket, and Elisha was talking to Diga-tiski. Solomon sat up and all attention turned to him.

"Diga-tiski has been telling me how you came to be here, Solomon," Elisha Brecht said. "He is a great man, eh, to keep you alive and well?"

"Yes," Solomon said. "He is a great man."

Diga-tiski, who had gained a fair understanding of English from his slave, beamed at the flattery; he was a man who deeply enjoyed hearing himself praised.

"And now our friend Diga-tiski will not mind it if two brothers talk alone?" Elisha suggested.

Diga-tiski complied, and when he was gone, Elisha leaned forward. "Take heart, Solomon. I intend to see you free of him soon."

Solomon Brecht felt a great burst of elation. It had been a long time since he felt any real brotherly love for Elisha; now he was overwhelmed with it. Elisha's return was like an answered prayer. Now no escape attempt would be required.

"How will you do it? I don't think he'll just let me go."

"No, but I know Diga-tiski—a few gifts, a little whiskey and money, and he can be persuaded easily enough."

"Thank God. Thank God."

" 'Pears to me it's Elisha Brecht who ought to get the thanks, brother. But don't fret. We'll talk more of it later, after I've probed a mite on Diga-tiski to see what it will take to buy you free. But for now, we've got enough to talk about, eh? It's been far too long since I've seen you, Solomon. Far too long."

The two young Chickamaugas left Running Water early in the morning to hunt. Their route took them along the river and into the rugged hills, following the remote game trails that no white men knew and even some Indians had trouble finding. It proved a disappointing hunt; they killed only small game.

Now the day was darkening and the hunters were on their way back to the town. They had just passed into a narrow, deeply shaded valley when they had sensed another presence near them. The realization brought fear, for the valley seemed a haunting, grim place in the waning light, a place one might encounter beings of the sort that were said to live in remote forest enclaves.

They stopped at the head of the valley, looking around them. They saw nothing, but the sense of a third presence grew stronger. Glancing at each other, each unwilling to admit the fear that gnawed in him, they continued into the valley, eyes flickering from side to side, hearts jumping at every whisper of the forest.

A noise ahead of them—both stopped in their tracks. A moment later a kiyu'ga, a ground squirrel, scampered from behind a tree and into the woods. A shared glance and smile, and the hunters stepped forward a mite more confidently.

And then there was a figure behind them, a figure that had come from nowhere, that had seemed to materialize like a ghost. The hunters wheeled, and the closest one gasped as a long blade gouged deeply into his heart. He slid to the ground, bleeding, and died before his last breath could fully escape his lips.

The second hunter stood transfixed, a rabbit staring into the face of a rattler, too frightened to move or even breathe. The figure advanced—tall, black-skinned, and speckled with the blood of his victim. A powerful hand reached out, yanked the rifle from the hunter's grasp and tossed it aside, then clasped upon the Indian's throat. The Chickamauga staggered back and fell; the black-skinned figure knelt atop him, his hand never leaving its choking grip. The Chickamauga felt the knife probe his throat.

"You talk English?" The black figure's voice was a low rumble. For a moment the grip on the Chickamauga's throat lessened, just enough to let him speak.

"Some . . . some English . . ."

"Tell me: Is there a prisoner in Running Water Town, a white man, an unaka?"

The young hunter didn't understand; he stared wild-eyed at the demon that held him.

"Talk to me! A prisoner—ahu'tsi—unaka! In Running Water! Is there such a one there!"

"Was . . . no more . . ."

There was a long, deathly pause. The black face became more fearsome. "What do you mean, no more?"

"Dead . . . he ran, he was killed."

The black man removed his hand from the Indian's throat and pulled the blade away as well. He was seated astride the young man's chest, and now he looked toward the sky, raised both hands above his head, the right one still clenching the bloody knife, and let out a chilling, animalistic scream that echoed through the hills.

The Chickamauga closed his eyes and prepared for death.

But death did not come, though the blade returned to his throat. He opened his eyes.

"Twenty lives!" the black man said, closing and opening his left hand four times above his captive's face. "Twenty Chickamauga lives will pay for that of Malachi Trent! Go! Go back to your town and tell it! Go!"

The black man stood and jerked the hunter to his feet; the young man started to run.

"Wait!"

The hunter dared not disobey. He stopped in place and watched as the black man, if man this fearsome being really was, went to the body of his dead companion and took the scalp. He heaved the bloody trophy at the survivor; it fell at his feet.

"Pick it up."

The Chickamauga knelt, rose, holding the scalp lock.

"That is the first. Now go."

The young hunter ran, as fast and hard as he could toward Running Water Town through the gathering gloom.

The black man turned away, still holding his knife, and walked into the forest. To himself at that moment he was nothing but a grieving man who had lost a friend closer than a brother.

But though Pontius Pilate didn't know it, to the Chickamaugas he was about to become something far more. He was about to become a legend.

24

If Ayasta had heard the story of the mysterious dark-skinned phantom in the forest that had sworn to avenge the death of the unaka prisoner, she would have recognized at once that the "phantom" was Pont. But she didn't hear the story, for by the time the hunters encountered the avenger in the forest, she and Walini were already well away from Running Water Town, riding, through a new-falling snow, along the Nickajack Trail that led to the Cumberland country.

She would not stay in the place where Malachi Trent had died. She would no longer consider herself sister to the man who had captured him. If only she had known earlier that the white prisoner of Ulagu had been Trent!

He must have come looking for her as he had promised. And he had found her—almost. The irony of that, the pain of it, was too much to bear.

So for the second time in her life, Ayasta was abandoning her own native life and people. There was nowhere for her to go now, as she saw it, but to the Cumberland settlements of the unakas. The Overmountain settlements were too far away, and carried too many bad memories besides.

Ayasta did not know how she would be received at the Cumberland settlements. She could only hope that somewhere there she and her girl-child would find a benefactor. She thought back to her time with the Colters and remembered talk of one named McSwain, a friend of Joshua Colter, who had gone to the Cumberland. He had been spoken of as a good man. Maybe she could find this McSwain, and he would show kindness to her and Walini.

The wintry world on this early January day seemed a vast, hostile place to the lonely woman as she rode along, Walini bundled on a cradle board loosely bound to her bosom. Ayasta had taken a musket and as much food as she could find, but how far it would be to the Cumberland settlements she did not know. And inwardly she was fighting a fear that this flight was futile; would not Ulagu track her down long before she could get far enough away to evade followers? To counter this, Ayasta had told several of the women in Running Water Town that she was going to the nearby town of Tuskegee to visit some of her kin. The story would give her some extra time to increase her distance from Running Water Town before Ulagu realized something was amiss.

But not much time. Ultimately Ulagu would follow her. He would move more swiftly than she could, burdened as she was with a small child. Probably would overtake her and her flight would come to nothing.

Perhaps so—but still she pushed on. She was driven by a sense of urgency, a need for escape, and deep grief, and nothing short of physical restraint would stop her.

A day after Ayasta departed, another person also fled from Running Water Town, intent on reaching the Cumberland settlements. It was Solomon Brecht, a man running because the brother he had counted on to save him had betrayed that hope.

While Solomon waited for Elisha to strike a ransom agreement with Diga-tiski and gain his freedom, Elisha conferred with Dragging Canoe, Ulagu—with whom he had made a tense peace—and various other Chickamauga leaders. What they told Elisha altered his intentions toward his captive brother.

Elisha at least had the decency to privately explain it all to Solomon—and the audacity to act as if Solomon should accept it without complaint. "Because you are my brother, I'll tell you something I'm not supposed to reveal: There'll be raids on the Cumberland settlements come spring. Dragging Canoe is determined to crush them out. So you can see the French Lick is no place you need be going."

"But I must, Elisha, especially if this is true. I must warn Repentance and the children and get them to safety before the spring."

"Aye, there's the very rub, eh?" Elisha said in a tone a little colder. "For you to be freed now would only send you scampering off to betray our plans, and I can hardly let that happen, can I! Such a thing would reveal that I had told you of the raids. I'm sorry, brother. Your freedom will come, but only after the springtime. You must remain patient until then."

Something fundamental changed inside Solomon Brecht when faced with this fraternal betrayal. All affection for his cold-hearted brother vanished, as did any lingering sentiment in favor of loyalism. Solomon was disgusted to think his own brother would gladly stand by and let Repentance and the children be endangered in the sprintime Chickamauga raids. If that was what being a Tory meant, Solomon would be a Tory no longer.

Inspired by the brave example of Malachi Trent, Solomon made his break without delay. He stole Diga-tiski's musket and ammunition, took the best of his two horses, and rode out. He expected to be pursued, and knew it was likely he would be caught just as Trent had been. But what else could he do? Solomon would rather die, even at the stake if it came to that, than stand by and let his family be slaughtered without him even trying to give warning.

Solomon Brecht would cower and grovel no more. For

him it was now freedom or death, and he was determined to face either one without flinching.

Back in Running Water Town, Diga-tiski was saddened, then angered, when he detected the disappearance of his well-liked captive. He did not know which direction Solomon had gone, but guessed the Nickajack Trail was the most likely route, for it led to the Cumberland country to which Solomon had been bound at the time of his capture. Diga-tiski took only two fellow warriors with him, knowing Solomon would be no challenge himself, and scoffing at the threat of the purported black-skinned avenger in the forests.

The snow-flecked corpses of Diga-tiski and his two companions came back into Running Water Town draped over the backs of their horses. Their scalps had been removed but not kept by the scalper. They were tied in the horses' manes.

The sworn debt for the life of Malachi Trent was now paid to the amount of four lives.

After that no one in Running Water Town seemed at all interested in setting out after Solomon Brecht. He had been Diga-tiski's slave, no one else's, and with Diga-tiski dead, no one had reason to risk coming to the same end just to recapture a mere escaped captive.

Elisha Brecht, the only person in the town who knew that Solomon was aware of the planned springtime raids, worried in secret, wishing he had never revealed the intelligence to his brother. Unlikely as it seemed, Solomon might just make it safely through to his kin and forewarn the Cumberland stations. Fearful the betrayal of that information might somehow be traced back to himself, Elisha considered leaving. But it was winter, and he only had a few men left to follow and protect him, so he stayed, hoping that his brother would die somewhere along his way, before he could reach the settlements. After a while that prospect began to seem so likely that Elisha's worries substantially drained away. Solomon had always been something of a bungler, and he was certainly no woodsman. He was probably dead even now.

* * *

Ulagu grew deeply angry when he realized that Ayasta had done again what she had done before. Feeling intuitively suspicious of his sister's abrupt decision to visit relatives in the midst of winter, Ulagu himself visited Tuskegee and found she had not been there at all. At first he was mystified, then decided that she must have headed back to the Overmountain settlements. Furious, Ulagu returned to Running Water Town long enough to inform Dragging Canoe of what had happened, then gathered what meager food and supplies he required and set out northwest along the course of the Tennessee River—going precisely the wrong direction to overtake his fleeing sister.

Unaware that she had evaded Ulagu, Ayasta pushed up the northwesterly route of the Nickajack Trail, feeling a sense of pursuit that sometimes made her almost frantic. At two points she departed the trail when she detected others near; in both cases the others were, indeed, Chickamaugas, but they were raiders returning along the war path and were not in search of her.

She had reached the mysterious, ancient stone fort that stood north of a river that crossed the Nickajack route, when she first detected that Walini was growing fevered. Worried, she stopped. The baby fretted and cried and grew hotter even as Ayasta held her. No, Ayasta thought. This cannot happen, not now!

The illness swiftly worsened. Unwilling to go on with Walini so sick, Ayasta made camp in the forest off the trail, and fought the despair that threatened to overwhelm her.

Solomon Brecht had no doubt about it now: Someone was behind him. He could sense it, feel it like a chill in his marrow. Whenever he left the trail and looked for his pursuer, he never saw anyone at all, but still he felt sure someone was there. Surely it was Diga-tiski, Solomon thought; for he knew nothing of his former captor's death.

He pushed on, driving himself all the harder. The sense of pursuit grew, filling his mind so that he could think of little else. That was one reason he was so intensely shocked when he stumbled upon two corpses in the road, so recently deceased that their body heat had melted the snow around them.

Chickamaugas, both of them. Solomon recognized them as residents of Running Water Town who had been among a band of raiders who had left the town some weeks before. They had been shot to death and scalped—and the scalp locks lay on their bloodied chests. Solomon was both repelled and mystified. Who would do such a thing? It was not the custom of either red or white scalptakers to leave their trophies behind.

He learned the answer some miles farther on, when he camped in the forest for the night beneath a sky that had cleared of clouds in the afternoon. He awakened and sat up, and saw a moonlit figure crouched at his feet, looking at him. Gasping, he leaped up and reached for his musket, only to find it gone.

"My name is Pont," the figure said. "Don't worry—I don't aim to hurt you. It's redskins that I hurt."

"What do you want with me?"

"Victuals, if you've got them. I'm empty as a hole."

Feeling that this was perhaps merely a vivid dream, Solomon Brecht shared food from his meager remaining supply. The black man, though obviously hungry, ate slowly, keeping his eyes on Solomon.

"Bad time for a white man to be in this country, 'specially on a redskin war trail," he opined.

Solomon was so awed and afraid of this intruder that he didn't even consider lying to him. "I was a prisoner of the Chickamaugas," he said.

"A prisoner? Where?"

"Running Water Town."

Pont stood so swiftly that Solomon backstepped. "Did you know another prisoner there, a white man name of Trent?"

"Yes . . . I carried him his food!" He paused. "But he's dead now."

"Yes. I know."

"He was a friend?"

"A good friend." Pont looked past Solomon into the forest, his jaw tightening. "A man whose death will cost the Chickamaugas a score of lives before I'm done."

"Trent tried to escape. He had no choice—he was already condemned to the stake. I helped him, what little I could. I gave him a knife blade. But in the end it did him no good."

"If you helped Malachi Trent, you are my friend." Pont stooped and picked up Solomon's musket, which he handed back to him. "Where are you bound?"

"French Lick, if I can get there."

"I'll get you there. What's your name?"

"Solomon . . . Smith. Solomon Smith." Solomon made up the false surname on the spur of the moment, a quick intuition telling him that as fierce a foe of the Chickamaugas as this Pont claimed to be, he might not react favorably to learning that the man he had encountered bore the same surname as the Chickamaugas' most infamous Tory ally.

"I'm at your service, Solomon Smith," Pont said. "I'll go with you as far as the Cumberland, if that suits you."

"It suits me fine." In truth, it rather frightened him, but he wasn't going to deny this big fellow anything he asked.

Solomon remembered the two scalped Chickamaugas. "I found two dead Indians beside the trail. Did you—"

"Indeed I did."

"What brings you out on this trail? It's dangerous for you too."

"If you want to shoot rabbits, you go where they run," he replied. "Anyway, they're bound to be looking for me down around the Five Lower Towns. I've killed four thereabouts already besides the two you saw on the trail. I'm ranging out to make myself harder to find." Pont stretched. "I'm going to sleep now."

He lay down and fell asleep within a half minute. Solomon slept no more that night, but sat up staring at his strange new companion, wondering if he should trust him. He had no reason at all to do so, but by morning he had decided that by putting his faith in Pont he really had nothing to lose but his life, which under the circumstances was a most uncertain possession anyway, and only safety to gain. If Pont was so capable a man that he could kill two Chickamaugas singlehandedly on their own war trail, he would be a protective soul to travel with. A kind of guardian angel—or guardian demon, if there were such things.

Pont rode directly ahead of Solomon the next day, mounted on a horse he had taken from his last two Chickamauga victims. Solomon was glad now that Pont, whoever he was, was here. In his presence he felt secure.

Near the stone fort, an obviously man-made structure that the Cherokees attributed to a legendary ancient white-skinned people called the "Welsh tribe," who purportedly had come across the great water long ago, Pont lifted a hand for a halt. Solomon paused and let Pont take the lead. Dismounting, Pont strode carefully into the forest, bearing his rifle. Waiting for him to return, Solomon found himself imagining that he heard the faint cry of a fretful baby somewhere in the forest. A few minutes later Pont emerged from the trees and signaled Solomon to follow him back in.

Leading the horses, Solomon trailed in after Pont and was surprised to come upon a well-hidden camp where an Indian woman was tending a baby. At first he was confused, then came a terrible suspicion that Pont was going to kill these two and wanted him to witness it. So appalled by that idea that he forgot to be afraid, Solomon stepped forward and protested.

"You have it wrong, friend," Pont said. "I won't hurt this woman, not ever. This here is Ayasta. She was Malachi Trent's squaw." The big man, smiling but managing to look sad at the same time, reached up and wiped the back of his hand across his eye. "And this baby, I can look in its face and see Malachi in it. This here is the child of my old partner, sure as the world."

He reached down and swept up the child and held it close. Solomon Brecht had never seen a sight like that of the black-skinned frontiersman holding the tiny child with such remarkable gentleness.

Solomon sank to his haunches and shook his head. After all the surprising things he had seen, he doubted anything could ever surprise him again. Then that notion was immediately given the lie when he realized that he also knew this Indian woman, knew her by appearance, at least. He had seen her many times in Running Water Town, though he had never met her. What was she doing out here, and how had she come to bear the child of Malachi Trent?

It was going to take a long time to make sense of it all, and at the moment Solomon had no energy even to try.

It had been an extraordinarily difficult fall and winter in the Cumberland settlements.

No one had anticipated the degree of Indian trouble that had come upon the new stations. Throughout 1780 it had been nigh impossible to gather harvests or to hunt in safety. Cattle had been killed in abundance by the skulking Indians, their cooling bodies found porcupined with arrows. Almost no one now dared live in their own cabins; instead they resided in the stockades, low on food and even lower on ammunition. In the prior year nearly forty men, including a son of James Robertson himself, had fallen victim to either the Chickasaws or Chickamaugas. Even now it was common to hear the imitated wolf howls or owl hoots by which the Indians communicated with each other in the surrounding forests.

It was a terrible time to live and a terrible place to be— but Hannah Brecht, living now inside the fort at Nashborough, or the Bluffs, had never been happier than she was this January day. Today a miracle had occurred, a grander miracle than she could have dared hope for.

James Robertson and three other Cumberlanders who had made a perilous journey to Kentucky to obtain direly needed powder and ball had returned today—and with them, incredibly, was Cooper Haverly.

There were no pretenses, accusations, or political strains to separate the couple now. Cooper swept Hannah into his arms and kissed her in full view of everyone there, and Hannah wondered if this could be real, or if perhaps she had died in her sleep and had been carried to heaven.

Callum McSwain, one of the three who had left the Cumberland settlements three weeks before with Robertson, introduced Cooper to those who did not know him and told what he could of Cooper's story, which Cooper had related in some detail to him during the journey back from Kentucky. Cooper was far too busy getting reacquainted with Hannah to tell the tale himself at the moment.

Fresh back from King's Mountain, McSwain related, Cooper had immediately left for the Cumberland to seek Hannah, but had made it no farther than Cumberland Gap before he became embroiled in some of the Indian troubles besetting settlers in Powell's Valley. Chickamaugas had been raiding extensively, and after stumbling upon the aftermath of one such raid, Cooper had volunteered his services to a band of armed valley frontiersmen who had set out in pursuit of the marauders. There had been a minor skirmish or two, with no one killed on either side.

Cooper had been eager to go on, but was persuaded to remain many days more to defend against anticipated new raids, which by good fortune never occurred. By now much delayed, he set out again, and on his way to the Cumberland came upon Robertson's band on the way to get the powder and ball. It was a happy meeting, and Cooper took up with the group, who were glad to have such a capable rifleman added to their number. The group made it back to the Cumberland settlements in much peril, but without incident.

Cooper's reunion with Hannah was not the only happy bonus of the return of the little ammunition-bearing party. James Robertson was told that his wife had borne him a son that very day and awaited him eagerly at nearby Freeland's Station. The child was the first born in the new settlements—and in a year in which so many had died, a birth was even more welcome than usual.

There was one more bit of news to be given the returnees that was not at all cheering. One of the Cumberlanders, a waggish and well-liked man named David Hood, had been killed and scalped by Chickasaws earlier in the day. Traveling from Freeland's Station to Fort Nashborough, Hood had come under unexpected attack. Three rifle balls had felled him; by the time other men in Fort Nashborough had responded to the gunfire, Hood was already scalped and lying in a heap in a snowy clump of brush.

Robertson's face showed his sorrow. "Where is he now?" he asked.

"Laid out in yonder shed. There was no opportunity to bury him, and we figure the cold will keep him."

"Aye," Robertson said. "Sad thing, sad indeed. I was fond of David." He turned. "Callum, will you see to the distribution of our ammunition? It appears we may need it even more than we anticipated."

"Indeed, Colonel," Callum said. "Are you off to Freeland's?"

"Aye—I'm eager to see little Felix."

"Felix, eh? A fine name for a young one. Congratulations to you on his birth."

Cooper, though exhausted when he arrived at the settlements, was remarkably revitalized by Hannah's company. The pair of them, seeking the farthest corner of the station for what little privacy a stockade allowed, talked intently for hours. Repentance was not about; she had developed a congestion of the lungs and remained abed in her cabin, being tended by her sons.

There was much for the reunited lovers to share with each other. Cooper knew no details of Hannah's river voyage to the lick beyond what fragments Callum and the others had told him secondhand, and Hannah knew nothing of Cooper's extensive military activity since their last parting.

Their talk inevitably came around to the apparent death of Solomon Brecht. Cooper hardly knew what to say about it. "I know it's a deuced sad thing for you and your family. How's Repentance taking it?"

"She's only recently come to understand the truth," Hannah said. "For the longest time she was . . . well, deceived about it all in her own mind." She briefly described Repentance's deluded mental state after Solomon's disappearance. "But that's past now, thank God," Hannah went on. "Bit by bit she's come to realize he truly is dead, and in the strangest way, I think knowing the truth has relieved her." Hannah smiled. "Now the prospect of marrying Callum McSwain is much on her mind—she's admitted as much to me."

"Callum!" Cooper smiled. "I'll be! Has he asked her?"

"Not yet . . . but he told me that he plans to, as soon as the Indian trouble is done and he can set her up in 'proper housekeeping,' as he puts it."

"He's more patient than me, then," Cooper said. "I don't aim to wait to marry you. I've already talked to Robertson about it—in the absence of a preacher, he has the power to marry us . . . if you'll have me."

Hannah put her arms around Cooper. "Have you? I never intend to let you out of my sight again, Cooper Haverly, and I don't want to spend a single day longer than I must without being your wife."

Cooper smiled, kissed her. "Tomorrow, then—if Robertson can."

"Tomorrow."

After midnight, new father James Robertson awakened in Freeland's Station, having heard an unusual sound, this one not made by tiny Felix. Rising, he fetched down his rifle and went into the station yard. Something was moving outside the gate—then the bar fell, pushed up from the outside, and frightening, savage-looking figures entered the stockade. Without hesitation he sent up the shout: "Indians!" Then he bolted back toward his cabin.

Within moments a battle was under way. The sound of gunfire cracked loudly and repeatedly within the stockade walls; the settlers firing from inside their cabins, every man glad for the fresh ammunition supply that had come not a day too early. Score after score of shots were fired before the sound of the swivel gun at Nashborough, the same gun that had been on Colonel Donelson's flatboat, boomed in the darkness. Help was on the way from the Bluffs.

The raiding Chickasaws had no desire to battle a new round of riflemen under these circumstances. They abandoned their attack and vanished into the woods, leaving the Freeland's Station occupants with two dead among their meager number, one white and the other a black slave. Both had died when rifle balls passed between the logs of their unchinked cabin and killed them as they rose from sleep at the onset of the fight.

Cooper was among the force that came from Nashborough, and was glad to find the Indians already gone by the time he arrived at Freeland's. This was no time to fall in battle, not with marriage immediately impending. He took advantage of the moment to request Robertson's services the next afternoon as marriage officiator, received Robertson's gracious acceptance, and returned to Nashborough by the light of dawn.

Robertson came to Nashborough at midday. Cooper and Hannah eagerly awaited him. "Be patient—I think we'd best see to burying the dead before we unite the living," Robertson said. "Come with me, if you'd like, Cooper. I'm going to see to getting poor David Hood properly beneath the ground."

Hood's body was a sad thing to look at in the little shed. His scalp was red and raw . . . and bleeding. Cooper and Robertson noticed it, realized the same thing at the same moment, and looked at each other in amazement.

"Alive! He's still alive!" Cooper whispered in awe.

And alive David Hood was, though terribly weakened and chilled. "David, forgive us—we didn't know," Robertson said. "Can you speak?"

"Aye . . . "

"You're hurt bad, David."

"I think, sir, that if I have half a chance, I can get well." Hood's voice was soft and raspy.

"David, my friend, you'll have a whole chance," Robertson replied.

Cooper ran to fetch help. Hood was carried to the closest cabin and settled into a bed near a roaring fire.

Cooper watched as Robertson performed a shocking but standard surgical procedure often used on scalping victims. With an awl he carefully bored a series of holes into Hood's exposed skull, just deep enough to allow a pinkish fluid to appear and overcrust the wound. Hood endured the pain with remarkable grace, saying afterward that as bad as it was, it was certainly not as bad as the scalping itself had been. The Chickasaw who had performed it had used a dull knife, requiring much hacking and sawing before the scalp lock came away—and this while Hood "played 'possum," as he put it. Cooper was astounded that anyone could have managed to lie perfectly still and unflinching while being scalped alive, particularly with a dull blade.

Hood's remarkable survival, horrifying as its circumstances were, cheered the settlers, and would earn for Hood the lasting nickname of " 'Possum." Hood was a popular man whose cheerfulness had often done much to brighten the Cumberlanders' grim situation.

When the awl procedure was done, Robertson patted Hood on the shoulder. "Good man, David," he said. "I suspect you'll walk with extra ginger about the Indians from now on."

The weakened man even then managed a smile. "I expect so, Colonel . . . but one thing I needn't worry about anymore. I know that at least they can't scalp me."

Cooper walked out into the stockade to get some fresh air, feeling a little squeamish about what he had just watched. He looked up and saw Hannah, Repentance, and Callum McSwain approaching him in a group. McSwain wore a big grin.

"Coop, would you be too angry at me if I stole a bit of your show today?"

"What do you mean?"

McSwain slipped his arm around Repentance's waist. "I've asked Repentance to marry me, and she's accepted. I'd thought of waiting for better times, but there's nothing gained in wasting the opportunity, with Robertson marrying you two up anyway. He can just as easy join two couples as one."

Cooper smiled and thrust out his hand. "Congratulations, Callum." Then he turned to Repentance. It was a difficult moment. Here was the woman who had so long gone along with Solomon Brecht's bitterness toward him. He wondered how she felt now. It didn't really matter; he would marry Hannah whatever Repentance thought of him. But he would prefer it happen in an atmosphere of favor, if possible.

"Mrs. Brecht, I wish you well in your marriage, and hope you will have a long and happy life as Mrs. McSwain. This is a good man who's taking you as wedded wife."

"Yes . . . and it is a good young lady who is about to become wife to you, Mr. Haverly."

"Indeed she is, and I hope our marriage carries your blessing, though I know it would never have been favored by your late husband."

Repentance Brecht smiled slowly. There was nothing in her gaze or manner now that suggested any lingering trace of the mental distresses that had plagued her. She looked strong and beautiful. "You have my blessing, Cooper Haverly," she said.

Cooper had never heard more welcome words. Repentance's acceptance of him washed away the strain and bitterness of the past. To Cooper, the winter day seemed as fresh as springtime.

The double marriage ceremony took place in the midst of the Nashborough stockade, with settlers from all around circling the couples and Robertson. When it was done, the assembled settlers sent up a great, congratulatory whoop and cheer.

The dancing was done to torchlight and fiddle, and lasted far into the night. If the revelers had allowed themselves to think about it, they might have found it odd to be dancing and laughing while Indians still crept in the forests around them. But such was the way of frontier folk: They celebrated when they could, for they never knew which opportunity for festivity would be their last.

In the midst of the celebration, Cooper took Hannah's hand and led her back to the stockade cabin set aside for them. A minute later McSwain similarly withdrew with his new bride.

And even as they closed the door behind them to enter the happy intimacy marriage allowed them, Solomon Brecht hid in the forests with Ayasta, her baby, and the ever-protecting Pont, very close now to the Cumberland stations.

Somewhere in one of the forts ahead he hoped to find his wife and children. The anticipation of that that reunion was so great that even Solomon's fear of the Indians haunting these forests could not overcome it.

Solomon Brecht was a man saved from captivity, a man given a second chance to live. He had run the gauntlet of the Nickajack Trail and survived, and now, if all went as he hoped, he would be rejoined with the ones he loved.

He had never realized until now how deeply he cherished Repentance Brecht, and how badly he had missed her.

25

Darcy Colter gave birth to a baby daughter in January, shortly after Joshua returned home from Sevier's campaign against the Overhill towns. The child, the image of her mother, was healthy and delightful to her parents, who named their daughter Hester, in memory of Joshua's late mother.

A few days after the baby's birth, Joshua was surprised to receive a visit from Israel Coffman and his family. It saddened him to see his old friend astride his big horse with a white bandage swaddling his eyes. Virginia Coffman had tied the leads of her husband's horse to her own saddle, and led him. Judah, swarthy and with features gradually shaping themselves into a living memorial of John Hawk, kept his own horse beside his father's, as if he was a protector of the blind clergyman.

Coffman held little Hester and touched her face gently, outlining its shape with his fingers and declaring her beautiful. Joshua found it difficult to talk to Israel without great sadness, and though he tried to hide it, Coffman detected it.

"Don't grieve for me, Joshua," he said. "I've grieved enough myself already. Now that I'm past it, I'm beginning to listen to the whispers of God in my ear. He's teaching me much. My spirit's eyes have grown keener even as my body's eyes have died."

"I don't understand why it had to happen, Israel. Why a man of God would be so stricken. It doesn't seem right, or just . . ."

"Aye, the wicked prosper while the faithful suffer—is that it? It's an ancient problem, my friend, one neither you nor I will resolve. Never finally doubt the goodness of

our God, Joshua. Question it if you wish, shake your fist at the sky as I have, but in the end, don't finally doubt it. It is a truth derived from revelation, not observance, accepted on faith, not argument. 'Where wast thou when I laid the foundations of the earth? Declare, if thou hast understanding. Who hath laid the measures therof, if thou knowest? Or who hath stretched the line upon it? Whereupon are the foundations thereof fastened? Or who laid the corner stone thereof; When the morning stars sang together, and all the sons of God shouted for joy?' "

"The book of Job, I believe?"

"Yes." Coffman smiled. "It's remarkable, Joshua, since my blinding, I've discovered I have the ability to pull the words of the scripture from my memory. Passage after passage, and those I can't remember, Virginia reads to me, and once I've heard them a few times, they're lodged in my mind to stay."

"I've heard that you've returned to your pulpit."

"I have, and the people of the congregation have been good to us, seeing to our needs now that I can no longer provide for my own as I did before. I'm moved so often by the good that has come from the evil that happened to me. It seems to be His way with me that with every hardship comes a gift, or a recompense."

"I'm glad."

"There's been another good thing . . . or I think it's good. I received a visitor some days ago, a fine old Presbyterian clergyman named David Moriah, from North Carolina. He had heard of me through Samuel Doak, who had met him through some circumstance or another. He has his eye set on Kentucky, not only for himself, but for his entire congregation."

"Sounds like the Exodus from Egypt," Joshua commented wryly.

"That's much closer to the truth than you realize. His people have suffered greatly from the Tories and outliers. They see Kentucky as a haven."

"A man can lose his scalp in Kentucky as quick as in Carolina, if not quicker," Joshua replied.

"Perhaps so, but in any case, Reverend Moriah feels compelled to go. It's not just to escape troubles in Carolina; he believes Kentucky is his destined field of service. But he is old and aged and doubts his life will continue long enough for him to achieve all he would like."

"What brought him to you?"

"He wants me to join him in leading the congregation, whenever it goes. I'll be Aaron to his Moses, and when he's gone, I would take his place. Of course, he didn't know until he met me that I had been blinded . . ."

"Did that change his mind?"

"Not at all." Coffman smiled. "He seemed to find me all the more interesting for it."

"Do you plan to go with him?"

"I don't yet know. Perhaps I shall."

The day was Saturday, so Joshua and his family, including Alphus and Zachariah, accompanied Coffman back to his home, where they spent the night, then continued on the next morning to the Newberry Hill Church near Jonesborough, a town that by now consisted of a notable collection of log buildings. Seated on the rough bench amid the congregation, Joshua was entranced by Coffman's preaching. The preacher had always been a capable and moving speaker, but something about him now transcended even what he had already been. About the preacher was an aura of wisdom deep and mysterious, of old prophets, ancient books, and things beyond the experience of the common man. Perhaps it was merely a perception somehow created or enhanced by the man's blindness, but whatever it was, Joshua felt it and could see that others did too. It put a shiver all the way through him.

It affected Alphus as well. The old man said little all the way home, seeming very thoughtful. Joshua feared he was about to descend into another of his spells, but this time it didn't happen.

Back home again, Alphus sat by the fireplace and stared into the flames as Joshua told him of Israel's talk of possibly going to Kentucky. Alphus looked up at him when he was through and said, "If the preacher goes, I think I'll go with him, by Joseph. What would you think of that?"

Joshua hadn't expected to hear anything like this. He wanted to respond that he didn't think much of the idea at all, that Alphus shouldn't consider such fool things, as old as he was. He ought to stay home, with his kin, and enjoy some serenity in his last years.

Something caught back the words at the last minute. He paused a moment, then said, "If that's what you want to do, Alphus, then I think it's fine."

Alphus smiled, just a little, then looked back at the fire and said no more, leaving Joshua wondering whether the statement was just another of Alphus's fleeting, impossible wishes, or if he had really meant it.

The rider, a young man named Sam Cochran, came to Nashborough from Buchanan's Station, bearing a most unusual message to James Robertson.

"There's three new people back at the station," Cochran said. "A white man, dressed mostly like an Indian, and an Indian woman, Cherokee or Chickamauga. And she's got a baby girl with her—that's the third. The baby looks to be half-bred, but she says the white man ain't the father. We can't ask him; he's too bad hurt."

"What happened?"

"Chickasaws got to them almost in sight of Buchanan's. They were making for the fort this morning when they sprung out on them, according to the woman. She grabbed the baby and made a run and managed to hide herself in a cave down by a creek, then make it safe to the stockade. The baby ain't hurt. The white man took two rifle balls through the middle and lost his scalp, but he's yet alive. We found him lying half in the water, all raving and saying 'Repentance! Repentance!' over and over again. A religious thing, I suppose."

"So it would seem. I wonder why the Chickasaws left him alive?"

"Well, there's the most peculiar thing of all, Colonel Robertson. The woman declares there was a second man with them, a Negro. She says he drove the Chickasaws off—and we did find some moccasin prints in the snow that looked bigger than any redskin foot I've ever seen. And there was blood too, a good ways off from where the white man fell, so we're thinking either this Negro shot him an Indian or the Indians got the Negro. Ain't no sign of any corpses, though."

Robertson gathered several other men and rode to Buchanan's Station. Within an hour Cochran was back again at Nashborough, asking for Cooper Haverly.

"You'd best come with me—the colonel wants you at Buchanan's quick, along with your wife and her family," Cochran said.

"My wife? I don't much favor the notion of taking her out of the stockade at such a time."

"It's important," Cochran said. He leaned closer and whispered, "The colonel says that man the Chickasaws shot is your wife's father."

"My God—Solomon Brecht, alive!"

"Aye—some who came with him on the flatboats say it's him indeed. He's so pox-scarred and scalpless they didn't know him right off. He's asking for his wife."

"His wife . . . Repentance . . ." Cooper shook his head at the irony. "Callum McSwain's wife now. God help us, what a situation!"

For the reunited Brechts there were tears in abundance, both of happiness and sorrow. Hannah was horrified by the sight of her father's scalp wound, which had already been awled over by Colonel Robertson. Yet she was overwhelmed with happiness that he was alive. For Hannah right now the world was a world of miracles, in which lost lovers return unexpectedly and dead loved ones are resurrected as if from the very grave.

She hadn't yet realized the complication created by her father's reappearance, now that her mother had married Callum McSwain.

McSwain had realized it, however, and paced about the Buchanan's Station yard with a face as pallid as death. Cooper dug for something to say to him and found nothing. He loitered around near the stockade cabin in which Solomon lay, and watched his own breath steam like smoke in the cold air.

Repentance appeared in the door, her face more pale even than Callum McSwain's. She too comprehended how deeply the return of Solomon altered her situation.

"Repentance," McSwain said, advancing toward her. "How is he?"

The woman's voice was drained of its usual music; she spoke in a peculiar, slightly shrill monotone. "Colonel Robertson believes he will live." Tears sprang to her eyes. "Oh, Callum, I waited so long for him to come back—just a mad dream it was . . . and now it's happened. He's back, and God forgive me, I wish he wasn't!"

"Hush, Repentance, hush! He might hear you." McSwain put his arm over her shoulder and led her away from the cabin.

"He knows already. I tried to hide it, but my face showed it—I could tell it by the way he looked back at me. Callum, God forgive me, I find myself wishing he had died!"

Cooper felt embarrassed and out-of-place. He walked away toward the far end of the fort, digging his pipe and tobacco pouch from under his coat.

McSwain and Repentance continued to talk, Repentance crying all the while and McSwain looking like a man at loose ends. What an insane place this world could be sometimes, Cooper thought, tossing people into situations that defy all sense and judgment, posing to them riddles that have no answers.

Hannah came out of the cabin, her eyes red, her face

blotched. Looking around the stockade yard, she located Cooper and motioned him toward her.

"He wants to see you," she said.

Cooper's eyes widened. "Me? Solomon Brecht wants to talk to a 'Colter'?"

"Please, Cooper, not now. Just go in and talk to him. Nothing is what it was before. He's changed."

Cooper entered the cabin with the attitude of a criminal approaching the justice bar of a particularly stern judge. Any trepidation he had was quickly overwhelmed by shock when he saw the pitiful state Solomon Brecht was in. His scalp wound was an ugly, jagged thing that had been covered by a hankerchief that had since slipped down and left everything exposed. Solomon was wan and pale and his breath rattled. His dark-rimmed eyes were closed. They fluttered open as the young man neared his bedside. There was no one else in the cabin but Cooper and Solomon.

"And here he is," Solomon said weakly. "The man who's made a Colter of my daughter."

Cooper curled his lip. Hannah had been wrong; nothing had changed. "I'm not a Colter—but what's the point of saying it for the thousandth time? You've never listened before."

Solomon smiled wanly. "Pay no heed, Mr. Haverly. Did you hear me that time? I called your name correctly. What I said before was nothing but the last gasp of an old habit. You'll find I've changed. I'm not the man you knew."

Cooper had nothing to reply, and wondered why Solomon had called him in.

"Hannah tells me she already is your wife," Solomon continued.

"Yes."

"And Mr. McSwain has taken Repentance as his bride."

"Yes."

Solomon squeezed his eyes closed and tears began rolling down his cheeks. "Forgive my tears, Cooper. I have suffered more than one kind of wound since coming here, and the worst wasn't inflicted by the savages. When

Repentance looked at me today, she showed no love, no happiness at my return. She regretted it. It was clear in her face. She doesn't love me now; in her mind I've been dead and buried and no longer have a place among the living."

"She waited for you a long time. She declared you were still alive and would come back. I reckon she loved you so much her mind couldn't handle the truth. The strange part is, it was her who was right."

"I was a fool for believing I could return and find all things as they had been. I've lost her, lost her."

"Not that I can see, Mr. Brecht. You're alive. Your marriage has never been dissolved. It's Callum who has lost a wife, not you."

Solomon lifted a blood-crusted arm and wiped at his eyes. "It would have been much simpler for everyone if I had died back in Running Water Town. Repentance would have never known the truth about me. She would be happy now with Mr. McSwain, and I would be a good memory to her, not an unwanted intruder from a life she's already put behind her." Solomon opened bloodshot eyes and looked at Cooper. "You want to know how you can be sure you truly love a woman, Cooper? When her happiness matters more to you than your own existence. That's how you know."

Cooper frowned, feeling he had detected some hidden significance in Solomon Brecht's words. "What are you saying?"

"Nothing that matters. I am a man who no longer matters, so there's naught I can say that means a thing, eh? Except for this: You take care of my daughter with all that's in you, Cooper Haverly. Love her more than you love yourself, and be loyal. I have not been the best husband to Repentance, but I have always been loyal. No matter what, I was loyal, and I'm proud of that. Do you understand me?"

"Yes. And you have my word: I will treat Hannah as you would want her treated. I'll love her more than any man has ever loved a woman. You watch, and you'll see."

Solomon shook his head, winced in pain. "No, I won't see. I doubt very much that I'll see."

Again Cooper was made uncomfortable; he didn't know how to respond to Solomon's seemingly pregnant words. He shifted on his feet. "Colonel Robertson says you'll recover from those wounds, Mr. Brecht. All you need do is lie still and rest."

"Yes, lie still. He told me that. He said that if I stirred about much, I could cause myself to bleed inside and then I would die. And wouldn't that be tragic? Lie still— that's what I need to do."

"Yes. And if the pain will let you, you should sleep."

"You're right, Cooper. I must sleep. When a man sleeps, he is free of all his own troubles, and brings no more troubles to those he cares about. If a man could only sleep forever . . . that would be the thing, eh?"

Cooper could stand this cryptic, strained conversation no more. He edged toward the door.

"Cooper."

"Yes?"

"Take good care of Hannah. Take her away from here— there will be Chickamauga attacks in the spring. Tell that to Colonel Robertson. And for what it counts, you have my blessing upon your marriage. May it bring you both happiness."

Cooper would have never believed he could receive a blessing from the lips of Solomon Brecht. Matters truly had changed after all—changed drastically.

"Thank you, sir. I hope you can rest well tonight."

"I will rest well indeed."

Cooper left the cabin, his heart racing. Hannah awaited him. "What did he say to you, Cooper?"

"Strange things. Things I couldn't understand. And he gave us his blessing. Can you believe that? Solomon Brecht blessing your marriage to one he's always hated as a Colter?"

"I can believe it. I've seen the man I love return to me when I feared I'd never see him again. I've seen a father I thought dead proven to me alive. Now I can believe anything."

* * *

Hannah cried the next morning when they told her what had happened in the night. Solomon Brecht, though warned to remain still, had rolled off his bed and onto the hard puncheon floor. The jolt had made him bleed into the cavity of his chest, and he had died within minutes.

Cooper felt guilty. Now Solomon's cryptic talk made terrible sense. How could he have failed to understand? Now that he did, it was too late.

Callum McSwain didn't seem to know how to take the news of Solomon's death. Suddenly the man whose life had erased his new marriage was gone, this time for good. But McSwain wasn't certain Solomon Brecht had left much behind him that was worth the having.

Repentance had changed. In the space of one day and night she had withdrawn into herself and would not even deign to look him in the eye. When he spoke to her, she ignored him; when he touched her, she shrank back. McSwain could hardly understand it; she had admitted that her love was now for him, not Solomon. Finally he realized that it was not love for Solomon that had changed her, but her sense of guilt because that love had ceased.

McSwain was left feeling helpless and hopeless. How could he battle a memory? How could he compete with an unstable woman's endless sense of guilt?

And the saddest part of all for him was that he truly and deeply loved her.

The year 1781 progressed, and time affected the lives of those in the Overmountain country, the Cumberland settlements, and in and around the Five Lower Towns of the Chickamaugas.

Joshua Colter joined John Sevier in Indian warfare in March. With the Overhill towns already subdued and burned, the new target was the Middle towns of the Cherokees, from whence several raids on Nolichucky farmsteads were believed to have emanated. Even as other frontiersmen gathered in North Carolina to take on the

British at a place called Guilford Courthouse, Sevier, Joshua Colter, and a band of about a hundred thirty men crossed the Alleghenies to ride against the town of Tuckasegee, plus some fifteen other, smaller towns. They killed about fifty warriors, made prisoners of their dependents, and burned their crops and grain stores. Joshua, having fewer emotional ties to the Middle towns, took a more active part in the destruction than he had in the raids on the Overhills, where his lack of participation had been so noticeable as to lead to angry whispers of court-martial. Nothing, however, had come of those threats.

Returning through the gaps and ranges of the mountains the Cherokees called "Land of the Blue Smoke," Sevier brought with him Indian hostages, several of whom would live on his lands for years.

The Chickamaugas remained untouched by these forays, but they continued to face an antagonist far more mysterious and subtle than John Sevier and his townburning riflemen.

Along the Nickajack Trail and in the rugged countryside surrounding the Five Lower Towns, Chickamauga warriors continued to turn up slain and scalped, and Indian children awakened in the night crying out in nightmares about a great black creature, in the shape but not the substance of a man, who preyed upon travelers in the forests. Warriors delved into the wilderness, searching for the vengeful scalp-taker, but those who returned reported either sign that trailed away into nothingness or no sign at all. Several who set out after the sworn avenger of Malachi Trent never returned at all.

Inevitably the Indians began seeing their antagonist in superhuman terms. By the time he had slain his eighteenth warrior, Pontius Pilate was perceived by his foes as a spirit-being who could transform himself into a giant black ka-gu', or crow. Others said he could vanish like a mist before any warrior who leveled an arrow or rifle against him.

Despite the distraction of the mysterious crow-man haunting the forests, the Chickamaugas continued to press their war against the settlers on the Cumberland.

While Nathanael Greene, now commander of the American southern army, took up the battle against the British east of the mountains, rising up to fight again each time his army fell, Dragging Canoe mounted his own campaign to drive out the deprivation-weakened Cumberland settlers. In March, while Sevier was giving his attention to the Cherokee Middle towns, Dragging Canoe led several hundred warriors—including Ulagu, who had long since given up on finding Ayasta and her daughter—toward the Cumberland settlements, intent on destroying Nashborough first, then the secondary stations. By the first of April the Indian army was ready for the attack.

Having been forewarned by Solomon Brecht's words to Cooper and by the unceasing smaller-scale Chickamauga forays that had taken place since the first of the year, the settlers anticipated an attack and continued to live in their stockades.

It had been Cooper's intent to heed Solomon Brecht's command and take Hannah away from the settlements before spring. McSwain had planned to do the same with Repentance, but Repentance refused to go. This was where Solomon had wanted her to be, and this was where he was buried. She owed it to his memory to remain here. And as long as Repentance remained, Hannah also was unwilling to go. When the spring came and brought the anticipated siege, all of them still remained residents of Nashborough.

The first shot was fired by a sentry the night of April 1 when a Chickamauga scout was spotted skulking near the fort, but the true battle didn't begin until dawn the next day. A handful of Indians raced toward the fort, fired off a volley, and retreated. Inside the fort, Colonel Robertson and a score of men, including Cooper and McSwain, mounted and raced out of the fort gates to pursue the Indians.

Once well away from the stockade, the mounted riflemen discovered they had been duped. The little group of Indians who had initially fired were joined by a much larger band, and the horsemen were forced to dismount or face being picked out of their saddles. In the meantime another large group of Chickamaugas appeared from hiding and came upon the stranded gaggle of frontiersmen from the rear.

The horses stampeded as yet another group of Chickamaugas appeared from the woods—and, ironically, it was the horses that helped turn the battle around for the frontiersmen. Many of the Indians set off in pursuit of the precious stock. And the horses, heading for the stockade, broke up the line of Indians that separated the stranded riflemen from the fort.

Meanwhile, Colonel Robertson's wife, Charlotte, seeing her husband and his companions in such peril, followed a wild inspiration and threw open the stockade gates. The men made for the opening, but more importantly, the large pack of dogs, all trained to sniff out and attack Indians, bolted out of the stockade and into the midst of the fray.

The pell-mell confusion allowed most of the twently riflemen to safely reach the fort, though five died in the attempt.

Once behind the protective palings, the men fought from the rifle platforms and drove the Chickamaugas back into the forests. All the next day sporadic fire was poured at the fort, the Indians' typically small powder charges making popping noises at the treeline, until at last the Nashborough residents grew weary of it, loaded their swivel gun with stones and shards of iron, and fired it off at the nearest visible Indians. The blast sounded impressive, and though the swivel gun did little damage to its targets, after it was fired, the siege was lifted.

When the battle was done, Cooper talked to Callum, then went to Hannah. "My decision is made," he said. "We're leaving here."

"But Mother is still—"

"We'll take her with us whether she favors it or not. Callum and I have made up our minds. It's for Repentance's own good to be removed from this place. Here she is constantly reminded of Solomon. Away from here, her mind can clear again. We're leaving, and soon."

Despite Cooper's declaration, it was another month

before the group actually departed. The forests were dangerous, haunted by Indian raiders, and Cooper and McSwain carefully gauged their departure to be at the safest time possible, as best they could determine it. With them they took a few other restless Cumberlanders, as well as Ayasta and Walini, who were under Cooper's willing protection. He remembered the kindness Ayasta had shown him when he lay wounded in Trent's cabin on the Nolichucky.

Hannah shed no tears to leave the Cumberland settlements. They carried few good memories for her now. Once away from them, the entire group seemed heartened; even Repentance was more her old self, as Cooper had predicted.

The party headed toward Kentucky by the usual route, going over the Cumberland River from the Bluffs, past Eaton's, Mansker's, and Bledsoe's stations, and into the Kentucky Barrens. Cooper wanted to continue east to Cumberland Gap and then down into the Holston and Nolichucky country and home, but McSwain had another idea. He talked privately to Cooper.

"I don't want to go back there," he said. "Not yet, at least. It would be no different for Repentance there than it was on the Cumberland—too many reminders both places. She needs a new home entirely."

"Where, then?"

"Right here in Kentucky. Logan's Station, Boonesborough, anywhere. There I can have my wife back again, like she ought to be. I'm convinced of it. But you needn't stay, Cooper. Go on back to your kin, if you want."

Cooper shook his head. "Hannah still wants to be near her mother," he said. "If it's Kentucky you're set on, then I'm with you."

On to Logan's Station they went, and with every mile Repentance seemed to shed more of her grim mental burden. By July, while far to the south on the Holston, the Cherokees were gathering at Long Island to make yet another treaty with the unakas who had chastised them,

Cooper and McSwain were building cabins in Kentucky, and life seemed good.

Even Ayasta seemed content here—but sometimes she would talk to Cooper about her long-unseen son Judah, wondering if he remembered his true mother. Cooper told her that someday, if she wanted, he would take her back to the Overmountain country to see her boy.

26

On a bright autumn day near the end of October in the year 1782, Alphus Colter gathered up rifle, ammunition, supplies, food, and dogs, and rode away from his home on the Great Limestone, without saying a word to anyone. At the time he left there was no one else at the Colter family stockade. It was late night before the old man was missed.

Darcy Colter didn't worry much at first; Alphus, though old, did sometimes go out for two or three days at a time to hunt in the forests. Joshua worried over him when he did it, fearing some accident might befall him, or Indians might find and kill him. But always Alphus either came back or Joshua was able to track him down and bring him home.

This time Joshua was not here to go after him. In September he had again ridden off on the war trail with John Sevier, to a rendezvous on the Big Island of the French Broad. The towns around Chickamauga that had been destroyed in 1779 had been gradually reoccupied under the names of Settico, Vann's, Bull Town, Tuskegee, and Chickamauga. Chasing out the Chickamaugas before them, the white men did their usual job of destruction, but were misled by their Indian guide and never even approached the Five Lower Towns, which were the heart of the Chickamauga country. Heading to the Coosa River, they burned more towns and then made peace overtures to the Cherokee headmen, who met them in Chota.

Joshua Colter was keenly aware of the passage of time when he saw the three chiefs, Hanging Maw, Old Tassel, and Oconostota, who gathered for the conference at Chota. In particular he noted how Oconostota had aged. Once stoutly built and as strong a man as Joshua had ever seen, now the old war chief was wrinkled and emaciated. When he mentally erased the lines of age from the face, however, Joshua could see the same striking visage that had awed him when he was a boy at Fort Loudoun, a fort that Oconostota himself had besieged.

Early in November, Joshua returned to the Great Limestone to find Darcy and Alphus's stepson Zachariah, now a stoutly built boy of eleven years, frantic with concern. Alphus had not returned, and through inquiring of neighbors, Darcy had learned that the old long hunter had spoken to some of them of going into Kentucky to hunt. "By Joseph, he had said, I'm wearied of waiting for Joshua to end his war-making and take to the mountains with me like he's been promising so bloody long. I'm off to Kentucky, and if Joshua wants, he can come after me."

"He'll get himself killed out there, Darcy," Joshua said outside of Zachariah's earshot. "If I don't find him—"

"You will. Joshua Colter can find anyone, at any place," Darcy said. "I'm loath to see you go off when you've just freshly come home, but I've worried for Alphus since he left. Go find him, Joshua, and bring him safe home."

Along with the frightening news about Alphus, Darcy had one welcome piece of news to give Joshua. A neighbor who had been away at the North of Holston settlements had returned with word that, on October 19, Cornwallis had yielded to a siege and surrendered eight thousand troops at a place called Yorktown, and in addition had put his pen to articles of capitulation.

Could the years of warfare against the mother country really be ending? Many seemed to believe it, Darcy said, but Joshua could scarcely accept the idea. And besides, with the fiery Dragging Canoe leading the Chickamaugas, there was no guarantee that a British surrender would end the troubles on the frontier border. As long as Dragging Canoe had a gun and scalping knife and even a handful to follow him, Joshua was convinced, he would raid until his last breath, just as John Hawk had. Even now Dragging Canoe was reported to be seeking new alliances with the northern tribes. Many months before, he had sent a band of warriors to reside with the Delawares in their main town of Big Spring, on the eastern bank of a creek called Tymochtee, and in return the Delawares had sent a delegation to live at Running Water Town. When the Delawares had executed one Colonel William Crawford at the stake in June in one of the most terrible death ordeals ever seen on the frontier, Dragging Canoe's exchanged warriors had joined the gruesome celebration as the man slowly expired, vainly pleading for the white renegade Simon Girty, a witness to the death, to shoot him and end his sufferings.

Joshua rode through a countryside filling rapidly with new cabins and barns. So busy had he been throughout the past year that he had scarcely noticed the great influx of settlers to the region, many driven here by the troubles of war in the east. There was no question now that the frontier as he had known it was gone, or rather, pushed farther west. Joshua's mind leaped ahead through the years, past his own life and the lives of his children and grandchildren. How far would the frontier ultimately be pushed? What lay in the truly distant west, the west beyond the big river that was said to slice through the wilderness from the far north? If only a man's life span was long enough to let him explore it all!

He came to the region of the Long Island and began inquiring to see if anyone matching Alphus's description had passed that way. Just when he was beginning to despair of ever picking up the trail, he located a family that lived along the Holston. Yes, the man of the house told him. There was an old fellow, traveling alone, who had come through with a packhorse and hounds, talking about heading across toward Bean's Station over below the south slope of the Clinch Mountain, and then up through Cumberland Gap into Kentucky to hunt. The family had put him up a day or so and tried to dissuade him, telling him that with the Chickamaugas still active, no one was traveling that direction except in large armed parties. The old man had refused to listen. What was his name? The man scratched his head. Colter, he thought. Albert Colter, maybe.

Knowing he had at last picked up Alphus's spoor, Joshua turned west and followed the Holston through Carter's Valley. Passing the mouth of Big Creek, he headed toward Bean's Station, keeping his eyes and ears open all the way.

Not many miles later he came upon a burned farmstead that was still smoking, and a lone man just finishing a burial in the yard. His heart heavy with dread, Joshua asked the man what had happened, eyeing the grave and wondering if Alphus was in it.

"Elisha Brecht and his damned outliers, that's what!" replied the obviously shaken man, who had a bloody bandage around his left forearm. "He came in alone, calling himself Jones and pretending to be a traveler who had been beset by the Chickamaugas, and like a fool I took him in, not knowing who he was. He ate my food and slept in my bed, and the next morning I woke up to find my cabin surrounded by redskins. That's when he told me who he was. They slaughtered my cattle, burned my cabin, and roasted the meat by the heat of it. Thought it was a real fine joke, I reckon. I figured my time had come—but the worst I got was a cut on the arm trying to fight off one of the redskins when it all started." The man swiped away a quick tear with his bandaged arm. "My old mother was here with me . . . now she's dead."

"They killed her?"

"As good as. I reckon the fright was too much for her. Her heart, it just quit on her and she died in my very arms. Brecht, he laughed. Damn his soul, he laughed to see her die!"

"I reckon you'll be going after them."

"Reckon I will."

"Ride with me, then. I'll help you."

The man's name was Edward Wallett, and he proved to be a good trail companion despite the grief that kept him blubbering and emotional. Wallett's rifles had been taken by Brecht and the Chickamaugas, so Joshua loaned him a spare he had brought. When Joshua told his own purpose, Wallett's eyes sparked.

"Aye! The redskins had an old man with them. At first I took him to be one of Brecht's bunch, but I finally saw he was a prisoner." He described the old man's clothing and looks, and Joshua shuddered to realize that it had in fact been Alphus.

They rode westward, the direction Brecht reportedly had gone. Wallett was talkative in his sorrow, so much so that Joshua several times had to tell him to lower his voice, for noise was dangerous under these circumstances. One of his stories, though, proved worth the hearing.

While Brecht was at Wallett's home, he said, still pretending to be the traveler Jones, he told a story he claimed to have picked up through the usual mill of rumors. Brecht had said that many months before, a white man named Trent had been killed by the Chickamaugas down in the Five Lower Towns, and since then a dark-skinned forest demon had been killing Chickamaugas one by one in that vicinity and along the Nickajack Trail. The Chickamaugas had begun living in dread of the killer, who was reportedly avenging the death of Trent. Then, abruptly, the killings had stopped after about a score of Indians had died. Wallett didn't know what to make of a tale like that.

"I suspect I know who this 'demon' might be," Joshua said, feeling again the chill of awe that Pontius Pilate had many times roused in him in the brief time he had known the man.

They found a trail left by many horses. It turned south, and they followed.

Alphus Colter tugged at his bonds, even though he knew there was no hope of loosening them. He was tied to a sapling at the edge of Elisha Brecht's camp, his old bones aching from the day's long ride and the clumsy posture in which he had been tied. But he made no complaint; he wouldn't give Brecht the satisfaction.

Brecht, drinking whiskey from a jug, walked over and looked down haughtily at him. "They're going to burn you, Colter. Roast you alive at the stake." He turned up the jug and took another swallow. "I confess I'm looking forward to seeing it. I knew I'd get you one day, old man."

Alphus gave Brecht a look of vain contempt so fierce it could set fires. Brecht laughed.

"See that Indian yonder?" Brecht asked, waving the jug at a warrior on the other side of the fire-lit camp. "His name's Ulagu. He's brother to the squaw your boy Joshua had with him for a time. What do you think of that, Colter! Reckon he'll enjoy burning you as much as me. Me and Ulagu, we fell out for a time because he kept me from getting your boy's scalp when I had a good chance, but we've made our peace now. We're good friends again. I can be a good friend to a man when I want to be. And I can be one hell of an enemy. Reckon you know that now."

"By Joseph, leave me be, you drunken old boar squat," Alphus muttered.

Brecht laughed, heaved a dollop of pleghm from his lungs, and spat on Alphus. Taking another swallow of whiskey, he staggered off and lay down to sleep.

Alphus tugged more at his ropes whenever no one was looking. Futile though it was, it gave him something to concentrate on.

Being captive, he had found, tended to clear the fog of age from a man's mind. He now realized how foolish it had been for him to set out alone to hunt in such uncertain times. Foolish indeed . . . old man foolish. Joshua had urged patience on him many times, saying that one day the long hunt he coveted so would be possible. Sheer exasperation and stubbornness had finally gotten the best of Alphus and he had set out alone. This is what had come of it.

His stomach grumbled and his head felt light. They had given him no food all day, and not being as young as he used to be, an empty belly took its toll quickly. He wondered where they were taking him. Probably back to the Chickamauga towns, where he could be executed with a proper-sized audience.

Alphus tugged at his ropes for another hour, then weariness began to drain his strength. He closed his eyes and dreamed of Sina. Awakening with the image of her fresh on his memory, he felt sad for a moment. Then again, he thought, maybe it's best she isn't around to know what a sorry end her man came to. Sina had lost her first husband to the wilderness. It would have tried her soul terribly to have lost her second to the likes of Brecht and his Indian cohorts.

It was deep night. Alphus looked around and was surprised to see no sentry posted. This was a relatively small group, consisting of Brecht and two other white men, and five Indians. All had been drinking fairly heavily, probably having raided a still-house somewhere recently. A little rested now, Alphus began working at his bonds again.

Something moved behind him, drawing closer. Animal or human, he could not tell. He froze, then twisted his head and tried to look.

"*Shhh!*" The faint command came from directly behind him. A warm burst of joy rippled through the old man.

"Joshua?"

"*Shhh!*"

A knife sawed at his bonds; it seemed to take half of forever to cut through them all. When his hands were free he still kept his position; he would not move until he was sure all in the camp were truly asleep.

At last he felt safe in moving, and carefully he drew his hands around in front of him. Joshua was still there behind him; he could feel his silent presence. Slowly Alphus pushed to his feet, grimacing when his aging and slightly rheumatic bones snapped loudly as he straightened his legs.

Quietly he edged back around the sapling, stepping

quietly on his worn-out moccasins. He turned and followed the faint figure of Joshua away from the camp, and they proceeded to where Wallett waited.

"Joshua, thank the good Lord above!" he whispered. "By Joseph, how did you find me?"

"We'll talk later," Joshua whispered back. "Let's make some tracks first."

"Not yet," Wallett said. "Not until I put a ball through Elisha Brecht's skull."

Joshua's whisper was sharp-edged this time. "Don't talk fool's talk, Wallett! Let's get away from here!"

With a curse Wallett lurched forward, toward the camp. Joshua grabbed at him impulsively, but missed. Wallett's foot cracked a fallen branch loudly.

"Run, Alphus!" Joshua ordered.

Alphus did run, as fast as aging legs would carry him, his face scraping branches and his feet catching on unseen vines and roots that almost pitched him over several times. Joshua was right beside him; Indian in his attitude toward warfare, he had no intention to stay around and fight a hopeless battle, whatever Wallett did. If Wallett had a grain of sense, he would run as well.

The camp was coming awake now, some of the closest Indians having heard the stir. If not for their drunkenness, the sleepers would surely have reacted even more quickly.

Wallett fired his rifle, aiming at a figure he thought was Brecht but which in fact was one of Brecht's cohorts. The shot struck home and the half-risen man pitched back dead on his blankets—but now Wallett was unarmed and his position had been revealed by the powder flash.

Joshua felt no qualms at running. On the frontier, fools paid for their own mistakes, and he was not willing to pick up this debt for Wallett. He and Alphus were well away from the scene by the time they heard Wallett's death yell. They paused only long enough to hear the responsive scalping cry of the Chickamauga who had killed the man, and with that confirmation of Wallett's fate, they mounted and rode off at top speed. Alphus was astride Wallett's horse. The original plan had been for him to ride double with Joshua; Wallett's death made that unnecessary.

They hoped no one would follow, but Elisha Brecht was not about to give up possession of a Colter so easily. He and the Chickamaugas pursued on horseback.

Darkness was the best friend Joshua and Alphus had at the moment, yet it was also an enemy, hampering them from seeing places where they might have hidden. And their horses, not as rested as those of the Chickamaugas, were beginning to tire. The gap between pursuer and pursued narrowed rapidly—and then a potentially fatal tragedy struck.

Alphus's horse stepped into an unseen depression in the ground and stumbled, pitching Alphus off and onto a slope down which he rolled, into a thicket. Joshua halted his own horse, rode back to the spot, and dismounted, grabbing his rifle and shooting gear. He could hear the Chickamaugas closing in behind him. He scooted down the slope, vainly trying to see Alphus in the darkness. At the bottom a familiar voice was groaning.

"I'm hurt, Joshua," he said. "I'm stuck bad."

Joshua kneeled and ran his hand over Alphus's body and was appalled to feel a warm flow of blood coat it. "My God, Alphus, what's happened?"

"There's a sharp prong sticking out of this log, and dogged if I ain't pegged it right into my gut," he said.

The Chickamaugas had reached Alphus's lamed horse and Joshua's riderless one now; Joshua could hear their exclamations. He knew they would soon descend on foot to continue their search.

"We've got to get you away from here—bear up, Alphus, and I'll pull you free."

Alphus bit his lip and made not a sound as Joshua pulled his body back and drew him off the impaling wooden prong. The blood flowed faster now.

"I'm carrying you, Alphus," Joshua said. "Don't flicker out on me, you hear?"

He picked Alphus up and hefted him over his shoulder

like he was a deer carcass. His right arm holding to Alphus and his left carrying his rifle, he moved deeper into the forest as Brecht and the Chickamaugas came swiftly down the slope in pursuit.

The morning light spilled into the woods. Joshua and Alphus, still alive, and amazed that they were, moved slowly along through the untrailed woodland. They had survived by hiding behind the great, gnarled root of a huge tree that had fallen of its own weight in a storm, pulling up a big mass of earth with it. The Chickamaugas had passed close and then vanished. Even after the daylight came, Joshua and Alphus had remained still for a long time, until they were sure their pursuers were gone.

Joshua had lost much of his food when his horse was taken by the Indians, but under his hunting shirt he carried a pouch of parched corn. He mixed the meallike grains with water from a spring and let Alphus drink. The grains, swelling in his belly, gave the old man a full feeling, but this only made the puncture in his groin more painful.

Joshua examined the wound, cleaned the grit and bark fragments from it with cold water, and ripped off a portion of his linsey-woolsey shirt to bundle against it. Alphus's trousers held the makeshift bandage in place.

They were afoot now, both of them, and Alphus was doing none too well. Joshua feared the exertion of movement was causing the wound to bleed. He had made Alphus a crutch out of a forked sapling, and this helped some, but not much.

"We'll make for Big Creek," he said. "There we can tend you and you can rest."

"What if Brecht is still about?"

"We can't worry with that now," Joshua said, "We've got to find you help."

Soon it was apparent that Alphus could walk no farther. Fighting despair, Joshua made a place for the old man to lie down. In his mind he pleaded with Alphus to hang on, to not give in and die. Externally he forced a calm expression.

"I'm going to make you a litter and drag you in the rest

of the way," he said, pulling out his belt axe. "In the meantime, lie still. Get some sleep."

He chopped two saplings and laid them side by side. Taking off his coat, which was made similarly to the hunting shirt beneath it, he tied the coat across the poles, which he had braced apart with a cross-stick lashed in place with strips torn from his and Alphus's clothing. At the base of the litter, where Alphus's calves would rest, he cut small rounded notches in the drag poles to accommodate more crosspieces that he similarly lashed down. He left a space of a few inches between the calf supports and the final, larger crosspiece on the bottom, so that Alphus could put his heels in the space, rest his feet on the bottom crosspiece, and not slide off the contrivance.

It worked even better than Joshua had hoped. Holding the upper ends of the drag poles on either side of his body—Alphus clinging to Joshua's rifle, in that Joshua could not carry it himself—the younger frontiersman pulled Alphus along behind him. Before long Joshua decided he would be glad to give all he owned for one good horse.

They created quite a tumult when they reached the fort at Big Creek. A previous newcomer had spotted Brecht and the Indians in the forest the day before and found the burned-out remains of Wallett's home, so the fort was already in a state of alarm.

Joshua was exhausted, but did not rest until he knew Alphus was as well-tended as he could be. When finally he did sleep, it was like the slumber of the dead.

Now that he was safe within sheltering walls, Alphus seemed to allow himself to finally give in to the trauma he had suffered. He became pale, feverish, and the wound in his groin festered and stank. The old man's closed eyes looked sunken in the sockets, and the people in the stockade began to talk of where best to bury him when he was gone.

Such talk infuriated Joshua. "He won't die," he declared. "He'll fight it out and live."

The looks he got in response were of pity and utter

disbelief. Joshua decided that he would vacate this place just as soon as Alphus was well enough to be moved.

He slept close to Alphus's side, awakening each time the old man groaned. He tried to make Alphus eat, but nothing would stay on his stomach. Two days passed, then three. Alphus seemed no better, but no worse either, so Joshua maintained his hope while all around him waited for the old man to die and be out of the way.

On the fourth day Alphus awakened and asked for food. An examination of his wound showed the swelling and putrefaction to be significantly less. Joshua fed Alphus bits of cornmeal bread and chunks of fowl meat. At one point the old man looked up at him. "Reckon you were right in that tale you told me: Now I'm little and you're big, and feeding me like I was a baby."

Joshua smiled. Alphus had heard his childhood recollection after all, that time he had sat by his bedside just like this, urging his recovery and sending up an unending string of prayers.

Two more days passed and Alphus was all the stronger, and Joshua all the more eager to leave Big Creek.

An unexpected opportunity allowed the men to leave the fort sooner than they had anticipated. A small flatboat laden with furs came poling up the Holston, bound for the Long Island, and stopped at the fort. Joshua's well-known name obtained him and Alphus passage on the boat. Stretched out in the shelter on a pile of blankets, Alphus was as comfortable in the flatboat as he had been at the fort itself. The flatboat crew was generous with food, seemed proud to have aboard such noted frontiersmen as the Colters, and were so eager to help that Joshua was able to buy a used but good rifle from one of them at a low price. He made a gift of it to Alphus, in replacement for the rifle taken from him by Brecht and his companions.

Upon reaching the Long Island region, Joshua knew he would have to find new lodgings for Alphus before continuing on by land to Great Limestone Creek and home. Alphus was not yet in shape for a land journey. He figured to build a half-faced camp or small cabin hut, like the station camp shelters he and Alphus had spent so many winters in years ago. But on the south end of the river island lived Joseph Martin, the Indian agent, and it seemed worthwhile to pay a call in hopes of possibly obtaining better quarters for Alphus than some crude shelter.

Alphus was weary after the flatboat journey, so Joshua stopped and built him a fire near the river's edge and made him comfortable while he headed for Martin's residence.

He encountered Martin himself, fresh in from a brief hunt along the river, before he reached the house, and was warmly greeted by the Indian agent. Martin, at six feet tall and about two hundred pounds, was a stoutly built man with an appealing face and manner. Joshua admired the man much, for Martin was an honest soul who tried to do his job as best he could, looking out not only for the welfare of the white populace he represented, but often for the beleaguered Cherokees as well.

"Alphus Colter is welcome under my roof as long as he wishes to stay," Martin said after Joshua explained his request. "It seems my home is a much-sought haven this year—come to the house and I'll show you what I mean."

At Martin's home Joshua was ushered inside by Martin's Cherokee wife, the former Betsy Ward, daughter of Nancy, and seated by the fire. Martin disappeared into an adjacent room. A little puzzled by all this, Joshua stood when he heard the door to that room reopening.

He was glad he did, for the figure who emerged was the sort that made a man rise at the sight of him. Standing beside Martin, looking back at Joshua out of his weathered, pitted, ancient face, was none other than the famed old war chief himself, Oconostota.

Of all the Cherokee head-men, Joshua had known the late Little Carpenter the best. Oconostota, a few years younger than Little Carpenter, had always seemed less approachable, and between Joshua and him, no personal bond had been forged. In fact, Oconostota had been a fearsome figure to Joshua during his boyhood at Fort Loudoun, and even as an adult he had seen the man in a harsh light for his instigation of the Fort Loudoun siege during which Joshua's mother had died.

But here in Martin's house on the Long Island, Joshua realized how much the years had tempered his feelings. Remarkable it was to hear Oconostota, who still was erect of spine despite his age, talk of his memories while Alphus, propped up comfortably near the fire, listened to Martin's easy translation of the old chief's tales.

Oconostota had come to the Long Island unexpectedly. In July, the month of the treaty-making at Chota, Oconostota had abruptly given up his rank as Great Warrior of the Cherokees, a position he had held for more than two-score years, and passed the title to his son, Tuckesee.

In the fall the aging warrior, his body thinned substantially from the two hundred pounds it had once weighed, climbed into a canoe and traveled to the Long Island. There, Martin had given him a welcome and invited him to spend the winter. Oconostota accepted readily; such had been his desire when he began the journey.

No man, except perhaps Little Carpenter, had exercised such influence among the Cherokees as had Oconostota. In the days when the French and English had been struggling for supremacy over the Cherokee lands, Oconostota had mastered the skill of subtle diplomacy. Above his house the French banner had sometimes flown, other times that of the British. Many times the war chief had made diplomatic journeys to the unaka cities such as Charles Town, and had enjoyed significant success in establishing British trade with his people in the early days—success he attributed to his stern and demanding diplomatic approach. "The Indian can expect nothing from the white men any other way," he said to Alphus through Martin. "The white man will do nothing through fairness, only through the force of strong talk."

He described his lengthy history of military exploits, for which he was famous. He told of his slow starving out of Fort Loudoun's occupants in 1760, of killing and scalping Pontiac's warriors in 1764, and of innumerable skirmishes and battles, small and large and against red men and white, in which he had taken part throughout his life.

He spoke of his worries over the steady encroachment of the white men in the 1770s, and of his reluctance to approve the 1775 land purchase by Richard Henderson, whom Oconostota called "Carolina Dick." He talked openly about the massive British-backed Cherokee onslaught against the Overmountain settlements in 1776, and of his own efforts since to help chart the best route he could find toward the best conditions for his people.

He spoke as well of his political activities, his differences through the years with Little Carpenter, who had often seemed bullheaded to Oconostota, and of his own acknowledged willingness to work in concert with or against French, British, or Americans, depending upon who could best help the Cherokees.

But mostly Oconostota simply told stories and anecdotes—tales of his 1767 journey by sloop to New York, where he watched a play entitled *Richard III* and engaged in diplomacy with the British and the six tribes of the Iroquois Confederacy. Throughout his life Oconostota had enjoyed influence not only with his own people, but also with other tribes, and he clearly was proud of it, just as he was proud of the fact he had never run in battle . . . though he did admit that he once "walked very fast down a creek" when the battle tide turned in the wrong direction.

And he talked of his deep friendship with Martin, whom he had protected from capture by the British in Chota the prior year. His affection for Martin would never end, he declared. Now that his life was drawing to a close, he wanted to be close to his good companion, who represented the "Long Knife," as Oconostota called Virginia. Joshua found it odd that Oconostota as an old man held such an obvious affection for Martin's employing state, Virginia, for it was well-known that once he had described Virginians as "bad men who love to steal horses and hunt deer."

Oconostota not only talked, but listened. He seemed to like Alphus, of whom he had heard, and the pair talked together until late in the night, one night after another, until Martin was weary of translating. Alphus healed as the days went past.

Joshua finally called Martin aside and asked him if he would consider allowing Alphus to remain the full winter with him, provided Joshua helped supply food. Martin was agreeable; he also had noted the mutually beneficial effect the old men had on one another. Joshua thanked him, bade good-bye to Alphus, and promised to return soon with meat. When he left, he found himself truly wishing he could have stayed. Martin's home seemed restful and healing, a haven in which Alphus was happy.

But he couldn't remain. By now Darcy and Zachariah were bound to be sorely worried. He rode home, eager to set their minds at ease and let them know that Alphus, despite his physical wound, was safe and well, and happier in the company of his distinguished, newfound Cherokee friend than he had been for many years.

Joshua Colter was thoroughly taken aback to find none other than the long-absent Cooper Haverly awaiting him when he arrived home. And not only Cooper, but also Hannah, with a baby boy named Ben in her arms; Callum McSwain; and—mystifyingly—Ayasta, and she had a baby as well, a daughter.

"They arrived two days after you left looking for Alphus," Darcy told Joshua. "Cooper and Hannah are married now. Solomon Brecht died on the Cumberland."

"But why is Ayasta here? And the baby . . ."

"It's a long story and as twisted as a vine," Darcy said. "Cooper can tell it better than me."

Joshua, thrilled to see his younger brother again, was eager to hear, for he knew virtually nothing of what had happened to each of these people since he had last parted from them. By now Cooper had become expert on all the individual stories that had so remarkably intertwined with each other over the past two or so years.

Joshua first shared the news of Alphus, greatly relieving Darcy and Zachariah. Then, aided by Hannah, Cooper began the long narrative of how the Brechts had traveled with such difficulty to the Cumberland settlements, and of the apparent death of Solomon Brecht. He told of Repentance's bout with madness, of Callum McSwain's subsequent marriage to her, and the complication of Solomon's surprising reappearance. Cooper described the sufferings and Indian fears the Cumberlanders had been subjected to, the attacks on the stations, and the wounding of Solomon Brecht by the Chickasaws outside Buchanan's. He told too, of how Solomon had died in what seemed to all a deliberate ending of his own life, apparently to leave Repentance free to remain McSwain's wife.

Ayasta herself shared her own story, telling of the birth of Walini, the death of Malachi Trent, the vengeance of Pont—confirming Joshua's earlier suspicions about the Chickamauga killer in the forests—and her own flight to the settlements and later journey into Kentucky with the

Brechts and McSwains. Now, she said, she had returned with them here, for she had long wanted to see her son again. And as for Joshua, she had come to understand that his killing of John Hawk had not been malicious, but inevitable. She had found it in her to forgive him.

Joshua felt a sense of profound relief. A burden he had borne for years now was gone.

"I'll take you tomorrow to Israel's house," Joshua told her. "Judah is a fine and healthy boy now, and it will be a good thing for you to see him."

Joshua turned to McSwain, who had been sitting silently beside Ayasta throughout all the talk. "Why is Repentance not with you, Callum?"

McSwain replied, "Because she is dead."

"I'm sorry," Joshua replied. "How did it happen?"

McSwain tried to answer, but his voice choked. Hannah spoke in his stead. "Mother died in Kentucky. It was an easy death, and natural. She became sick over the winter; it affected her lungs, which had always been weak, and she couldn't overcome it. It was hard when it happened, but it could have been much worse for her. In Kentucky she had the most happiness she had ever known. Callum was a good husband to her, gentle and kind. If not for him, she would have never overcome her grief at what happened to Father."

"I don't deserve all the credit. Repentance had the gift of some fine children who did much for her far longer than I did," McSwain said.

"Where are your brothers now, Hannah?" Joshua asked.

"Still in Kentucky, living and working with a farmer there. It's a life they seem to like, and they chose to keep it. So we came on without them. We don't know yet if we will return or stay."

Joshua talked privately to Callum that night. "I don't know what comfort to give you, my friend," he said. "It's a trying thing for any man to lose a wife, and now you've suffered it twice."

"Aye. There's been some hellish times for me," he said.

"But there is one comfort I have even yet—and it's not the whiskey jug."

Joshua paused, then hesitantly ventured, "Ayasta?"

"Indeed. She's quite a woman, that Cherokee. It may be that I find myself a married man for a third time—if she'll have me." He chuckled. "I never would have thought myself one to cast an eye on a red-skinned woman, God knows!"

The next morning, Joshua kept his pledge to Ayasta. With McSwain accompanying, he put her and Walini on a wagon and drove them east to Coffman's house near Jonesborough. When they arrived, the yard was full of horses, and Coffman was seated beneath a tree in his front yard, talking to an elderly man who looked quite distinguished despite the noticeable stoop of his back.

Ayasta was holding Walini very close to her. Though her expression was as stoically uninformative as always, Joshua sensed the tension in her. There was the potential here for a happy reunion with her son, or an unhappy one. It all depended upon the attitude of young Judah himself, and the Coffmans.

Israel Coffman stood as he heard Joshua striding toward him.

"Hello, Israel."

"Joshua!" Coffman beamed, recognizing the voice. He no longer wore the cloth sash across his eyes, and the scar left by Patrick Ferguson's saber was stark and evident, a straight slash across his eyes. His eyelids were so tightly closed that Joshua suspected they had healed in place.

The man with Coffman was the Reverend David Moriah, pastor of the North Carolina congregation that had been planning so long to transplant itself into Kentucky. Joshua and Coffman greeted the man politely, then Moriah turned his attention toward Ayasta, who was still seated on the wagon. He was obviously curious about what an Indian woman was doing in the company of two white men.

When Coffman realized McSwain was present, he lifted his hands skyward. Coffman's gestures had become bigger and grander since he lost his vision.

"Callum McSwain, my dear brother, it's marvelous to see you again!" Coffman exulted. His use of the word "see" unsettled no one, except perhaps McSwain himself.

"Hello, Preacher." McSwain was fascinated by Coffman's scarred visage, and looked so closely at it that Joshua had to smile. Coffman, of course, was unaware of the staring, for which McSwain had good cause. Even apart from his scar and tightly closed eyes, Coffman looked much different than the last time McSwain had seen him. His hair had begun turning white, and he had grown a beard that was almost snowy. He was also more corpulent, not being as active as when he had his vision.

Coffman launched into an excited description of the planned Kentucky migration and talked for a full five minutes before Joshua could cut in to explain the main reason for the visit. When he realized Ayasta was present, Coffman went completely, unnervingly silent, making Joshua wonder if bringing the woman had been a mistake. He glanced around. So far Virginia Coffman and Judah were not anywhere to be seen.

"Bring her to me," Coffman said quietly.

Ayasta walked in a straight, tense posture at McSwain's side toward the preacher. Coffman extended his hand toward her.

"Ayasta Hawkins?" he said. "Are you there?"

"Yes."

"Come here, child. Come to me."

Ayasta extended her hand. Coffman's fingers closed around hers, then he pulled her forward and threw his arms around her. Moriah's brows shot up a full inch and he stepped backward in surprise.

"Dear lady, dear, wonderful lady!" Coffman said. "You have given me more than anyone except God himself and my own dear wife! Come inside, dear woman, and see your son!"

Returning home that night, Ayasta was a woman at peace, and more sure than ever she had done what was right. Judah had remembered her, which pleased her greatly, even though the boy now clearly regarded Virginia Coffman as his mother.

Bouncing along on the wagon seat, Joshua also was at peace. Alphus was safe, healing, and happy at the Long Island. As Coffman himself had put the sentiment, using his habitual scriptural quotes, Joshua felt his lines had fallen in pleasant places. Those he cared about were well, at least for the moment. Darcy was safe at home with their two fine children; Cooper and Hannah were married, and now parents; McSwain, though twice-bereaved, was clearly happy in the presence of Ayasta; and Israel Coffman was joyful in anticipation of the exodus to Kentucky.

At the moment, life was good, and he hoped it could stay that way.

Ulagu withdrew the knife from the throat of the trembling unaka who knelt before him. He could hardly believe what the mortally fearful man had just said to him.

"He lives?" Ulagu said. "Wasi lives? Tell me how you know!"

Russell Proud felt a great wash of guilt, but it was not nearly as strong as his fear. His voice trembled as badly as his body as he answered. "Joshua Colter himself told me long ago, told me the whole story," he said. "Your sister lied to you—her son isn't dead, but living under the name Judah as the adopted son of the blind preacher Coffman, over near Jonesborough. She wanted him raised as white, and she lied to you to keep you from coming after him."

Ulagu let the information sink in. He had not expected to encounter such a revelation when he and his band attacked the camp of these two unaka hunters. The raiders had kept well-hidden for many days after the old Colter man had escaped them, fearing they would be searched out by some band of responding frontiersmen. That had not happened, and the group had begun making a winding way back toward the Five Lower Towns. They had stumbled upon these two hunters entirely by accident.

"How do you know me?" Ulagu demanded.

"I've seen you in battle," Russell replied. "I knew from all that Captain Colter has told me that you have wanted the return of the boy. Please, I beg you, spare us! That's all I ask in return for telling you!"

Ulagu turned to Elisha Brecht. "Wasi is alive!"

"He's lying," Brecht said. "Trying to save his own neck."

"No," Ulagu answered. "He is too frightened to have made up such a lie. I believe him."

Brecht sighed. Though he and Ulagu had settled their differences and reunited, he still found the Chickamauga's unpredictable ways frustrating sometimes. He was for killing these two and going on, but clearly that wasn't going to happen.

"Where can I find the home of this Coffman?" Ulagu demanded.

"Close to the town, so close you could never safely reach it," Russell said. He was beginning to realize how terrible a thing he had done. What if this Chickamauga harmed or killed the Coffmans because of what he had revealed?

Ulagu stepped back and paced about, his mind reeling. What a fool his own sister had made of him! He was still bitter toward her for her flight from Running Water Town; now he was even more angry for her deception about Wasi.

He looked at the unconscious but living form of the other unaka on the ground. He had gathered from the talkative one that this was a kinsman named Jacob. Inspiration struck. Ulagu returned to Russell Proud.

"If an Indian cannot capture Wasi, a white man can," he said. "A white man could move freely near the town."

Russell's eyes widened as he caught the implication. "But I can't—"

"If you wish to see your kinsman live, you can," Ulagu coldly replied. He put the knife again to Russell's neck. "You will go to the house of this Coffman and capture the boy. You will bring him to me here at this place within three sleeps—or your kinsman will die a slow and painful death, and his blood will be on your hands, and his screams in your ears forever."

Russell Proud felt like he might faint, but he nodded.

Brecht, irritated at the prospect of delay in returning to the Chickamauga towns, swore and stomped off.

Russell Proud was given his horse and sent away. As he rode he felt a growing sense of guilt. He had just betrayed the confidence of Joshua Colter, who had indeed told him the entire tale of Ayasta, her son, and her brother. Yet now it was too late to change his course, for he couldn't let his cousin Jacob die.

Ulagu watched him depart. "Now we wait," he said.

Elisha Brecht swore again and wished he hadn't already drunk all his whiskey.

Joshua held Darcy in his arms as they lay together on their bed, talking quietly of the day's events.

"Israel's all swole up with eagerness to head for Kentucky," he said. "That preacher Moriah, he's a quiet old soul, and I don't know what he thought of the way Israel wrapped his paws around Ayasta, but he seemed to be a good man. He told me a few of the congregation are already encamped over at Sycamore Shoals, and more will come over the mountains when the weather warms. Preacher Moriah, old as he is, has been staying with the Coffmans. The lot of them will be off at the first sign of spring."

"It will be different once Reverend Coffman is gone," Darcy said. "He'll be missed."

"Aye, and no one will miss him more than I will," Joshua said. "I've known him many a year now. I reckon that once he's set up in Kentucky, I'll just have to head up there to see him from time to time. The day's coming when that kind of thing will be a lot easier and safer than it is now. I believe the war's truly ending. Once it's done, men like Elisha Brecht are going to be got rid of. War feeds vermin like him. Peace will starve him out."

"I wish I could believe there really will be peace," Darcy said. "I don't believe peace can come until the last Chickamauga is dead."

Joshua sighed. His good humor was making him unrealistically optimistic. Darcy was right; even if the war with Britain ended, peace would not follow on the border, where the real ground of war was the unending dispute between whites and Indians over use and occupancy of the land. And the fact was, the Chickamaugas were growing ever stronger, welcoming new seceders from the Overhills and Creeks by the day.

Joshua slept well that night, and awakened the next morning feeling strong and fit. Another day or two at home, and he would kill some game and bear the meat back up to Martin, as promised, his payment of sorts for Martin's care of Alphus.

Darcy cooked a big breakfast for all the big group, which so crowded the cabin that Joshua made jokes about the walls bursting outward. After breakfast he, Cooper, and McSwain took their rifles and headed into the woods, where they hunted away the day and returned about dark. A big supper, an evening of conversation, and they retired again.

The next morning Joshua was awakened by the sound of hoofbeats outside the stockade, then by the ringing of the bell he had mounted at the gate for those seeking entrance. After dressing quickly and grabbing his rifle, he left the cabin and loped toward the gate. Cooper and Hannah had been sleeping in the loft and McSwain at the fireside, and both men came out after Joshua.

The man at the gate was Eli Candle, the same neighbor and member of Coffman's church who had come looking for him the time Virginia miscarried her child. "Captain Colter, the preacher wants you to come quickly," Candle said. "There's been some bad trouble."

"What is it?"

"The Reverend Moriah is dead. Shot to death. And little Judah is gone."

"Gone? Run off?"

"No. Taken away, and not by Indians. It was a white man, the same who shot Reverend Moriah when he tried to stop him. Do you know a man named Russell Proud, Captain?"

"Know him? He's one of my own rangers."

"Well, sir, Virginia Coffman swears it was Russell Proud who's responsible."

Joshua swore beneath his breath. This made no sense; why would Russell Proud, of all people, murder a visiting preacher and take Judah Coffman captive?

"Cooper, Callum, it appears you've picked a handy time to come home. Get Darcy to fetch us up some food that will travel, and I'll see to the horses." He paused, realizing something quite unpleasant. "But first, I reckon, I'd best tell Ayasta."

Virginia Coffman was, understandably, in a state of agitation and some confusion, but on one matter she was firm and unwavering: It indeed had been Russell Proud who took away Judah.

It had all happened in the strangest way. Hoofbeats in the yard, and knock on the door . . . Virginia herself had answered and found Russell Proud standing there, tears streaming down his cheeks. Fearing he had come bearing news of some calamity, she quickly ushered him in. Israel and Reverend Moriah were seated near the door when Proud entered. Coffman, having heard his wife call Proud's name, stood and asked him what was wrong.

"I've come to take your child away," he said.

Virginia told Joshua that she had been so surprised by the statement that she didn't have a reply. Israel Coffman had been equally confused and silent, but Reverend Moriah had pushed himself up and advanced toward the corner in which his rifle stood. At that point Russell Proud lifted his own rifle and trained it on Moriah.

"Don't touch that gun," he ordered. But Moriah, who didn't know Proud and thus was responding to him more forcibly than were the bewildered Coffmans, picked up the rifle anyway and began to level it at the intruder. Russell Proud let out a great sob and fired, killing the old man on the spot. He then pushed in, knocking Virginia to the floor, and took up Moriah's weapon. Drawn by the commotion and gunfire, Judah walked into the room, and Russell Proud immediately grabbed him.

Virginia wiped her eyes, swallowed, and went on. "Captain Colter, Russell Proud seemed so distraught, so crazed—and it honestly seemed he didn't want to be doing what he was doing. He cried the entire time, saying he was sorry but that he had no choice—else 'they' would kill his cousin Jacob."

"Who is 'they'?" Joshua asked.

"I asked him the same thing, and he said . . ." She paused, beginning to lose her voice to emotion, but regaining it quickly. ". . . he said that Jacob was being held by a Chickamauga who was Judah's uncle and who was demanding that Judah be brought to him if Jacob was to live. And he said, oh God, he said Elisha Brecht was there too!"

Joshua rose, so angry he could hardly control his rage. "Damnation!" he bellowed. "Ulagu! How could he have found out about Judah's identity—unless Russell himself told him? Damn his eyes, Russell must have done it, likely trying to buy his life. If that's true, I'll kill him myself for it! I'll hang his arse from the highest limb I can find!" He knelt before Virginia Coffman. "Did you have any hint of where he might have taken Judah?"

"Captain Colter, there's the most singular part of it all: He told me himself that I should send for you, and that if you would go to the head of Boone's Creek, he would blaze a trail for you from there. He said you should follow quickly, or the Indians would be gone with Judah . . . and he said that if you found him alive, you could do with him what you wanted. He said he was a Judas and didn't deserve to live, but he had to do what he was doing for the sake of Jacob."

McSwain said, "Joshua, I don't like the sound of it. Likely Elisha Brecht is behind this, and trying to get you to a place he can get his hands on you."

"I don't think that's it," Joshua replied. "I suspect that the trail-blazing notion was Russell's alone. It makes sense. If Jacob is captive, Russell wants to get him free, but at the same time he doesn't want Ulagu to get so far with Judah that they can't be found. Damn it, I wish he had come to me to begin with. We could have ridden out in force and surprised them."

"And Jacob Proud would have been the first to die,"

McSwain said. "That's how Russell would have looked at it. I can't justify what he's done, but I do understand it."

There was no time now for gathering rangers. As they were about to mount and leave, however, several neighbors appeared, armed and mounted and ready to help. Joshua smiled and nodded his acceptance.

Joshua went to Israel Coffman's side. The preacher was seated in the corner, head lowered, his unseeing eyes shielded in his hands. Joshua put his hand on Coffman's shoulder. "I'll bring him back to you, Israel," he said. "Trust in God . . . and in me."

As he rode away at the head of the party of horsemen, heading for the headwaters of Boone's Creek, Joshua wondered if he would be able to keep his promise to Israel Coffman. He hoped so, with all that was in him, for the promise had not been made to Coffman alone. That morning, before he left his own home, he had promised the same thing to Ayasta.

28

Russell Proud moved as if in a nightmare, feeling cut off from the truth of what he had done back at the preacher's cabin. He had killed a man, a stranger, and had kidnapped an innocent boy who he would now turn over to a savage band. It was intolerable, inconceivable . . . but he was doing it, for Jacob's sake.

If only the child would quit crying! It made him feel even worse, having to hear it. "Shut up," he said gruffly to Judah. "Dry up those tears and shut up!"

Some yards farther on he stopped and dismounted. With his belt axe he scored a mark on a tree, clear enough that even a poor tracker could spot it—and Joshua Colter was far from a poor tracker. Russell had struck upon the idea of notifying Joshua Colter while on his way to the Coffman house. Initially he had planned to fetch the boy, deliver him to his Chickamauga uncle, then go off and fetch Joshua at that point. Then he had realized that he might not be alive to fetch Joshua at all. Ulagu, Brecht, or some other of the ruffians might do him in even though he fulfilled his end of the bargain. So he had fallen upon this more certain plan.

He mounted and rode again, trying not to think about what would happen to him if he did survive the Chickamaugas and went on to face Captain Colter. Likely as not he would hang for what he was doing. There was no way out now; Russell faced intolerable options no matter which way he turned.

He had begun blazing his route at the hill at the headwaters of Boone's Creek, then had headed northwest toward the remote area where he and Jacob had been attacked. Now he stopped once again and scored a beech trunk, turning the point of the score mark in the direction he was going, like a pointer arrow. This was the last mark he would make. A little farther and he would be too close to the Chickamauga camp to risk more scoring; they would probably be watching the trail and would see him do it.

Hardly had he gone another hundred yards before a lean warrior stepped out of the brush and faced him. Russell's heart thumped like a drum. "I brought the boy, like Ulagu wanted," Russell said, waving back at Judah, who was tied to the saddle on a horse linked to his own mount.

Either the Indian spoke no English or was in no mood to answer. He waved his rifle to indicate Russell should disarm himself. Russell reluctantly handed down his own rifle. "Well, reckon we can go on in now," he said.

The Indian trotting before him, Russell proceeded. Judah was still crying, but silently now. Russell wondered what the boy was thinking. Surely he remembered virtually nothing of his early life among the Indians; despite his native heritage, this experience was certainly no less horrifying for Judah than it would be for any white-skinned child. He was now the son of a white preacher, a resident of a new kind of world. To Judah the life of the Chickamaugas from which he had sprung would now be thoroughly alien.

Russell Proud scanned the Indian camp as he entered it, looking for Jacob. There he was, tied to a tree, but conscious and alive. Jacob's head was drooped at first, but he lifted it and looked at Russell, then at Judah, and back at Russell again, and the second glance conveyed horror, for he understood what his cousin had done and obviously disfavored it. It would be just like Jacob to scorn his own life and die nobly refusing to let himself be traded for the child, Russell thought with a rising perturbance that made him momentarily forget his own sense of guilt. Likely he won't appreciate at all what is being done for him here. Hah! It would serve him right if they went ahead and killed him.

Ulagu's eyes swept quickly over Russell Proud and focused on Judah, or as Ulagu still thought of him, Wasi. He walked back to the boy and stood beside his horse, staring him up and down. His nose wrinkled slightly in disgust as he examined the white man's clothing Judah wore, but when he walked up to Russell, there was satisfaction in his expression.

"It is Wasi, as you said. You have kept the bargain," Ulagu said. "And now I will keep it too. You and your kinsman are free to go."

Russell took a deep breath and nodded. Ulagu waved his head; the warrior that had met Russell in the woods drew a knife and walked back toward Jacob.

Elisha Brecht came riding into the camp from off the same route by which Russell had entered. "Ulagu!" he said. "Don't let this bugger go—he's betrayed you! The bastard's blazed marks all the way to the camp!"

Ulagu looked up fiercely at Russell; Russell blanched and lifted a hand placatingly. "It's not true! I swear it . . ." and he trailed off, realizing how foolish it was to lie when all Ulagu had to do was go investigate Brecht's claim for himself.

Ulagu required no such confirmation. He reached up, grasped Russell's coat, and dragged the frontiersman from the saddle. Wordlessly he shoved the man to his knees, pulled a tomahawk from under the sash around his middle, and killed Russell Proud with one swift blow.

The warrior who had been ready to free Jacob Proud had stopped when Brecht rode in; he looked to Ulagu for instruction. Ulagu spat some words to him in Cherokee; the warrior went on to Jacob Proud, cut his bonds, and pulled him to his feet. He shoved him toward Ulagu, who still stood beside Russell's body. Elisha Brecht, grinning, dismounted and strode in closer for a better view.

Jacob Proud was stiff and sore from injury and many hours of confinement, so he surprised everyone with the swiftness and dexterity with which he grasped the Indian who had just freed him. His left hand shot out and deftly took the knife from the Chickamauga's hand; in a moment he had driven it into the Indian's heart. Now he dived at Ulagu as the others circled about, yelled, and moved in toward him. Ulagu dodged away. Almost without breaking motion, Jacob Proud turned on his toes and made for Elisha Brecht instead.

The knife dug into Brecht's stomach with the sharp side of the blade turned up. When the knife was fully buried, Jacob Proud pulled up with a rapid sawing motion and laid open the Tory's sizable midsection all the way to his sternum. Brecht made a hideous noise in his throat and staggered back, away from the blade, and fell. He writhed a couple of moments, blood gushing from him, and died speedily.

The killing of Elisha Brecht was the last act of Jacob Proud's life. As Brecht made his final spasm, Jacob fell beneath a flurry of blades and tomahawks. He died swiftly and with little time to think, but the last impression that flashed through his mind was that in taking the life of Elisha Brecht, he had done a service for the world that he could take pride in, even if only in his dying moment.

Hours in the Coffman household had extended themselves into what felt like days, and the minutes had seemed like hours. Now, in the darkness of a new night, Israel Coffman sat silently in his own unending darkness, listening to his wife cry and hearing words of encouragement from neighbors and friends, words as unhelpful as they were well-intended. Blindness now seemed a blessing, for it blocked one more route by which he could be intruded upon by those around him. Even when they touched him and spoke to him, he could hide within the shielding darkness. Perhaps, he thought at one point, this is something like the place of mental escape that Alphus Colter so often reserved for himself.

"Israel.".

Go away, Coffman thought. Leave me be.

"Israel, it's Joshua. I must talk to you."

Coffman, with great reluctance, broke out of his brooding state. "Did you find him?"

"No, Israel. They were already gone. We found the bodies of Jacob and Russell Proud. And also Elisha Brecht. He had been cut open with a knife, and how it happened I don't know, except that Jacob Proud had blood on his right hand and arm. But Judah was not there. The Chickamaugas were already long gone with him by the time we reached their camp."

Coffman stayed silent for a while. "Where will they take him?"

"Back to their towns, I expect."

"Then I'll go after him. I'll talk to this Ulagu and tell him why he must return Judah to me."

"You can't do that, Israel, not without your eyes. But don't fret. I'll go after him."

Israel Coffman nodded. "Thank you, Joshua. Thank you."

Joshua left the Coffman home and rode to his own house, where he related the same unwelcome news he had just given the preacher. Darcy was horrified at the thought of Joshua going to the Chickamauga towns. "You mustn't! They'll kill you!"

"Darcy, what if it were one of ours?" Joshua asked. "Think of that, and then you'll know what the Coffmans are going through right now."

She didn't argue with him after that. "You'll go alone?"

"I'd like to take along Cooper and Callum if they're willing."

"Aye," both men said almost in unison.

"And I'm thinking of talking to John Sevier," Joshua went on. "I have a notion he'll be able to give me some guidance on how to go about it. Lord knows I need whatever help I can get."

Ayasta strode up to him. "I'm going with you."

"No, Ayasta. I can do this without you."

"No. I know the places they might take him. I know the lower towns. When this John Sevier came through to burn the Chickamauga towns, he didn't even find the main ones, he was so misled by his guide. I can give you more help than he can. And Judah is my own flesh. I must go."

Joshua looked questioningly at Darcy, remembering how Ayasta had driven them apart before. Darcy, touching her withered hand with her good one, seemed torn for a moment, then nodded. "If it were mine, I'd want to go too." She turned to Ayasta. "I'll be glad to care for Walini while you're gone—if you'll allow it."

After a few hours' rest, Joshua, Cooper, McSwain, and Ayasta set out for John Sevier's house on the Nolichucky. Sevier had already heard a somewhat confused rumor of what had happened at the Coffman house, so was eager to know the true details. When he learned of the death of Elisha Brecht, Sevier slapped his thigh as if Joshua had told him a good joke.

"By the eternal, there's one death I won't bewail!" he exclaimed. "If it was Jacob Proud who did that devil in, he died in a way that did justice to his surname. But that's not our main point of discussion, is it? You're wondering, I take it, how best to approach trying to bring the boy back."

"Aye."

"A trade of prisoners would be an option in some such circumstances, but any captives I hold are from the Middle Cherokee towns, not Chickamaugas. And I doubt Ulagu would have any interest in trading back the boy for any amount of ransom or exchanged prisoners. I'm afraid I have little hope to extend the good Reverend Coffman and his wife. Your only hope may lie in the pleas of Ayasta herself to her brother . . . though I fear even that might fall on deaf ears."

Joshua was disappointed, but stood with extended hand. "Colonel Sevier, I thank you. We'll do what we can."

"Godspeed to you, Joshua."

They were mounted and leaving Sevier's when the colonel waved Joshua down. "Think me a fool if you wish, but there is one other possibility that has just come to mind. A mile down the river, in a small cabin of mine, is a man named Francis McCarthy, a former trader among the Chickamaugas. He's a temporary renter, and won't remain here long, for he has his eye on Carolina. But he does claim to have stood in good favor with Dragging Canoe himself. Perhaps if I ask him, he might lend some help."

Joshua smiled. His intuitions had told him it would be worthwhile to confer with Sevier; it might just be that this McCarthy would prove the key.

When he met the man, his confidence lessened. Short, long-maned, and bearded, McCarthy had one squinting eye and one that was a blind hollow pucker, the result of what McCarthy called a "vexacious disputation in a tavern when I was yet a fresh young soul." McCarthy's look and bearing called to mind every dishonest trader Joshua had ever seen, and he knew the breed well, his natural father having been a prime specimen.

Nevertheless, McCarthy proved a willing man. "I'd be proud to do what I can," he said. "But it will be dangerous doing for us all, particularly those of us of the white flesh."

"I can offer you no payment other than whatever return service I can be to you, or perhaps some livestock," Joshua said.

"I don't recall talking of payment. I know of this preacher Coffman. The 'Blind Prophet' I've heard some call him. They say he's a good man." McCarthy leaned forward and spoke in a confidential tone. "The day's coming when I'll leave this tearstained vale, and when I stand before the Almighty I figure it can't do me harm to have helped out a preacher at least once in my time. The last preacher I run across I didn't help at all. I stole his horse. His clothes too. They was laid across the horse, you see, the preacher being in the river swilling himself clean. I left him to scamper through the forest in the naked innocence of Adam. Hah!"

They went on. John Sevier watched them leave, shouted another Godspeed with uplifted hand, then rode slowly back to his home on the river.

Callum McSwain caught the look on Joshua's face and knew what it meant. A glance over at the ragged-bearded McCarthy revealed the same sharp expression.

"Where?" McSwain asked.

"Somewhere behind you," Joshua replied softly. He stood. "Come with me, Cooper."

They were camped within five miles of the site of Chickamauga, Ayasta's former town. Rebuilt since it was destroyed in 1779, then burned again by Sevier, it now lay vacant once more, its populace having moved, along with almost all other residents of the outlying Chickamauga towns, into the Five Lower Towns farther down the river. Ayasta was sure that her son was now among the residents of Running Water Town.

Joshua and Cooper explored the woods around the camp and found no sign of anyone. "Reckon you were wrong," Cooper said.

"No," Joshua replied softly. "There was something—"

They turned at once, leveling their rifles. The sight that met them sent Joshua's mind flashing back to a dark riverside scene in 1779 and a tall figure who was part of the night around him, rising beside Ayasta when first she came looking for Joshua Colter. The image now was much the same.

"Hello, Colter," Pont said.

"Hello, Pont." Joshua lowered his rifle, and Cooper did as well. "Didn't expect to find you still haunting these forests." Joshua stuck out his hand. "I've heard much talk about the Chickamaugas' vengeance killer. They say the Chickamaugas see you as some sort of spirit."

"Maybe I am. Maybe they killed me and I came back to haunt them."

"Or maybe they just killed Malachi Trent, and you're making them pay the debt. A score or so of them dead now, I hear."

"You hear right."

"Why are you still here?"

"A man's got to live somewhere, don't he? And for me, that's got to be the wilderness. The way I look at it, I might as well live where the Indians are scared to death of me instead of where they're not. And I'd rather risk the Chickamaugas than the slave-catchers."

"Come into the camp. Ayasta is there."

"I know. I saw her."

McCarthy's eyes went wide when Joshua led the ebony-skinned frontiersman back into the camp. By now the legend of the Chickamauga's crow-man had spread widely, and McCarthy immediately made the connection. "Gawd!" he exclaimed.

"Don't worry, McCarthy. This here's Pont, a friend of mine . . . or so I hope he'll let me consider him."

Introductions were made, but Pont's chief interest was Ayasta. He knew nothing of what had happened to her since the day he had taken her and Solomon Brecht to the vicinity of Buchanan's on the Cumberland, only to become embroiled in a skirmish with Chickasaws. He now learned of Solomon Brecht's brief survival, of Ayasta's move to Kentucky, her recent return to the Overmountain settlements to see her son—and lastly, of the boy's capture by Ulagu.

Understanding the reason for the presence of these people here, Pont told Ayasta: "If it comes to no other way, you leave it to me to get your boy back. You were Malachi Trent's woman, and what I do for you is the same as doing for him."

Pont made no effort to keep the others from hearing what he said. Joshua glanced at McSwain. The Scotsman looked none too happy, no doubt because of Pont's reference to her as "Trent's woman."

A dour look on his face, McSwain filled his pipe vigorously and put it to his mouth before he realized he had no fire with which to light it.

The rest of the journey was made by McCarthy and Ayasta alone, for no others could safely approach the Chickamauga towns. For Joshua, Cooper, and McSwain, the time of waiting was tense and difficult. Only Pont seemed fully at ease.

In these circumstances, Joshua had much time to observe the man as well as talk to him. Pont was as fascinating and awe-inspiring as ever. Though he was in Pont's presence, Joshua had the feeling that he was not in Pont's company. Back when Malachi Trent was living, he and Pont had seemed two aspects of a single unit, separate and yet not separate. Now Trent was gone, and Pont stood alone. Utterly alone. Joshua expected never again to meet a man so naturally a part of the forests and mountains, a man who was not only a law, but an entire world, unto himself.

When Pont talked, it was mostly of Ayasta. He had no interest in discussing his now-completed vengeance against the Chickamaugas; that task, being done, no longer held any meaning for him. Pont lived fully in the present, and the issue at present was to obtain the return of Judah.

Three days passed before Ayasta and McCarthy returned late in the afternoon. Judah was not with them.

McCarthy told the tale. As they had neared the towns, they were observed—which was their intent—and intercepted. Both were known by those who took them, so when Ayasta requested to be taken to her brother, the request was quickly granted.

Dragging Canoe himself gave audience to Ayasta and McCarthy, largely out of his liking for the one-eyed trader. McCarthy, though a cheat when it served him, was smart enough to be honest when cheating wasn't prudent—and with Dragging Canoe he had always been highly generous, figuring one day such coddling might pay off.

This didn't prove to be the case this time, however. Ulagu remained determined to raise his regained nephew according to the wishes of his late father, and Dragging Canoe, who had been mentor of John Hawk, refused to try to dissuade Ulagu. No ransom, no exchange of captives, would be considered. Ayasta had deserted her own people twice and had proven to be deceptive. No. Wasi could not go back to the unakas. Nor was Ayasta welcome any longer among her own people. She had made her heart white, and with the white men she would remain—but without her son. And on those terms she and McCarthy had been sent away from Running Water Town.

For the first time since Joshua had known her, Ayasta was unabashedly sorrowful of expression. There was no stoicism now. Her grief was like that of one bereaved. The sight roused an aching sympathy in Joshua—but there was nothing to be done.

Pont stood to the side, observing it all in detail. That night Pont called McCarthy aside and talked to him softly, out of the hearing of all others. Joshua saw it, and wondered . . .

In the night, Joshua awakened to see Pont and McCarthy edging into the forest. He followed. Pont heard him and turned.

"Where you going, Pont?"

"Just going."

"What about you, McCarthy?"

The old trader seemed at a loss, fidgeting and gnawing on the end of his tongue. "Going with him," was all he said.

Joshua stood silently a few minutes, looking at Pont's tall figure in the night. He knew that Pont and McCarthy were going to the Chickamauga town. Pont would not simply desert the group. And that could mean only one of two things: Pont was going to take Judah back by force, or . . .

Joshua understood now. He put out his hand. "I'm glad our paths have crossed, Pont."

"And so am I, Joshua Colter. But every path comes to its end. Or so I hear."

"So I hear too."

"A man might as well make that end as glorious as the sunrise, eh?"

"Reckon so."

Pont turned away and looked into the forest. He looked back no more. His course was set.

Joshua said to McCarthy, "I'll be waiting. Watch your hide out there."

Pont and McCarthy vanished into the forest. Joshua returned to his bedroll and lay awake for the next two hours, fingering the Roman coin that hung around his neck, and thinking to himself that a world that handed men so much sadness and loss and suffering also gave them opportunity for things much finer—for nobility beyond description, courage big as the mountains, and love that was as hard as iron.

Only with much effort did Joshua convince Cooper, McSwain, and Ayasta to go on back toward the Overmountain settlements without him. Trust me, he urged them. I must stay here for now, and there is some danger in it, danger that need not be shared.

Cooper questioned Joshua closely, asking why Pont and McCarthy had disappeared. Joshua refused to answer, and at last it was McSwain who pulled Cooper aside and told him that if Joshua Colter said to trust him, then by heaven, trust him they would just have to do.

"I'll be on soon—and, God willing, everything will be well," Joshua said.

Joshua waited for two more days, alone and restless—and thinking much of Alphus. Was he still faring well at the Long Island? Joshua had intended to return there, but the kidnapping of Judah had changed his plans. As soon as he was home again, Joshua would go on to the island. Perhaps he would spend the rest of the winter there himself, sharing time with Alphus, while there was still time to be shared.

Joshua Colter, knowing what Pontius Pilate was doing, was very conscious of human mortality right now. And human greatness too.

When McCarthy came back, Ulagu was with him, and at his side on a slightly smaller horse rode Judah. McCarthy caught Joshua's eye and nodded, almost imperceptibly, and Joshua sent up a silent prayer for the soul of Pont.

Ulagu rode up to Joshua and looked at him up and down. Last of all he looked at the Roman coin that hung around his neck. "John Hawk had much admiration for you, Joshua Colter," Ulagu said.

"No more than I had for him." His eyes flickered to Judah in silent question.

Ulagu looked at the boy, then gave the answer with a movement of his head that indicated Judah was to join Joshua. Judah clicked his tongue, rode around to Joshua's opposite side and sat facing Ulagu now, rather than beside him.

"The black one was no spirit. He was a man," Ulagu said. "His death was hard, for there were many who owed him blood vengeance for the twenty warriors he had killed. But he died bravely. He died well."

"And bought the boy's freedom."

"Yes. He was the only one who was great enough to make such an exchange."

"I will see your nephew safely back to his home," Joshua pledged. "Perhaps there will someday be peace between us, Ulagu."

With Judah between them, Joshua and McCarthy began the long ride home.

29

The return of Judah brought great happiness to all the Nolichucky countryside. Few had expected that the child would ever be returned to the Coffman household. The story spread across the settlements, gathering accretions and exaggerations all the while, until in the end most believed Joshua Colter and Francis McCarthy were almost solely responsible for the boy's recovery. McCarthy himself helped this process along, stretching the story each time he told it, and making himself more and more its hero. Joshua found it terribly frustrating to see the central truth of the story— Pont's self-sacrifice—being overlooked.

The day would come when he would sit down with Darcy and dictate to her the true details, which she would record in her even scrawl. "We'll keep that, and pass it on after us when we're gone," Joshua said. "I'll not see what Pontius Pilate did washed away in a flood of lies."

Joshua waited only two days after reaching home again to head up to Long Island and Alphus. He found his foster father similarly situated as before, his wound healing beautifully. The frontiersman and Oconostota were great friends by now.

In privacy Joshua told Alphus about all the remarkable events that had happened since he had seen him last. The story of Pont's self-sacrifice moved Alphus deeply, and Joshua knew why: It reminded Alphus of the circumstances of the death of his son Gabriel, who by refusing ransom for himself when he was a condemned prisoner of the Overhill Cherokees in 1776, opened the way for the freeing of his fellow captive, Cooper Haverly.

Joshua feared that his story might cause Alphus to begin brooding again, and in a way it did. But this brood was different, healing instead of harmful. In the quiet peace of this Long Island cabin, built on land the Cherokees believed sacred, Alphus was finally able to come to peace with the death of Gabriel Colter. Joshua's story of the death of Pont had given him a perspective he had lacked on the sacrifice his own son had made.

But Pont's story alone was not the only source of perspective for Alphus Colter. "I've learned much from that old Cherokee sitting in yonder," Alphus told Joshua. "He's made me understand a simple thing I knew already, but have fought all my days. You know what it is, Joshua? It's that this life we live comes to an end. A man has his time, and then his time passes, and all the clawing and looking back he does can't change it. Time was made to pass through our hands, not to be held by them, and when it's gone, you don't grieve for it or try to get it back. You hold your head high, and when death comes in, you don't flinch. You look it in the face." He smiled. "I reckon that's what this Pont fellow did. And Gabriel too." He paused. "When the spring comes, Oconostota will do the same."

"I don't understand."

"Oconostota has told me that when the winter ends, so will his life."

Joshua did spend the rest of the winter at Martin's home with Alphus and Oconostota. He hired a rider to carry word to his family that he would be remaining, and that Callum McSwain and Cooper should see to the care and support of all while he was gone, and be ready to respond with the rangers should need arise.

The winter passed and spring came. Alphus was healed now, not only in body but in mind and spirit. On a cool day when the first dogwood blossoms appeared in the forests, Oconostota, Major Joseph Martin, Alphus Colter, and Joshua climbed into a long canoe and began a long river journey that would take them to Chota. It was there that Oconostota wanted to be laid to rest.

"Bury me as the Christians are buried, and turn my face toward the Long Knife," he instructed Martin.

Chota was a mere relic of the great town it once had been. Since its burning, it had been partially rebuilt, in no small part through the work of Nancy Ward, but never again would it bear the glory of past days. Time had sapped its vitality, as it had Oconostota's.

The old war chief's life had been lived in the noise of battle and the frequent tumult of diplomacy. His death, however, was quiet. As he had said he would, Oconostota passed away shortly after his party arrived at Chota. Aided by Joshua and Alphus, Major Martin constructed a coffin from an old canoe and buried Oconostota as requested, with his face toward Virginia. In the makeshift coffin, Martin placed Oconostota's knife, siltstone pipes, iron cup, beads, vermilion, and various other items. Then, feeling subdued by the passing of the great chief, the white men turned their faces toward home.

Joshua had assumed that the death of Reverend David Moriah and the capture of Judah Coffman would have negated the planned congregational migration to Kentucky. It hadn't. Across the mountains the pilgrims streamed, converging in a great camp around Coffman's home near Jonesborough. The "Blind Prophet" had already been accepted as the proper successor to the late Moriah. Already an advance party had gone ahead to put in crops on land Moriah had obtained near Logan's Station. When the congregation arrived there in the summer, they expected to find the crops well along in growth.

A guide and scout had been found: Callum McSwain

himself. The Scotsman, moved by the safe return of Judah and grateful for the loving relationship that was growing between him and Ayasta, was eager to lend his help to what he saw as a divine mission. And what better man than himself to guide the pilgrims to the Logan's Station region than one who already held lands near there?

Alphus Colter was going too. It was his choice, and Joshua did not try to change his mind. "They'll be needing a good hunter along the way," Alphus said. "I'm old, but I can still draw a bead." He laid his hand on Joshua's shoulder. "Come with me, by Joseph. We'll hunt together. It's not the long hunt we've talked of, but it will be time shared as we used to share it, and in furtherance of a good purpose."

"And at the end, will you stay or return?" Joshua asked.

"Let's don't talk of ends," Alphus said. "Ends come when and how they will, and take care of themselves. Come with me, Joshua, and bring Darcy and the children. Leave the farming to Cooper—he's set on staying here now, anyway. Come with me, while we've got the chance. You can always return afterward."

When the congregation of the Exodus Presbyterian Church, as the body named itself, set out from Jonesborough, Joshua Colter and his family accompanied them. The great body of pilgrims advanced toward the Long Island. Some men rode, and many who lacked enough horses for all walked in order to allow their womenfolk to ride. Babies were carried in baskets, and goods of all types on packhorses. Israel Coffman, mounted on his big Chickasaw, rode symbolically at the front of the party, led by Zachariah Colter. Callum McSwain rode farthest ahead with a handful of selected scouts. He had asked Joshua to be one of them, but Joshua had declined. On this journey he intended to stay near Alphus all the way.

Ayasta, carrying her baby, rode near Darcy, who was similarly burdened with Hester. It cheered Joshua to see the animosity his wife had held toward the Indian woman fading away. Before the journey ended the two would be friends, he believed.

Past the Long Island the pilgrims traveled down the

Holston, past the fort at Big Creek—where Alphus enjoyed greeting some of those who had waited for him to die—and on to Bean's Station, fifty miles west of the Long Island. Turning northward, they passed over Clinch Mountain and into the valleys and hills that lay beyond, fording the rivers on rafts, though some of the younger and more adventurous riders often swam their horses across. In Powell's Valley they approached the looming Cumberlands and entered the famous gap.

All along the way Joshua and Alphus made side trips into the forests to hunt game, which supplemented the beeves occasionally killed and roasted, and the other food supplies that had been brought along. In the Yellow Creek valley they made one such venture, heading west into the rugged mountains.

Joshua had hunted here alone many years before, while he was in grief over the death of a beloved girl named Tilly Hampton. Being here brought back the feelings of those days and made his mood somber.

Alphus, meanwhile, was in the opposite mood. Though not boisterous, he seemed quietly happy, charged with an inward excitement. Joshua was glad he had chosen to accept Alphus's invitation to accompany the Kentucky-bound pilgrims. It was worth it simply to see Alphus in such a contented state. The old man had purpose now. He was in his element, and in his favorite company.

The sun westered behind the rugged green mountains. The hunters had wandered far, too far to return to the camp tonight. Alphus had led the way with an energy he had not displayed in years. A time or two Joshua had started to ask him why they were pushing so far and so hard, but some intuitive sense had stopped him.

Miles behind them, the pilgrims of the Exodus Church were gathering on the Yellow Creek Flats beneath a splendid sunset, and around the base of a small knoll. Atop it stood Israel Coffman. He was a happy man tonight. Facing the people he had been called to serve, he lifted his arms.

The words of the Ninetieth and Ninety-first Psalms spilled from his memory as easily as if he were reading them: "Lord, thou hast been our dwelling place in all generations. Before the mountains were brought forth, or ever thou hadst formed the earth and the world, even from everlasting to everlasting, thou art God. . . ."

In the waning light of day, far off in the mountains, Alphus Colter paused, cocking his head. Joshua nodded. He too had heard the familiar sound of a browsing deer.

". . . For a thousand years in thy sight are but as yesterday when it is past, and as a watch in the night. . . ."

The deer came into view, crossing the crest of the next ridge. It was a magnificent buck, the largest and finest Joshua had ever seen. The animal, sleek and beautiful, looked back at the men. It showed no fear, made no sign of bolting.

Joshua lifted his rifle. "No," Alphus whispered. He had a peculiar expression. "This one has come for me."

The old man lifted his rifle. Still the buck did not move. Clicking back the lock, Alphus sighted down the long barrel.

The preacher's voice rose higher, his blind face turned upward, his hands extending to the blood-colored sky. ". . . teach us to number our days, that we may apply our hearts unto wisdom. . . ."

Alphus pulled the trigger. Powder flared in the pan and cracked in the rifle. The ball hurtled through the dimming evening, and the buck crumpled and fell.

". . . Let thy work appear unto they servants, and thy glory unto their children. And let the beauty of the Lord our God be upon us . . ."

Alphus lowered his rifle and slowly nodded. "It is a fine one, by Joseph," he said. "The finest I've ever shot."

"Aye," Joshua replied. "A fine one."

". . . I will say of the Lord, He is my refuge and my fortress: my God; in him will I trust. Surely he will deliver thee from the snare of the fowler, and from the noisome pestilence. . . ."

Alphus did not reload. Neither did he go to examine the buck he had just killed. Seeming suddenly weary, he walked slowly to a nearby tree and sat down, holding to his rifle as he lowered himself to the earth.

"I'm feeling right weak, Joshua," he said.

". . . Thou shalt not be afraid for the terror by night; nor for the arrow that flieth by day; Nor for the pestilence that walketh in darkenss; nor for the destruction that wasteth at noonday. . . ."

Alphus Colter closed his eyes. "It's good to be here, Joshua," he said. "And good to be with you, by Joseph."

Joshua knew what was happening, and that he couldn't stop it, and that it wouldn't be his place to stop it if he could. But it hurt terribly, for what was being taken from him was too much a part of him to be wrenched away without pain.

". . . There shall no evil befall thee, neither shall any plague come nigh thy dwelling. For he shall give his angels charge over thee, to keep thee in all thy ways. . . ."

The light was almost gone now. Alphus closed his eyes.

"Alphus . . ." The tears rolled from Joshua's eyes. He reached out and touched the shoulder of the man who had been father to him most of his life. Alphus slid slowly to the side, his weight against Joshua's hand, his eyes still closed.

". . . Because he hath set his love upon me, therefore will I deliver him: I will set him on high, because he hath known my name. . . ."

Joshua gently lowered the body of Alphus Colter to the earth. Kneeling beside him, he looked at him until the light was completely gone.

". . . I will deliver him, and honour him. With long life will I satisfy him, and shew him my salvation."

The preacher lowered his hands, "Amen," he said.

The congregation answered in ragged, soft unison: "Amen."

Joshua skinned the buck by the light of dawn, and wrapped the hide around Alphus's body. In a hillside nearby he found a small cavern, and this became the final resting place of Alphus Colter, frontiersman, dead after more than seven decades of life.

Joshua Colter worked for the next two hours carrying stones to the mouth of the little cavern. He piled them over it, like a cairn, until the opening was fully covered. There would be no marker for this place of burial. Alphus's bones would lie here in secret, until at last the body that had once borne his spirit would be nothing but part of the mountains he had loved all his years.

To Joshua Colter, that seemed appropriate. He looked at the stone-blocked cavern a few minutes more, then went to the horses, mounted, and rode east to join the pilgrims on the flats of Yellow Creek.

AFTERWORD

T HE BORDER MEN contin-
ues a saga begun in THE OVERMOUNTAIN MEN, published
by Bantam Books in 1991. Readers who wish to learn the
early history of Joshua Colter and his family, friends, and
foes on the Carolina/Tennessee frontier, are referred to
that volume.

Like its predecessor, THE BORDER MEN is a work of
fiction woven around a framework of fact. Many of the
characters in the story actually existed or are based on
people who did. Many events depicted happened substantially as described, and the settlements and frontier com-
munities named are historical, with the exceptions of
Colter's Station and Colter's Mill. All Indian towns named
are historical except for the briefly mentioned Tikwalitsi,
a fictional Overhill Cherokee town that entered the story
in THE OVERMOUNTAIN MEN.

A list (not exhaustive) of characters in THE BORDER MEN
who come directly out of history include John Sevier and
his kin, the Shelby family, the Robertsons, the Donelsons,
Dragging Canoe, and Oconostota, plus many of the more
secondary characters, such as the Reverend Samuel Doak,
the officers involved on both sides of the King's Mountain

campaign, most of the voyagers in the Cumberland-bound flotilla, and many of the named residents of the Cumberland settlements. Many characters whose appearances are very brief, such as Nancy Ward, Joseph Martin, and Archy Coody, to name but three, are historical persons.

Fictional characters include the Colter family, Cooper Haverly, Callum McSwain, Israel Coffman, Ayasta, Ulagu, Pontius Pilate, Malachi Trent, the Brecht family, and various minor characters. Concerning the Brechts, I wish to note that the family depicted in THE BORDER MEN is in no way connected with the actual Brecht family that settled on the Tennessee frontier, and whose surname evolved into Bright.

Comment is appropriate on two of the key portions of the story: the voyage of John Donelson's flotilla of flatboats and pirogues to the Cumberland settlements, and the King's Mountain campaign.

Tennessee historians have long praised the memory of Colonel John Donelson in gratitude for his foresight in keeping a diary of the thousand-mile river voyage from what is now East Tennessee's Tri-City area to the French Lick, now Nashville. Donelson's diary, though containing large gaps and lacking detailed explanations, nevertheless is a remarkably clear portrait of a voyage that faced a staggering number of difficulties and dangers. The diary provided the basis for the portion of THE BORDER MEN pertaining to the river voyage. I have fictionalized that voyage only to the extent of involving the fictitious Brechts and their boatmen.

Donelson's daughter Rachel, incidentally, grew up to become the wife of a man who some years after the period of this novel was to ride into Jonesborough to enter the practice of law. He was Andrew Jackson, who became seventh president of the United States.

The anecdote concerning David " 'Possum" Hood, who was scalped alive by Chickasaws while pretending to be dead, is a true story. To be scalped and survive was a fairly frequent occurrence on the frontier. At one point early Nashville boasted more than a score of living citizens who had given up scalp locks to the Indians. Often, scalped survivors suffered lowered mental and physical capabilities, but this was not always the case, as David Hood's example demonstrates. One touching anecdote concerning him involves the tenderness he showed to a little girl who, like him, had lived through a scalping. Hood visited her, and through gentle play, jokes, and self-depreciating humor, helped brighten the child's unhappy situation.

Concerning the King's Mountain campaign: This episode alone could easily be developed into a large novel; my treatment of it in this broader-scoped work is brief and somewhat simplified; I have, however, striven to make a substantially accurate portrayal. My principal source of facts was Lymain Draper's *Heroes of King's Mountain,* a classic historical work. The anecdotes concerning various participants are all historical, though to further the plot I have incorporated fictional characters into some of them (as in the blinding of Israel Coffman, and having Joshua Colter find the brain-injured, but living, Tory).

Lore of King's Mountain, though containing uncertainties, mysteries, and contradictions, is widespread and highly treasured by descendants of the original "backwater men." King's Mountain is one of those events that, like the sinking of the Titanic, the assassination of Lincoln, and the Civil War, continues to fascinate no matter how thoroughly it is explored. One organization, in my opinion, deserves particular credit for keeping alive awareness of the history and significance of King's Mountain. That is the Overmountain Victory Trail Association, Inc., headquartered in Elizabethton, Tennessee. The members of this organization have contributed untold time and effort toward preserving and promoting this important piece of our heritage.

I close this afterword with notes of thanks to all those at Bantam Books who are involved in publishing and promoting my books—especially Greg Tobin, Don D'Auria, Tom Beer, Shawn Ortiz, and Joan Shulhafer. Thanks also go to my capable agent, Richard Curtis, and his staff.

And as always, I especially thank my wife, Rhonda, and

children, Matthew, Laura, and Bonnie, for their continued love and support. They make life in our household a
lot of fun.

Cameron Judd
Greene County, Tennessee
August 28, 1991

It was hard to know who to side with: the skinny fiddle player with the missing ear or the hefty trail bum with the harelip. The former was taking some fierce punishment from the latter, but then, he had brought it on himself by his heartless teasing. I am a man with little sympathy for anyone who taunts another because of his looks, for there's not a one of us who can control what nature gives us, or fails to.

Of course, I couldn't stand by and see a small man beaten to death by a big one, either, no matter what the circumstances. That made my decision for me. I hefted up a big cuspidor, advanced, and brought it down as hard as I could on the back of the bigger man's head. It made for quite a messy explosion.

I had hoped it would drop him. It didn't. He turned and glared at me in disbelief, stinking cuspidor muck running all down both sides of his wide head. He had eyes that drilled like augers. His nose was wide and flat, like his face; his whiskers were coarse as wool and thirstily soaking up the foul stuff I had just baptized him with.

The whiskers hid his mouth deformity fairly well, but his speech betrayed it. I couldn't make out all he said—mostly just catch cuss words that came out with their edges rounded off. His general point came through even if his words didn't, that being that I had been mighty foolish to cut into his business in so rude a manner.

His partner had been holding the fiddler from behind during the beating. He gave me the ugliest, most threatening grin I had ever received. He was a shrimpy man with a beard worthy of Elijah; his eyes were bright with the prophecy of my impending doomsday.

The fiddler was the only one who welcomed my intrusion. He took advantage of the distraction to wriggle free and dance off, very spritely, to the corner. From there he poked fun at his interrupted tormentors, obviously having gained no wisdom from suffering.

I felt inward surges of both anger and fear. I had butted into this situation only because I had thought that the fiddle player was about to be killed, for he had howled pitifully at every blow he took. Yet now it seemed he hadn't been hurt at all—in other words, I had endangered myself for darn little reason. That accounted for my anger. The fact that the harelipped man was big enough to separate me from my limbs singlehanded accounted for my fear.

"Have yourself some tobacco, rabbit-mouth, have yourself a chew!" the fiddle player chortled from his safe distance. His fiddle and bow lay at his feet, kicked into the corner earlier by the two hardcases. The fiddler stooped and snatched them up. The rosiny bow dragged the strings and made a high, scratchy drone that melted into music. The fiddler's voice rang out, shouting more than singing in raucous jubilee—"Well, I went down in Helltown, to see that devil chain down . . ."

Now I knew how the Romans felt as Nero fiddled while their world crumbled to ash around them.

The hardcases advanced and I backed up, promising myself that if I lived to get out of this place, I'd never lend a hand to any more one-eared fiddlers for the rest of my days.

"Here now, let's have no more trouble!" pleaded the wiry barkeep from behind his protecting counter. He had been yelping and begging for peace throughout the whole thing.

The harelipped man said something to me that I couldn't understand. Elijah the Prophet interpreted: "Peahead says he's going to pluck out them curls of yours like the feathers of a roasting hen."

Meanwhile, the exuberant fiddler was scratching and shouting away, ". . . Johnny, won't you ramble? Hoe, hoe, hoe . . ."

I wanted to ramble myself, not that there was any way with these two between me and the door. If the side window had been open I would have made a dive out of it, but it wasn't open, for outside the February cold still crawled over the western Nebraska landscape, leaking in through the panes.

"Listen, friend, you've got my apology," I said placatingly. "I thought you were getting a little rough on the fiddler, that's all."

Another muffled statement, another interpretation: "Peahead says the fiddler made fun of his mouth. Peahead don't stand for nobody making fun of his mouth."

"I don't blame you, Peahead, I don't blame you at all," I replied. "He had no right to tease you. Listen, I'm mightly sorry about the cuspidor. I'll pay for you a bath right out of my own pocket, I promise."

The white-bearded one shook his head. "You shouldn't have called him Peahead. Peahead don't like noboby but his friends calling him that."

"Peahead!" yelled the fiddler at once, having heard the last statement. His fiddle droned up high like an excited bee. "Well, I went down in Helltown, to see old Peahead chain down! Peahead, won't you ramble, hoe, hoe, harelip!"

"Here now, don't do that," the barkeep said feebly.

The fiddler's mockery proved helpful to me this time, for it snatched the attention of Peahead and his partner away from me for a moment. In that moment I balled up my fists and lunged forward, striking two blows in tandem, the first pounding into Peahead, the second into his companion.

The effort jolted me worse than my victims. These fellows were solid, even the little one. My attack did no more than draw their attention back my way.

"Fiddle man!" I yelled, backing up again, wishing my gun belt was hanging around me, not on that wall peg behind the bar. "Fiddle man, this is your fight, not mine! Get over here and help me!"

". . . Peahead, won't you ramble? Hoe, hoe, hoe!" He was so caught up in his mocking music that I'm not sure he even heard me.

They fell upon me then and the world became a confusing whirl of grit, muscle, motion, and the stink of the tobacco spittle that dripped from Peahead. Then came pain, the dull pain of repeated blows that pounded me like spikehammers and made me sink toward a floor that was beginning to spin beneath me. I tried to fight, but there can be no fighting when your main foe weighs twice what you do and doesn't mind using it to full advantage. How long this went on I did not know; time had come to a halt.

I heard my voice yelling for help, calling out to the fiddle player, the barkeep, anyone at all, to give me aid, but aid did not come. A fist struck my jaw and I called out no more. I felt tremendous weight atop me, felt the floor hard as an undertaker's slab beneath my back. My eyes, already swelling, opened enough to let me see the fearsome faces above, the massive fists that went up and down like shafts on a locomotive—and then a bare blade, glittering and sharp, that sliced open my shirt and explosed my chest. For some reason I noticed right then that the fiddle music had stopped.

I didn't hear Peahead speak, but he must have, because his partner said, "He says he's going to carve his initials on your chest for you to recollect him by."

I was near passing out when the knife pricked my chest. Writhing, I tried to pull free, and couldn't. The blade was cold and stinging. My eyes began to flutter shut and the images above me were almost gone when a third figure appeared behind the two that leaned over me. A heavy chair hovered, descended, crashed against the rocklike skull of Peahead. My last light dwindled and everything turned black. All I could hear as I sank away was the voice of the barkeep saying here now, don't do that, here now, don't do that, over and over.

The face that slowly put itself together before my blurry eyes was slender and brown and wore a mean expression. I groaned and swiped a hand across my eyes, and when I looked again the face was in sharper focus, and glittering somewhere down below it was a badge on a blue shirt.

"What's your name?" the man with the badge demanded.

"McCan . . . Luke McCan," I answered in a whisper-voice.

"Luke McCan, you think I need your ilk drifting through our town and stirring fights with the locals?"

"I . . . didn't stir any fight . . . just tried to help out . . ."

"You've helped yourself into a cell, that's what you've done. The barkeep says you lit into Peahead Jones with a spittoon, then fisticuffed with him and his brother before they raised a hand against you. Is that true?"

"The fiddler . . . they were slapping that fiddler . . ."

I pushed up a little and groaned. Somebody had put me

on a bed in a small room. It might have been a spare bedroom in somebody's house, or maybe the sickroom of a doctor's office.

"It was to help out the fiddler that I got into it," I reaffirmed. I found a window to my right and looked out it. The sun was edging down.

"Well, this fidder was gone when I got there, and the barkeep seemed to hold you most at fault," the man with the badge said.

"He's a coward, then. Blaming it on me because he's afraid the other two will come back on him if he tells the truth."

"You can argue about it with the judge. Mr. McCan, you're under arrest on a charge of brawling, City Ordinance Number Fifteen. However, if you'll make restitution for the saloon damages, I'll drop the charges and let you go. Fair enough?"

"Restitution? I'll pay no restitution for a fight I didn't start."

"Have it your way, then. If you won't do the responsible thing on your own, we'll let the city judge make the decision for you." The lawman reached over to a chest of drawers and fiddled with a pile of bills and change lying atop it. I recognized the prior contents of my pockets. "Let's see—three dollars and seven cents, a folding knife, and a handkerchief. Not a lot, but the cash I'll take to be applied toward your fine, and the knife I'll take as a potential weapon. The hankerchief you can keep."

"Thanks very much. You're too kind." My attention was somewhat diverted from the lawman at the moment because I was examining my chest to see if there were any initials carved onto it. There weren't. The fiddler had brought that chair down on my attackers in time to save me a slicing.

"Old Doc says he wants you to stay here a few more hours so he can keep an eye on those bumps and bruises. I'm going to chain one of your ankles to the bed, in case you think you might like to run away. Tomorrow morning I'll move you to a cell, unless you've had more cooperative thoughts about paying that damage bill. Do you own a horse and saddle?"

"No." It wasn't really a lie, because the horse and saddle I possessed technically were property of my brother-in-law. In a way, you might say, I had stolen them from him, but not really, for he was dead when I took them. And he would have gladly given the horse and saddle to me anyway, had he been alive. We had gotten along well, my brother-in-law and I.

Without more talk the lawman produced a chain and linked me up firmly to the metal footboard. "That will do, and that's all for now. Good evening, Mr. McCan."

I gave an ill-tempered grunt in response, and closed my eyes. Every inch of me hurt, and from the feel of my face, I knew I was probably no beautiful sight. But at least I was alive and uncut.

A little later a black boy brought me supper on a tray. It must have been provided by the doctor, whom I had yet to talk to, rather than the jail, because this was better food than any jail would put up for a small-time prisoner like me. It was hard to chew the chicken because the left side of my jaw hurt every time I moved it. As I ate I wondered what had become of my pistol and gun belt, which I had left hanging on the peg in the saloon. The lawman had not listed them among my personal effects, which must mean he was unaware of them.

After supper I dozed off. A pecking on the window beside the bed awakened me. I sat up.

There was a face looking back in at me. It was lean, battered, familiar . . . the fiddler. He pecked lightly on the window again and made motions to indicate I should be careful and quiet.

The window was stuck, my muscles sore, and my ankle chained to the footboard; sliding up the lower window section proved difficult. With help of the fiddler outside, I finally got the job done.

"Come on—I got your horse out here—we can ride out of this sorry town!"

"Not with me chained to a bed, I don't reckon."

He looked in over the sill, saw my situation, and swore beneath his breath. He clambered in through the window, making too much noise even though his thin, Lincolnesque form moved with the lightness of a windblown feather.

There proved to be strength as well as suppleness in those long limbs. He squatted at the end of the bed, wrapped a hand around the picketlike metal post I was chained to, and with a few grunts and twists worked it out of the footboard top piece. My ankle chain slid off. The fiddle player stood and grinned.

"The name's J. W. Smith, but call me Fiddler," he said in a low voice. "You're . . ."

"McCan. Luke McCan."

"Pleased to know you, McCan, and thanks for your help today. This here's my way of repaying the favor."

"What's going on in there?" came a gruff voice from the other side of the door. The knob began to turn.

Fiddler Smith turned and dived headlong out the open window. Without a moment's hesitation I followed, hitting the ground with a grunt as the wind was knocked from me. I rose and ran, ankle chain jingling, struggling for breath that would not come, as behind me I heard the exclamation at discovery of empty room and open window. It gave me a joyful feeling, and as soon as breath returned, I laughed.

We rode like wind blowing through a narrow mountain gap. For a long time we did not speak to each other and looked behind us often to see if there was sign of pursuit. There was none, and at last we slowed our pace to a lope, then a walk. Fiddler Smith's violin bounced on the side of his horse, hanging from the saddlehorn in a large flour sack.

"Reckon I'm not enough of a criminal to merit a chase," I commented.

Fiddler Smith grinned. "Reckon not." He dug into his pocket and pulled out a twist of hot tobacco. Carving off a chew with his knife, he shoved the twist at me. I declined.

"Thanks for helping me out," I said.

"No, sir, it's me who owes thanks to you. Them two in that saloon might have done me in if you hadn't stepped in."

"You didn't look much scared, not with the way you kept on teasing that Peahead gent."

"I never had much sense, I admit. Once somebody pushes me, I push the other way. He gave me a hard time about my fiddling, so I gigged him about the lip." He grinned again. "Right mean of me. A man can improve his fiddling, but he can't change a harelip."

I reached down and touched the butt of my pistol, finding it reassuring to have it there again. "You must have took my gun belt off the peg," I said. "I didn't figure I'd have it again."

"A man needs his weapons. Hey, that is your own horse I

gave you, ain't it? It was the only one tied out front of the saloon. I figured it for yours."

"It's mine. Thanks for fetching it."

We rode awhile longer, me sizing up Fiddler. He was an interesting-looking man and as ragged a one as I had ever seen. He wore nankeen trousers that had gone out of fashion a decade and a half back, a shirt that once had been yellow and now had faded to a sickly tan and white, and a dark broadcloth coat that hadn't been sponged down for a year or more. His hat was a battered derby greased from much handling. It fit his head as perfectly as a cartridge case around a slug.

We made camp in a grove beside a little stream. Fiddler gathered wood and built a roaring fire. I commented that maybe the fire was a bad idea, in that followers were still a possibility. Fiddler just shook his head.

"Never could abide to camp without a big fire," he said. "A man needs the comfort of light and heat out in the wilderness."

Fiddler had several cans of beans in his saddlebags and broke out two of them. I was glad to see them, being down to dried-up biscuits and a bag of jerky. My plan had been to resupply myself in town, a plan ruined by the row in the saloon.

After we had food under our belts we fell to talking. Fiddler Smith spoke cheerfully—he seemed one of those types who are always cheerful—and told of a most unillustrious past.

"The mountains of West Virginia's where I come from—that'll always be home to me, though I doubt I'll ever again live in them. Never had a thing as a boy except two good parents. But they died young and left me alone, and that's how it's been for me ever since. My daddy left me nothing but that old fiddle yonder. My two sisters are dead these six and seven years, and the only brother I've got lives up in Powderville, Montana. I ain't seen him in twelve years.

"I took to roaming when I was sixteen. Even though I'm a slender fellow, I was a lot stouter in my younger days, and I've always been strong. The only two things I've ever known how to do is fight and fiddle, and that's how I've made my living. I'd fiddle in saloons, and toss out drunks who got too rowdy and such. Every now and again I'd serve as deputy or policeman in this or that town back East. Mostly I roamed through the cities, doing whatever I had to do to keep body and soul together. I was in Colorado awhile too, at a little mining camp called Craig City. You might have heard of it."

"I think I have."

"McCan, I'll tell you: I ain't seen a bright prospect in a long time, not until now. Back when I was living in Chicago, I got myself fired from a saloon over a bit of trouble. Well, right after that, into town comes this fellow named Walden, Ike Walden, a big white-haired man who called himself a 'freethinker for temperance and health.' He lived in a big house and had some sort of bee in his bonnet about closing down this saloon that had fired me—he claimed it was destroying the community or something like that.

"He held a big rally to close the place down and drew the biggest bunch of old women and teetotalers you ever saw. I was at the rally because of the food they were handing out. Things got hotter and wilder, and before you know it, here goes Ike Walden and an army of these axe-carrying liquor haters down to bust up the saloon. I went along, hoping to see the fellow who fired me get his comeuppance. Things got hotter and hotter, and before you know it, Ike Walden was staring down the barrel of a pistol. He decided to fight and was just about to get his brains blown out when I jumped up and wrestled my old boss to the ground and took the gun. To this day I ain't sure why I did it.

"Ike Walden declared me the finest fellow he had run across. He gave me a job doing general work around his place for almost a year. I got restless then and left for the West, but he told me to keep in touch with him and I did.

"Well, about two weeks ago I got a message from him, offering me new work. He's in Colorado now, and has built himself a town about forty miles west of Fort Collins."

"What's the new work?"

Fiddler beamed with pride. "Town marshal. Town marshal of Walden City, Colorado mining town. Bound to be the best durn job I've run across."

"Can you handle it by yourself?"

Fiddler cocked his head and looked closely at me. "Don't know. That's a good question. I'll tell you this—Walden's not allowing saloons or gambling in the town. He says that draws 'undesirable' folks. It seems to me that marshaling in a town without saloons and gambling halls ought to be a right easy job."

"Sounds like it."

Fiddler loaded and fired a corncob pipe. "Well, that's my story. Let's hear yours. You got family, McCan?"

There's no way Fiddler Smith could know the stab of pain that question brought to me. I doubt it showed on my face, for pain had been a constant companion of mine for months now, and I had grown accustomed to hiding it. I didn't want to answer his question, but given his openness with me, I felt obliged.

"I had a family," I replied. "No wife, just a sister and her husband. And there would have been a wife by now, except . . ." My will failed me and I trailed off.

He gave a perceptive look. "She's dead?"

I nodded. "Not only her. My sister too, and her husband. They were together on a train in Chatsworth, Illinois. It was last August when it happened. A railroad bridge caught fire and collapsed beneath the train. More than a hundred people died." I paused, my voice growing tight, as it always did when I talked of this. "I was going to go with them at first, but at the last minute I had to stay behind. I was running a hardware store in Independence with my brother-in-law, you see, and our clerk quit on us just in time to knock me out of the trip. It saved my life, but when I think of what that accident took from me, I swear that sometimes I wish I had been on that train too. Life without Cynthia hasn't been much of a life."

"I'm sorry," Fiddler said.

"Me too. Me too."

"So what brought you out here in the midst of this godforsaken territory?"

I rolled a smoke as I talked. "I wasn't brought out here. I was driven. Loneliness, mostly, and bad memories. After Cynthia, I didn't want to stay in Independence. The business didn't matter to me anymore, even though it passed to me after the . . . tragedy. I sold out, tucked some of the money into the bank to draw on as I needed, then took out roaming. Just like I did during my younger years. Roaming, working here and there. Mostly gambling. I gamble a lot. Too much. I had given it up for Cynthia, but after she was gone, it kind of reached out and took hold of me again."

"You tell a sad story, McCan. Too sad to have happened to a fellow young as you. You can't be out of your twenties."

"I'm well into the thirties now, Fiddler. I've always looked boyish, everybody tells me."

"Losing a woman is hard for a man of any age. Look at it this way, McCan: there'll be other women. Odds are the next one you won't lose."

"I've already lost two in my time."

"Two?"

"Yes. Before Cynthia, there was a girl in Montana. Maggie Carrington was her name."

"She died too?"

"No, but as far as cutting herself off from me, she might as well have died. She married another man, name of Rodney Upchurch. Your talk about this Ike Walden and town-founding put me in mind of Upchurch. He set up the Upchurch community near Timber Creek."

"You talked about roaming in your younger days. Was that in Montana?"

"Mostly. I started out in Dakota. I freighted into Deadwood from Pierre during the big boom and stayed on to mine for a time with a man named Caleb Black."

"Caleb Black . . . sounds familiar." Fiddler drew on his pipe and his eyes suddenly lit up. Wasn't it a Caleb Black who trailed the outlaw Evan Bridger for so many years?

"One and the same."

"No! You mined with him? Well, I'll be, I'll be!"

"More than mined with him. We rode together up in Montana. I worked for the Timber Creek Cattle Enterprise, then finally just drifted out of the business and went back to Independence. That's tended to be my way, just drifting in and out of things, never settling down. Kind of funny, in a way. I thought when I met Cynthia that my wandering days were over. Now here I am, drifting again, shiftless as ever. I've already gambled away half of what I got from selling off the store."

"Montana," Fiddler said thoughtfully. "Sure got to get up to Montana myself one of these days, and see that brother of mine. Lord knows he might even be dead by now."

Fiddler sat quiet with his thoughts and eyed me through his pipe smoke for a while, then got up, stretched, and pulled his fiddle from its flour sack. He sat by the fire and played a couple of slow tunes, real minor and strange and pretty, then laid down his bow and put the fiddle across his lap. I had gone to work on the ankle chain with a file from Fiddler's saddlebag. When at last the chain fell free, we both grinned. I rubbed my ankle in relief.

"Think you might want to cut out the drifting for a while and settle into some steady work?"

I shrugged. Fiddler must have found more yes than no in it, for he spread his easy grin again.

"In that case, why don't you stick with me and go to Walden City? Town marshaling might be too hard a job for one man after all. I could use a deputy."

He surprised me with that one, I admit. "I don't know, Fiddler . . . this Ike Walden might not have in mind to hire more than you."

"Why, he feels he owes me. I can talk him into it or I ain't Fiddler Smith. What do you say, McCan? I like your company. You're good folks—I can spot it right off."

"Well . . . I got no other offers pending."

"That a yes?"

"Just a maybe. I can ride in with you and see how the place feels, and what this Ike Walden has to say."

Fiddler grinned all the broader. Picking up his fiddle again, he sawed out a new tune, this one lively and bright. I lit up my cigarette and lay back, smoking and watching the sky and wondering what kind of place Walden City would be, and whether I would stay there for any length of time.

A little later Fiddler brought out a bottle and took a long swallow. He waved the bottle at me but I turned it down.

"What's a champion of temperance like Ike Walden going to think of a town marshal who pulls on a flask on the side?" I asked him.

"Why, Ike Walden don't have to know everything," he replied. "And I don't have to be no angel of teetotalism to safeguard a town—at least as long as everybody else stays sober."

I chuckled, but the incident gave me my first pause as to the likelihood of Fiddler's success as a town marshal. Surely Ike Walden wouldn't put up with an enforcer who broke his own rules, not if he really was the authoritative type that Fiddler painted him.

We slept a little while and rode out with the dawn, crossing into Colorado just south of the South Platte. It would take some long traveling to reach Fort Collins, especially in that Fiddler planned to get there by way of Denver. Clearly he was in no real hurry to claim his new job, even though he seemed to be looking forward to it.

The longer we rode together, the better I got to know Fiddler Smith, and the greater my doubts about his ability to perform his awaited job became. He drank too much, usually not to the point of full drunkenness, but enough to become tipsy by sundown. "Don't worry," he reassured me. "I can hide it. Anyway, maybe a town without saloons will give me the nudge to throw the bottle away once and for all."

"Maybe so," I said. "And maybe a town without gambling halls will break me of my card habit."

Hours rolled into days, and miles stretched behind us. We reached Denver and remained there three days, then rode north to Fort Collins and west into the rugged mountains, following the narrow trails that led to the new mining town of Walden City.

CAMERON JUDD

Writing with power, authority, and respect for America's frontier traditions, Cameron Judd captures the spirit of adventure and promise of the wild frontier in his fast-paced, exciting novels. In the tradition of Max Brand and Luke Short, Cameron Judd is a new voice of the Old West.